From a Distance

Matthew

Thanks and Enjoy

Merry Christmas 2011

♡

From a Distance

CL Hart

P.D. Publishing, Inc.
Clayton, North Carolina

ISBN-13: 978-1-933720-75-3

9 8 7 6 5 4 3 2 1

Cover design by Stephanie Solomon-Lopez
Edited by: Day Petersen / Verda Foster

Published by:

P.D. Publishing, Inc.
P.O. Box 70
Clayton, NC 27528

http://www.pdpublishing.com

Writing a book is a lonely endeavor, but no one does it alone. It's the people around you who offer assistance and support, that without their help these pages would only hold part of the story. My gratitude and heartfelt thank you to the following:

First and foremost, **Marcia Hotvedt** RAHT and "thee" **Dr. Cathy Wilkie** DVM. BS; their veterinary advice and expertise was invaluable. I'll never call it a Veterinarian hospital again.

The "chick in the yellow shirt" for all her support, advice and contagious excitement that has pushed my writing beyond what I thought I was capable of.

My parents for their guidance, wisdom and support. Your place in San Diego was also very pertinent and helpful. And for accompanying me to Tijuana – you would have bailed me out if I got caught – right?

My editors - **Day Petersen** and **Verda Foster**; for your patience, understanding and over all professional guidance. You filled the holes that I created, even when I was too stubborn to admit it. My readers and proofreaders – **Marcia, Judi, Gord, Lori, Shelley, Heather and Kathy**. Your input helped my output.

Linda and **Barb**; you *are* PD Publishing and I'm grateful to call it home.

Stephanie Solomon-Lopez for your fortitude in designing such a wonderful cover.

To all my family and friends for all your continuing support both in my life and in my writing.

To **Dude** for all the laughter and smiles as I wrote (who knew I talked out loud as I typed). You inspired me to look at the world through your eyes, and I'm a better person for it. RIP Little Man

To the fans – without you there would be no reason – you inspire me.

* please note – No dogs are harmed inside the pages of this book, you have my word. CLH

~ For Marcia ~

The world is no longer considered a big place; instead, it has become more like a global community. Due to the powers of the Internet and the ever prying eyes of the glossed over news media reporting twenty-four hours a day, international incidents become household discussions. However, not all of the world's problems are reported to the public at large. Sometimes the "powers that be" twist events to tip the scales of truth and justice in their favor; other times there is a mere whisper in the shadows and the problem ceases to exist. These people migrate to each other, creating a core of influential authority, pockets of power spread throughout the world in such cities as London, Paris, Toronto, New York, and Washington. They live and work within the fabric of government, the military, and large corporations. They are identified only as "Global Engineers".

Are you a pawn or are you a knight?
Do you move forward, or do you move right?
Some say it's a game, but it may be your life;
You can't walk forever on the edge of a knife.
You best be aware of all that's around;
Death can sneak up without making a sound.
Can you trust a shadow that's not your own?
Who has your back if you're standing alone?
The truth that you find may not set you free.
From a distance, the future is not what you see.
~ CL Hart

Chapter 1

Kenzie's weathered soul was as worn as the stones of the pathway leading to the south entrance of Paris's Luxembourg Park. The City of Love was all around her, but she was not there as a tourist. She was there to do a job. Trained eyes looked over the lay of the land, taking in locations, distances, exits, and any patterns in the daily activities of the Luxembourg Palace security. The observations were not necessary, as the famous palace and park — constructed in 1615 for Marie de Medici — were already etched into her mind. She knew every inch of it before arriving in France, having pored over maps and pictures upon receiving the assignment. Once she had landed, she explored the park grounds extensively until she found the best spot to wait for her target. The vantage point she chose provided her the easiest and quickest escape.

This morning she strolled along the pathway with her canvas bag slung lazily over her shoulder. Already, a few people gathered on the benches and chairs that lined the walkways of the park. Not one of them gave her a second glance. One of the tools of her trade was to blend in with those around her, and she was good at what she did. She was of average height and stature, looking common, almost ordinary, with the exception of her exotic gold-colored eyes hidden behind dark sunglasses. What made Kenzie special were her skills as a hunter. She stalked her targets with unwavering determination, never showing emotion, or care, or concern for anything around her. She was silent and lethally dangerous.

Unseen, she slipped into the thick foliage, opened her bag, and quickly assembled her rifle with practiced precision. With the weapon in its deadly form, she climbed into one of the trees, searching for the right spot. Years of training and experience enabled her to make herself comfortable and invisible. With her shot lined up, she closed her eyes and relaxed. She opened them again, confirming that her natural point of aim was still on the empty chair next to a chess table.

She rechecked her rifle and was confident it would do the job. Though the gun was not the caliber she trained with, it shot straight and true, nothing special, nothing unique, nothing traceable. Satisfied that everything was ready, she waited with determined patience for her target to appear.

There was no change in her demeanor when she saw him coming down the sidewalk toward his chair. He sat down and she primed her body for what she was about to do. She breathed in and out rhythmically, then took one last deep breath and released it slowly, silencing her mind. There was a large clock tower in the center of the park, and at one minute to nine, she squeezed the slack out of the trigger, everything in her focused on her target. She sensed more than heard the heavy iron hand move into place over the XII. There was a churn and a click as the gears aligned noisily. The ancient tower erupted with a bong of the first bell, signaling the hour. There would be nine, and she counted. Two, three...fire. She didn't wait; she didn't need to. The job was done. She was out of the tree before the clock tower chimed its final bell.

She left the park and headed for the Charles de Gaulle airport. She patted her plane ticket, secure in the inside pocket of her jacket as she travelled northeast through the narrow streets of Paris on an old, used motorcycle. Several times she turned to make sure no one was behind her. Once she was certain she was alone, she turned down a back alley, and then slowed the bike to a stop next to the River Seine. Quickly, she descended the stone steps to the wide walkway next to the river. Without a second thought, she separated the scope from the rifle and dropped them both into the obligingly murky waters, then scampered back up the steps and sped away. Her assignment finished, she could disappear back into the darkness, her only respite from what she had become.

The plane was only half filled to capacity, but she still felt slightly claustrophobic as she leaned back into her seat and settled in for her long flight home.

Home. What a concept. She sighed deeply as she closed her eyes. Home was just a place to wait for her next job.

Her given name was Katherine, but nobody called her that. She had never known a real home, not even as a child, nor had she had a real family or friends, just different places with different faces. Her mother, of Egyptian descent, had died when Katherine was young, bequeathing her daughter dim memories and the looks of an exotic princess. Her father had gone to fight in Vietnam and when he did not return, Katherine went to live with her elderly grandmother, Helen, who called her by a shortened version of her middle name, Mackenzie. Well intentioned, Grandmother Helen had no idea how to deal with a rambunctious, rebellious teenager. The total lack of parenting only added to Kenzie's moral decline and frequent troubles. She trusted no one, respected no one.

With no adult guidance, her sharp mind and bad attitude landed her in Juvenile Hall many times. Just when she was about to fall through the cracks of the system, she found herself in front of Judge Benjamin Woodward, a hard-nosed man with little tolerance for disrespectful, out of control teenagers. A widower for more than twenty years, he had learned to hide his emotions. However, occasionally, behind his mask of stone, he found himself wanting to reach out to those who needed a little extra help. Tough, but fair, Judge Woodward commanded respect from those who respected few.

He watched with interest as the latest rebellious young woman stood in front of him, surveying her surroundings in cocky arrogance. With her full lips, dark skin, and almond shaped golden eyes, her looks were as intriguing as her body language. It was easy to tell that she thought her present predicament was a waste of her time, and she wanted everyone around her to know that. The opposing counsel shuffled papers and the defendant split her attention between the clock on the wall and the hole in her jean jacket. She impatiently ran her fingers through her long, curly dark hair and sighed loudly.

For Judge Woodward, it was not hard to see why Kenzie had been in trouble with the law several times. She stood defiantly in front of him, reached into her pocket, and fished out a cigarette and lighter. She placed the cigarette between her lips and glanced down at the lighter in her hand. With an ease born of practice, she flipped open its lid to light her cigarette when her eyes caught the stony face of the judge.

"Don't...you...dare," he said slowly and clearly, leaving no doubt in Kenzie's mind who was in charge of this courtroom. Judge Woodward watched and waited, and finally the Zippo clinked shut without its flame ever touching the end of the teenager's cigarette.

Judge Woodward looked over her lengthy juvenile record, then glanced at her. He saw something more than just defiance in Kenzie's eyes. Checking her birthdate, he realized she was almost an adult, almost — but not quite. He studied her strong features and her obstinate attitude, then leaned back in his chair and pulled off his glasses.

"What do you have to say for yourself, young lady?"

Kenzie stared back at him. "Is this going to take long? I've a previous engagement."

"I think you're going to miss it." He put his glasses on and read from her file. "Would you care to explain yourself?"

She crossed her arms and looked suspiciously at the judge. "In regards to?"

"Why don't we start with the stolen car?"

Kenzie shrugged her shoulders. "I needed a ride."

"Twice?"

"There and back."

"And the assault?"

"The guy wouldn't give me his car. I wanted, I needed...I took it."

"Why?"

"I told you, I needed a ride."

The judge sat quietly studying her as she ran her fingers through her unmanageable hair. Years later, he would look back at this moment, trying to figure out what made him do what he did. Kenzie appeared no different from the thousands of other young offenders who were marched before him, but something told him she was.

Judge Woodward adjourned the court for lunch and went back to his chambers to see if he could pull a few strings with an old Army buddy. The colonel and he had remained friends long after the judge had exchanged his uniform for a black robe, and he was quite willing to listen to the judge's idea.

After lunch, Judge Woodward called the teenager and her public defender into his chambers. He waited for them to take a seat across from his desk. Once they had settled, he started. "You, Miss LeGault, are almost an adult and you've been in and out of the system like it's a revolving door. Well, the revolutions are about to stop. Tell me, young lady, have you had any thoughts about your future?"

Kenzie crossed her arms and remained silent.

The judge flipped through some papers on his desk. "You're no longer a juvenile, young lady. It's time you started to take some responsibility for yourself as an adult. Two counts of grand theft auto, one count of aggravated assault. You have two options: two years at Washington Correctional Center for Women or—"

Shocked at the judge's proposal, Kenzie's public defender slid forward in her seat. "Your Honor WCCW is—"

The judge cut her off. "Let me finish, counselor."

"Your Honor, with all due respect, that's a women's prison...for adults. You can't send her there—"

"It is within my power to do so, and believe me, I can and I will. She's old enough to do the crime, so she's old enough to do the time. It's time for her to make some of her own decisions." He leaned over his desk and stared straight into Kenzie's eyes. "Your choice?"

Her steady gaze never faltered. "What's my other option?"

"Four years serving Uncle Sam." This little maneuver was going to cost him a couple of bottles of forty-year-old Scotch, but something told him the young woman in front of him was worth the effort he had made.

Kenzie sat impassively as her court appointed lawyer pleaded with the judge. "Your Honor, this is highly irregular. You can't force her—"

"Counselor, I would advise you to sit back and shut up. No one is forcing anyone to do anything. I'm simply giving her options. She's old enough to understand the law, and to know the consequences of breaking it. What I'm doing is offering her a choice. Turn her life around, or continue on the road she's currently on."

Judge Woodward stared at Kenzie. She gave no outward indication of where her mind was going but he had his own suspicions. "If you're thinking of going AWOL once you're in training, the two years at WCCW will be on the table until you have served your entire obligation to the military."

Kenzie, her arms still crossed over her chest, raised one eyebrow. "A few years playing soldier? Not a problem. Where do I sign?"

Forty-eight hours later, Katherine Mackenzie LeGault stepped off a bus at Fort Lewis and into the care of Sergeant "I eat recruits for breakfast" Carter. He knew who she was and why she was there, and he wanted to make damn certain she knew there was no "playing soldier" under his command.

Kenzie thrived in the military. It taught her discipline and responsibility, two things her life had been seriously lacking. She got three meals a day, a place to hang her hat, and a chance to make something more of her life. Academically it was challenging at first, since she had never applied herself at school. However, she was top of her class in all the physical training, even though she was smaller than most of her fellow recruits. Soon everyone knew her name, and the direction her military career was heading.

Halfway through Kenzie's training, two monumental things happened. First, her Grandmother Helen passed away, leaving her with no family and making her feel quite guilty for all of the trouble she had caused her. Second, she sent a letter of thanks to the man who had changed her life. A few weeks later, she was surprised to receive her first piece of civilian mail. The return address surprised her even more: Judge B. W. Woodward, Seattle, Washington.

The letters between them started out short, but soon their length grew, as did their friendship. Kenzie liked having someone in her life, and Judge Woodward liked the spirited fire he had seen beneath the young woman's anger. Since she excelled in all levels of her training, he was not surprised Kenzie graduated top of her class.

With no family left to invite to her graduation, she sent an invitation to Judge Woodward. She could not hide her smile when she saw him sitting in the second row.

The U.S. Army was where she belonged and somehow Judge Woodward had known that. He was there when she received her first promotion, clapping proudly, shoulder to shoulder with the others who were there to see their family members promoted. On her twenty-first birthday, the judge was there to watch her open an envelope that had come from the legal firm of Broughton, Greene, and Hanson. Unbeknownst to Kenzie, her grandmother had set up a trust fund for her. It was not a lot of money, but it was enough for Kenzie to purchase her first off-base residence — a twenty-eight-foot Catalina Mark II sailboat. No one knew about it but the judge. It was the first thing she'd really owned, and it was a home without roots, just like her. In honor of her grandmother, she named it *Helen's Gate.*

The judge was there for Kenzie, cooking her dinner before she left to begin training at Fort Bragg. Soon after, her duties took her all over the globe, opening her eyes to many of the misfortunes that the rest of the world endured. Kenzie wrote the judge often, but she wrote less and less about what she was doing and where she was doing it.

The first time he saw her after she returned from Europe, Judge Woodward was surprised at the maturity in Kenzie's features. He saw her in a new light. The short-cropped dark hair he was accustomed to was starting to lengthen, showing off her natural wild curls. She had always been a beautiful, intelligent woman, but now there was a different side to her, an inner awareness of who she was and a new attentiveness that told him some of what she had seen. It was also the first time he saw how quickly she could change her outward appearance, slipping into another language, almost changing her personality. Judge Woodward knew then that the Army were grooming her to be something more than an average soldier. The next time he saw her, he was not surprised to see Kenzie sporting a new set of stripes on her uniform.

It was over a year before he saw her again. Her hair was a little longer, her demeanor a little quieter. He noticed more ribbons of action decorating her uniform, and her eyes bore the darkness of someone who had seen death — close up.

Only those in the highest ranks of the chain of command knew Kenzie had been training as a sniper, one of the few female snipers in the world. She loved it, even though it entailed long hours of lonely work. Friends had never been a part of her life, and she didn't miss what she'd never had. Girlfriends were a rarity and those there were, were discreet and disposable. It was the military after all — don't ask, don't tell.

But someone in her life did know, a young man from South Dakota, Corporal John Mifflin, the other half of her sniper team. Miff, as she called him, was her spotter and her first real friend besides the judge. Only a few years younger than her, Miff's job was to overlook the area, assess the wind speed, and clarify the distance to the target while she lined up the kill shot. His eyes were her eyes when she took aim through the scope. They were a great team, and with time had learned to work as an efficient unit; two people who worked together toward one goal — bringing down the enemy target. They took pride in what they did. It called for a special kind of person to crawl around in some of the worst conditions the world had to offer, to lie in wait for hours, sometimes days, for that one clear shot. Nerves of steel, attention to detail, and the patience of a saint were some of the primary attributes of a sniper.

In those long hours of waiting, hidden within the shadows, camouflaged from life, they spoke to each other in veiled whispers. Things she had never even said aloud to herself, she told to him. They shared their dreams and aspirations, and spoke of the women who had come in and out of their lives. Miff never judged her. She always knew he had her back and her trust.

In no time, LeGault and Mifflin were the top two names in their field. If the military wanted a target out of the picture, they were high on the list to get the job done. Until something went wrong during an assignment, very, very wrong. They were waiting in the mud in the driving rain in South America, watching for their target. They didn't move or speak, communicating only with hand signals. Without warning, two shots rang out under the canopy of the jungle, echoing deep into the night. Corporal J. Mifflin died instantly. A high caliber bullet hit him in the eye, splattering his brain matter all over his partner. Kenzie survived with a near miss, the bullet slamming into her shoulder, inches away from a kill shot. Badly wounded and devastated by her partner's death, Kenzie barely made it out of the jungle alive. Regrettably, all she could bring back for his family were his dog tags.

There was a cursory investigation, but so much of the incident was confidential the only answer the government gave was that Mifflin died in the line of duty. His family received a medal for his bravery and a crisply folded flag. Kenzie had a hard time after his death and took a leave of absence, during which she had many long phone conversations with the judge. However, due to the sensitive issue of security, she couldn't speak about what was really bothering her. He tried to console her, but survivor guilt was a hard thing to get over. Having served in Vietnam, he understood that.

When Kenzie was finally able to see Judge Woodward, he knew by the look in her eyes how painful it had been. He couldn't help her, but that didn't keep him from wanting to try. When her leave of absence was over, she returned to the only life she knew.

One afternoon she received a message to report to a Colonel Manuck off base, which was unusual. However, in the military, she had learned not to question, but to follow, orders. She had heard of him — a man of color, who wore his rank proudly on his uniform. She knew he was a man who required the utmost respect and that had nothing to do with his rank. He had a reputation of being a good soldier, a quiet man who let his actions do most of his talking. However, she also recalled some disturbing stories she'd heard about Colonel Manuck, rumors about covert operations and a very high mortality rate among the soldiers under his command. The mortality rate didn't scare her, and the thought of covert operations sounded like an intriguing challenge.

Kenzie found the address that she was looking for belonged to an old, rundown office building. She double checked the piece of paper in her hand and confirmed the location was indeed correct. She paused outside the door, took a breath, and straightened her uniform before she knocked. The door opened immediately and Kenzie entered the nearly empty room. She was surprised to see two men there.

"I'm looking for Colonel Manuck?" she said, looking at each man.

"I'm Manuck," the man with the large barrel chest said.

"Colonel." Kenzie started to salute.

Manuck waved off the pomp and circumstance. "Not needed. You know who I am?" the colonel asked as he offered her one of the three chairs in the room.

"Yes, sir," she said as she sat down on the cold metal chair.

The other man wasn't introduced, but after a quick observation of his crisp dark suit and tie, athletic build, and military haircut, Kenzie guessed he was a Fed. He was a Kevin Costner look-alike, and she decided to call him Kevin, since no name was offered.

Kevin sat down, his eyes never leaving Kenzie's as Colonel Manuck quietly laid out the reason as to why she was there. Manuck did most of the talking. Now and then Kevin would supply a few details. At first, the colonel explained a military career change; however, as she listened longer, it became plain that it was more than just a career change. Many times over the following years, she would wonder what would have happened that day if she'd declined their offer.

FBI, CIA, SSA — the initials didn't matter to her. She would be performing the same function, but the proposition came with strings attached. She weighed the offer very carefully. More responsibility, less military operations, and it all came with a fat pay raise and a security clearance at the highest level. Kenzie was ready to jump at it until Kevin made one final statement. He cleared his throat dramatically and then informed her that any perceived benefits would come at a very high cost.

"Your life in the civilian world will come to an end."

"Meaning?" She looked to Manuck for clarification.

Manuck hesitated for a moment, weighing his words as he studied her face. "Any and all contact with persons not within the unit will cease."

"Your existence will be terminated — permanently," Kevin added coldly.

Kenzie glanced from one man to the other, not sure what to ask, but somehow she knew there would be nothing more forthcoming.

That afternoon Judge Woodward received a call from Kenzie, asking if she could meet him for dinner. It had been a while since he'd seen her, and when she walked through his door, he couldn't help but notice the concern creased into her brow. He was surprised when Kenzie brought up the subject of her financial estate. Money was not something she typically discussed. He listened carefully to her words and wishes, and though she had not mentioned anything specific, he suddenly had his suspicions. The mood became happy and light as they made and ate dinner together, and then enjoyed one of their highly competitive games of chess. When Kenzie pulled on her black leather jacket to leave, the dark foreboding feel from earlier in the evening returned. They hugged tightly to one another at the front door and again in the driveway. It was hard for her to leave, but she tried not to show emotion as she climbed onto her motorbike.

With a simple nod, she was gone and the elderly judge stood and watched as Kenzie rode out of sight. Somehow he knew this good-bye was different.

When Kenzie reported to Colonel Manuck the next morning, she handed him all her signed papers, her dog tags and identification. He gave her a new security clearance ID card — with no name and no picture, just a laser scan of her thumbprint. Just like that, Katherine Mackenzie LeGault ceased to exist.

Two days later, Judge Woodward was reading his morning paper when a small article caught his eye.

United States Army Press release — Fort Lewis, Washington. Officials at the Fort announced the death of a local soldier. Sergeant Major Katherine Mackenzie LeGault, a highly decorated member of Special Forces, was killed in the line of duty. She leaves behind no immediate family.

A feeling of unbearable sorrow tore at his chest. He laid the paper down in utter disbelief as tears filled his eyes, blurring his vision. It couldn't be true. Surely, if she were dead, someone would have called him. The tears fell as he closed his eyes and recalled their dinner just the other night. His breath caught as he remembered her strange demeanor that evening. Reaching for the paper, he read the death notice again, wondering whether his sudden insight was the truth or just what he wanted the truth to be.

Weeks after the judge read the obituary, a package arrived for him at the courthouse. He was hesitant about opening it without a postmark, but curiosity got the better of him. Inside he found a small jewelry box, and when he lifted the lid, a smile instantly spread across his face. Inside was a Zippo lighter embossed with a black and white yin-yang, the same as the lighter his Katherine had flippantly attempted to use in his courtroom so many years before. He smiled broadly. Katherine was alive. It was all he needed to know.

Months later, another package arrived, another Zippo lighter — no note or return address, but he knew it was from her. It was her way of telling him she was okay.

Kenzie quickly became one of Colonel Manuck's favorites. She spoke less than he did, but was far more accurate with a rifle at five hundred meters. When he met with her, their meetings were short and to the point. Kenzie knew he had to report to someone higher up, but she didn't ask who it was. It was irrelevant to her job. He gave her orders and she followed them. Killing became easy. It was her job. It was what she did.

In her new posting, Kenzie only met Colonel Manuck in nondescript buildings or underground parking lots. At times, she found the whole cloak and dagger thing almost amusing, but there was little humor in what she was doing. She followed her orders to the letter. The first few jobs were a lot harder than she had expected. In some way, she felt vulnerable without her dogtags and military backup, although the job itself was not much different from what it had been before. If anything, her situation was better because she had more freedom to move under the radar, and she answered only to Colonel Manuck. She liked the fact that sometimes she would spend months in one location just gathering information. Kenzie considered herself a specialist in her field of global security. When a problem arose and all other avenues of solution had failed, they would bring her in to handle it by whatever means necessary. She followed all protocols, as per her orders. It was a different life and she was learning to enjoy it, although she soon realized that the cost of her anonymity was a world of solitude.

With the luxury of money, she had two residences, but neither of them was a home. One was a house in the Pacific Northwest and the other was her sailboat, for which she changed the mooring often. Kenzie's only interaction with the world outside of her true existence was the polite conversations she had with the strangers in her life, the overly happy Asian woman who giggled and bowed every time Kenzie came into her small produce store, and Jack, the skateboarding mechanic who looked after her bike. Nobody knew her real name, where she lived, or what she did. She was living her life as a ghost. There was no one to notice that, even though Kenzie had quit smoking years earlier, she still purchased Zippo lighters on a regular basis.

Chapter 2

Kenzie's cell phone warbled a text message. Flipping it open, she read the text — ACTIVATION: PREP MODE/ARMED AND READY FOR TRANSPORT; WHIDBEY ISLAND NAVAL BASE/HANGAR 11. ASAP. She read the message again before punching in her confirmation code. Closing her phone, Kenzie absorbed the information as she grabbed her helmet and backpack.

Kenzie arrived at the heavily fortified front gates of the naval base, flashed her high-level clearance ID, and they waved her through without even a salute. No one saw her face beneath her helmet as she cruised her bike toward Hangar 11. Several armed Marines secured the entrance, and directed Kenzie where to park her bike. Keeping her helmet on, she nodded as one of them indicated the waiting plane. The sound of the powerful engines whined as Kenzie climbed the stairs. The flight crew said nothing as they closed the doors, muffling the sounds outside as she took her seat.

Once her flight leveled off, one of the flight crew came back and handed her an envelope. Not even making eye contact, he returned to the cockpit. Alone, Kenzie turned the envelope around to reveal the words **Omega 3** written boldly on the front.

"Omega," she whispered to herself. She had heard of them, but until that moment, it had never occurred to her that she was one of them.

The Omega Squad was the silent little brother of Delta Force. Their military actions were unrestricted by any legal limitations, military or civil. They were the few, the proud, the non-existent. Delta Force soldiers were hand picked from within the military elite, Omega soldiers rose above that. They followed their orders and then never spoke of their assignments again. According to the government, the only difference between Delta Force and the Omega Squad was that the Omega Squad did not exist.

Her finger traced the words on the envelope. "If I'm three, who the hell are one and two?" she whispered as she ripped open the envelope. Scanning the document quickly, she learned that they were heading for a military base in the Middle East. Further orders would be provided upon her arrival. Then her eyes fell on the bold type at the end of the document, and an eerie feeling settled in the pit of her stomach.

Upon arrival, rendezvous with additional personnel

Kenzie didn't like the idea of working with someone again. It was something she was not comfortable with, but knew there was nothing she could do about it.

When the plane landed, Kenzie was hustled out and was taken into what she assumed was the commander's office. There were several people there, and even without introductions, Kenzie knew which ones were other non-named personnel. One stood about 6'3", with a football player's neck and shoulders. The other was a little shorter and had a slightly thinner build, but the same intense stare. That, and the lack of emotion on their faces, told her who they were.

There were no introductions offered between the soldiers, only slight nods of acknowledgment. The commander explained the situation as the three soldiers listened intently.

Kenzie thought it strange that they were brought in to deal with a military operation the commander's own men could have handled, but she kept her assessment to herself as she studied the map on the wall.

The three listened in silence as the commander finished the details of the mission. "My orders were to get you people down here and let you handle it."

"Yes, sir. That's what we do," the smaller of the two men said firmly. Apparently he was in charge.

"Now you understand that this information is highly classifi—"

"Sir, our classification is of the highest level," thick neck fired back.

"The job will be done as directed," the smaller man said impassively. "We'll be ready in ten minutes, sir. Please be certain that a helicopter is ready for our insertion and our extraction."

The commander nodded and left, leaving Kenzie and the other operatives alone.

Kenzie mulled over the mission in her mind, feeling a sense of uneasiness growing inside her. The two men, who seemed familiar with each other, didn't seem to be bothered by what they were told. She looked them over, assuring herself they were as equally trained as her and more than capable of doing what had been ordered, so why was she feeling so uneasy?

The two men changing knew more about the operation than she did and that made her even more uncomfortable. "Does this seem strange to anyone besides me?" she asked. When the men remained silent, Kenzie looked to the second agent, the shorter of the two men, and he appeared to be looking at her. When she arrived, she'd caught a glimpse of recognition on his face, but the expression quickly disappeared.

"Do I know you?" she asked him.

The question caught him off guard but he covered quickly. "No," he said abruptly and turned his attention to his preparation. The fact that he did know her wasn't of any importance to their present situation.

She realized that she still didn't know what their names were or what to call them. "Are you going to tell me your names or should I just make some up?"

"I know what to call you — split-tail, so it doesn't really matter," thick neck, the taller man, said snidely.

Kenzie chose to ignore the derogatory slang directed at her.

"Funny, I thought you'd be taller," the man continued.

"How tall do you have to be to pull a trigger, Einstein?"

"You don't have to be tall, but you have to be a...a guy." He glared at her in frustration. "It's a man's job, not a job for a woman, and my name's not Einstein, either."

She raised an eyebrow in surprise and then looked at his partner. "It would appear not." Her sassy sarcasm got a small smile from the shorter one. Kenzie slipped into the shoulder harness that held her twin 9mms.

"Where are your .45s?" thick neck asked. "Or is that too big a gun for a little girl?"

"The 9s work for me," she said as she leaned over to pull a small backpack from her bag.

"Will this work for you, too?" Thick neck gazed lewdly at her figure while grabbing his crotch.

Kenzie looked over at thick neck and sneered. "I guess that would make you asshole number one."

Thick neck stood up after fastening his backpack, his eyes lingering on her on his way to a mirror on the wall. "Actually, number two, code name Cobra." He began to darken his face in front of the mirror. "The quiet one over there is Viper. He's number one."

"I'm working with a couple of snakes — nice." She reached down and retrieved her black balaclava from her bag. "Kind of a cocky son of a bitch, aren't ya, Cobra?"

When she straightened up, she was not surprised to see he had turned around to face her. A foot and a half apart, they stood eyeing each other.

"Nice tits," Cobra said. Suddenly his right hand shot out, reaching for one of Kenzie's breasts, but before his fingers could touch even the wool of her shirt, she turned to her left, striking out with her right hand, driving her fingers up into his armpit. Stepping out with her right foot, she lifted him over her hip and Cobra landed soundly on his back.

"Try that again, asshole, and I'll break your fuckin' arm."

"Hey...hey, knock it off, you two." Viper rushed to break them up, but it was already over.

Kenzie stepped over Cobra and brushed past Viper to stand in front of the mirror. With her black smudge in her hand, she glanced over to see Viper offer Cobra a hand up.

"I'm not here to be you boys' secretary."

"And we're not here as your enemy," Viper said as he brushed off Cobra's shirt.

"I don't call anyone friend." Kenzie plucked her balaclava off the floor where it had fallen during the scuffle, and pulled it over her head. "So we can forget having a beer when this is all done." In stilted silence, the three boarded the waiting helicopter. A short but dangerous flight took them over a border they should not have been crossing. Moments later, three black figures rappelled silently to the ground.

Chapter 3

A phone rang, interrupting the thoughts of the lone occupant of the large office. The man sitting at the desk reached for the handset. It was too early for the call to be good news. "Yes?"

"We have a problem and it needs to be dealt with immediately."

"Explain." His voice was void of emotion. The voice on the other end of the phone spoke in a gravelly whisper. He didn't like what he was hearing. He glanced down at the paperwork on his desk, "Is she a threat to Maquinar?" The voice did not reply immediately, and he could almost see the frustration on the caller's face.

"I'm not sure."

"That, to me, sounds like we have a problem."

"I just think—"

"No! I'm not willing to put my ass on the line..." His voice trailed off as his finger traced the Federal Government seal embossed on the letterhead of the letter he was holding. "That other little problem we talked about before..." He ran his hand over the stubble on his chin while his mind spun off in a different direction. "Eliminate one to eliminate the other, and both problems cease to exist. Get it done, clean and fast. Can you do that?"

"Consider it done," the caller said and the line went dead.

After what seemed like a lifetime, Kenzie landed back at Whidbey Island Naval Base. The silence on the plane ride home was almost unbearable. There was no one there to talk to, and for the first time in her life, she realized there never really had been. She was alone — no partner, no companionship, no one to share her life's ups and downs with — except for the man she called "Judge". Looking out at the lights of Seattle, she fingered the fresh sutures on her cheek. Even in the distorted reflection of the plane's window, she could see the swelling and the discolorations on her chin and cheek. She wished it hurt more. The physical pain would keep her mind occupied.

She was alone and it was more than her conscience could bear as she tried to forget the images burning in her mind. She needed someone to tell her that she'd done what needed to be done. What she didn't need was to face the man who had put her into that position. Flagrantly flouting policy and procedures, Kenzie deplaned and left the base.

She sped through the empty streets on her bike, running from the memories and the shadows in her mind. She had no idea where she was going — she just needed to drive, to get away — but she couldn't run from herself and from what she had done. Hours later, she pulled up in front of a convenience store just as the bundle of newspapers arrived. She waited impatiently for the elderly man to pull one from the pile. Walking back to her bike, she flipped madly through the pages until a small article caught her eye.

After reading it a second time, she folded the newspaper in half and tucked it inside her leather jacket. She sat on her bike, struggling to decide between following her principles or her training. A moment later, she fired up her bike and roared down the deserted roadway.

Kenzie parked her bike and walked a short distance through the quiet, urban neighborhood. Silently, she slipped into the shadows and made her way along the side of a house. Within seconds, she disappeared through a ground level window into the basement. Making her way up the basement stairs and through the house, she was as soundless as they had trained her to be. Without a noise, she moved down the hall, pausing only for a moment at a picture hanging on the wall. It was obviously taken many years earlier, a young Judge Woodward standing with one hand in the air and the other on the bible as he swore an oath of duty and justice. Moving on, she took a chair in the kitchen and waited.

A long, patient wait later, she heard a familiar creak coming from the carpeted stairs leading to the second floor. The swinging door opened into the kitchen and a hand reached for the light switch.

"Leave them off, Judge."

He froze at the sound of her voice and flattened himself against the opposite wall. "What? Who's there?"

His startled voice tugged at her and she realized just how long it had been since they had spoken in person. "A ghost," she answered solemnly.

The judge hesitated, but even in the dark, he knew who it was. "Katherine?"

No one but the judge ever used her first name, and it sounded strange. She had almost forgotten it was hers. "Yeah."

The judge noted that she sounded tired. "My God, girl, what are you doing here?" he said, reaching again for the light switch. "It's been so long. Let me take a look at you?"

"Leave 'em off." She regretted the demanding tone in her voice. "Please."

Judge Woodward did as asked, crossed the dimly lit room and took a chair opposite her. "Katherine, you're sounding awful good for a dead person." Squinting in the low light, he didn't like what he saw in the shadows. "Rough work you're in?" He nodded toward her bruised cheek and the row of stitches. He watched in painful interest as her eyes went down to a scratch on the table she was picking at with her nail.

"Yeah, well, you should see the other guy," she said.

The judge waited, hoping she would say more. When she didn't, he could wait no longer. "Katherine, what's wrong?"

She took a deep breath, but said nothing as she glanced out the back window. There was a long moment of profound silence before her low whispered words crept from the shadows. "I shouldn't have come here."

"Well, you are here and you can't change that now." He watched her with knowing eyes, waiting, probing. "Something happened that was bad enough for you to risk coming out in the open." She turned back and looked at him, and he understood. "I have a military background, my dear. I have a pretty good idea what you're doing."

"I wish I did." There was an awkward moment of silence and it penetrated deep into her subconscious. Never before had she felt uneasy around the judge.

"Katherine?"

The concern was evident in his voice, but she didn't know what to say or how to say it. He watched her in the shadows, waiting long enough to know she was not going to answer him.

"I know you can't tell me what happened, but maybe I could help if you give me something to go on."

Her eyes darted around the room, telling him just how uncomfortable she was, but he wondered if her nerves came from whatever had happened or from who she had become. He waited and finally she spoke.

"Who am I?"

The judge leaned closer, knowing there was more to the question than the obvious. "I'm not sure how to answer that. Who do you think you are?"

There was a long silence, a palpable pause to have come from such a simple question. "I don't think I know anymore...I don't think I ever really did. I've just followed orders." She stopped and the only sound in the room was the steady tick of the kitchen clock. "Because that's what a good soldier does...but at some point I stopped thinking for myself...I stopped caring." It was the most she had spoken all at once in a long time.

"That's your job."

"What?" she said as she stood up quickly from the table. "Not to care?"

"No." He wanted to reach out to her, but had no idea how. "Katherine, your job is to follow orders, because if you don't follow those orders, people will die."

Kenzie slowly unzipped her jacket. "People are dying whether I follow orders or not." She tossed the folded newspaper onto the table.

Picking it up, he moved to the light over the sink. Judge Woodward quickly scanned the paper, knowing it was her way of communicating without giving him information. The moment he spotted the military press release, he knew he had found what he was looking for.

"That was no accident."

He read the article quickly. "Are you sure?"

Kenzie nodded and waited for him to finish. When he was done, he returned to the table, put the paper down, and sat across from her.

"I was there."

"At the base?"

Kenzie stared into nothing, recalling the sights and sounds where she had just been — the flames, the heat, and the sound of gunfire, the stench of death as it rose into the night sky. Her conflict then was almost as bad as the conflict she was experiencing now. Kenzie looked at the judge as she fingered the injury to her face. "Those men didn't die on any base." She reached for the paper and zipped it back into her jacket.

"Katherine?"

Kenzie noticed the growing gray of twilight and knew her time was up. "I gotta go."

"But you just got here. Stay for a bit, let's talk."

"I can't." She rose from the table, uncertain of what she was going to do. She did know that she should not have come. Her being there put her only friend at risk. "I, ah, I'm sorry...but I gotta go."

"Where are you going?" the judge asked.

She walked over to the door at the edge of the hallway, which would take her back to the basement. "I don't know. I have to deal with this myself."

"It was good to see you, Katherine. I've missed you — and our chess games."

She tried to smile but couldn't muster one. She didn't know whether it was because of the wound on her cheek, or the confusion in her conscience.

"Can you come back?"

"It might be better for us if I didn't."

"I'm here if you need me. Be careful."

"Always."

He watched as the basement door closed silently, and just like that, she was gone. Standing alone in his kitchen, Judge Woodward made his own decision and reached for the phone. Dialing a number, he listened to the ringing until a sleepy voice answered.

Kenzie had no idea what possessed her to go and see the judge, knowing she should not. Regardless, it had made her feel a little bit better. She kept her mind busy on the long drive back, and when she pulled into her driveway, she was certain she had made a decision.

With confident strides, she made her way up the stairs and stopped to unlock the back door, but it was already unlocked. Someone was in her house! Startled and apprehensive, she reached for her weapon. Crouching down, she pushed the door open from the bottom as a large figure filled the doorway in her kitchen.

"Where the hell have you been, LeGault?" Colonel Manuck said. "Have you got any goddamn idea what goes on when someone like you doesn't show up for a debriefing? Especially after a mission that was almost a disaster."

"Almost a disaster? It was a disaster!" She fought to calm her rising anger.

"We do what we have to do. We do what we're asked. People live and people die, for God, for country—"

Kenzie glared at her commander. "They didn't die for their country. They were murdered!"

"Sit down and shut up, LeGault. You do what you're told to do, and that's the end of it. You're not here to think, you're here to do, because we've trained you to do it — period!"

"I didn't sign up for this."

"No one ever does, but someone has to do the dirty work and that's what we do."

Kenzie couldn't help looking down at her hands, knowing just how dirty they had become. She picked at her bitten fingernails, digging at the rough skin around the edges. "Did you know what we were being sent there to do?"

"You do what you're told to do — period. What we do here is highly sensitive and classified. We can't afford the actions of one person to destroy the delicate balance of our nation's safety and security."

Kenzie crossed the room and looked out the window, her eyes scanning the busy streets below. She crossed her arms, but it felt uncomfortable and unnatural. "So what happens now?"

"That depends on you." Manuck sat down at her desk, ignoring the thin layer of dust covering the unused work area. Pulling herself from the view out her window, she turned to watch him. He felt her stare. Wiping his hands off, he turned his attention back to her. "I need to know — are you an asset or a liability?"

"Meaning what?"

Manuck picked up a briefcase and placed it on the table. Keeping his attention on Kenzie, he opened it and looked down at the two large envelopes with her name on them. He pulled out one and offered it. "Your next assignment." He never took his eyes off her.

As she studied the lines in his face, Kenzie knew it was a test. "What if I don't take it?" There was no answer as his dark eyes returned her questioning stare. "What if that was my last assignment and I wanted to...let's say, take an extended leave, without a return date?"

"Extended leave? You mean quit?"

"Whatever you want to call it — leave, quit, holiday... What if I want to resign? What if I've had enough? What if I want out? What happens?"

Manuck studied the grain on her dusty table and was silent for too long a time before answering. "There are proper procedures, steps to be taken, but it isn't going to happen overnight. We would have to establish an identity for you, and that takes time. We have spent a lot of time and money training you. We can't just let you leave."

"But I can get out?"

"If that's what you want, but in the meantime there are jobs that need to be done." He reached back into his briefcase for another envelope and held it out to her, waiting to see if she was going to accept it. When she didn't, he laid it on the table and pushed it toward her. "We need confirmation within forty-eight hours." He slipped the first manila envelope he had offered her back into his briefcase.

Reaching for the envelope, her hand stopped and she pulled it back as if she had been burned. "Forty-eight hours?"

"We need to — eliminate the problem — quickly." Manuck's eyes bored into hers. "And we need the best."

Kenzie finally picked up the envelope and broke the seal. The colonel watched her with interest as he clicked shut his briefcase. Kenzie pulled out the documents, perusing them quickly. "It's a woman," she said flatly, looking at the picture of a young woman sitting on what appeared to be a park bench. The photo had obviously been taken with a telephoto lens, but Kenzie could clearly see the features of the young woman's face.

"Is it a problem?" Manuck asked. "I need to know."

Kenzie flipped through the pages, absorbing the information without even realizing it. Though the thought of killing a woman weighed heavily on her mind, she reminded herself that she was a soldier.

"Can I count on you?"

"Where?"

"Guadalajara, Mexico. There's a plane standing by."

Kenzie didn't answer him. She walked over to her bags and looked around her bare living room. There was nothing personal in the room, nothing she really cared about. How could she? She didn't exist. Aside from the judge, she had no one in her life and never had. This was not a home; it was just a place where she waited for her next assignment.

"I need an answer, LeGault," he said impatiently. "Can I count on you to eliminate this problem?"

Walking over to the fireplace mantle, she picked up the only photograph in the room. Staring into Judge Woodward's face, she spoke in a distant voice. "Have you ever heard the fable about the frog and the scorpion?" She didn't wait for an answer. "You see, this scorpion wants to cross this river, but he can't. He sees a frog out swimming in the river, so he asks the frog for a ride on his back. The frog says, 'No — if I give you a ride on my back, you'll sting me.' The scorpion replies, 'Why would I do that — we would both drown.' The frog thinks it over and then decides it seems safe enough, so he lets the scorpion on his back. Halfway across the river, the scorpion stings the frog and as the frog starts to sink to his death, he says to the scorpion, 'Why did you do that? Now we're both going to die.' The scorpion says, 'I couldn't help it — it's what I do.'"

Kenzie replaced the photo, picked up her bag, and walked over to the colonel. "Of course I'll eliminate your problem. It's what I do."

Manuck stood on the tarmac and watched Kenzie's plane ascend to the skies before he climbed into his black Suburban. With one eye on the blinking taillights, he picked up his cell phone and dialed a number. "It's Manuck. She accepted the second envelope, so I would consider the problem solved. Yes...the best man for the job."

Chapter 4

Cori Evans. The name meant nothing to Kenzie, just another notch on the butt of an imaginary gun. Still, something kept drawing her to the photo she had folded up inside her pocket. The information she'd been given was sketchy at best, but that was typical. It was her job to find the person, the patterns, and the best method of disposal, though this time is was different and she knew it. She had a deadline, and the countdown had already begun.

The plane landed on a strip that was non-military, non-commercial, and definitely nondescript, but it was Mexico. If one flew low enough and fast enough, no one was any the wiser. Kenzie glanced at her watch. "What's our evac time?"

The pilot looked at his own watch and shrugged. "Twenty-three hundred hours."

"Don't be late," she said as she climbed from the plane.

The sun was high and hot by the time she reached her destination. She undid one more button of her thin white cotton blouse, thankful she had changed into her khakis. A large component of her job was to blend in, and clothes and fashion were all a part of the cover. Unfortunately, most of the time she found herself in the desert of a third world country or deep in a bug infested jungle. When the opportunity presented itself, she liked to dress up rather than down.

Her target was located in a small apartment building crowded within the bowels of Guadalajara. With a dense population of five million, there were few places one could observe unnoticed. A vacant lot situated across the street from the four-floor apartment house would have made a good place to lie in wait, but a quick examination of the area told her there was little coverage for a sniper shot. Kenzie repositioned the heavy canvas bag on her shoulder as she decided to see where Cori Evans lived before she found a spot to watch Cori Evans die.

Mexican and American music blared loudly outside and inside the apartments as Kenzie made her way down the narrow hallway. Doors opened and doors closed, but no one paid her any mind when she stopped in front of apartment 307. She knocked quietly then tried the knob. It was locked. No surprise. A quick glance left and right and Kenzie had the cheap lock picked and was quickly inside. A wave of warm air engulfed her as she closed the door behind her and looked about the room. It was basic and plain with simple furniture. There was a hint of jasmine in the air and she wondered for a brief moment if it was the woman's perfume.

Kenzie looked around the apartment. In some ways, it reminded her of her own house. It was neat and tidy, but didn't have a lived-in feel. There was no real warmth, no feeling of home. The kitchen was clean, the tables were spotless, and the door to the bedroom was open. The smell of jasmine grew even stronger as she glanced inside at the made bed. A quick, but thorough search of the room revealed little about the woman in the photograph in her pocket.

The woman's passport was taped to the underside of a dresser drawer — a predictable hiding spot. Kenzie flipped through the blank pages. Not a traveler. She looked at the lone photograph on the dresser next to a set of keys in a basket. Kenzie picked up the photograph and looked at the picture of Cori with her arms draped around an older woman. *Her mother,* Kenzie guessed. *Who are you and what are you into?* Kenzie looked at the smiling, fresh face of the young woman. *A terrorist threat? No, not likely,* she answered her own thought. *Then what? She doesn't look like the type to be starting a revolution. Maybe she's sleeping with a terrorist. Maybe she is the terrorist. Whatever... That's someone else's problem, not mine. I'm just here to fix it. Just do your job, soldier.*

Kenzie was careful to leave the apartment just as she'd found it. She paused on the front stoop of the apartment building and looked around for her best position, somewhere high and out of sight. She scanned her options and then made her way across the street and onto the rooftop, unseen. Within minutes, her rifle was together, sighted, and ready, then she made herself as comfortable as possible. Hours passed in the heat and she felt the fatigue of the last week grow heavy on her eyelids. The Middle East and back, and now Mexico — a lot of miles and a lot of thinking. The heat radiated off the brick ledge and she did her best to ignore it, but she couldn't ignore the memories replaying in her mind. Kenzie shook her head, more to eradicate the thoughts swirling in her head than a weak attempt to stay awake. *Stay focused — stay on target.*

Wiping the sweat from her face, she watched and waited, but there was no sign of Cori Evans. She checked her weapon, tweaked the sights slightly and then peered through the scope. The rim of metal rubbed against the fresh stitches on her cheek. It didn't hurt but it did remind her of what had happened on her last assignment. Repressing the memories, she pulled the picture from her pocket and then looked over the smattering of pedestrians in the area. *Cori Evans, what are you doing in Mexico? Why does someone want you dead?* The thought furrowed her brow as her fingers traced back and forth along the raised ridges of the skin on her cheek.

She reached for her bottle of water and took a long drink, then wiped the excess from her lips as she spotted her target. Cori's bright honey-colored hair contrasted sharply against the brown streets and sea of dark hair surrounding her. Dressed in a soft pastel green, cotton, sleeveless top and matching pants, Cori was easy to watch as she walked toward her apartment. She was taller than Kenzie had envisioned and a lot more athletic looking, with broad shoulders and narrow hips. She carried a bag in her arms and laughed as several of the local children playfully ran circles around her.

A deep breath in...a long breath out as Kenzie focused on her target, her finger lying in wait on the trigger of her rifle. She squeezed in the slack, then waited as Cori stopped and talked to the children. Kenzie pursed her lips in irritation as she moved her finger off the trigger. She would never fire with the children there, no matter what her training. There was time. As she watched and waited, Kenzie concentrated on her firing sequence and her escape plan. She prided herself on being the ultimate soldier — no muss, no fuss, and no screws ups. Mistakes, mental or physical, could not happen. Her training had taught her that. She was a professional, someone who killed without thought and without remorse, but... Her mind's eye took her back to where she didn't belong: that night in the desert.

Kenzie shook her head but she couldn't rid herself of the past. She had to focus, she had to get her head back in the game, but it was not a game and she knew that better than anyone. Opening her eyes, she steeled herself against any thought that might distract her. Kenzie pulled her rifle in closer, leaned into her sights, and adjusted the crosshairs. This job needed to be done. Taking a deep breath, she blew it out slowly as she brought Cori Evans back into focus.

Watching the interaction between her target and the local children, she found herself questioning the validity of her orders. There was nothing here to convince her that Cori Evans was a threat to national security, or to anyone else, for that matter.

"What the hell am I doing?" Kenzie pulled back from the scope and watched Cori enter her apartment building. Kenzie was questioning orders, something she could ill afford to do, but nothing about Cori Evans gave any indication that the woman was a threat.

Your opinion doesn't matter. You do what you're ordered to do, or people die. Get it done, LeGault. It's why you're here. You're a soldier. Now...do...your...job.

Sweat trickled down her back, and she was aware it wasn't just because of the heat, but also the pressure of her fraying ethical fiber. The voice in her head kept telling her this was wrong. Kenzie looked around the small collection of apartments and something caught her eye. A cool breeze blew over her as the sun caught the glass and reflected a flash of light from a silhouette across the way. Someone was scanning the rooftops with binoculars.

What the—?

Kenzie dropped out of sight, pulling her rifle with her. She rolled away from where she had been lying, and scurried across the rooftop dragging her bag and gun. Unclipping her scope, she used it to peer over the edge of the roof.

"Where are you? Where are you? Where are you?" she whispered as she looked back and forth from window to window. The sun was now casting long shadows, as the sounds of the street below grew louder and louder in Kenzie's ears. "There."

Whoever it was had moved back into the cover of darkness deep within the room. She could make him out, but she couldn't see his features.

"Hello, and just who the hell are you? And what are you doing?" As if to answer her questions, the dark figure moved closer to the window and laid a hand on something next to it. With a slight adjustment to her scope, Kenzie could make out the long, black barrel of a rifle.

She rolled over onto her back, and quickly reattached her scope to her rifle. *It's a goddamn sniper convention! What the hell is going on?* She moved to a new location before she dared to look over the edge again, fully aware that she was making herself an easy target, as she sized up the other sniper. The dark figure was now standing next to the window. The binoculars were gone and this time his hands held a rifle — trained on Cori's apartment.

"What the..." So many expletives went through her mind she couldn't put her tongue on just one. *Someone sent a backup. Someone doubted my ability to do the job.* Looking back at the other gunman, Kenzie knew the time had come for her to get off the fence. Systematically, she rechecked the bullet in the chamber, the fit of the scope as she dialed in the approximate distance and wind, and then brought her weapon up for the kill. It was her job and she was going to finish it.

Finger on the trigger...breathe in...squeeze in the slack of the trigger...breathe out and...

She couldn't do it. Her mind was too unsettled by the voices screaming inside her head. Pulling back from the roof edge, she tried to sort out the conflicting echoes inside her. The only thing she knew was that she couldn't pull the trigger until she knew the "why" of this assignment, even if it went against everything she'd been trained to do. If being ordered to kill an innocent person was a test of her allegiance, then it only confirmed her earlier quandary. That was no longer who she was or wanted to be.

Looking across the way, she found no sign of the second gunman. She was not sure whether that made her feel better or not. A decision had to be made, and she was making one. Without even realizing it as she quickly disassembled her rifle. She slung her bag over her shoulder, and moved toward the fire escape on the far side of the roof. She didn't have a plan and didn't have time to stop and think about it. The soldier in her was simply acting and reacting.

Quickly and quietly, she descended the flimsy metal staircase until she made her way down into the heat at street level. No one paid her any attention as she slipped into the back entrance of the apartment building, away from the prying eyes of whoever else was watching. Kenzie stopped in front of Cori's door and paused for a moment to think about what she was going to do. She reached into her bag, pulled out one of her 9mms, then knocked loudly on the door. She glanced both ways down the hallway, thankful she didn't have an audience as she waited.

"*Ola*," a cheerful voice called from the other side of the door.

Kenzie grasped the cool metal doorknob and waited for the lock to be disengaged. The moment the handle moved, Kenzie pushed the door open and forced her way into the apartment.

The young woman from behind the door fought back, screaming in fear. They struggled for a moment, smashing into the cheap kitchen table. Kenzie had to drop her bag as they wrestled on the floor amongst the splintered wood. The young woman was surprisingly strong, but no match for Kenzie's strength and training. The end came quickly as Kenzie overpowered her and brought her gun up and into the young woman's frightened face. It was Cori Evans and it was all she needed to know.

Pull the trigger, LeGault, and get the hell out of here, the voice in Kenzie's head screamed, but those were not the only words she was hearing.

"*Qué usted quiere...qué usted quiere?*" Cori screamed in Spanish.

Kenzie rose to her feet and motioned with her gun for her intended target to rise. "Get up."

"What do you want?" Cori pleaded, this time in English.

"Shut up!" Kenzie ordered, pressing the gun against Cori's forehead. Her own head was pounding with second thoughts. One could not do that in the military. It just did not happen.

Cori seemed surprised Kenzie spoke English. "Who are you? What do you want?"

Kenzie grabbed Cori by the hair and Cori held her tongue.

Pulling them out of the line of sight of the window, Kenzie dragged her hostage along with her as she crossed the room and pulled down the blinds. Whoever was out there would no longer have a view inside, or a target. Shifting her eyes away from searching the outside, Kenzie looked down at her captive.

Cori's fear flooded face stared back at her. Kenzie was unsure of what to say as she watched the rapid rise and fall of her chest. It was easy to see her heartbeat pulse just below the surface of her neck. Kenzie looked away. Everything felt unreal, distant, almost as if she were watching some else's life.

"You're an American, so what are you doing in Mexico?" Kenzie asked, as she turned back to look into the young woman's eyes. Cori gave her no answer, returning the stare with a staunch air of defiance. This not only surprised Kenzie, it also annoyed her. She pulled back on Cori's hair and pushed her gun within inches of her face.

Cori stared into the black hole at the end of the gun's barrel. She closed her eyes for a moment, as if waiting for the gun to fire. Instead, Kenzie pressed the cold metal hard against her forehead.

"I'll ask you again — once. What are you doing in Mexico?"

"I'm...I'm a student at the Universidad Autonoma De Guadalajara," Cori answered as calmly as she could.

The information surprised Kenzie, and she didn't like surprises. "Taking what?"

"Why? What does it matter?"

Without a thought, Kenzie responded as she would have with any other person she was interrogating. She struck Cori hard in the face, splitting her lip. Cori lifted her hand to the corner of her mouth.

"Don't make me ask again," Kenzie said, releasing her grasp on Cori's hair. Walking to the window, she pulled back the blind and searched for the other gunman. She scanned the area to no avail. *Where did he go? Has he gone?* "What are you studying at the University?"

Cori gingerly touched the corner of her mouth and looked down at the bright blood on her fingers. "Computer programming."

Computer programming, Kenzie pulled away from the window. *Why would someone want a computer programming student dead?* The whole situation was taking a bad turn and all Kenzie wanted was out — finish the job, then find out who the other shooter was and why they were there.

Kenzie saw Cori watching, swallowing with difficulty, as Kenzie tensed and tightened her finger on the trigger. Her conscience tugging at her, Kenzie stopped. She lowered the gun and Cori dropped her head into her hands. Kenzie couldn't hear her crying but she was certain she was.

Reluctantly, Kenzie realized she would have to take Cori with her. "We need to get out of here, now."

"We...what? Why?" Cori appeared panicked. "I'm not leaving here," she added boldly.

"We are leaving!" Kenzie reached down, grabbed a handful of Cori's hair and dragged her to her feet. "It wasn't a suggestion. Do you own a car?"

"No." Kenzie pushed the barrel of the gun harder against the flesh of Cori's face. Then Cori reluctantly acknowledged, "Yes."

A hardened glare formed on Kenzie's features as she struck Cori's cheek with the back of her hand. "Don't lie to me again." She holstered her gun and went to her bags on the floor.

Cori raised her hand to her face and glanced quickly at the door.

"Don't even think about it," Kenzie warned, seeing the consideration of flight on the young woman's face. "I could have killed you, but I didn't." Pausing for a moment as if to reflect on her own comment, Kenzie sighed loudly before walking over and crouching down in front of Cori. She was tired and needed time to think, but there was no time to think. There was someone else out there hunting Cori Evans and Kenzie had no idea where he was.

"Look," Kenzie said as she licked her lips, "I don't want to hurt you, but I need answers."

Cori looked incredulous. "You don't want to hurt me?" she echoed, as she touched the cut on her lip that Kenzie gave to her. Cori's eyes quickly flicked around the room, as if searching frantically for a way to save her life. "I don't have any answers for you. Hell, I don't even know what the questions are. I don't know who you are or why you're here, but I'll give you whatever you want...just, please don't take me with you."

"Believe me, you're safer with me than you would be staying here. We need to leave — now." Kenzie rose to her feet and placed a hand on Cori's shoulder. She felt Cori instantly pull away.

"You're crazy. I'm not going anywhere with you. You bust into my home, shove a gun in my face, split my lip open," she touched the corner of her mouth as if to emphasize her point, "and you think I'm going to leave with you. No way. Whatever it is that you think I have, or whatever answers you think I can give you, you have the wrong girl."

Kenzie leaned down to within inches of Cori's face. "I don't care. I said I don't want to hurt you, but I will if I have to." She spoke slowly and clearly as she pulled her gun from her holster. "Now, get the keys to your goddamn car, pick up my bag, and let's go."

"But you—"

Cori never got a chance to finish as Kenzie grabbed her by the neck, shoving her thumb into a pressure point just behind Cori's ear. The pain brought instant tears to her eyes and Cori fought back. Bringing her elbow up, Cori fought to turn her body away from the pain. The maneuver didn't surprise Kenzie, as Kenzie turned her wrist, driving her thumb deeper into the soft tissue behind Cori's ear.

"I know more ways to hurt you than I do to kill you, so just do as I say." Kenzie released the pressure point.

Cori gasped as the pain was instantly released, holding her ear and jaw.

"Let's go." Kenzie gestured toward the door.

Cori silently complied without further resistance. Kenzie pulled her second gun from her holster, quickly checking the rounds in both. Holstering one gun, she turned to Cori. "Where's your car?"

"It's in the lot across the street, a red Honda," she said, frustration apparent in her voice.

"Okay, this is how it's gonna work. We're leaving here. You're going first and I'll be right behind you." She nodded toward the door. "Don't do anything stupid or heroic. I saw how you enjoy the neighborhood children and I'd hate to have to come back here. Understood?" Kenzie aimed her gun at Cori's side until she saw Cori nod. "Once we're in your car, I want you to go east on Anillo

Periferico, and then out of town on the 54. Understood?" Cori nodded again.

"All right, grab my bag there and let's go." Cori picked up the duffle bag and the two left.

Kenzie was on edge. If she were the shooter, now would be the perfect time to take the shot. The sun was about to set. They would be in the light and the shooter would be in shadows. One shot and then he could easily dissolve into the darkness and be gone. Alert and observant, her eyes swept quickly over the neighborhood.

Shuffling out and away from the apartment building, she kept one hand on Cori, the other tightly gripping her gun. Though her attention was on their surroundings, she also watched the frightened woman with her. Everything in her told her she had done the right thing, so why didn't she feel better?

"It's over there." Cori pointed out the small older Honda parked in the vacant gravel lot across the street.

Cori's direction pulled Kenzie's mind back to the moment. Her lack of focus concerned and annoyed her. Silently scolding herself, she kept her eyes moving like she had been trained. Rooftops, open windows, and the busy streets of Guadalajara, it was all too much for her to take in. Feeling overwhelmed and vulnerable, she gave Cori a nudge with her elbow as they crossed the street. "Hurry up."

They reached the car and Cori struggled to get the key into the slot as she shifted the bag on her shoulder. Kenzie knew she had brought more than she'd needed for this job. It was Mexico, fifty bucks could buy her just about anything, but the merchandise was not always up to her standards.

Cori seemed to delay getting into her car. Fumbling with the keys and the lock, her head looked around desperately.

"Come on," Kenzie demanded, aware of her delay tactics.

The shot was not audible, but a millisecond before it was fired Kenzie saw the red line from the laser sight refracting on the car. Instinct took over and she tackled Cori to the ground just as the side window of the Honda exploded. "Stay down," Kenzie ordered as they huddled together, the shattered glass raining down upon them. Moving away from the side of the car, Kenzie brought her guns up and fired rapidly in the direction of the source of the laser.

The loud noise of the big guns echoed through the neighborhood, filling the streets with screams from frightened people, including Cori who was crouching down, her hands over her ears, looking too stunned to move.

"Open the car door," Kenzie yelled as she ducked down to reload.

Cori didn't move.

"Open the fucking car door, now!"

Cori reached through the shattered window, unlocked the door and pulled it open. With the car door now open, Kenzie holstered one of her guns and pushed Cori forward. "Get in, get over, and get down."

Kenzie picked up her duffle bag, and threw it into the back seat just as two holes exploded into the frame of the car. Kenzie hurtled into the driver's seat and then emptied her handgun at the muzzle flash in the shadows. Quickly switching guns, she holstered the empty one as she reached for the keys gripped tightly in Cori's hand.

"Give me the keys," Kenzie demanded as she ripped them from Cori's fingers. Firing up the engine, she shoved it into gear and stomped on the gas pedal. The tires squealed as the small car shot backward out of its parking stall and into the street. Kenzie spun the steering wheel with one hand and the car bounced and slid sideways as she slammed it into a forward gear.

Cori crouched on the passenger side floor watching as Kenzie maneuvered the car with one hand while reloading her guns with the other. "What was that?" Cori yelled over the noise of the car. "What the hell was that? What's going on?"

Kenzie was too busy refilling clips and trying to drive to answer. Her eyes darted from her lap to the road in front, and then to the vehicles behind them. Kenzie shoved an ammo clip into the butt of her gun. "Somebody wants you dead. That's why I'm here." She holstered her gun and looked down at Cori. "Why would someone want you dead?"

"You're here to protect me?" For a moment, Cori's face held a look of relief, but that soon disintegrated. "You're not here to protect me, are you?"

To Kenzie it sounded like a rhetorical question, so she offered no answer. "Why would someone want you dead?"

Cori rubbed at her face. "I-I don't know. No one... I'm just a student. I haven't been down here long enough to piss someone off that badly. I'm not into drugs, and my mother doesn't have any money, so there's no point in kidnapping me." She sniffed loudly as she looked around her at the shattered glass. "I don't know why anyone would want me dead."

Kenzie was thinking about Cori's disclaimer as they approached Anillo Periferico, the main road that looped around Guadalajara. Studying every vehicle behind her, she tried to decide if she should go directly to the rendezvous point or follow a circuitous route to make sure no one was following them. *The rendezvous point... What am I going to do with her? How am I going to explain her? Maybe I can smuggle her onto the plane. Yeah, right, and then what? I need to find out who wants her dead. Then what, LeGault?*

Cori, struggling to stay calm, said, "Excuse me."

Her thought processes interrupted, Kenzie looked down at Cori almost as if she had forgotten she was there.

"What just happened? What exactly is going on?"

After a pause, Kenzie finally said matter-of-factly, "Someone just tried to shoot you." She reached over and brushed away some of the shattered glass. "Sit in the seat."

"I think I know that, but why are they shooting at us?" Cori's voice reflected surprise and fear.

Kenzie reached around into the backseat and unzipped her duffle bag. "Not us — you." Keeping her eyes on the road and behind them, she felt through the bag with her fingers. "Now get up and sit in the seat."

Cori didn't attempt to move. "You shot back at them."

"That's what I do." Déjà vu took her back to when she was standing in her own home talking with Colonel Manuck. *Was it Colonel Manuck? Does he not trust me?*

"But you could have—" Cori paused and looked at Kenzie in naïve astonishment. "You could have killed an innocent bystander."

"That really isn't my concern. Now get in the seat."

"It isn't your concern that you just shot at innocent people and someone could have died!"

Kenzie's jaw muscle tightened as she looked in the rearview mirror, "People die all the time. It's not my problem. Now move your ass into that seat before I make you!" Kenzie found what she'd been looking for in her bag and dropped the extra clips into her lap.

"Not your problem—"

Kenzie turned and glared at her. "I'm still alive, and that is my first priority." She reached down, grabbed a handful of Cori's hair, and started to pull. Cori screamed and snatched out at Kenzie's wrist with both hands, digging her fingers into skin. Kenzie ignored the pain and continued to pull. Cori had no choice but to slide into the passenger seat. The moment she was seated, Kenzie let go of her hair and Cori rubbed at her scalp.

"Now, since you feel like talking, maybe you can explain to me why someone wants you dead."

Cori's mouth opened, but she just as quickly closed it. "I don't know. You don't understand — you must have the wrong person."

Kenzie knew she didn't have the wrong person. She had seen the assignment — the name and the picture matched. Still, an overwhelming sense of wrong was growing inside her. In the meantime, she kept her eyes moving. There was someone out there looking for them; she just didn't know where. Cori was upset, but Kenzie reminded herself that was not her problem. She had a job to do. So why hadn't she done it? She had orders, so why had she not followed them? *What am I doing?*

A flash of white darted out from behind a delivery van in the rearview mirror and Kenzie saw it out of the corner of her eye. It was a white Renault and it was moving rapidly in their direction. Kenzie pressed down on the gas pedal and the Honda sped forward.

Cori glanced behind them. Turning back, she noted, "What's going on?"

The Renault was closing the gap and Kenzie didn't have time for questions as she steered the little Honda in and out of traffic. There was no doubt in her mind now — the white Renault was after them.

Cori glanced from Kenzie to the rear window. "Is it them?" The rear window exploded in a shower of glass, answering her question.

Dipping and bobbing her head, Kenzie kept sight of the white Renault in the mirror. Try as she might, she couldn't catch a glimpse of the driver or tell whether there was more than one person in the car.

Kenzie pushed the accelerator pedal to the floor and the little car responded. They were now weaving in and out of the traffic at a dangerous rate of speed. Pulling a gun from one of her holsters, she tucked it under her leg as they sped through the streets. Narrow roads combined with slow moving farm vehicles, and speedy little taxis made maneuvering difficult, but Kenzie kept ahead of their pursuers. She spotted an opening in traffic, and the next corner they came to, Kenzie pushed the little Honda to its limit, pulling quickly in front of a large bus chugging out plumes of diesel smoke. The large vehicle blocked the Renault's view as the driver of the bus leaned on his horn.

"Jesus Christ, you're insane!"

Cori braced herself against the door and the dash as Kenzie whipped the Honda into the next lane, letting the bus roar past them. She slammed on the brakes, and horns blasted and tires squealed as she gunned the Honda and swung back in behind the bus and then in behind the white Renault. It was a gutsy, crazy move, but it worked. They were now behind the little white car.

Roaring down the road, the driver of the Renault was unaware he was now the one being followed. Kenzie squinted to get a look at the lone occupant, but she couldn't identify the person. Bracing the steering wheel with her knee, she pulled the gun from beneath her leg and slid a cartridge into the chamber. Kenzie gripped the gun tightly; resting the barrel on the side mirror, she calculated her shot. The driver of the Renault must have seen her in his mirror and slammed on his brakes. The rear tires of the Renault smoked as the brake lights flashed on.

Kenzie slammed on the brakes. Needing both hands on the steering wheel as she fought for control, she threw the gun into Cori's lap. The Honda swayed recklessly back and forth. "Son of a—" she said, taking her foot off the brake and slamming it back onto the accelerator.

Powering the car past the Renault, Kenzie made a sharp turn to the left, darting down a narrow road. Coming out into a busy intersection, she barely slowed as she zipped in and out of traffic before turning down another street. The oncoming traffic honked and snarled to a quick stop, but Kenzie ignored them, turning a hairpin right onto a side street, scattering pedestrians in both directions. The Honda banged harshly over a curb, flinging the two women about inside the car. They heard the brakes and the horns of the vehicles they left behind, but, so far, the Renault had not turned the corner.

Cori looked down at the gun in her lap and picked it up.

Without any warning, Kenzie slammed on the brakes and made a sudden right turn, then a left, and then gunned the car again, bouncing and banging it along the potholed road. Cori had no choice but to brace herself against the jostling, dropping the gun to the floor.

They roared down roads she didn't know, barely slowing down for the traffic. Most of the roads were scarcely wide enough for the car, but it didn't seem to faze the woman behind the wheel. People and animals fled as Kenzie maneuvered in and out of side streets. It was only when they returned to the main street that Kenzie finally slowed down.

Kenzie squinted into the setting sun. "You okay?" she asked without taking her eyes off the road or the rearview mirror. "I think we lost 'em." Kenzie reached up and readjusted the mirror as she drove the Honda cautiously down the narrow, bumpy street.

Once again on their way to the rendezvous point, Kenzie looked around the car for her gun and caught sight of her shell-shocked passenger. "You should put your seatbelt on." Without waiting for a response, she reached over and grabbed the seatbelt. Pulling it across Cori's waist, Kenzie snapped the restraint into place.

A hysterically frightened Cori slapped and pushed away at Kenzie's arm. "Get away from me — get away. You're fuckin' insane!" Cori's wide eyes glared at Kenzie in disbelief. "Are you kidding me? Tell me you're kidding. You bust into my apartment, slap me around, then force me to leave at gunpoint, where I'm shot at as you drive like a maniac on meth through the streets of 'Lajara, and now you're worried about my goddamn seatbelt?"

"We need to get out of here and out of the city," Kenzie said calmly, ignoring Cori's tirade. "They obviously know your car."

"How the hell would they know my car?" Reaching down to the floorboard, Cori kicked at the gun and tried to retrieve it off the floorboard. "And who the hell are 'they'?"

"Let me have the gun," Kenzie demanded as she maneuvered the Honda around some serious potholes and life-risking pedestrians.

Cori lifted the gun, but before she could even think about aiming it, Kenzie had snatched it out of her hands. Cori struck out, punching and slapping at Kenzie with all her might. Her blows were erratic, but several landed, hitting Kenzie in the hand, shoulder, and her already damaged cheek. The car swerved erratically as Kenzie held up a hand to shield herself. Horns honked as the little Honda swayed back and forth, in and out of their lane of traffic.

"Son of a bitch!" Kenzie dropped the gun into her lap. She backhanded Cori, sending her hard into the passenger door. Kenzie steadied the out of control car before holstering her weapon. Reaching up, she touched her face and then looked down at the blood on her fingers.

"Are you kidding me?" Kenzie's brow furrowed and her glare darkened. She returned her attention to the road but her eyes lifted for a glance in the rearview mirror. A ribbon of blood was curling down her cheek. Her head hurt, her cheek throbbed, and she'd had enough. Instinctively Kenzie pulled her 9mm and pointed it directly into Cori's face. Her icy stare intense and devoid of emotion, she looked closely at the face of her intended victim. The two women locked eyes but no words were needed. Kenzie had made her intentions very clear.

With no forewarning, Kenzie stomped on the brakes. Her hands on the steering wheel stopped her momentum, but Cori didn't have time to brace herself as she slammed full force against the restraint of the seatbelt. The thick strap bit into her neck and waist, stunning her into submission.

Kenzie didn't say a word, just holstered her weapon. Cori settled back into her seat while Kenzie pulled out into traffic. The tension in the car was thick but the message was clear. "I won't kill you, but that won't stop me from inflicting a lot of pain on you," Kenzie finally said.

Cori sat quietly in her seat, awkwardly attempting to get her seatbelt back into proper position. She looked to the road ahead of her, all the while shooting glances at the stranger driving her car. She couldn't think and she couldn't concentrate. Her body ached in pain as her mind tried to make sense of the alternate reality that had become her world.

When the car passed the University, Cori turned and looked at her. "What are you going to do with me?"

The driver looked at Cori and then turned her attention back to the road in front of her. The traffic was getting lighter as they drove out of the city and she adjusted the rearview mirror unnecessarily.

"Can't you just let me go? I won't say anything."

"No," Kenzie said without hesitation.

Cori looked down at her hands and then out the shattered passenger window. She watched as the centuries old twin towers of the Cathedral of Guadalajara disappeared from sight. She wondered if she would ever see them again.

"Somebody wants you dead, aren't you curious as to why? I know I'm a little mystified." Kenzie glanced over at the young woman and Cori looked back at her. Her face was battered and bruised, her hair rumpled, her clothes and her car had seen better days. Cori looked every bit the victim that she had almost become. Kenzie felt something she had felt days earlier in a remote desert in the Middle East — remorse. It was not the first time she didn't like who she had become. Looking at this young student, she knew there was no way Cori Evans was a player. Someone screwed up somewhere, and Kenzie just hoped it wasn't her.

She turned away from Cori and looked straight ahead, then did something completely out of character and very unprofessional. "My name is Kenzie."

Chapter 5

The rich mahogany wood and the long, thick curtains swallowed up what little light there was inside the small office/library. Book-laden shelves lined the walls from floor to ceiling. They gave the room the appearance of being loftier than it was. The lone occupant was leaning back in the chair at the desk, pipe smoke curling upward over his head. The massive desk was strewn with papers — faxes, documents, and a long yellow legal pad filled with handwritten notes. The day's newspaper was folded just within arm's reach, but he didn't have time to read it, not today.

Lifting his hand from the armrest, he spun his watch around for the umpteenth time. His phone should have rung by now. It hadn't, and that confirmed what he already suspected. Sitting up, he placed his pipe in the holder on the far side of the desk as he reached for his thick Rolodex. He was well aware that the more people he got involved, the greater the chance he might tip his hand, but he had no choice. With the decision made, the question remaining was whom he could trust when lives were at stake.

The light on one of the phone lines flicked red, and then the phone warbled an incoming call.

"Yeah?" he answered quickly into the handset, his eagerness showing through his normally stolid demeanor. "Is it done?" There was a long pause as he listened. He reached for the papers on his desk, scattering them around until he found the one he was looking for. "Son of a bitch! Where is she right now?"

Tossing the document down, he rose from his chair and paced to the window. "And what can we do about it?" He pulled back the heavy curtain and looked out into the night. "Where's the plane? Oh for the love of Mary...how hard is it to kill one woman?"

He threw back the curtain and rubbed his hand over his face as he listened to the voice on the other end. "This is becoming a bigger problem than it's worth. I asked for your best. Who exactly did you send?" He walked back to his desk and looked over the scattered papers. "Where is she — right now?" The answer he heard from the party at the other end of the phone annoyed him. "Then find out!"

Cori had no idea where they were going. For a while they traveled north on Highway 54, and then turned off onto a narrow paved road that she had barely seen in the dark. The pavement gave way to hard packed dirt and the rough road and abundance of potholes jarred her back, but making any kind of comment about the road conditions would have been pointless. Tired, exhausted, and beyond functional, she knew there was no point in trying to escape. Everyone knew that in Mexico, if you wanted to be safe, you didn't go anywhere after dark.

The instrument panel of the Honda gave off an eerie glow of green, enough light for her to see the driver. She had said her name was Kenzie, but she had not said anything since. She was an interesting woman, quiet and calm, but very much in control. Cori could tell a strong current was churning below the hardened surface. She watched the strong fingers holding tightly to the steering wheel as the car bounced unrelentingly down the dirt road. Cori was a hands person and she always noticed them first. She often wondered if it was because she had wanted to be a surgeon at one point in her life, though that had been a long time ago.

The mountains were to their right, which meant the ocean was in front of them, but a long way off. The moon was high and the stars were out in abundance when Kenzie pulled the car off the road and killed the engine. The dust settled, and Cori could taste it in her nose and mouth as the sounds of the motor died away into silence.

"Where are we?" Cori's voice sounded strange and raspy so she licked at her dry lips. She winced when her tongue touched the swollen corner of her mouth and tasted the iron in the dried blood. Everything was unreal, like a dream, and she was floating beyond it. Nothing about this made sense. She was not rich, and neither was her mother, but then again Kenzie had said it was not a kidnapping.

Kenzie reached into the back seat, pulled out a large bottle of water and offered it to Cori. Cori accepted the bottle and muttered a quiet "thank you" before she took a drink. There was a waiting silence inside the car, interrupted by the gurgle of water as Cori took another drink. With her thirst quenched, she reluctantly offered the bottle back.

Kenzie accepted it without a word, took a long drink, and then placed the bottle on the console between them. Opening the car door, pieces of glass cascaded to the ground as Kenzie pulled herself from the confines of the vehicle.

"Can I get out, too?" Cori asked cautiously.

Cori noticed Kenzie studying the landscape. "No," she answered finally, her tone low and emotionless as she slowly walked around to the back of the car.

With nothing else to do, Cori sat and listened to the noises of the night — some she knew, some she did not. The wind rustled through the countryside, filled with the sound of crickets. She picked remnants of glass from her clothing and tossed them out the window. How had this happened? More to the point, how had this happened to her? She watched as Kenzie moved around to stand in front of the car. The woman's thoughts were obviously miles away.

Time ticked away, giving Cori lots of opportunity to study her captor. She moved with silent confidence, but Cori could tell she was not at ease. Kenzie paced...and she waited. Several times Cori was certain she heard the woman talking to herself. It didn't take her long to realize they were waiting. The question was, waiting for what — or for whom?

Many possibilities circled around in Cori's mind. Some were plausible, some unbelievable, but each supposition baffled her more than the last. She closed her eyes and fought to maintain some rationality in her thinking. "What exactly are we waiting for?" Cori finally asked as Kenzie looked at her watch for the umpteenth time.

The wind lifted Kenzie's long curly locks and she brushed them out of the way in annoyance. She walked to the back door of the car and yanked it open. "We're waiting for a ride," Kenzie said as she unzipped her duffle bag, obviously irritated by the intrusion on her thoughts.

A ride? Cori was surprised by the answer, mainly because she had not really expected to be given one. "From whom? From where?"

Straightening up from the back seat, Kenzie pulled on a baseball cap and pulled her curly hair through the opening in the back. Reaching into her bag, she pulled out what looked to Cori like a thick pair of binoculars.

"Who are we waiting for?" Cori asked again as she watched Kenzie scan the skies.

Kenzie ignored the question as she searched the horizon and then back down the road they had traveled.

"What are we waiting for?" Cori asked. Kenzie brought the glasses away from her eyes and Cori saw that they were not typical binoculars.

Kenzie glanced down at her watch again. "I'm looking for a plane."

"A plane? Here?"

"Yes." Kenzie lowered the night vision binoculars, scanning the horizon with her naked eyes. "And they're late," she added, raising the expensive binoculars to resume her search.

Cori watched her, frightened but intrigued by the quiet woman with the lethal skills. She wondered just how one became a hired killer. Was there a sign-up sheet outside the main hall in some university? As if her question was asked aloud, Kenzie lowered the night vision glasses and looked over at her. She felt the darkness of Kenzie's eyes and was reminded of what had transpired just that afternoon. This woman did not hesitate to shoot at people.

Feeling uneasy and very vulnerable under Kenzie's intense stare, Cori looked away. She wondered whether she could kill someone if she were put into the right situation. Without hesitation, Cori knew the answer was no.

Time dragged on and there was still no sign of a plane. It was quiet, until somewhere far off in the hills, a coyote cried out, breaking the silence of solitude.

Cori looked over at Kenzie, her eyes hidden behind the binoculars that were continuously sweeping back and forth over the distant mountains. "Why are you here?" Cori asked, waiting for an answer as she studied the woman with the gun. The question received no immediate response. After a long moment, Kenzie turned tired eyes to her. Unnerved by the hardened gaze, Cori began to chatter nervously. "I mean — why here, why me, I don't understand. Who am I? I'm nobody. I'm just a girl trying to get by. So why me? What did I do?"

Kenzie said nothing, but for once she didn't look away. The questions Cori was asking were the same questions she had been asking herself...and they were the only things keeping Cori alive.

"You're some kind of hired killer, one with serious connections and the money to back up your mission — night vision glasses, your own plane." She looked around into the darkness. "Is this even a runway?" Cori waited but Kenzie didn't answer. She was not really expecting her to.

Returning her attention to the skies, Kenzie was grateful for the silence that finally fell between them.

Dejected, Cori tried to keep to herself inside the car, but time was not a comfort to her and neither was the quiet. "Can I ask you a question?"

Kenzie turned around and faced her. "I haven't been able to stop you yet."

Cori ignored the sarcasm. "Who sent you here to kill me?"

Kenzie didn't answer, though several thoughts crossed her facial features, obvious even in the dark.

"Can't you tell me who? I think I have a right to know. I mean, someone wants me dead and you must know who it is."

Cori waited, she wanted answers, some kind of dialogue, but her captor would not oblige. "Okay, don't answer... At least tell me why? Can you do that? Can you tell me why someone would want me dead?"

"That's more than one question." Kenzie turned away from her and went back to watching for the plane.

"Why don't you just let me go? I mean it's obvious that you have the wrong girl. It is possible you know — somebody somewhere mixes up a name. Maybe the wrong address..."

Kenzie turned and glared at her through the broken back window of the car. "You don't get it, do you?" The question came out harshly. "If I wanted you dead, you'd be dead, period. You're alive because I need you to answer some questions for me. I want to know why someone would want you dead, and why they chose me to do it!" Each word was a demand. Kenzie took a deep breath, as if to clear her thoughts. "Look...the only way I'm going to be able to figure things out is with your help. I'm not going to hurt you."

Cori studied the woman outside of the car. "Am I supposed to take your word for that?"

There was silence as Kenzie looked up to the stars. Kenzie stepped up to the driver's window and bent down to look squarely at Cori. "I have no reason to lie to you."

For a brief moment, everything else was forgotten as they looked into each other's eyes, searching for answers and the truth that lay beyond their grasp. It had been a long, hard day for both of them, and the toll etched in their distressed and weary faces.

Cori looked hard at Kenzie, eager to find something to give her hope, any sign that she might survive this ordeal. "You want me to trust you? Then tell me what happens when you find the answers. Are you going to kill me?"

Kenzie backed away from Cori and her persistent questions.

"Well?" Cori's courage was growing with her frustration. Throwing open the car door, she stepped out into the night and challenged the woman who was holding her captive. "That's what you were paid to do, isn't it? You were paid to kill me, weren't you?"

Kenzie looked down at her watch again. "Nobody paid me anything. Now will you shut up? I'm trying to think." She started to walk away from the car, but she didn't get far enough.

"What do you mean, nobody paid you? You're doing this for free?" Cori sounded confused by Kenzie answer. "I don't understand? Why would someone—"

"I'm not that kind of a—" She searched for the right word, but none of them seemed accurate. Killer, assassin, murderer — the words were accurate all right, but she wanted to scream that they were not who she was. She did what she did because someone told her to, but suddenly that explanation seemed feeble and inept, and that frustrated her even further. Turning around, her eyes ablaze in fury, she sputtered out, "I don't work that way...I'm not that kind of — I do what I'm ordered to do."

Shock registered on Cori's face. "What you're ordered to do? What does that mean! Exactly who do you work for?"

It was not just a question, it was a demand for information, but Kenzie refused to answer. Instead, she moved further away from the car, away from the questions she couldn't, or didn't, want to answer. All she wanted was for the plane to show up, but she had no idea what she was going to do when it did. Her level of frustration boiled over, "Get your ass back in that car!"

Cori did as ordered, but that didn't settle Kenzie down. She began to pace in front of the car and then beside it. Her mind was a mélange of questions and doubts. She had so few answers, leaving her to question what she had done. Orders were orders, and it was not up to her to decide which ones was going to follow. When Manuck found out she had botched another assignment...

"Aw shit," she muttered in exasperation, wiping hard at her face.

Hours passed in silence as Kenzie kept her gaze on the empty sky. Thankfully, Cori was sitting quietly in the front seat of her beat up car, giving Kenzie time to mull over the endless questions swirling in her mind. The assignment was a bust — again. Her extraction team had not shown up, stranding her in a foreign country. *Why?* She had no phone, no means of contacting anyone, and even if she had, who would she call? Moreover, what would she say?

Looking at the young woman in the car only added to her dilemma. It was easy to see that Cori had spent the better part of the last few hours crying quietly. Kenzie tried not to care. She had too many other thoughts in her head and she didn't have the time to feel badly about Cori's tears.

Feeling eyes upon her, Cori looked into the haunting gold eyes of her would-be killer. "What?" It was mostly a plea, but Kenzie remained silent to Cori's question. "Why are you looking at me? Answer me! What are you doing?" Cori demanded. "What happens if your ride doesn't show up?"

Yeah, Kenzie! The thought screamed inside her head and she did her best to ignore it. The gray twilight of the predawn was beginning to lighten the vast Mexican sky. It would not be long before the sun would be up and they would be standing out in the open like sitting ducks with no place to go. *We can't stay here forever.* Kenzie looked down at her watch and knew that decision time was approaching fast. *Think...think! What am I going to do?* Kenzie looked at Cori and pondered the questions rolling around in her mind. *Why? ... Who? Now that's a better question. Who would want this woman dead?*

Kenzie turned back toward the car, stepping awkwardly on a stone that made her stumble. That sudden movement saved her life. A bullet she didn't hear coming sliced the skin along her temple just before she dropped to the ground.

The sudden flurry of action startled Cori. She screamed because it was all she could do.

"Shut up and stay down," Kenzie ordered touching her temple. "Son of a bitch," she grumbled angrily, wiping the blood off her fingers and scrambled to the car. "Close, way too close," she cursed to herself as she opened the back door of the car and pulled out her duffle bag.

There was a ping of metal as another shot searched for its target. Cori screamed again, hunching herself into a ball and slipped to the floor of the car.

Kenzie paid her no attention as she concentrated on acquiring her weapon. Within a minute, she had her rifle out, assembled, and the telescopic sight clicked into place. There was no time to re-zero the sights. She hoped her assembly of it onto the sniper rifle was true. She crawled carefully over the ground toward the rear of the car. Kenzie turned her ball cap around, settled into the familiar position, and began to ready her mind for what she did best. Everything around her grew soundless and disappeared as she searched the distance through her scope.

Several minutes of stressful silence had gotten to Cori. Kenzie heard a quiet whisper. "Can you see anything? I can't see a thing."

Kenzie continued to scan the horizon. "You won't. It's a high-powered rifle. Now shut up and stay down." Kenzie closed her eyes and relaxed, tuning out everything around her before she opened them again. This is what she did, what she excelled at. She searched with all her senses, looking for shapes in the distance, something innately human, something shiny. Mother Nature didn't make things shiny — man did. She sought out the shadows, looking for something that didn't blend in, for a silhouette against the skyline that shouldn't be there, and she listened for a sound nature didn't make. The five Ss had been drilled into her until they were a part of her. Shape, shine, shadow, silhouette, and sound — these were the basic principles of hunting an individual, and they paid off.

The rising sun reflected off something down the road that they had traveled the night before. Kenzie focused in and saw a shadow where there shouldn't be one. She checked the wind, and then estimated the distance. Not an impossible shot, but still... When the shadow moved again, Kenzie let go a breath, squeezed the slack from the trigger and fired the shot. She wished for a moment that she had a silencer, but by the time the shot was heard, it would be too late. The crack of the rifle echoed around the car and throughout the low valley as the distant shadow slumped into a heap.

Kenzie disassembled her rifle, put it back into her duffle bag, and threw the bag into the back seat. "Let's go."

Cori was curled up in a ball on the floor. She looked at Kenzie in startled disbelief as she climbed into the driver's seat. "That's it? Let's go? What if they're still out there? What if they shoot at us again? They aren't going to shoot again, are they? You just shot someone! You just killed someone, didn't you? You just killed another human being. Who was it?"

Kenzie didn't answer, not because she didn't want to but because she didn't have an answer. She turned the key and the Honda's overworked motor whirled to life. She had no idea where they were going, but she knew they could not stay where they were. Plane or no plane, they had to go.

They had traveled only a few minutes when Kenzie stopped the car. Cori lifted her head just enough to see Kenzie pull one of her guns from its holster. Climbing from the car, she walked across the dirt road and stood at its edge. Watching in puzzlement, Cori was shocked to see her pull back some of the vegetation to reveal the white Renault. How Kenzie had seen it, Cori had no idea. She hadn't had any inkling the car was there, but Kenzie had. Then Cori saw the body crumpled on the ground next to the car. She had seen a dead body before, but it still made her stomach roil as she watched Kenzie rummaging through the dead man's pockets. When she returned to the car, Cori could see she was angry about something.

"That's nice, first you murder him and then you rob him."

Kenzie turned to face her but didn't answer as she put the car into gear. A moment later they were back on the dusty, bone-jarring road. Cori had no idea where they were going, and she really didn't care.

After a few minutes, "I didn't rob him," Kenzie said flatly. "And I didn't murder him."

"Really? You put a bullet through his head and then rifled through his pockets. What the hell would you call it?"

"I didn't murder him. He shot first, remember?"

"He shot first... Is that how you justify it? You're a murderer, and no matter what you say, that's what—"

Kenzie snapped. "Will you just shut up?"

Kenzie's explosion was enough to silence the questions in the car. Cori was scared. She could feel it from the pit of her stomach to the shakiness in her hands, but watching Kenzie's steely confidence settled her somewhat. She looked at her profile again and saw the fresh wound on Kenzie's temple, "You're hurt."

Cori heard a quiet compassion in her own voice, and it appeared to calm Kenzie's simmering anger. Kenzie reached up to touch her injury. Leaning forward, Kenzie looked at herself in the rearview mirror. The bleeding appeared to have stopped, and Kenzie attempted to wipe away some of the dried blood. "I'm fine," she muttered as she looked back to the road.

There was an uneasy silence in the car for a long while, as if each one was waiting for the other to speak. Then softly, Kenzie stated, "I wasn't robbing him."

Cori was lost in her thoughts and didn't hear her clearly. "Pardon?"

Kenzie cleared her throat. "I said I wasn't robbing that..." she hooked a thumb back towards the Renault, "...that guy."

"Could have fooled me."

"I think...I..." Kenzie paused, choosing her words carefully. "I was looking for his identification."

"Why would it matter? Are you going to notify his next of kin?" Cori saw the muscles tense in Kenzie's jaw as she considered the question.

Cori leaned back against her seat and looked at the road unfolding before them. As Guadalajara's majestic skyline rose in front of them, she realized they were going back the way they'd come the night before.

Kenzie gingerly touched her throbbing temple and then rubbed her eyes. She sighed deeply, resting her head against her hand for support. "I didn't know him," Kenzie finally said, "but I know his type, and they don't usually have family."

"Know his type? What does that mean? What? Does he work for the same people you do?"

Kenzie glanced in the rearview mirror again, "Meaning we need to find another way out of Mexico."

"Who exactly do you work for?"

Kenzie hesitated, then answered, "Let's just say I follow orders."

"You said that before. But whose orders?" Cori was scared, confused, and exhausted. "I mean, why would they send you down here to kill me?"

Sighing deeply, Kenzie turned to look at her, "That's the answer we need to find."

Further down the road, Kenzie suddenly veered off onto a frontage road and Cori braced herself against the car door. "A little warning might have been nice," she said as they pitched back and forth inside the car.

Kenzie made no comment as she maneuvered the car toward a Pemex gas station. Cori glanced around at all the people and then back at her captor. This was the chance she'd been waiting for. There would be no way for Kenzie to stop her from fleeing without making a big scene. *Could it be as easy as that?* Her freedom and her life had seemed to be beyond negotiation, but now she might just have a chance. They rolled forward toward the pumps and a young Mexican came up next to Kenzie's door.

"Fill 'er up." He nodded with a broad smile and reached for the hose. She watched him with annoyance. "Clear the pump before you start," Kenzie said in perfect Spanish as the young man looked over the shattered, bullet-riddled car. He nodded his understanding and turned to zero out the pump before starting to fill the car.

"I'm going into the gas station to clean up...and to get a map and some supplies." Kenzie turned and looked at Cori. "You're free to go."

"What? Just like that you're letting me go?"

"Just like that...or you can choose to stay." Kenzie opened the car door and exited the vehicle. Closing the door, she leaned down and looked at a startled Cori. "But keep in mind, no one ordered a hit on me."

Cori had her hand on the door handle, but didn't move as the comment resonated in her thoughts. If she didn't stay with Kenzie, where was she going to go? A thousand unanswered questions clamored for her attention. The "who", "what", "why", and "where" seemed secondary to her absolute desire to run, but she had nowhere to go. Her eyes went to a man on a telephone next to the rundown gas station. Outside phones were commonplace in Mexico; however, one that was working was a rarity. This one obviously was and she watched the man hang up and walk away. She could make a call, but to whom?

Minutes later, Kenzie came out of the station's convenience store carrying a brown paper bag and a six-pack of bottled water. She handed the attendant some pesos for the gas and then climbed into the car.

"I guess we have an understanding." Kenzie placed her purchases into the back seat. Cori nodded reluctantly. Kenzie started up the car as she studied Cori's face for a moment. She pulled the car up next to the gas station and then turned the car off. "Go clean yourself up. I'll wait."

There was no compassion in her voice, then again, Cori had not expected any.

The dim light flickered on in the bathroom and Cori looked at her reflection in the dingy mirror. She looked tousled, dirty, and bruises were coloring her cheek and chin. Splashing some water on her face, she was briefly taken aback by the coolness of the water. She patted her face tenderly with a paper towel. *Better, but not good*, she thought as she combed her fingers through her hair. Moments later, she slid back into the passenger seat of her car.

"Thanks," she said as she snapped the seatbelt into place. "Now what?"

Kenzie didn't reply as she reached around to the paper bag in the backseat and pulled out two pairs of sunglasses. "Here." She offered a pair to Cori. "You're gonna need these."

Tired and resigned, Cori took the glasses. "Not much of a disguise."

"It's not meant to be a disguise," Kenzie said as she slid her new sunglasses into place and fired up the car. "They're for protecting your eyes. We're heading west, into the sun."

Silence fell between them. The traffic grew heavier but it was not the zany, out of control rush hour to which most North Americans were accustomed. This was Mexico, where there was a different pace for doing things, and that included driving. There were no horns honking, no tailgaters. If people wanted to pass, they flashed their lights or used their hazard lights and other cars moved out of the way. It was a different life down here, and that was what drew many people. However, it was not the pace Kenzie was used to, and the trudging traffic only added to her frustration and aggravation. In utter exasperation, she slammed her hand down on the horn.

"That won't help any," Cori said. "People aren't in a hurry here, and they sure don't pay much attention to horns."

Kenzie swung the car out and around a slow moving farm truck and squeezed in front of it, barely missing an oncoming taxi.

"Jesus, that was close. Are you still trying to kill me?" Cori said as she looked over her shoulder at the taxi speeding away.

"I'm not trying to kill anyone," Kenzie said quietly.

"Really? Or did you mean at this moment?"

Kenzie didn't respond to the sardonic comments. As the car turned onto Highway 15, Cori looked back at the city of Guadalajara. "The way I've got it figured is..." she finally said, "you said you were following orders, and there are only so many kinds of people who get those kinds of orders. Organized crime, but I highly doubt that, so either you're military or you're government."

There was a long moment of silence before Kenzie finally answered, "Yeah." There was hesitancy in her voice.

It was an answer, but not the answer Cori was expecting. She wanted more. She turned to look at the woman driving her car. "Well, which is it?"

Kenzie contemplated the question for a moment before she answered, "Both."

Settling more comfortably into her seat, Cori focused her eyes on the road. "Whose?" she finally asked.

Kenzie's grip tightened on the steering wheel and the muscles of her forearms flexed. "Whose do you think?"

Cori didn't want to think about that, not if the answers were as scary as the questions. It just couldn't be possible that someone had put out a hit on her, but if it was, then... "I don't understand. Why would they want me dead?" Her head hurt. "That doesn't make sense."

"You're telling me."

For a long while, neither of them spoke. The little car's motor vibrated roughly, the tires clicked rhythmically over the cement highway as they headed westward — away from the city, and headfirst into the unknown.

Cori broke the silence. "So now what?"

"I'm not really sure. I'm kinda making this up as we go."

"Great, that makes me feel a whole lot better."

The morning sun rose high and hot as the landscape around them became less populated and more humid. With the car windows missing, there was no use trying to use the air conditioning and the heat became stifling. Kenzie pulled her paper bag of supplies from the back seat; a mix of fruit, nuts, and some packaged jerky, and offered it to Cori. She refused and Kenzie didn't push it. She knew hunger would win Cori over — eventually.

Kenzie was right, but it was well into the afternoon before Cori reached for a piece of fruit. Peeling the skin from an orange gave Cori something to do as she watched the Sierra Madres in the hazy distance.

"Where are we heading?" Cori asked as she noted the sign indicating they had crossed over from the Central Time Zone into the Mountain Time Zone.

"Mazatlán," Kenzie answered.

"Mazatlán? Why not Puerto Vallarta? It has an international airport like Guadalajara." She bit into the fruit, painfully splitting her already sore lip.

"Because we're not flying."

"But I thought we — were we not waiting for a plane back there before you shot that guy?"

Kenzie pulled the map out from behind the sun visor and glanced over it.

"Are we not flying back to the States?"

"No." Kenzie stowed the map back to its previous location.

"But I thought you said—"

"You'd do better to think more about why someone would want you dead than to focus on what I might have said."

Cori repeatedly ran her fingers through her honey-colored hair as she thought about Kenzie's admonition.

The calm Kenzie was exhibiting was a far cry from the turmoil inside her. The quiet gave her time to think, but the longer she thought, the more she realized how bad their situation was — little money, no ID, and no idea where they were going or what they were going to do once they got there. The situation was grim, and something told her it was not going to get better any time soon.

The wheels on the road were turning as fast as Kenzie's mind was searching for answers neither of them had. The silence grew heavy in the car. Trained to be detached, Kenzie did whatever needed to be done without thinking about the human cost. Nevertheless, she was starting to realize she was still human after all. She felt sorry for Cori and the position she had put her in.

"The reason we can't fly," Kenzie said suddenly, breaking the silent tension in the car, "is that we don't have tickets. In order for us to get tickets, we would need to show ID. You can't show yours because that would tip off whoever is after you, and I can't show ID because...well, I can't show ID. So we're going to have to drive."

Cori gingerly touched her sore face. "Drive...all the way!"

"I figure our best bet is to take the ferry out of Mazatlán to La Paz, then up the Baja to Tijuana and over the border to San Diego."

"All the way to San Diego," Cori said in disbelief. "That's like...a thousand miles."

Kenzie glanced at her watch. She was hoping they would reach Mazatlán by sundown. "Pretty close. I figure it's about 900 miles, give or take a few."

"How long is that going to take us?"

"A few days."

Cori leaned back against her seat. "But what about the border? We'll need ID there, won't we — ID and visitors' visas or passports?"

"I've got a connection in Tijuana." Kenzie had reviewed every available avenue of escape, but they were in a foreign country, a country that required proper identification. They wouldn't be able to use Cori's because that would send a red flag to whomever was behind the hit, and as far as she herself went...

With a sigh, Kenzie put her elbow on the window's edge and rested her head on her hand. She wasn't even sure she had enough money with her to make it out of Mexico, never mind to buy ID for someone who didn't exist. She knew what that meant, but was hoping they wouldn't have to deal with it until they reached Tijuana — if they were lucky.

As they drew closer to the coast, the lush green vegetation began to change. At her first glimpse of the distant waters, Cori sat up at little straighter in her seat. "There it is."

"What?" Kenzie asked as she wiped the ever-present sweat from her brow and dried it on her pants.

"The ocean."

Kenzie glanced over at her for a moment before she commented, "You act like you've never seen it before."

"I've seen it, but I'm originally from Missouri, so it's always a big deal." She sat back down in her seat, a little self-conscious and taken aback.

"Missouri?"

"Born and raised."

"Whereabouts?" Kenzie asked.

"Springfield, Missouri."

"Your family still there?"

"My mom. My dad died when I was a kid, so it was just mom and me for the most part. She's still there."

"And let me guess, you were a cheerleader at Springfield High," Kenzie said derisively.

"Actually, well...yes, but I went to school at Kickapoo High—"

"Kickapoo?" Kenzie asked with raised eyebrows. "Seriously?"

"Yeah, Kickapoo, or Kick-a-shit as we used to say," she said with a chuckle, forgetting for a moment where she was. "Kickapoo. It was named that because of where it was located, Kickapoo Prairie. It has a whole Indian background thing and...anyhow, it's where Brad Pitt went to school."

Kenzie stared out the windshield. "Who?"

"Brad Pitt." It was easy to see Kenzie had no idea who the actor was, "You don't know who Brad Pitt is?"

"Should I?"

"Brad Pitt, the actor. You know, *Interview with a Vampire*, *Troy*, *Legends of the Fall*." She looked at Kenzie and could tell the titles meant nothing. "Just had a baby with Angelina Jolie?"

Kenzie shook her head. "Sorry."

"Actually, you kinda look like her," Cori said as she studied Kenzie's profile.

Kenzie turned to face her. "Like who?"

"Forget it," Cori said, and then questioned in an afterthought, "What was the last movie you saw, anyhow?"

It was an innocent question, but to Kenzie, it reinforced the reality of what her life was, or rather, was not. It was not normal and it never had been. She didn't see movies, she didn't date, she didn't do a number of things. Follow orders...that's what she did. Her life was her job and her job was her life. She had given everything to the military and had never looked back — until recently. "I-I don't remember," Kenzie answered honestly.

"I suppose you don't watch TV either, do you?"

Kenzie's thoughts went to her home in Seattle. There was a television there, but she couldn't recall if she'd ever actually sat down and turned it on.

"You must have watched some as a kid, or gone to the movies for fun when you were a teenager?"

As Cori watched the changes in Kenzie's facial expressions, Kenzie was suddenly feeling very uncomfortable.

"You did have fun, didn't you? Or, at the very least, a childhood?"

Fun? It wasn't really a word in her vocabulary. *Has my life ever been fun?* The more she listened to Cori talk, the more she realized there had been a lot missing from her life.

"I don't remember much about my childhood, but I know I didn't watch TV or go to movies."

"Well, what did you do? You must have done something for fun — hobbies, sports, boys?" The question resulted in a subtle change in Kenzie's demeanor, and Cori dropped her sunglasses to get a better look at Kenzie.

The scrutiny made Kenzie pause for a moment before she answered. "I didn't have time for that stuff."

"For boys?"

She turned and looked at Cori. "Actually, it was girls...but I didn't have much time for them, either."

"Really?"

Kenzie was looking at Cori wondering what the woman thought about that revelation. Then Cori asked without more than a little hesitation.

"What did you do with your time, then?"

"I stole cars."

The conversation in the car was mostly one sided as Cori related the story of her life as Kenzie pursued any reason for Cori being a target. Nothing made sense, at least not to Kenzie. After hours of listening to Cori's normal childhood, she was even more confused.

"What about work?"

"You mean since high school?" Kenzie nodded and Cori thought a moment, then shook her head. "I delivered pizzas and then flowers for a while after graduation. Then I moved away from the Midwest and came out to the coast. I did a number of different odd jobs, just about anything to pay the rent and put food on the table, until I landed a good job working as a secretary with Trillium International, which has offices all around the world, including Mexico. They're the ones that helped me get into the University of Guadalajara."

"Helped you...how?"

"They have this in-house program that helps people at the lower income levels advance their education."

"Really?" Kenzie chewed on that information for a moment. "So, they're paying for your education? Why would they do that?"

"They say if they invest in their employees, then the employees are more loyal and will do a better job. I suppose that's partially true, but I think the real reason is because they get a big tax break. Either way, I don't care. I get an education and a good job to go back to once I'm finished with school." Cori paused in her recollection. "I was lucky. I owe Trillium a lot."

"I would guess it was the result of a lot of hard work on your part rather than luck. What does Trillium International do?"

"I'm not really sure. They're one of those big conglomerates that seem to have branding irons in a lot of different fires. You've heard of them, haven't you?" Cori turned to Kenzie and registered her blank look. "Where exactly did you grow up, in a cave?"

"In Seattle."

"Seattle! That's where I was, that's where I was working for Trillium, in their head office. That's something we have in common. You've never heard of them?"

"Who?" Kenzie asked.

"Trillium International."

"Nope."

"Have you actually been living this life?" Cori asked. "You lived in Seattle, so you must have at least heard of Bill Gates."

The name did ring a bell for Kenzie. "You mean that computer guy?"

"Yeah, that computer guy. You really need to get out more." Cori shook her head in disbelief. "Calling Bill Gates 'that computer guy' is like saying Wayne Gretzky was an ice skater." Even that name was unfamiliar to Kenzie. "Never mind," Cori said. "Anyhow, I liked Seattle."

"Yeah, it's okay, if you can handle the rain. What exactly did you do at Trillium?"

"Secretarial stuff mostly."

The questions and answers died away and Kenzie was actually a little disappointed to see the port of Mazatlán in the distance. It had been relaxing, listening to Cori talk. All the same, the more she heard, the more Kenzie was reminded that her own life had been anything but conventional. Robbed of a childhood, she had learned the art of survival on the streets, picking fights instead of picking outfits. Stealing cars had been a lot easier than stealing hearts. She didn't have a mother to teach her how to be a woman, she had the military, and they taught her how to be a soldier and then they taught her how to kill. Gingerly, she rubbed at the dried blood that matted the hair at her temple as she thought about her most recent trip to the Middle East. She was not aware that she winced but Cori saw it.

"Is your head okay?"

"I've had worse," she answered as she removed her sunglasses and looked at the side of her head in the mirror.

"I can look at that if you want. I wanted to be a doctor for a while, until I realized how much schooling it was going to take...and how much it was going to cost. I tried med school for one semester but it didn't work out, so I left school and kept looking for a job. Are you sure your head is okay?"

"It's fine." Kenzie put her glasses back on. "Thanks," she added, barely above a whisper, but loudly enough for Cori to hear the attempted nicety.

At the outskirts of Mazatlán, Kenzie looked sadly at the rubble that some people called homes. Everything seemed to have a layer of dust, even some of the people. Cement buildings with their chipped paint and unfinished fences contrasted sharply against the backdrop of fancy hotels where wealthy foreigners came to play. Money bought color, she realized — the more money spent, the more vibrant and vivid the colors. The poor seemed to exist in grays and browns, while the wealthy basked in the energy of blues, oranges, reds, and greens.

"Welcome to Mazatlán, the Pearl of the Pacific," Kenzie said. In order to cross traffic at the next light, Kenzie pulled the car over into the right-hand lane.

The city roads, more pot-holed than paved, were made of cobblestones that had been there since before time, or so it felt as they swayed back and forth inside the car.

"So, what didn't work out?" Kenzie asked.

Cori seemed surprised by Kenzie's sudden question. "Pardon?"

"I asked what didn't work out...with being a doctor?"

Looking down at her hands, Cori recalled with vivid clarity. "I couldn't stomach it." She turned back to the window, attempting to hide her embarrassment. "Watching the surgeries made me vomit."

Kenzie maneuvered the car through the city until they reached the road that traveled alongside the ocean. Mazatlán's harbor was home to the West Coast's largest fishing fleet, making it easy to find. Kenzie pulled the car into a vacant lot. Driving through the long grass, avoiding the piles of rubble and discarded refuse, she stopped at the edge, parking just above the ferry terminal. Killing the motor, they sat and watched the fishing vessels come in and out of the harbor.

Cori sat quietly for a while, periodically glancing at her watch. "Would it be okay if I went to find a bathroom?" she asked hesitantly.

"I told you this morning, you're free to do as you please." Kenzie climbed from the car and then leaned in through the window. "You may want to try back there." She jerked her thumb back toward the main road.

Turning in the direction indicated, Cori started walking. Climbing onto the hood of the car, Kenzie leaned back against the windshield and closed her eyes for the first time in days. She wondered whether she would ever see Cori again.

Chapter 6

The morning started with fog and a light drizzle. It kept the judge inside for most of the day. That was okay with him. He had enough paperwork to work through to keep him busy for a month.

He closed the curtain and turned back to the boxes of files stacked up around his library. It was actually his office, but he thought it sounded better to call it a library. Frustration and anger etched his careworn face as he sighed loudly. He had been searching all night and most of the day, but so far he had not come up with anything. However, if he couldn't find Kenzie, then maybe—

The phone warbled and its intrusion startled him. "Hello?" The voice on the other end of the phone surprised him, but then he realized it probably should not have. "What did you find out?" He listened intently, nodding and taking notes but saying little.

"But is it possible?" He listened some more. "No, don't get them involved. We need to find another way."

There was a long pause, then the judge jumped to his feet in anger. "I don't care! Might I remind you who you're talking to?" He pounded his desk. "Find out...now!"

Unaware that thousands of miles away the judge was looking for her, Kenzie was lying atop the hood of the car, fighting off fatigue, when she spotted Cori in the distance. Taking a long drink from the water bottle next to her, Kenzie waited for her to get closer.

"Did you find what you were looking for?"

"Yeah, finally," Cori said as she made her way through the long grass, past a pile of discarded kitchen sinks. Kenzie offered her the bottle of water and Cori took it. She unscrewed the cap and took a long, greedy drink.

"Who were you trying to reach?"

The questioned surprised Cori as she almost choked on her swallow of water. Kenzie knew Cori had gone to look for a phone, not a bathroom, but she wasn't sure until she saw Cori's response.

"My mother. With everything that's been going on, I wanted to be sure she was okay."

A young Mexican boy about seven or eight years of age appeared out of nowhere by the pile of sinks. Kenzie saw him but kept her attention on Cori. "And?"

The young boy's appearance captured Cori's interest and she ignored Kenzie's question. "Hi, there," she said, smiling brightly.

"Hello, *señorita*." He smiled at Cori. "You American, from USA?"

Cori looked to Kenzie and the young boy mistook the response. "You Canadian, *sí*?" He looked from one to the other. "From Vancouver...Toronto?"

"Vancouver," Kenzie answered quickly. She opted for the West Coast, knowing it was far more likely than the East Coast.

"Ah...I like Canadians." His smile was seemingly honest, but the women were wary. Young children worked hard for their money, finagling anything at any time in hopes of making a few coins to take home to their family. This barefoot and bare-chested young man was no different. "What you want? I can get. José, number one go-getter."

"Thanks, but I don't think so," Cori said, returning his infectious smile.

Kenzie watched as he looked over the cute little woman with the honey-colored hair, showing concern over her bruised face. "Anything you need," he offered, but Cori gently shook her head.

José then turned his charm on Kenzie as she sat on the car. "You want your hair done like Bo Derek? For you, cheap, almost free."

Cori chuckled. "Don't waste your time. She has no idea who Bo Derek is, never mind what her hair looks like." Kenzie shot her an icy glare but with the dark glasses on, Cori couldn't be certain.

"You want silver, I can get you silver. Blankets? Cowboy hat?" He looked hopefully at the two women. "You want, José go get."

Kenzie kept her attention on the harbor. "No thanks, José," she answered in an impassive voice.

"We're actually waiting for the ferry," Cori said politely, her smile quickly fading as she must have felt Kenzie's eyes boring into her.

José was smart. He had to be to survive on the streets. Sensing some tension between the women, he hoped he could resolve whatever their issue was and maybe make a peso in the process. He turned toward the ocean to see what they were looking at. "You wait for the ferry from where?"

Kenzie was hesitant to answer him, but his knowledge of Mazatlán might be of some use. "La Paz," she said.

"That ferry not here for a long time. You have long wait. You have someone on that ferry? You want something while you wait. *Cervecería*? Soda? I can get you Coca Cola."

Realizing the woman on the hood of the car was the one he needed to deal with, José moved closer to Kenzie, continuing his best sales pitch. "You wait, *señorita*, you need good Mexican blanket. My cousin makes good Mexican blanket, the best in Mazatlán. José get you one, cheap. For you, almost free."

Kenzie turned her attention to young José. "What time does the ferry get in, Mr. Number One Go-getter?"

José smiled and stood his ground under her scrutiny. "The ferry from La Paz gets in seven, sometimes eight." He shrugged his shoulders and bobbed his head. "Could be nine." His smile got bigger. "Sometimes even ten."

Kenzie watched him, his body language, his eyes, his movements. "I'm not paying you to find out when the ferry gets in."

"No, no señorita." He waved his hands as he spoke. "José not looking for money. The ferry," he smiled broadly, "she runs on Mexican time. Sometimes she comes in at seven, sometimes not. Sometimes eight, sometimes—"

"Yeah, yeah. I get the picture."

"You wait for *marido masculino* or *novio masculino*, boyfriend?"

Kenzie watched the young boy in amusement. He seemed so anxious to please, that she wondered whether he could be of some assistance. "We're not waiting for someone. We're waiting to take the ferry back to La Paz. Do you know anything about the ferry?"

"*Sí, señorita*, but you will have a *mucho* long wait. The ferry does not leave tonight. It does not leave Mazatlán until tomorrow afternoon."

"What?" Kenzie sat up and pulled off her sunglasses. This was not good news. The last thing she wanted to do was to sit and wait. The longer they were in one place, the greater the chance that someone would catch up to them.

"*Sí, mañana.*" He nodded and smiled at Cori. "Tomorrow, three o'clock, right on time. And you have a permit, *sí?*"

Kenzie noticed Cori looking at her to see if this was news to her as well.

"What kind of permit?" Kenzie asked.

"*Señorita*, you will need a permit for your car." He gestured at Cori's ravaged Honda.

Sliding off the hood of the car, Kenzie went and stood in front of José. If she intimidated him, he didn't let it show. "Explain."

"You have to have a permit to take a car on the ferry, a permit for you and your car. You show car's paperwork, your visitor papers, and your ID, and you go." Cori's shoulders sagged. "And you have to pay in plastic, ah...credit card, not *pesos*."

"You're sure about this?" Kenzie turned to face the harbor. They'd come so far to catch a ferry they couldn't get on. "Credit card only?"

"*Sí, señorita*. José knows. You ask, you want, José knows."

"Son of a bitch," Kenzie said through gritted teeth as she kicked at the tall grass. She walked away in anger and frustration. She stopped at the end of the desolate lot, hands on her hips as she pondered their situation. Her head was pounding, her body was aching, and the last thing she wanted to do was to add two or three days drive to their trip. Besides, driving straight north from Mazatlán would have them deep into the interior of Mexico, far away from other tourists, and they definitely didn't have the money for that. They would stick out like the targets they were. Weighing their options, she returned to the others.

When she arrived she heard Cori ask, "Is there any other way to La Paz, or over to the Baja?"

"No, *señorita*. Sorry. That ferry is the only way."

Kenzie knew José was telling the truth just by the look on his face. "What about fishing boats?"

"No. They aren't allowed to land except for here." He pointed to the harbor.

Kenzie followed his finger and her eyes stopped on the loading docks where there were stacks of shipping containers. "What about those?"

José looked at Kenzie and then to what she was pointing at. "Those ones go on the ferry," he answered.

"So, the ferry takes people and cargo?"

"*Si, señorita*, except for *Carga Negra* — Black Cargo."

"What's Black Cargo?" Cori asked.

"Twice a week the ferry takes black cargo: gas, dynamite, butane, cattle — things like that."

"Really?" Kenzie's mind was working and she chewed at the corner of her lip as her eyes stared off into the distance. A small smile spread across her face as she turned to Cori. "This could work, but we have to find the right cargo with the right owner. José, do you know anyone who ships over to La Paz?"

"José knows everyone." He thumped his chest proudly.

"Somehow, that's what I figured Mr. Number One Go-getter." Kenzie looked at Cori. "How about someone who ships livestock?"

"*Sí*," he answered with a quizzical look.

Kenzie turned to Cori. "We're going to have to sell your car."

The ferries used to travel between La Paz and Mazatlán were Danish-built crafts from the 1970s. Some were designed for passengers and had modern conveniences such as restaurants, bars, and staterooms, but the cargo ships were designed for cargo only. They were large, cumbersome, and very slow moving, transporting upwards of one hundred trucks across the Gulf of California. The crossing system itself was quite complicated, even to many locals, never mind what the tourists thought. The daily departures were something one could not set one's watch by, nor could a predetermined arrival time be expected, which gave Kenzie some small measure of comfort.

True to his word, José knew someone shipping cattle over to La Paz, his uncle, and Kenzie rewarded him handsomely for the introduction. Using most of what little money they got for Cori's car, they convinced José's uncle to hide them in a plywood box camouflaged with hay within a trailer of moving and mooing cattle. When Kenzie climbed into the four-foot by eight-foot box at the bulkhead of the cattle trailer, she suspected she and Cori were not the first passengers Jose's uncle had smuggled across the Gulf. The hiding spot was assembled too quickly for it to be a one-time thing. In Kenzie's mind, it was money well spent. As long as the cattle didn't need to be unloaded for an industrious inspector, they should have an easy, if not comfortable, passage across the Gulf of California.

Once the human cargo was in place, the bulky beasts were moved into the cattle trailer, filling the large space to its maximum capacity before the double doors were slammed closed. Cori and Kenzie would not be getting out until they had crossed the Gulf and were delivered to a farm outside of La Paz, on the peninsula of the Baja. It was going to be a long, hot, stuffy journey.

"Are you sure this is going to work?" Cori whispered to Kenzie as the trailer came to a stop outside the inspection booth at the ferry terminal.

Kenzie held her finger against Cori's mouth to silence the talkative young woman.

Cori closed her mouth. *My life is in danger and I'm hiding in a trailer with a bunch of cows — and a professional killer,* Cori thought as she unintentionally held her breath as they waited. They could hear voices outside but the guard at the inspection booth waved them through without a second look. The truck and trailer rolled slowly onto the deck of the ferry, swaying and creaking until it came to a stop. Lifting the lid of the box, Kenzie peered beyond the cows to see they were one of the last vehicles boarding the ferry. They were on edge the entire time, as they and their cargo of cows were loaded onto the deck. Big diesel motors lumbered their cargo into place and then, one by one, their motors shut down. The only sound left was the vibrating hum of the massive motors below the deck of the ferry. It seemed to take forever before the waters churned and the ferry began to pull out of Mazatlán. The activity on the lower decks slowly ceased and they were alone with the rest of the cargo. The movement of the large boat rocked them gently as the ship and its lading groaned and moaned. The animals that were initially restless, soon settled in for their journey across the open sea.

"You should get some rest, it's going to be a long crossing," Kenzie said as she wiped away the sweat from her face with her forearm.

"Yeah, maybe if I go to sleep, I can wake up from this nightmare. I was sure someone was going to see us, Kenzie."

"Well, they didn't. Just close your eyes and listen to the boat. You'll be asleep in no time."

"What about you? You haven't slept either."

"I will." Kenzie lifted the lid of the box again and stood up. Hidden from view inside the trailer, she looked through the slats, feeling the cool ocean breeze on her face. "I'll get some sleep once we're further out. I won't feel safe until I know the harbor is behind us."

As best she could, Cori snuggled into the coarse, itchy straw inside the box.

With Cori quiet and Mazatlán fading into the distance, Kenzie hoped to get some much-needed rest. She knew it would be hard to sleep with all the unanswered questions stirring in her mind. Once they got to La Paz, what then? They no longer had transportation and they had very little money left over from the sale of Cori's car. Would it be enough to buy a ride north? And then what? Maybe it would be better if she just disappeared. It wouldn't be difficult, considering she no longer existed. Once they got back to San Diego, she had enough money to tide her over for a while, at least until she decided what to do.

She sat down and reluctantly pulled the lid back on the box, sealing away the cool breeze. Lying back in the hay, she closed her eyes against the storm of questions pounding away.

Chapter 7

Surrounded by the rush of cars heading homeward, the Bentley Continental Flying Spur sped along the turnpike. Its windshield wipers slapped hard against the driving rain as the driver maneuvered the heavy car through the thick traffic. The luxury class vehicle had a few after market accessories, including bulletproof glass and a rally G3 suspension, but the lone passenger in the back seat could easily afford all of that and more without a second thought.

It had been a long, stressful day, filled with questions for which Winston Palmer had no answers, and that irritated him. With his power and position, he was used to asking the questions. He was beyond having to answer to anyone.

He unsnapped his leather briefcase and pulled out a thick envelope with, MAQUINAR — PRIVATE AND CONFIDENTIAL, boldly written in red. He flipped it over and unwound the string that fastened the envelope. Several color photos slid into his lap. He picked one up and studied the face staring back at him. It was obvious the woman in the photo had no idea the picture was being taken. He turned the photograph over and glanced at the name, date, and location printed neatly on the back. With a slight grunt, he gathered up the pictures and thrust them back into the file. Picking up one of the file folders, he flipped his way through the papers, but there was nothing new for him to see. Winston Palmer knew her file, and he knew her story. Slapping the file folder shut, he glared out at the passing rain-soaked scenery. His irritation simmered to the surface when the phone built into the birds-eye maple console interrupted his thoughts. He shoved the file into the envelope, then threw it into his open briefcase and slammed it shut.

"What?" He made no attempt to curtail his anger and frustration.

"We have a problem," the voice said.

Derek, the young Asian driver of the Bentley, glanced in the rearview mirror at his employer's pursed lips. Their eyes locked, and Derek quickly turned his attention back to the road.

Palmer pushed a button and a soundproof privacy window began to slide upward, separating him from his driver. He waited for the window to be in place before he spoke again. "I'm aware we have a problem. What I don't understand is why we still have a problem!" He reached for his pipe.

"Vasquez is dead, Senator."

His hand stopped in midair as he listened to the silence on the phone. "I'm sorry," Palmer said, voice dripping with disdain. "That is my problem because... Oh wait, it's not. I really don't give a damn." He wearily rubbed a hand over his face. It had been a long night and an even worse day. "What you're really telling me is that the job is not done. Correct?"

"Correct."

"So now she knows we're after her...and that changes things." Palmer thought for a moment as he looked out the window. *Not necessarily.* "Has she contacted anyone?"

"As far as I know, no one."

"What do you mean, 'as far as you know'?"

"As far as I know." The voice on the phone faltered. "We have to be careful here, Senator. We can't just go in guns blazing. There would be too many people, too many witnesses. Every moron has a digital camera these days, and I don't care to see our faces sprawled across CNN."

"Then eliminate the witnesses."

"It's not that easy."

"Make it that easy. Just put a fucking bullet in her head!" Palmer ordered.

The voice on the other end of the phone was silent for a moment. He had more information to convey, but was reluctant to be forthcoming with it. He never backed down from a confrontation or shirked from his responsibilities, but this situation was different. "That's the other problem. We're not exactly sure where she is."

"What the hell? What do you mean, not exactly?"

"She's somewhere in the Gulf of California, on a boat."

"Jesus Christ, Colonel! What kind of operation are you running?" Palmer dropped the phone to his chest and shook his head. It was supposed to have been such a simple job. He sighed loudly and counted to ten before returning the phone to his ear. "What kind of boat?" he asked deliberately, trying to control his anger.

"We think she might be on the ferry that runs between Mazatlán and La Paz, or maybe even a private boat or something."

"Something?" Palmer rubbed at his chin and then ran the edge of his pipe over his teeth, making an irritating clicking sound. Counting to ten silently in his head was not curtailing his temper.

"A private boat or something? You're kidding, right?" His sarcasm didn't require an answer. "With all of the resources you have at your disposal, I cannot fathom your response. You think... Maybe... Something. I would expect more from you, Colonel. Where exactly," he enunciated clearly and concisely, "is she now?" Palmer listened to the computer keys clicking distantly over the phone.

"Latitude twenty-four point one three..."

"If you know the location that precisely, Colonel," the senator interrupted, "why can't you get someone there? Or is there something additional you need to tell me?"

"It's not that easy. According to these numbers, that puts her—"

"Do I sound like I care, Manuck? Because I don't. And I don't need to remind you that this job needs to be done. There is no leeway here for mistakes, and believe me, she is a mistake, one that we can ill afford to have walking around. Maquinar is too important."

"Too important, or too profitable, Senator?"

The senator ignored the comment. "Get it done, and get it done right. Make the problem go away, Colonel."

The *Pichilingue* left a broad wake on its sluggish journey through the Gulf of California to La Paz. Something woke Kenzie from her light slumber. She wouldn't sleep soundly until she felt safe, and right now, she didn't feel safe. However, she did feel the warm body next to her. Cori had inadvertently curled up to her in her sleep, her head resting comfortably against Kenzie's side. For a moment Kenzie felt a little envious of her soft snore. She wished she could sleep so easily, but there were too many things on her mind and too much blood on her hands.

What happened? What went wrong? She reviewed Manuck's orders, point by point, but none of it made sense. Killing Cori did not make any sense. She was supposed to be protecting the innocent, not killing them, and Cori was innocent, she was sure of it. *Innocent and gorgeous.* Closing her eyes, Kenzie rested her head against the wall of the plywood box and took a deep breath. Another place and another time, sleeping with this woman would have been the first thing on her mind — *Get your head on straight, girl. You're on the run, not on the make.*

The shooter in the desert hadn't carried any ID, but she knew one of her own when she saw one. The rifle he had was high powered and very expensive, which bothered her almost as much as the thought of how he had come to be there. And why had her extraction team not shown up?

When she rummaged through his clothes, she had not been looking for ID. What she had been looking for was a contract or a photograph, something that told her who he'd been aiming at. There had been nothing — no note, no picture, not a scrap of paper telling her who he was working for. For a moment, she regretted not searching his car but there was no point in agonizing over it. The chance that there would have been anything there was now a moot point. *Move on soldier* — that brought her mind onto another subject. Colonel Manuck. Had he not trusted her to do the job? Then again, she hadn't done the job he had ordered her to do. She had gotten too close to her target, and fear and paranoia had begun to consume her. Maybe it was time to get out, finally have a life away from the military.

She could feel the warmth of the sleeping woman beside her, and Kenzie knew she could never go back. But what could she move forward to? She was exactly what they had trained her to be — an assassin without connections. They had taken the emotion out of her, drilled her to become a killer without a conscience, with no moral guidelines other than loyalty to the people who gave her orders. She was a killing machine who did not feel like killing anymore.

What could anyone do with someone who possessed her lethal skills, someone who had witnessed things that in the public's mind had never happened? Maybe it wasn't possible. She couldn't recall having heard of a retirement home for morally bankrupt assassins. Financially, the military had looked after most of her needs, so she had managed to save a small nest egg. She wasn't rich, but she could survive on what she had put away, at least for a while. Then what?

Her moral compass was spinning out of control. She knew she was walking on the edge of a knife and if she didn't make a move soon the results could be lethal. She had never trusted anyone, and for very good reason. She was not willing to take a risk with anyone's life but her own. It was only then she fully understood that she had not killed Cori because it went against the very core of who she was. For reasons she could not comprehend, she was finding herself drawn to the woman. "Chatty Cathy" Cori was constantly on her mind and Kenzie knew that this time she was disobeying orders for entirely different reasons.

Kenzie finally fell back to sleep, but she didn't sleep well. In the shadows of her mind, caught in the twilight of dreams, the war between right and wrong continued. Faces of those she had killed haunted her, whispering to her conscience. With vivid clarity, she recalled the locations she had visited, places were she had taken the lives of strangers without ever a question — in the heat and humidity of the jungles of South America, or the hot stinging sands of the Kuwait desert, or even the quiet of Paris' Luxembourg Park. The jobs were over, but they continued to play in her mind. There were so many, too many, and she wanted out.

Voices in the distance woke Kenzie from her nightmares. Her first thought was for the woman who had been sleeping beside her. "Cori," she said in a whisper.

"What's going on?"

Kenzie could hear the fear in her voice and the rustling of hay as Cori moved about inside the box.

"Shhh," Kenzie brought her finger to her lips and then reached into her bag. She felt amongst her belongings for her silencer. Finding the cold metal cylinder, she screwed it into place. "Stay here and stay quiet," she said as she pushed the plywood top off the box.

Kenzie peered out from the protection of their camouflage box, but there was nothing for her to see except cows. Not wanting to spook the cattle, she slowly and carefully climbed from their hiding place. It took her a few moments to squeeze past the cows' beefy bellies, but finally she made it to the outer wall of the cattle trailer. She peered cautiously between the slats, looking for the source of the voices she could hear. Night had fallen and the deck of the ferry was dimly lit, making her task all that much harder.

"What's going on?" Cori asked in a hushed whisper.

Kenzie quickly turned and brought her finger to her lips, then tapped her ear.

Moving away from the side of the cattle trailer, Kenzie leaned over the back of one of the cows. "I heard something."

"I figured that," Cori said with a hint of sarcasm as Kenzie turned her attention back outside. Cori scrambled from the box. Pushing her way through the press of cows, she made her way to where Kenzie was standing.

"Voices," Kenzie said, "but I don't know from where. What are you doing?" Kenzie whispered angrily.

Cori was peering through the wooden slats. "The same thing you're doing — looking for whoever is talking." All she could see were the vehicles parked around them. A five-ton truck with a canvas tarp, a white panel van, and a red Freightliner...the line of trucks and trailers went on and on. A movement on the far side of the open ferry deck caught her eye. She rested her forehead against the wooden slat to get a better look. Before she could say anything, Kenzie tapped on Cori's shoulder and pointed in that direction. Cori nodded.

The two women watched and waited, but there was no explanation for what they had heard or seen. Cori changed her position, looking through several different slats, but still could not see where the voices were coming from. Just as she stepped away from the trailer wall, Kenzie raised her hand and pointed to the rear of the trailer. Ducking and dodging, Cori did her best to see beyond the cattle, but was unsuccessful.

Kenzie saw the look of frustration on her face. Holding up two fingers, she indicted to Cori that she had seen two men. Walking her fingers, she indicated that they had moved just beyond the rear of the cattle trailer.

Moving up beside Kenzie, Cori finally saw the two men moving slowly in and out between the vehicles just beyond their trailer. One was dressed in dark blue work overalls, while the other was dressed more casually in khaki pants and a white t-shirt. The men were speaking too softly for her to make out what they were saying. They appeared to be searching the vehicles — looking in windows and peering into the back of truck beds. Cori whispered to Kenzie, "They're looking for something."

"José's uncle said it was against the law for anyone to be below on the car deck after we left port," Kenzie said as she chambered a round into her gun. "So the only thing they would be searching for is us."

Cori watched the men — their movements, their body language — and didn't come to the same conclusion. "I don't think so. Looks to me like they work here."

Kenzie brought her weapon up in search of her targets. This was what she knew, what she was trained to do, and her reflexes responded accordingly. Taking a deep breath, she slowly released it, relaxing her nerves and steadying her aim. Focusing only on the two men, Kenzie ignored the cows and the smell of the stale diesel fumes as she raised her gun and took aim.

"What are you doing?"

Kenzie heard the question but didn't think it was worthy of an answer.

"Stop! What the hell are you doing?" Cori said in a harsh whisper. "You can't just shoot those men."

Lowering her weapon, Kenzie turned and glared at her. "Why not? People have been shooting at us."

"Well, so far, these guys haven't. Let's just wait."

"Wait for what? For them to find us and shoot us? I don't think so."

"Kenzie, let's just see what they're doing."

"It doesn't matter what they're doing. They aren't even supposed to be down here," Kenzie said flatly, as she turned her focus to the two men.

As she raised her weapon, Cori reached around and put her hand on the gun, pushing it downward. "No," she said, her features drawn in determination.

They were only inches apart, both stubbornly sure of what they believed.

"Shoot first and ask questions later, that's what I live by."

"Make a mistake and you'll have to live with the consequences," Cori responded quickly. "Sooner or later you're going to have to stop shooting people." Cori stared deeply into the gold of Kenzie's eyes, "Just...wait."

Kenzie broke the stare first, pulling her mind back from the desert of the Middle East. Rolling her tongue along her teeth, she glanced over Cori's shoulder, searching for the men. She located them standing next to a cargo van. One of them lifted the tarp that covered the back of a five-ton work truck, but the taller of the two men was not interested in its contents. He moved away from the work truck toward the cattle trailer.

"And if you're wrong?" Kenzie said without taking her eyes off the man as he approached.

"Then you can go ahead and shoot them," Cori whispered into Kenzie's ear from behind. "I won't say a word. Hell, I'll even help you dump the bodies."

Kenzie didn't respond, mainly because she didn't know whether or not Cori was kidding. She watched the taller man getting closer and turned to Cori, pressing her finger to her lips. The man moved down the length of the trailer, and Kenzie was sure she heard a catch in Cori's breathing when he stopped almost directly in front of them. Without hesitation, Kenzie brought her weapon up level with the man's head just on the other side of the worn wooden slats.

Neither of the women moved as they waited to see what he was going to do. The longer he stood outside the trailer, the more slack Kenzie squeezed out of the trigger. The shot would be silent, but the sound of the bullet tearing through the wood might alert his companion.

A short whistle from beyond the trailer drew the man's attention and he turned away from his impending death. Cori let out the breath she had been holding as they watched him join his partner at the open railing of the ferry.

"Can you see what they're doing?" Kenzie asked in a hushed voice as the two men huddled close together. They were speaking to each other, but the noises from the ferry mixed with the sounds of the ocean masked their words. They appeared to be warily surveying their surroundings, which made Kenzie uneasy until she saw the men turn their backs to the salty winds and place cigarettes in their mouths. As their swirls of smoke dissipated into the air, she relaxed and turned her back to the men.

"It's just a couple of slackers stealing from cars and sneaking a smoke," she whispered in relief as she turned back to Cori.

"And you were ready to blow them away," Cori whispered back.

"I live by my instincts. I've survived this long because I don't trust anyone," Kenzie said as she slid her weapon into its holster.

"Well, your instincts were wrong this time."

"Were they?"

"You almost shot two innocent men. I would say your instincts were wrong." Cori said as she made her way back to their hiding spot. "But I guess you don't really care, do you?"

"They aren't exactly innocent. They're breaking a ton of laws by smoking on the car deck of a ferry transporting dangerous goods."

"Oh yeah, I forgot..." Cori leaned back against the plywood wall of the box. "Smoking is punishable by death in Mexico."

Kenzie glared at her but didn't respond as she took a seat. Reaching up, she slid the lid back over their box, but left it open enough to allow in some light and a slight breeze.

Cori watched with interest as Kenzie pulled out her weapon and checked it over. Dropping the clip, she slid the mechanism back, ejecting the unspent shell into her hand. She fed the bullet back into the clip, shoved the clip back into the butt of the gun, and then returned it to her holster. She moved with precision, confident of herself and her surroundings. The muscles in Kenzie's forearm rippled, her hands and fingers were long and strong, and her eyes — Cori had never seen anyone with gold-colored eyes before. She was more than a little unnerved to realize that she was finding herself attracted to a woman who had such an affinity for killing.

Kenzie reached for a bottle of water. As she glanced up, she noticed that Cori was watching her. Actually, watching was not the right word — more like — ogling.

"How much longer before we reach the Baja?" Cori asked quickly, hoping to cover her embarrassment at being caught staring at Kenzie's body.

Slightly amused at the situation, Kenzie slowly unscrewed the cap from the bottle. She took several long gulps of water, enjoying the attention from the obviously embarrassed young woman. When Kenzie finished, she looked at her watch. "I think we should be almost halfway."

Unconsciously licking at her lips, Cori gave a brief nod. She suddenly didn't care how long the trip was going to take. Looking through one of the air holes in the box, she watched the smokers huddled in the distance as the bright moon lit up the car deck with a silvery glow. The sun had long since set, but it was still hot and humid inside the cattle trailer. The muscles in her arms and legs burned with fatigue, making them heavy and shaky. She tried her best to get comfortable in the straw. Beads of sweat rolled down her body, leaving her feeling damp and dirty. Uncomfortable as it was, the heat and conditions were not what was on her mind.

Kenzie watched as Cori rolled first on one side and then the other. It was obvious that she was having difficulty falling back to sleep. As she continued to stare at the young woman, Cori opened her eyes. Kenzie didn't look away, instead she faced the fear and apprehension that clouded Cori features. She had gotten too close to her target, close enough to see into the reflection in her eyes, and she found herself in a new role — protector.

Cori wanted to look away, but something in Kenzie's stare held her. An uneasy silence fell between them as they swayed with the rhythm of the ship, each looking to the other for something indefinable. Without a word, Kenzie looked away and Cori was sure she was going to roll over onto her side. Much to her surprise, Kenzie raised her arm, inviting her back to where she had fallen asleep before. Cori said nothing, but the desire for comfort was a strong pull for her tired body. She hesitated for a moment, and then crawled over to nestle against Kenzie's side. It was not long before she drifted off into an exhausted sleep.

Leaning back against the straw, Kenzie enjoyed the warmth of the body next to hers. It was the first time in a long time that something felt right in her world. After a while, Cori's steady breathing lulled Kenzie into her own slumber.

The cattle were moving restlessly, rocking the trailer, shaking Cori awake. Looking around, she could tell that some time had passed since she had fallen asleep, but she had no idea how much. The moon was high and the stars were bright, adding natural light to the eerie yellow glow from the few working lights that hung over the car deck. Turning her head, she was not surprised to see Kenzie was also awake.

"What's going on?" Cori asked over the noise of the anxious animals.

"I'm not sure, but something's wrong." Kenzie got to her feet and cautiously opened the plywood lid all the way off their hidden hay-box.

"I hear voices," Cori said with alarm.

"So do I, but that's not my only concern. I smell smoke."

"What?" Cori peered out over the edge of their hideaway. The smell of smoke resistered with Cori and the sudden sound of loud, panicked voices in the distance. A wave of anxiety heightened her senses as she heard the growing commotion. "Those voices are getting closer. Do you think they know we're here?" Cori's question was cut off as the trailer swayed abruptly with the sudden movement of the frightened cattle.

Kenzie pulled her weapon from its holster. "I doubt it, but I'm not taking any chances." Kenzie's eyes narrowed and she wrinkled her nose as a stronger whiff of smoke reached her nostrils. The clamor of hurrying feet was growing louder.

"They're coming this way," Cori said as she turned back to face Kenzie. The cattle were thrashing and crashing about, violently shifting the trailer back and forth. She reached out to brace herself and gripped Kenzie's bare bicep. The combination of softness and strength took her a little by surprise.

Ignoring the hand on her arm, Kenzie looked at Cori with concern. "Something is definitely burning."

With so many things going on, it took Cori a moment to focus on what Kenzie was saying. "What?"

The cattle's fear was growing and the trailer continued to rock wildly to one side, throwing Kenzie off balance. She grabbed at Cori to keep her from falling. "Something's on fire!"

Turning away from Kenzie, Cori saw flames bursting from the rear of the trailer. "It's us!"

As if responding to Cori's realization, the cattle surged toward the women, fearfully moving away from the smoke and flames.

"Son of a—" Kenzie pushed Cori away from the shifting mass of cattle as she reached back for her duffle bag. "Don't get pinned, they'll trample you!" Kenzie yelled as she pulled her silencer from her bag and screwed it into place. She leveled her gun at the closest cow and fired.

"What are you doing?" Cori yelled as she looked from the fallen cow to the flames licking at the rear of the trailer.

"Saving our lives." Kenzie glanced out toward the dark waters beyond the wooden slats. Between the oceanic crosswinds and the movement of the ferry, the smoke was billowing upward and outward, away from them and the crazed animals.

Screams of "Fire!" were shouted in several languages just beyond the trailer walls, as well as panicky orders from the crew and deckhands.

Cori didn't hear Kenzie's shot, but she saw the second cow crumple before her. "Stop shooting them, Kenzie!"

"And what...get trampled by these animals?" Kenzie aimed at her next target. "It's us or them, Cori. Take a look around you...we don't have many options. If I shoot enough of them, their bodies will make a barrier and the rest won't be able to get to us." Kenzie shot another wide-eyed cow and then bent down to look through the slats of the trailer. Some of the crew had unraveled the fire hose, but there was no water coming from it. It was apparent that this was not a well-trained safety crew as people ran about the deck in panicked disarray.

Cori turned back to Kenzie. "We have to get out of here."

"I'm open to suggestions," Kenzie yelled back through the chaos as she shot another cow. It fell on top of the others, creating a makeshift blockade between them and the trampling cattle.

It was then Cori saw José's uncle, the owner of the cattle trailer, appear amongst the few spectators on the car deck. "Our problems just got worse," Cori said. "José's uncle is here."

Kenzie peered through the slats. She saw him, too, and knew instantly by the look on his face that they were not the only ones in a life and death dilemma. *Will he tell anyone that he's smuggling people?* She holstered her weapon. "He has his own problems to deal with. We need to find a way out of here, and fast."

Kenzie scrambled back toward the front of the trailer, reaching for her bag as she went. By the light of the growing orange glow, she could see Cori struggling past the carcasses as the flames snapped and crackled.

Outside on the car deck, several of the ferry employees had come up with a plan and were quickly moving to unhook the cattle trailer from the truck. When they pulled the release arm and uncoupled the connection, the entire trailer lurched backward as the weight of the back end lifted the front. The cows bawled in fear and pain as the flames seared their hides. The sudden movement sent Kenzie and Cori tumbling into the mud and manure covered floor. Cori landed hard on the still warm body of one of the dead cows as Kenzie slid toward the stumbling herd, grabbing wildly for the side of the trailer.

Cori scurried in next to her, looking as fearful as the cows at the growing flames. "Kenzie, I'd rather die in prison than burn to death. Hell, I think I'd prefer to be shot than burn to death," She said, her eyes wide with fear. "We need to get out of here."

The trailer was moving, that part was easy to feel, but the question on Kenzie's mind was, where were they moving it? As if answering her silent question, the truck that was parked in front of them backed its bumper up against the gooseneck hitch of the trailer. The two vehicles made contact and the truck's engine roared above the noise as it began to push. Only then did Kenzie realize what was happening.

"I don't think we have a choice anymore," she hollered over the metal on metal noise. The two women struggled to stay standing as the truck pushed the cattle trailer backward.

"Where are they pushing us?" Cori screamed.

Kenzie slung her bag over her shoulder and reached for one of the rings fastened to the front wall of the trailer. Grasping Cori's forearm, she pulled her hand up to the ring. "Hang on!"

The rear of the trailer was now fully engulfed in flames. The cattle were screaming in panic as a sudden gust of wind whipped the flames into a frenzy. Cori saw the opening edge of the ferry coming alongside of them as the rear axle of the trailer dipped down toward the moving waters. She turned to Kenzie in fear. "They're pushing us out to sea!" Cori screamed over the noise.

"I know."

Cori's eyes darted around, seeking another way out, but like Kenzie, she knew their only hope was to hold on. "What about José's uncle? He knows we're here! They can't do this!"

"They have no choice. If they don't get this fire out, the whole ferry could go up in flames!" Kenzie yelled. "When we hit the water, we'll hit hard. If you let go," Kenzie's eyes held the reality of the situation, "you'll die."

Without warning, the trailer reached the pivot point and the weight of the cattle slid them off the ferry deck. The dark waters of the Gulf pulled at the back of the trailer, flipping it almost vertical. The trailer lurched violently, shaking and banging them brutally against the wooden slats. The flames were doused with a steamy hiss, as the cattle bellowed and screamed into the night air. Everything in the trailer that was not attached tumbled down into the churning waters as Kenzie and Cori held on for their lives. The trailer bobbed in place for a moment and then began a rapid descent into the ocean.

"KICK THE SLATS! KICK AT THE SLATS!" Kenzie screamed. They would be trapped unless they created a hole.

Cori didn't want to look at the cows splashing and screaming below. The trailer was sinking fast. She began kicking desperately at the old wood, trying to break out of their impending doom.

The weight of the duffle bag swung hard and pulled on Kenzie's shoulder as she felt the wood splintering under the onslaught of her feet. Kicking hard for their very lives, she could see the lights of the ferry becoming smaller as it continued toward La Paz. Except for Jose's uncle, everyone on board was completely unaware of the two stowaways left behind to die.

Kenzie began to rip away at the broken boards with her hands. She could feel the spray of the water against her face as she glanced down at the roiling water rushing toward them. "We need to go!" she yelled.

Cori couldn't have agreed more, but as she started toward the opening, the trailer shifted violently, breaking Kenzie's grip on the steel ring. Cori reached out a saving hand, but it was not necessary, Kenzie had already grabbed hold of one of the wooden slats. Her body slammed hard into the side of the trailer, dislodging the heavy duffle bag from her shoulder. Kenzie struggled to hold on as she grappled for the strap of the bag that held all the tools of her trade.

Leaving the hole she had created in the side of the trailer, Cori reached out to rescue the bag, but as she did, her foot slipped on the wet wood. She cried out in surprise and fear as she wildly searched for a hold to keep her from falling into the rising sea. A powerful grip on her wrist brought her to a muscle-wrenching stop.

"Don't move," Kenzie said between clenched teeth.

Cori had to move. The water was rising fast and she could feel her feet touching the carcasses of the dead cattle. She turned to see that Kenzie had her by the wrist, the other hand holding tightly to the side of the trailer, while still managing to hold the strap of the duffle bag against the edge of a slat with her toe.

"I can't hold both of you!" Pain seared through Kenzie's arm and shoulder as she tried to hook her bag onto her foot. "Grab hold of something."

The rising waters were pushing the dead cows up against Cori's legs as she tried to reach for the side of the trailer. The jostling movement was more than Kenzie could handle. She had to let go of one or the other. The duffle bag sailed passed Cori's face and landed nearby with a splash. Reaching out, Cori strained to grab the bag, but before she could secure it, she felt Kenzie pulling her up and out of the salt water. Her fingers grasped at the air. "But..."

"Let it go!" Kenzie commanded as she pulled Cori up next to the hole she had busted out. "Quickly!" The water was rushing up to meet them, its foaming waves climbing up the trailer walls, sucking everything downward. "Go."

Kenzie didn't have to tell her again. Cori kicked and dragged herself through the opening in the broken slats. The ocean was rising inside, bringing with it the remnants of the trailer, dead cows and piles of floating hay. The flotsam was making her escape much more difficult.

"Now or never, get moving!" Kenzie pushed Cori upwards as the waves and the debris banged against her body. With every ounce of energy she had left, Kenzie pulled herself through the small hole as the chill of the ocean sucked at her waning strength. A slicing pain ripped at her side as she cleared the hole and kicked her way to freedom. They were not out of danger yet. The foamy water swirled as it claimed the wreckage of the trailer and the dead animals it encased. The two women splashed to the surface amongst the debris, both thankful to be alive as the waters finally began to calm.

Cori looked at the distant lights of the ferry as it moved off, dipping below the horizon. She wiped her face as she looked at Kenzie. "Now that was interesting," she gasped turning away from the disappearing ferry. "I can't believe they just kept going."

"What did you expect them to do?"

"I don't know...something."

"As far as they know, it was just a burning trailer and some dead cows. They didn't know we were in there," Kenzie said as she took stock of the damage to her body. She felt her gun banging loosely against her sore side. The holster had been torn sometime during their escape, and she could not chance losing her gun. She reached to take it out of the holster and a zing of pain sliced through her shoulder. She glanced at her companion, but if Cori heard the hiss of pain, she made no comment. With her other hand, Kenzie carefully pulled the gun out of the holster and slid it firmly into the waistband of her pants.

Treading water was painful for Kenzie, but she said nothing as they bobbed up and down with the rise and fall of the ocean. Soon the only sound was the slosh of the water against their bodies.

"What would you suggest now?" Cori asked.

Kenzie frowned and looked at the stars, and then around at the vast darkness. "I'm not sure, but my first suggestion would be to stay afloat."

"Funny." Cori wiped away the water on her face.

"I was being serious. I'm too pissed off to be making jokes. I lost my bag down there. It contained everything we were going to need. Everything. And now we have nothing. Christ!"

"What do you mean, everything?"

"Just what I said, everything. That bag held my life."

"That's kind of pathetic, isn't it? Even for you."

"It means we have nothing — no money, no food, and no water."

Kenzie touched the gun in her waistband for reassurance. "And only one gun." *One gun, with how many rounds left?* She tried to recall how many cows she had shot.

"Great. Could this get any worse?"

Kenzie moved her hand around her right side where she felt a gash along her ribcage. Swallowing her pride, Kenzie admitted through clenched teeth, "We might have another problem. I think I'm bleeding." She pulled her hand from the water and touched her fingers to her lips. Blood.

"You're hurt," Cori said with concern as she swam closer to Kenzie. "How badly?"

"Bad enough to bring sharks." Kenzie searched the waters around them. "They can smell blood for miles."

Cori studied the serious look on Kenzie's face. "How badly?" she asked again.

"I'm not sure." She could hear the fear in Cori's voice. Kenzie thought it was a little ironic that she might be responsible for Cori's death after all. The ferry was all but out of sight, leaving them surrounded by blackness.

"Can I see," Cori asked.

Kenzie focused on the woman next to her. "Probably not."

"Can I at least have a feel?"

The set up was too good to pass up. "Women usually offer to buy me a drink before they ask that question." Even in their present predicament, Kenzie was certain Cori was blushing.

"I'll put that on my list of things to do, once we get out of this mess," Cori said as she cautiously reached out for Kenzie's side.

With her eyes and concentration on the horizon, Kenzie felt gentle fingers probe her side.

In the darkness, Cori had to rely on what she felt to tell her the extent of the injury. The goose bumps on the tight skin told her Kenzie was as cold as she was. Exploring upwards along the ribcage, she felt the jagged edge of the torn flesh. "It's not good. It feels deep, and long," Cori said with her eyes closed. "Try not to move too much. It will only make you bleed more and stir up the water."

Something in the distance caught Kenzie's attention. "I'll do my best," she said, searching the darkness. She didn't tell Cori about her shoulder because there was nothing either of them could do about it while they were in the water.

Cori opened her eyes. "Well, look on the bright side, at least we're all alone out here in the middle of the ocean and no one is shooting at us."

"It's actually the Gulf of California," Kenzie said, keeping her eyes on the distance. "And I hate to be the bearer of bad news, but I don't think we're alone."

Chapter 8

By the time the helicopter picked him up, Cobra had his orders and was eager to eliminate the assigned target. He had killed women before, but never a child, that was his only rule. He pulled the picture out and studied her face again. *What a shame. She's quite a looker.*

There was no interaction with the pilots during the flight that took them to La Paz. Cobra stared out the window at the water far below. The ocean was dark, but the moonlight illuminated the tips of the rolling waves. Reaching into his vest pocket, he pulled out his Blackberry and began punching away at the buttons until he received the information he had been waiting for. She was still out in the Gulf somewhere. The ferry had not yet reached port and would probably be a few hours longer before arriving. He had time.

Unbuckling his seatbelt, Cobra leaned forward and unzipped his large black duffle bag. Though he had packed it only a few hours earlier, his training led him to check and recheck that he had everything he might need. Running his large hand through his assorted equipment, he satisfied himself that he was ready. He zipped the bag and kicked it off to the side. Leaning back in his seat, he stretched out his long legs and relaxed. If he was lucky, he could catch a few winks before they landed.

Cori felt the panic churning in her stomach, "What do you mean, not alone?" she said, spitting out the salt water that splashed into her mouth when she spoke. The dark water washed over her as she bobbed, making it impossible to see anything. Searching the waters around her for the fin that could mean death, she asked fearfully, "Did you see a shark?"

"Not a shark," Kenzie said as Cori turned to face her. "A boat." She nodded her head in the direction of Cori's left shoulder.

Spinning around, Cori craned her neck above the water. There was a break in the waves and she saw the black silhouette of a fishing boat against the moonlit sky. Cori was certain she had never seen anything so beautiful. "Can we make it?" she asked, keeping her eyes on the boat in the distance, fearing that if she looked away she would never see it again.

"It's further than you think."

Cori heard the doubt in Kenzie's normally confident voice. "But can we make it?"

Kenzie gave her a gentle push in the direction of the boat, "If we don't," she took a breath to spit out a mouthful of seawater, "we'll die trying."

A feeling of dread shivered down Cori's back. "We can't swim too fast or we'll attract the sharks, not to mention you might bleed to death."

"If we don't get to that boat before they fire up their motors, it won't matter."

That lone realization sent another shiver down Cori's spine, but this one went all the way to her toes. The two set out in the direction of the fishing boat in silent determination, both knowing failure was not an option.

Manny Javier was a third generation fisherman. He considered himself an honest man, but recent times had not been good to him and so he had taken to doing some illegal night fishing. It paid a lot better because he could keep whatever he caught with no concerns of limits or species. All he had to do was to keep an eye out for other boats. Thankfully, there were typically not many, just the slow-moving ferries that could easily be seen from a great distance. When he or his crew spotted another boat, they shut down their motors, turned off the lights, and waited for the vessel to pass. In the meantime, everyone kept their eyes on the water. With no light and no motor, there was always a chance that something could go wrong.

"The ferry is almost out of sight. Get ready to fire her up, Al," Manny hollered down to his small crew of relatives.

"Aye, aye, boss man," Al called to his older brother. With a wave of his hand, he headed up to the wheelhouse to start the massive motor.

Young Ramon began his descent from the back arm of the boat, where the roller fed out the fishing line. The lights of the boat suddenly flooded the deck and the surrounding waters, and something white caught his eye in the ocean, just beyond the light. "There's something in the water," he yelled over the grinding motor, pointing toward the starboard bow. "I think...I think it's a body!"

Manny did not hear exactly what his cousin said, but he could see Ramon's distress and the direction in which he was looking. Moving swiftly to the bow of the boat, Manny scanned the dark ocean before laying his hand on the switch for the large searchlight anchored to the side of the wheelhouse. He was hesitant to turn on the light for fear the bright beam would be seen by other boats, but as far as he could see, they were alone. Moreover, if someone was in the water, being seen was a risk he was willing to take.

"There," Ramon said as he scurried up to the railing to stand next to his uncle. "I think it's a body." He pointed to where he had seen it, keeping his eyes glued to the area for fear of losing his bearings.

Manny swept the light over the black seas. "It is a body," he said suddenly. "All stop! All stop!" he yelled toward the wheelhouse as he held the searchlight on the body. As an arm rose from the dark depths, he widened the beam, fixing the light on the bobbing body in the water. "Ramon, grab some blankets from down below. Francisco, pull out the life preserver. Al, shut down the motor." Everyone scurried to follow their captain's orders, as he focused the light on the waving arm.

As the big diesel engine began to wind down, Manny leaned over the railing to get a better view. He was surprised to see it was a woman, and she was not alone. He squinted into the night. "*Idios mío!* It's two women!" he said in surprise. "But where did they come from?" He scanned the area but saw no sign of any wreckage. All he saw was a haze of smoke left behind by the long departed *Pichilingue. Had they fallen off the ferry during the fire?*

The fishing boat drifted toward the two women in the water. Within minutes, Manny and his crew of four had them safely on board. The seasoned captain looked the two women over as he draped a blanket around each of them. They had both suffered scrapes and scratches, most of which appeared to be new, but they also had injuries to their faces that were older. With a suspicious eye, he looked at the row of stitches on Kenzie's cheek.

He crouched down in front of them. "How did you two end up floating in the ocean in the middle of the night? Did it have anything to do with that fire aboard the ferry?" The blonde's teeth were chattering and she hunkered down further into her blanket. Silently, she shifted her gaze to her companion. "Well, how about it? You don't look like you've been out on a cruise."

Manny's eyes traveled down Kenzie's torn shirt and the fresh blood staining it. "And what do we have here?" He reached forward to pull aside her blanket for a better view. He wasn't expecting to see Kenzie's 9mm pistol pointing directly at him.

"Suppose you don't ask us any more questions and we won't ask you why you're out here fishing in the dark." Kenzie's voice was low, her words slow and deliberate.

Manny looked from the gun to the hardened eyes of the woman holding it. The two stared at each other in silence as everyone else on board watched and waited.

Cori slowly reached over and placed a hand on the barrel of the gun, pushing the weapon down and away from their interrogator. "He just saved our lives. How about a truce?" Everyone waited, unsure of what to do. "Please," she whispered.

It was a moment longer before the gun was lowered. Kenzie kept her eyes on Manny as she tried to return it to her waistband. The movement caused a slight grimace of pain and Cori saw it. She gently touched Kenzie's forearm. The tender touch was enough to make Kenzie take her eyes off the apparent captain as she turned to look at Cori. No one had ever touched her like that before, not mentally or physically.

"She's injured," Cori said without taking her eyes off Kenzie.

The captain looked from one woman to the other. He didn't like having women on his boat, especially women with a gun. He was unsure of what he should do, and that was something he wasn't used to.

Cori turned to face him. "Can you help us? My friend is hurt. She's bleeding."

"Let's get you down below." Manny gestured toward the door below the wheelhouse.

The women helped each other to their feet. On unsteady legs, they followed the captain toward the door that led to the living quarters below.

"Fire up the diesels," Manny said to his brother before he stepped through the door. "Let's get out of here. Al, take the wheel and head due north."

Kenzie scanned their surroundings as they cautiously made their way down the steep steps. Alert and observant she was, but her mind was on something Cori had said. *Friend; she called me her friend.* The smell of fish, diesel, and hardworking bodies was overwhelming. The captain obviously took a lot of pride in his boat, but it was a working fishing trawler and it smelled like it. Taking one step at a time, Kenzie kept her right arm pinned against her side, using only her left to keep her balance. She was doing her best to ignore the pain that was ripping through her right ribcage and shoulder. At the bottom of the stairs, Kenzie found herself standing next to Cori and the captain in the middle of the galley.

The captain sat down on the bench that wrapped around the galley table. "Let's see what we got here." Manny motioned the taller woman over to where he sat. Kenzie dropped her blanket, exposing the tattered, bloodstained shirt. "Holy Patron Saint of Travel, you're lucky you weren't shark bait." Without hesitating, he pushed back the shredded material of Kenzie's shirt with his finger and peered at the torn flesh. "Pretty nasty wound you got there. I'm not going to ask how you got it. You were lucky the tides were with you tonight. If they had been going out, well..." He let go of her shirt and sized up the two fortunate women. Whatever they were up to was not his concern, but not many law-abiding people were plucked from the ocean in the middle of the night. "The name is Manny, and we can leave it at that."

Cori laid her blanket on the bench on the other side of the table. "I'm Cori, and the silent shark bait here is..."

"Kenzie." Her voice was just above a murmur as she held out her left hand to the man who had saved them. "Thanks for the lift. I think we have an understanding."

Manny looked at the offered hand and hesitated for a moment. "Those are pretty mangled up, too," he said, noting the cuts and scrapes on both of her hands. He glanced at Cori's hands, but they were nowhere near as injured as Kenzie's.

Kenzie reviewed the damage her hands had sustained while trying to escape the cattle trailer and was surprised she hadn't felt them earlier. At the moment, they were the least of her concerns. She offered her hand again and the captain took it. "This your boat?"

"*Sí.*" Manny was impressed. The woman with the dark curls was not a big woman but even with her injuries, her handshake was solid. It told him a lot, especially when he saw her grimace.

"Okay, enough of this. Excuse me," Cori said as she moved in front of Kenzie, blocking the captain's view. "I need to take a look at your side and, apparently, your hands. Just how bad is it?" Lifting the bottom of Kenzie's shirt, Cori grabbed both edges of the material and tore it apart. The t-shirt ripped all the way up the side.

Kenzie frowned at the action. "I could have just taken it off. It's not like I have another one."

"I can't imagine how it would have hurt to get out of that shirt," Cori said as she examined the area. Blood was again starting to ooze from the large gash, and there were several smaller scrapes made by the splintered wood. Squinting in the dim light, Cori could see there were also slivers in the skin covering her ribcage.

"What do you have for medical supplies?" Cori directed her question to Manny, not taking her eyes off Kenzie's side. "I'm gonna need something sharp, like a needle, something I can use for stitches, and some kind of dressing." Manny mumbled something and left in search of the requested materials. "And alcohol," she yelled after him.

"For cleaning or drinking?" his voice bellowed from beyond the small galley.

"Both."

Kenzie liked the feel of the gentle hands that were moving along her side. It felt good, and it gave her a chance to study Cori's face. Her eyes were so focused, her brow fixed in a stern look of concentration as she examined the injuries. Kenzie's eyes kept going back to the dark bruises she had left on Cori's face, twisting the guilt in her stomach.

The boat swayed heavily in the waves and Cori grasped Kenzie's waist for support. Kenzie clasped Cori's shoulder with one hand and reached out for the table with the other. A hiss escaped her clenched teeth as pain speared through her shoulder.

Cori stood up and looked at Kenzie with deep concern. "What else hurts?"

"Nothing," Kenzie lied as the two women locked eyes. "Just fix up my side...please."

You're not as tough as you think you are. Cori looked up into the eyes of her would-be killer. Their gazes held for a few moments as Cori bit at her lip in contemplation. It was only then that she realized her hands were still holding Kenzie's waist. She could feel the warmth of the firm, toned skin radiating beneath her hands.

Kenzie felt the change in the pressure of Cori's touch as she tilted her head back in challenge.

"What...else...hurts," Cori asked. When Kenzie did not reply, Cori moved her hands along her ribcage and gave each rib a forceful push. The woman's stoic expression never changed, but her eyes sparkled with gold. *She's enjoying this*, Cori thought, and that spurred her on. Slowly sliding her hands down Kenzie's firm flesh, she stopped on her hips and pressed hard, looking for any sign that something else was giving Kenzie pain.

"I said, 'nothing'."

Cori's eyebrows furrowed in frustration. *That hiss came from somewhere.* Thinking back to their plunge into the water, she recalled Kenzie's death-defying grab. With her eyes focused on Kenzie's face, Cori reached up and pressed on her right shoulder.

"Son of a bitch!"

The sudden intake of breath and the color draining from Kenzie's face gave Cori the information she was searching for.

"Don't tell me 'nothing'," Cori commented, deliberately poking her shoulder again.

Kenzie's eyes rolled in pain as she reached out and grabbed Cori's arm. "What the hell was that for?" she said in anger.

"That was for the back of your hand when we were in my car — and for your fist in my face in my apartment. We need to get the rest of your shirt off."

Kenzie licked at her lips, certain that she saw a twinkle of satisfied revenge in Cori's eyes.

Manny came back into the galley with his makeshift medical supplies. "I got wha..." He stopped short at the sight of the half-naked woman. He was a tough old seaman, but a young, good looking woman in a bra still made him blush. He cleared his throat and made the sign of the cross over himself. "I got what you asked for... Hope fishing line will ah...work. I threw everything into some...um boiling water, so it's as sterile as you're gonna get on a fishing boat." Kenzie showed no sign of modesty or embarrassment as Manny did his best not to gawk at the sight of her bare skin above her skimpy bra.

Cori was concentrating on her examination of Kenzie's shoulder, and paid little attention to his discomfort. "I'm gonna need a hand here Manny, assuming you're up to it." Cori stepped back from her patient. "She's dislocated her shoulder and I won't have the strength to perform the reduction."

Manny took his eyes off Kenzie's cleavage and looked at the unnatural bulge at the front of her shoulder. He carefully placed the items on the table and reached into his back pocket, pulling out a silver flask. "You're gonna need this," he said, offering the alcohol to Kenzie.

"What is it?"

"Tequila."

She accepted it, but hesitated before taking a drink. "Before we carry on with this, I think we need to talk."

"I think we need to do this first—"

Kenzie cut Cori off. "No, we need to deal with this first." She turned to the captain. "As uninvited guests aboard your boat...how long will you let us stay on board, and how far will you take us?"

"Depends. How far you want to go, and," he eyed her suspiciously, "who you're running from?"

They were fair questions. Kenzie answered, though it made her feel uncomfortable. "I'm not really sure who's after us, but I can tell you, they aren't amateurs." She looked at Cori before continuing. "I don't have the money now, but I'm good for it.

Unfortunately you'll have to take my word for it, but I'll pay you handsomely...if you're willing to take us north...at least as far as you can?"

The captain didn't answer right away, so Kenzie took a long drink of the tequila. A shudder went through her body as the alcohol burned down her throat. She had to swallow several times before the fumes left her mouth.

"You want mainland or Baja?" the captain asked as she took several smaller sips from the silver flask.

"Baja." Kenzie wiped tequila from her lips. Keeping one eye on the captain, she watched Cori prepare what few medical supplies there were. She knew her pain was going to get worse before it got better.

Manny removed his hat to scratch his head. Taking his unexpected passengers across the Gulf to the Baja of California was a risk, a big risk, but if the financial reward they were offering was real... He looked the two women over and considered his options. The blonde was a bossy little piece of dynamite, but he knew the one with the gun was in charge.

"I can take you as far as San Felipe, but it will be dangerous...and costly," he added.

"Fine." The boat pitched wildly to starboard and without thinking, Kenzie reached out to steady herself. A flash of searing pain exploded through her unstable shoulder. This time she couldn't conceal her pain, letting out a loud hiss from between clenched teeth.

"Okay, enough of this talk, we need to fix this shoulder," Cori said.

Kenzie's face grew pale and Cori was certain she was going to faint, so she slid her hands around Kenzie's bare midriff. "Trust me," Cori whispered into her ear as her hands tightened their hold.

Kenzie studied the upraised eyes. Didn't Cori understand that she was not really the trusting kind? She hadn't relied on anyone since she had been teamed with John Mifflin. Still, this was different. She had little choice. Not only was her body in need, but something stirring inside made her want to believe Cori.

Manny took in the situation and made a decision. "I think we should do this in my quarters. There's not nearly enough room around that table."

"Okay," Cori said, while the silent Kenzie only nodded.

Surprisingly the tequila was already affecting Kenzie, so Cori slid her hands around her waist and guided her down the narrow hallway to the captain's quarters. It was a small room, but there was more than enough space to work on Kenzie's injuries.

Cori carefully deposited Kenzie on the bed. "You need to drink more," she said as she handed over the flask.

Kenzie was going to protest, but the look in Cori's eyes told her she didn't have the strength or will for that much of a fight. Putting the tequila to her lips, she took several large gulps and then placed it on the night table next to the bed. The alcohol shook her body sending another sharp slice of pain through her shoulder. "Errrggg!" she grunted through clenched teeth.

"Okay, let's get this shoulder back into place. Hope you're ready." Cori sat down on the bed next to Kenzie. Bringing her legs up, she carefully maneuvered around Kenzie's waist and locked her ankles together. As she brought one arm around Kenzie's chest and the other around her back, she noted how warm Kenzie was. Carefully, she wiggled tightly against Kenzie's side, trying not to think about her forearms pressing into Kenzie's breasts. She looked at Manny and nodded. "Alright." The captain moved to Kenzie's side and took her hand. "Have you done this before?" Cori quickly interjected.

"*Sí.* Working on a fishing trawler, you have to be ready to do just about anything, but I ain't sticking around while you sew her up. I've got a boat I've got to get back to."

"Fair enough. Okay, Kenzie, lean over into me." Cori tightened her hold.

Kenzie started to relax into Cori's care, but something sharp and hard, forced her forward. "Hang on." Pulling her 9mm from her waistband, she leaned past Cori to place it next to the tequila. As an afterthought, she took one more long pull on the nearly empty flask. "Okay." Closing her eyes, she leaned over into Cori's damp shirt as Manny's calloused hands circled her arm.

Cori felt Kenzie shiver in her grasp. She squeezed a little tighter, pulling Kenzie's uninjured shoulder against her chest. Cori could feel her tense just as Manny pulled her arm. A gut wrenching *thunk* filled the small room as Kenzie did her best to muffle a cry. Cori whispered a shushing sound into her ear, but she was unsure if Kenzie heard it as her head flopped over onto Cori's shoulder.

"She's out," Manny said as he laid her arm against her side. "I suggest you sew her back together before she wakes up. You can stay here in my room, just don't make a mess." Manny laid Kenzie's limp body out on his rumpled bed as Cori looked around the cramped quarters. *How on earth could we possibly leave it any messier than it already is?*

"You two are in real trouble, aren't ya?" he asked, watching Cori as she laid a towel over Kenzie's chest. She was awfully young to be in this much trouble, but it didn't matter. He had already decided to help them, more for this little one than for the sullen woman on his bed.

Cori nodded slightly to Manny's question as she turned to face him. He looked to be in his sixties. His dark skin weathered from the elements, his eyes dark from years of struggle, but he appeared to be streetwise, and, in Cori's opinion, friendly.

"We didn't do anything wrong," she said, her voice strong, "but we seem to have attracted the attention of some bad people."

"You were on that ferry weren't you?"

Cori nodded reluctantly.

"But they didn't stop when you went over the side?"

Cori was quiet for a moment, pondering how and what to say. "Can we say that they didn't even know we were there, never mind that we went overboard, and leave it at that?"

He accepted what little she offered with a dip of his head. "Where exactly are you headed?"

Where? Good question. Cori was not sure, but as far north as they could get in Mexico. "Assuming you take us to San Felipe, we'll make our way to Tijuana, then San Diego. Beyond that, I'm not really sure."

Manny nodded. "I'll do what I can, but I won't promise." With that, he left the young woman to care for her friend.

The door shut with a soft click and Cori turned back to tend to Kenzie's wounds. The light in the room was not very good, so she pulled the overhead lamp closer to see what she was doing. Pre-med had been a long time ago. She hoped she could remember what little she'd been taught. Kneeling down beside the half-naked woman, she removed the towel from Kenzie's chest, uncovering her wounds. After a quick examination to determine the full extent of Kenzie's injuries, Cori decided it would be better just to cut off her soiled bra. Once that was done, she used a clean, damp towel to begin wiping away the blood. The view in front of her was far more pleasant than she could have imagined as she ran a needle and fishing line through the jagged edges of flesh.

When the make-do stitches were finished, she sat back and looked over what she had done. The sutures were ugly and unprofessional, but she figured they were better than leaving the skin gaping open. Checking over Kenzie's hands, she decided none of the dozen or so cuts were deep enough to require stitches. Her next undertaking was to remove the many slivers of wood they both acquired while crawling through the hole in the cattle trailer. When her body was free of wood splinters, she started on Kenzie's.

It took her longer than she anticipated, but eventually all that remained were red and swollen scratches over much of Kenzie's body. She gently ran her hand over the taut skin of Kenzie's abdomen, feeling for any slivers she might have missed.

It had been a long time since she'd had her hands on a woman's naked body, and she could not help the feelings that touching Kenzie was stirring in her. There were several scars marring Kenzie's strong body, but they appeared to be old and well healed. Kneeling closer to Kenzie's head, she parted the hair to get a good look at where the bullet had grazed her temple a couple of days earlier. The swim in the ocean had cleaned the scab from the wound, leaving behind a small gouge of skin, which should heal easily. Cori swallowed hard at the realization of how close that bullet had come to ending Kenzie's life. She reached out and lightly brushed the old bruise and stitches on Kenzie's high cheekbone. *And where did you get these?* She tenderly fingered the sutures. Cori decided they had been in place long enough. With a couple of snips, she removed the dark thread and then sat back to study Kenzie's face. *Thirties? Late thirties*, she decided. *Hard to tell, but regardless, she sure is beautiful.* "Especially when you're not pointing a gun at me," Cori whispered.

Her eyes traveled down Kenzie's body, noting what she guessed to be a healed bullet wound on the shoulder they had just relocated into its socket. There was a small red scar on Kenzie's lower back that appeared to be recent. Cori knew that the scar left behind by her stitches would not be as clean and unnoticeable. Her fingers traced the disfigured flesh of the old wound on Kenzie's shoulder. Cori had never met anyone who had been shot, at least not someone who had lived. The scar was thick and raised, and very close to one breast. Cori's eyes drifted toward the dark, erect skin of Kenzie's nipple, and she unconsciously licked her lips.

"Just what did you have in mind?"

Kenzie's mumbled words caused an instant blush on her face. She looked to see Kenzie's golden eyes were barely open. "Hi," Cori said shyly, forgetting that she had just had her hands all over this woman's body. "How are you feeling?"

Kenzie's eyes scanned the room before coming back to look at Cori's face. She blinked slowly, feeling the full effects of the tequila. "I don't know." Her tongue felt thick. "How do I feel?"

Impossibly, Cori blushed an even deeper red. "I...ah..." Her eyes traveled to Kenzie's injuries. "I was looking for more splinters. I think you had half of that trailer in your side and hands."

"Hmmm." Kenzie closed her eyes and nodded.

Cori noted the small bead of sweat on her upper lip and reached for a clean towel. Kenzie opened her eyes and gazed at her.

"I did say you had to buy me a drink before you could cop a feel."

Cori was embarrassed beyond words and she struggled for something to say. "I was not copping a feel. I was just going to..." She held up the towel. When no response came from Kenzie, she took it to mean she had permission. Leaning forward, Cori lightly patted her face. "Are you okay?"

Kenzie licked at her dry lips. "I think I'm drunk." She focused on Cori's face. "But not too drunk. Did you get kicked out of med school for groping your patients when they were unconscious?"

"No," Cori said firmly.

"Hmmm." Kenzie closed her eyes and drifted with the alcohol running through her body. After a moment, she opened her eyes again. Lifting her hand, she concentrated with all that was left of her sobriety and reached for Cori's face. "Thank you," she said softly and was instantly rewarded with a small smile.

The ache of loneliness Cori had felt for years swelled up inside of her. She leaned into Kenzie's gentle touch. This woman was a stranger who came into her life and turned it upside down. Now she felt drawn to her. For the sake of human companionship or protection — either way, it made Cori feel the safest she had since this all started.

Try as Kenzie might to keep her eyes open, they disobediently drifted closed. Somewhere in a tequila-induced fog, she basked in the memory of a look of desire and a spoken word. Cori had called her friend, something no one had called her in a very, very long time.

Cori gingerly laid the arm back onto the bed, knowing Kenzie would be feeling the pain in the morning. "Thanks for saving me," she whispered as she leaned down and kissed her forehead. With Kenzie taken care of, Cori became acutely aware of her own damp clothes. She pulled a thin blanket over Kenzie's body, gathered the supplies, and left the room.

The captain found Cori some dry clothes. They did not fit her but they were clean, and for now that would have to do. She curled up on one of the benches in the galley and fell fast asleep as the

Juanita Rose motored its way northward. Deep in slumber, her mind tumbled with the rise and fall of the ocean waves.

Cobra was fuming. He had watched each vehicle as it disembarked from the ferry. Nothing. How could anyone lose someone who was on a ferry? There was no way he was reporting back that he, too, had failed. Moving off to the side, Cobra pulled his Blackberry from his pocket and punched in a series of numbers.

A canvas-covered cargo truck pulled over to the side of the disembarking ramp to exchange drivers. Cobra paid them little mind as he waited, his eyes glued to the small screen in his hand.

The driver of the truck got out and greeted another man that had been waiting alongside Cobra. "Lucky you even have a truck to drive, Hector," the rotund man said as he handed the keys to the other driver. "There was a fire on board, almost caught the truck on fire." He pointed up to the box of the truck and Cobra looked up to see where the flames had blackened and singed the canvas.

"Fortunately, the entire ferry didn't go up in a blaze of glory, Danny," Hector said as he examined the damage.

"It was quite a commotion, very scary."

"Excuse me." Cobra slid the Blackberry into his pocket and walked closer to the truck. "A fire, you said?"

Hector was checking the contents of the load as Danny, the driver, told the gathering tourists about the excitement on board.

"A fire!" one woman exclaimed, fearful about her impending crossing aboard the next passenger ferry.

"Did anybody die?" Cobra asked cautiously.

"No, *Señor*." Danny shook his head.

"So, no passengers were hurt?"

"There are no passengers on this ferry, only cargo, but there are a lot of dead cows floating out there." Danny quickly explained the fire and the frantic ejection of the cattle trailer, exaggerating his own part in the whole affair.

"Dead cows, huh?" *Maybe she's already dead.* The Blackberry in his pocket beeped. "So the whole trailer went into the water?" He pulled the PDA from his pocket and looked at the screen. *Son of a bitch.* His lips curled in annoyance as he read the flashing message.

The *Juanita Rose* powered through the water of the Sea of Cortez, transporting its illegal cargo. The bright rays of the sun broke over the mountains of the mainland and streaked across the gray of the morning sky. Manny was the only one awake, his calloused hand lightly holding the wheel as his boat sliced through the ocean waves. He took a sip of his strong, cold coffee and checked his navigational dials. They were making good time northward, but he had not relaxed since the women had come aboard.

Down below, near the bow of the boat, heavy eyes opened with a subtle groan. *What happened to my head?* Kenzie attempted to lift her right arm, but the ache in her shoulder made her think otherwise. Surveying her surroundings, she recalled the last few days in an instant, but where she was at that precise moment was a little foggy. Tequila. That much she remembered. She repeatedly opened and closed her swollen hands, working out the stiffness as she recalled each and every sliver that had been embedded in them. Her left hand brushed through her curls, the pain in her scalp reminding her that she had drunk too much of the liquid painkiller. Kenzie was not much of a drinker and now she remembered why. Sliding her hand down over her face, she lightly touched the spot where the bullet had grazed her head. She'd had worse. Moving her fingers downward, she felt for her stitches. Her eyes widened as she realized the sutures were gone.

Images broke through her hazy fog and she sat up with a muffled moan as she looked around the small cabin. *Cori.* There was no sign of her, and for a moment, Kenzie was grateful. *What are you doing, LeGault?* She leaned back in the bed and recalled the caring eyes and the warmth of being called "friend". Several long moments passed as she recalled more of what had happened, and only then did she remember the tender touch of Cori's lips on her forehead. A long forgotten feeling flooded her body and Kenzie was not sure if that was a good thing.

She pulled back the blanket and was a little surprised to see she was completely naked. *Where the hell are my clothes?* Looking around the small cot, she saw nothing that resembled what she had been wearing. Glancing down at her side, she noted the stitches knotted asymmetrically along her wound. She ran her fingers over them, stirring up warm, comforting memories of small hands against her skin. The ache between her legs unnerved her.

There was a pair of old coveralls hanging on the back of the small door, and she put them on. Zipping up the front, she patted the pocket out of habit. She turned and looked back at the cot. *Forget my clothes...where the hell is my gun! Son-of-a-bitch, get your shit together, girl!* Searching the small room to no avail, she left the room feeling naked and unsettled.

Kenzie moved past the sleeping crew in their bunks and found Cori curled up on a bench in the galley, asleep. *She called me "friend"*. The thought felt uncomfortable as she studied Cori's relaxed features. *She looked so innocent — too innocent to be involved in all of this.* Looking back toward the captain's quarters, Kenzie made a decision. When she lifted the small woman, her shoulder and side screamed in protest but she ignored them as she relocated Cori to the captain's cabin. Cori never stirred, not even as Kenzie gently placed her onto the cot. Pulling the thin blanket over Cori, Kenzie realized that she liked the feeling of being a protector far more than she had ever liked being a terminator. *If things were different...*but they weren't and they never would be. Kenzie leaned down and placed a tender kiss on Cori's forehead. Her mind awhirl with "if onlys", she silently left the room.

Moving back through the galley, she spotted her 9mm tucked under the pillow Cori had been using. She instantly felt better as she collected the weapon and dropped it into one of the deep pockets in the coveralls.

Up on the deck, in the wheelhouse, Manny saw a shadow pass over the window in front of him. He knew without looking, the dangerous one was on the prowl. He returned his attention to the sea, knowing that eventually, she would seek him out.

Kenzie licked at her dry lips as she looked over the ocean beyond the boat. The wind whipped her curls and the cool spray felt good on her face, but it did nothing for the throbbing in her head. That ache was more from the hangover than the swirl of questions in her mind. Stiff and sore, her body ached all over and she gave in to it for moment, taking in all the fresh air she could inhale. A while later, she went in search of the captain. She stepped into the wheelhouse and was taken aback by the strong smell of grease, diesel, and fish.

"*Buenos días, Señorita,*" Manny said without turning around.

"Good morning, Captain."

"Feeling better?"

Taking her eyes off the distant shores of the Baja peninsula, Kenzie looked at him without changing expressions. "Feeling like shit, actually."

He nodded with a smile as Kenzie moved inside the wheelhouse. "Nice outfit," he commented. He watched her slow and halting movement. She was sore. "How's the shoulder?"

Standing next to him, her gaze automatically went to the ocean before them. "Better." She considered for a long moment. "I assume I have you to thank for that."

"I looked after your shoulder," he said. "Your friend looked after the rest."

Silence fell between them as Kenzie contemplated his description of Cori. "Either way...thanks," she said as she looked down at his thick, black coffee. "Got any more of that?"

"Last cup, sorry. But," he reached over to a cupboard next to him and pulled out a small bottle of what appeared to be more tequila, "this might take the edge off."

"No, thanks." Kenzie looked at the bottle and her unsettled stomach churned. "I ah...I actually don't drink."

Manny chuckled as he put the bottle back. "Could've fooled me, *Señorita.*" *That explains the green around her gills this morning.*

She managed a weak smile, but that was about it. "What do you have for ship-to-shore communications on this boat?" He pointed a thick finger at the radio above his head. "And when you're out fishing at night?" Her eyebrows rose in question as she watched his face.

There was a moment's hesitation, but he knew he wasn't fooling her. He slid back the door under the wheel and reached up inside, his hand searching for something his eyes could not see. He smiled at her as he pulled a satellite phone from its hiding spot. It was an old phone, and that was being polite. It was larger than a masonry brick and weighed about the same.

"Give it a moment," he said as he pushed a few buttons and then handed her the heavy phone. "It's old, but it works," he said, noting her skepticism. "Your friend used it last night."

"Cori called somebody?" The information unsettled her, but she would deal with that later.

He gestured to the open door and the rear of the wheelhouse. "Want me to step out?"

"Nah." She shook her head as she dialed a series of numbers. "Did she say who she called?" Kenzie asked.

"She said it was her mother."

Manny turned his attention back to the sea as Kenzie put the phone to her ear. She was a little surprised to hear a clear ringing coming from the antiquated phone.

"*Hola,*" a gruff voice grumbled.

"Big Polly there?"

"Who's callin'?"

"Kenzie." She reached out to steady herself against the gentle sway of the boat as she waited, but she didn't have to wait long.

"Kenzie, is that really you?"

She smiled as a warm feeling rushed over her. Big Polly had a way of making anyone feel safe. "Yeah, but I need to make this short. I need some help."

"For you...anything."

"I'm coming in, and I'm coming in hot."

Big Polly's playful banter turned serious, "Not a problem. Tell me where and when."

Moving the phone away from her mouth, Kenzie turned to Manny as she wiped at her tired eyes. "Where are we?"

"We were passing Isla Carmen when the sun came up, a few hours ago."

Nodding, she brought the phone back to her mouth, but Manny held up a finger. "Hang on," she said quickly into the phone, and then to Manny, "What?"

"I understand your real destination is San Diego, by way of Tijuana?" Though his eyes were on the ocean, he could feel her bristle at his words.

Kenzie squinted into the distance as she rolled her tongue against the inside of her cheek. She didn't want anyone to know where they were headed, but it appeared that Cori had not been as discreet. "That's one option."

Manny wondered exactly who this stoic woman was and what kind of trouble she was in. He considered himself to be an honest, hard working man who was only fishing illegally because he needed to provide for his family. Breaking the law was not something he wanted to do, but he found himself wanting to help her.

"I have family in Santa Rosalia."

"I'm listening,"

"He has a plane."

Kenzie turned and looked at the salty captain. Her golden eyes began to shine as a slow smile spread across her face. "Really?" She raised the phone back to her ear.

The fishing boat moved swiftly through the water and Kenzie leaned against the steel railings, casting an eye on the white foam running alongside them. Her head had started to clear but she still felt like she had gone a few rounds in the ring with a gorilla. Taking a deep breath, she looked at the coast of the Baja moving slowly in the distance.

"Mind some company?" Cori asked as she came alongside her.

Glancing over her shoulder, Kenzie looked Cori over from head to toe. She had a blanket still wrapped around her shoulders and her hair fluttered around her face. She looked tired and haggard. *I wouldn't mind your company at all,* Kenzie thought, but she only nodded and turned back to watch the view beyond them.

"How are you feeling?" Cori asked loudly over the sound of the chugging diesel motor and the ocean wind.

"Fine." She waited for a moment before she asked the question that had been nagging her mind. "Captain said you made a phone call last night." Kenzie didn't want to ask, she wanted to trust Cori, but she had survived this long by listening to the persistently cautious voice in her head. *To who?*

"Yes. I know I probably shouldn't have, but I had to call my mother and make sure she was all right. With everything that's happened, I just couldn't...I just wanted to know she was all right."

"I understand," Kenzie said. "Was she all right?"

Cori nodded. "She's concerned. I haven't phoned this often since I left Seattle."

"You didn't tell her where we were, did you?"

"No."

The conversation died, but Cori had something else to say. "How's the shoulder...and your side?" she finally asked.

"Good," Kenzie answered too quickly, showing she too was feeling a little uneasy.

"And your hands?"

Kenzie looked down at her swollen hands. "They're stiff and sore, but they'll be fine in a day or two. Like the rest of me," she said as she opened and closed them several times. "A little banged up, but I'll be fine, thanks to you."

Not wanting to look into Kenzie's eyes, Cori kept her attention on the horizon. "I did the best I could with what I had." Kenzie turned to look at her and Cori could feel her stare.

"You did just fine." Kenzie moistened her lips as Cori turned to face her. "Thank you," Kenzie said with a rare smile. "And thanks for taking my stitches out, and for taking care of me. I'm not used to that. I haven't had to rely on anyone in a very long time and ah..."

"You're welcome. That's what friends are for."

"Yeah, about that..." Kenzie ran her fingers through her curly hair.

"What? You're going to tell me that you didn't have friends, either?"

"Well, I have, but, ah...um," Her finger picked at the peeling paint on the railing of the *Juanita Rose.*

The smile on Cori's face faded as she watched the intense stare of her would-be assassin. "Something tells me you haven't had many. Did you have anything normal in your life, Kenzie?"

Thoughts and memories flashed through her mind as flecks of paint drifted downward and into the water below. "It's had it moments." Kenzie lifted her eyes to the horizon and she took a deep breath. No one had to tell her that her life had not been typical. John Mifflin had taught her that. He had been the golden boy of his high school, and had joined the service upon graduation. In truth, he had been her only friend, aside from the judge. All of that seemed so long ago, and so very far away. This with Cori, this was different, and she could feel it in the raw ache in her stomach.

Kenzie turned to face Cori, studying her every feature and, for the first time, really seeing the beauty of the woman beneath the bruises. It would be one of those moments that she would remember for the rest of her life. Even after all they had been through, Cori still had the fresh look of innocence, one that under different circumstances she would have liked to get to know better.

"Why did you call me your friend?"

"Well," Cori pushed her flapping hair out of her eyes, "you haven't held a gun on me for almost two days now, and...well, you've saved my life twice, and..." Cori's smile faded as she looked deep into Kenzie's eyes and answered her honestly, "Because I think you need one."

Their eyes locked for several long heartbeats, until Kenzie had to look away. There was too much communication in the silence and it made her extremely uncomfortable. Looking down at the railing, she began to pick at the paint again until Cori gently laid a hand on top of hers. Kenzie stopped her picking and flattened her hand out on the railing, allowing Cori's fingers to intertwine with her own.

Hours later, the *Juanita Rose* pulled into the safe harbor of the tiny town of Santa Rosalia. As per their arrangement, Manny's cousin Fernando was there to meet them. The fishing trawler returned to sea, its captain at the helm hoping Kenzie would reward him as she had promised. If she did, he would not have to fish illegally for a very long time.

Fernando regarded the two women in the front of his pickup. "So, I know Manny said not to be asking a bunch of questions, but do you need anything in town before we head out to the airstrip?" The one with the curly hair was a real looker with her exotic gold eyes, but the woman with the honey-colored hair made his eyes shine. Neither of them had spoken much, but that was okay by him, as long as they didn't mind him looking.

Kenzie held on to the frame of the window as they bounced painfully down the pothole riddled road. "We need some clothes, but we don't have any money."

"*Sí*, that's not a problem. Manny said to look after you, so I'm gonna look after you. There are a few stores in town that will carry what you need. *Sí?*"

"That sounds fine," Kenzie said as she continued to scan their surroundings. "I also need to know where we'll be landing, then I need to find a phone. I need to make a call to have someone pick us up."

"*Sí, sí.*" Fernando smiled and pulled an old cell phone from his pocket.

Looking at the shape and the apparent age of the phone, Kenzie suggested they find a landline.

Chapter 9

In a nondescript building on the south side of town, three men waited silently around a folding particleboard table. The walls of the office were bare, with the exception of a calendar that was two years old and a faded picture of the Seattle Space Needle. A single lopsided aluminum blind hung over the only window, partially obscuring the view outside. The florescent light flickered overhead, its noisy hum the only sound in the room. Situated in the center of the table was a black, three-legged, speakerphone, designed for conference calls. The only other thing on the table was an ashtray holding a smoking pipe.

Winston Palmer reached for his pipe and placed it between his tightly pursed lips. Drawing deeply, he blew several large puffs of smoke into the already warm room.

Terry Bucannon was sitting to the left of Palmer, Manuck to his right. Terry constantly waved the pipe smell away from his nose. Being a Deputy Director in the CIA afforded Bucannon the authority to command others, but there was nothing he could do about the smoke coming from Palmer's pipe. When Palmer rose from his chair, Terry thankfully waved away the smoke as he watched the senator move to look out the window.

"I wouldn't be standing in front of any windows if I were you, Senator," Manuck said to Palmer. "She can take the eye out of a quarter at about 500 yards, and she'd be gone before you hit the floor." Before Palmer could comment, a light on the black box on the table flashed red and began to hum.

Moving quickly away from the window and taking his seat back at the table, Palmer told himself he had moved because the call they had been waiting for had finally come, not because he feared for his own safety.

Manuck leaned back in his chair as Terry slapped at the connect button. "Tell me it's done," Manuck demanded.

A crackly voice filled the room. "No, sir. I've run into another problem."

"God damn it!" Manuck slammed his hand down on the table. "What's the problem? Can't you just shoot her in the head?"

Senator Palmer rubbed his face, trying to wipe away the preceding forty-eight hours of tension.

"It seems there was an incident on the ferry, and — well, I thought she was dead..."

"You thought? Your orders are not to think, but to do as you're commanded."

"The intel I had yesterday—"

"Is she dead or not?"

"Apparently not, sir."

"Apparently? Since you're calling us, I'd say probably not. Where is she now?" Manuck said between clenched teeth.

"Near as I can tell...somewhere on the east side of the Baja... Possibly Santa Rosalia, sir."

"Possibly? Can you get this job done or not?" Terry asked Cobra, his eyes locked on Manuck's red face.

Cobra resented the inference of incompetence. He was not used to failure and the indignity that came with it. "I'll phone you when it's done, sir." The connection ended.

Terry Bucannon rose from his chair and slid it back into place next to the table. "Call me when this is done, then I think we need to take a break and let things settle for a while." He nodded at the two men and departed in silence without waiting for a response.

Senator Palmer glared at the closed door, "Who the hell does he think he is?"

"I don't know, but I know what he's becoming...a liability," Manuck said, his thoughts on the present problem.

"I don't think we have to guess that she'll be heading for the border."

"Don't worry, Senator, she won't get across it."

"What about Maquinar?"

"Let's just leave it alone for now."

In a town the size of Santa Rosalia, almost everyone was related, either by birth or by marriage. Everyone knew everyone else. The small seaside town was renowned for the metal church designed by Gustave Eiffel, the man who designed the Eiffel Tower, and for its famous El Boleo Bakery. Everywhere one went, the warm aromatic smells of freshly baked rolls filled the air. Pushcart hot dogs and handmade tacos were available on almost every street corner. It was a quaint Mexican location, though it retained a definite sense of its French heritage as well.

Fernando pointed out a few tourist shops selling ponchos, blankets, and piñatas. "Most *turistas* don't come here to shop, so we tend to cater more to our own. That is fine by me," he said as he pulled his pickup truck up to the sidewalk. "We'll find what you need here."

The two women exited from the truck and went into the store. It was a small store. Many types of clothing were stacked high on unseen tables. A wide variety of pants, tops, blouses, and dresses also hung layered against the walls. Chatting with Melita, the shop clerk, Fernando watched as the two women wandered through the small store.

"What about this?" Cori pulled out a white cotton dress and held it against her chest.

Eyeing the selection, Kenzie could not help the small smile that snuck onto her face. Something about Cori was so engaging, so contagiously energetic, but now was not the time to be thinking about that. "It's nice, but I think we're looking for something a little more practical, and probably cheaper." Kenzie quickly picked out a shirt for herself, some underwear, a bra, and a pair of knock-off designer jeans.

Fernando held out a dark woolen poncho to her. "You might need this, Señorita. The nights get cold."

She did feel a slight chill in the air. "Thanks," she said quietly as she accepted it.

Melita directed Kenzie toward a curtained area in the back of the store where she could change into her new clothes. Parting the shabby curtain, Kenzie stepped into what could only be referred to as a cubbyhole. She unzipped the coveralls, then peeled it off her shoulders, letting it fall to the ground. Now standing naked in the changing room, Kenzie ran her hand over her side, gingerly fingering the fishing line sutures. The area around the wound was angry and red, but she was not too concerned. Even her hands were already improving, swollen and sore, but improving, and she was thankful for that.

Kicking the coveralls to the side, Kenzie donned her new underwear and jeans, and instantly felt better. She was trying to manage the bra's hooks when a shadow fell across the curtain. She could tell by the outline that it was Cori.

"Kenzie?"

"Yeah?" she answered as she tried to get her bra fastened. Normally she could do it up behind her back or hook it in the front and swivel it around, but with her injured hands and painful shoulder, she couldn't do either. And it didn't help that her bra was so close to the stitches on her side.

"Are you okay in there or do you need a hand?"

Kenzie noted the movement of the curtain that separated them. *A hand*? Her thoughts flew to the evening before and Cori's gentle hands on her body. *I'm not sure if I have the strength for that.*

"Kenzie? Are you all right?"

The concern in Cori's voice made Kenzie swallow her pride and the thoughts that went with it. "Come in," she said. She brought her arms up to cover her chest as Cori stepped into the change room.

Cori anxiously surveyed her medical handiwork. "Are you okay?"

Kenzie did her best to ignore the wandering gaze and gestured at the bra cupping her breasts. "I can't get it done up. My fingers aren't that nimble at the moment, and with my shoulder, I can't get my arm around..." Her voice trailed off in frustration.

Smiling shyly, Cori wiggled her index finger in the air. "Turn around. I'll get it."

In the close proximity of the changing room, Cori almost felt like she was having a normal moment, just shopping in a boutique with a friend. Except this was not a shop in some mall. She examined the mottled bruises on Kenzie's back, and reminded herself that they were in a changing room in a shop in the middle of Mexico. Cori latched the bra into place. "There," she said as her hands inadvertently brushed against Kenzie's skin. It was warm to the touch, she noted, as she traced one of the long scratches that ran down Kenzie's back. Cori saw the goose bumps that rose in response to her touch. She turned Kenzie around, putting them face to face.

Cori lifted her eyes and Kenzie leaned toward her. Studying the golden eyes, Cori wanted so much to reach out and gently brush back the hair that covered Kenzie's forehead. "You have gorgeous eyes," Cori finally said, breaking the silence.

The tough girl loner image Kenzie had nurtured most of her life crumbled with the rise of the blush to her cheeks. She was not used to compliments, never mind the scrutiny and attention of a beautiful woman. "Thanks," she murmured, barely choking the word out.

There was not enough space for two people inside the changing room, and Cori could feel the heat radiating from Kenzie's body. It made her uneasy, but only because of what she was feeling for the woman she barely knew, feelings that she had to get under control.

"I ah...we should...I need to...um, put some clothes on." Kenzie felt the need to maneuver away from the woman studying her every move. She leaned toward the chair where she had set her new honey-colored, sleeveless polo shirt. Kenzie selected the top and then straightened up, only to find herself face to face with Cori again.

"Here, let me. You must still be hurting." Cori plucked the top from her grasp and gathered the bottom edge in her fingers. Kenzie held her arms in front of her and Cori awkwardly steered them through the holes. She tugged the shirt up over Kenzie's head and then down over her toned body, ultimately resting her hands on Kenzie's waist.

The heated atmosphere of the tiny room was suddenly charged with a palpable tension. Once again, Cori felt a sexual attraction to Kenzie. However, this time Kenzie had her eyes closed, and for that, she was grateful. Cori shook her head, trying to remind herself of the reality of their present situation. They were on the run. This was not the time. When she looked back at Kenzie, she realized that the golden eyes were still closed.

"Hey," Cori said softly. Eyelids opened and Cori saw a look of desire she was not expecting. "Are you okay?"

"Yeah," Kenzie answered with a husky whisper, "For a moment there, I almost forgot." She stopped, and her gaze drifted away from Cori's face.

"Forgot what?" Cori asked as she rested her hand on Kenzie's arm.

The touch felt like a caress. Cori's soft fingers squeezed with gentle concern, and it was more compassion than anyone had shown her in a long time. The one-night stands Kenzie had in her past had not been about passion or emotions. The encounters had been about sex and nothing more, thanks in part to the military's archaic "don't ask, don't tell" policy. Kenzie reveled in the moment, knowing better than most that in a blink of an eye, it could all be gone.

"Kenzie?"

Kenzie's look of smoldering desire was all the invitation Cori needed and she leaned in, within inches of Kenzie's lips. She hesitated. As her eyes drifted downward toward Kenzie's parting lips, she could feel the tension in her rising. Her gaze rose to Kenzie's. Neither spoke, but Cori knew the wanting was there as she moved to close the distance between them. Their lips met cautiously, tenderly touching as if each was seeking permission from the other, and then, in a moment, the kiss ended. Pulling away, Cori averted her eyes and hurriedly stepped out of the changing room, leaving a stunned Kenzie behind.

What was that? Her lips still parted, Kenzie watched as the thin curtain fell back into place, leaving her alone with her confused thoughts. *Holy crap, Cori feels the same way I do. But this is not the time, and definitely not the place!*

Cobra parked his rental car on one of the lively streets of Santa Rosalia. His gaze skimmed over the colorful seaside town. She was close, so close he could almost taste the success. He scanned the many handcarts selling food and the lines of people around them, then checked the clip of his gun. Stepping from the car, he slipped the gun into his holster and then pulled on a lightweight jacket to cover it. He closed the door of the car and went in search of his target.

Cori stood for only a moment outside of Kenzie's dressing room. She couldn't believe what she had just done. *What was I thinking? A few days ago, I would have given anything to be as far away from this woman as I could get, and now...* She reached for the new clothing that she had left in a pile.

"They're paid for, *Señorita*," Fernando said as he tried on a hat. He looked at himself in a mirror, but decided the look did not suit him.

"I...ah..." Cori cleared her throat and held up her new clothes to the young woman tending the store. "Do you have another place to change?"

Melita pointed to a stall on the other side of the shop and Cori fled. Inside her small change room, she dropped her clothes and pressed a hand to her mouth. *I can't believe I just did that.* Her pulse raced and her hands were shaking as she tried to calm herself. *Just breathe. It's okay. At least she responded — kind of.* Her thoughts jumbled, Cori quickly stripped off her borrowed clothing and donned her new khaki pants and white sleeveless cotton shirt. Once dressed, she felt better. There was a small mirror hanging from a wire and she turned it to look at her reflection, still conflicted about what she had done.

"Smooth, Cori, falling for a trained killer," she said just under her breath as she looked at her mirror image. Turning first left and then right, she examined the bruises that Kenzie had made just days earlier. The swelling in her lip was gone, but the bruise around her cheek was still very colorful. Letting go of the hanging mirror, she caught sight of Kenzie's reflection just before the mirror spun back into place.

The woman she had just kissed was leaning nonchalantly against the frame of the door to the change room. Her face was expressionless, but her eyes spoke volumes. "I'm sorry about that...the bruises," she said, her voice low and contrite. "I shouldn't have hit you."

Confused by the feelings swirling in her body, unsure of what to say, Cori turned to face Kenzie. Without thinking, she pressed a hand against her own cheek, feeling the soreness of the bruise that lay beneath the skin.

The look on Cori's face was enough to prompt Kenzie to take another step into the change room. She laid her hand over Cori's. "I'm sorry."

Cori took the last step separating them and studied Kenzie's eyes, searching for an answer to any of the questions her mind and body were asking.

This time it was Kenzie who took the initiative. Kenzie's hand moving with an assurance she didn't feel, surprisingly gentle fingertips traced the outline of Cori's lips.

Cori didn't pull away from the warm touch as it played over her lips. The swinging mirror behind her reflected the light into Kenzie's eyes, making the golden highlights sparkle brightly. The intensity of Kenzie's stare made Cori's heart flutter, causing her to surrender a small breath.

The slight parting of Cori's lips was enough for Kenzie. She trailed her fingers downward until they rested just below Cori's chin, and then ever so tenderly tilted her face upward. Inclining her head slowly, Kenzie gently brushed her lips over those that had kissed her moments earlier. The connection between them was warm but tentative, and it only lasted a moment. Pulling back, she looked to Cori for a response. "But I'm not sorry that you kissed me."

Cori reached up to touch Kenzie's face. The woman fascinated her. She didn't know why, but right now, she really didn't care. Mere inches separated them as Cori's fingers drew Kenzie down for another kiss. Their lips met with greater desire, and the intensity of the kiss grew.

Kenzie's fingers were under Cori's chin, but she wanted more. Sliding her hand downward, she caressed Cori's body as their kiss became more impassioned and more demanding.

The rough texture of Kenzie's battered hand only served to heighten the sensitivity of Cori's skin. Her breathing became shallow and quick. Pushing her body against Kenzie, Cori's fingertips inched toward the lean waist, drawing her closer. Then

Cori's hand touched the cool metal of the gun tucked into the waistband of Kenzie's jeans, and the reality of it backed her away.

"I...ah..." Cori swallowed her desire and looked away.

Kenzie felt the movement of her gun, and was pretty sure its presence was the reason for Cori's sudden shutdown. "Hey..." she said, but then didn't know what to say after. Her past relationships had been based solely on a need for sexual release. Suddenly the world looked a whole lot different to eyes that had never known true passion. A slow, sly smile slid across her face.

The swaying mirror behind Cori caught an image in its reflection and it instantly turned Kenzie to ice. The familiar face she glimpsed was not one she would likely forget. A flash of anger and a sense of dread churned within her as her past rushed into her present. It was him. *Cobra!* The mission, the memories, and the feelings of frustration flooded back to her.

The last time she had seen him had been in a desert in the Middle East, when she had refused to pull the trigger on a target and the two of them had gotten into a fistfight. Kenzie had been winning until Cobra used the butt end of his rifle on her face. By the time she had recovered, the mission was over and the soldiers were dead. The wound he had inflicted was the one from which Cori had just removed the sutures. The scar would forever remind her of what they had done.

In one fluid motion, she pulled Cori deeper into the dressing room. Clamping one hand over her mouth, Kenzie pulled the curtain closed. Cori's eyes were wide with shock and confusion as Kenzie put a finger to her lips.

"Son of a bitch! Where the hell did he come from?" Cobra's appearance in Santa Rosalia couldn't have been a coincidence. Obviously Manuck had sent him to finish the job she had refused to do. But why? And more importantly, how had he found them? For the briefest of moments, she recalled the phone calls Cori had made in Mazatlán and on Manny's boat.

Pulling her gun from her waistband, she racked a round into the chamber.

"What...who?" The fear that had been momentarily forgotten hurtled back into Cori's life.

Kenzie thought about her options. Looking at Cori, she realized following her instinct to confront Cobra was not possible, and her moment of doubt regarding Cori's innocence had to be wrong. There was no way she could have feigned that fear-filled response. So no, rushing out with guns blazing was not an option. She was now responsible for both of them, not just herself.

"Someone I know," Kenzie said, moving the curtain aside. Cobra had stopped outside the shop on the sidewalk, giving her a chance to get a good look at him. Their skirmish in the desert had left a few marks and bruises on his face, she noticed with a smirk. It was obvious that he was looking for them. *But how did he find us?* And then another thought occurred to her. *Where is his partner?* Kenzie quickly scanned the area for Viper.

"Here...in Santa Rosalia?" Cori whispered, her throat suddenly dry as her heart hammered against her chest.

"Yes," Kenzie said, her mind spinning with options.

"Who?"

"A snake," Kenzie said as she looked around the small change room. It was only about the size of a telephone booth. *How did he find us?* She ran her fingers through her hair as she tried to formulate a viable plan.

Cori looked at the ground in panic, expecting to see a slithering reptile. "Where?"

"Not that kind of snake," Kenzie said, seeing the fear her comment had evoked. "The two-legged kind, and he's just outside the door of the store."

Cori relaxed, but only slightly, as she moved to peer around the curtain.

"No." Kenzie quickly stopped her. "I'm not sure whether he saw us, but if he did, he won't hesitate to kill everyone in here." Continuing her situation analysis, she noted that the walls of the change room did not go to the ceiling. "Come here," she directed as she slid her gun back into her waistband. "I need a boost. Can you make a stirrup with your hands?" Cori nodded and interlocked her fingers for Kenzie to use as a step. With one foot on an unstable small shelf and the other in Cori's hands, Kenzie reached for the dangling mirror and slowly lifted it above her head until the angle of the reflection cleared the edge of the wall. Cobra was still on the sidewalk, just outside the shop door. By the looks of his demeanor, he had not seen them, but he was facing in their general direction. At the moment, he appeared to be alone.

"Okay." Kenzie jumped down from her perch. Landing with a jolt, she fought to ignore the sharp pain that ripped through her side. She drew her weapon and reached for the curtain. "Call to Fernando, not too loud, and make it sound sweet."

Cori nodded her understanding, though she was not sure whether she could do it.

Kenzie saw the hesitation. "Take a breath and let it out slowly. You can do it."

Cori did as she was told, but it didn't stop the quaking in her stomach or the pounding in her chest. Taking another breath, she called out, "Fernando, dear, could you come here, please?"

Waiting outside of the curtain, Fernando was a little surprised by the endearment, but he complied with her request. "*Sí.*"

It was Kenzie's voice that came through the thin curtain in response. "Don't make it obvious, but there's a man on the sidewalk — military haircut, dark hair, a big thick neck supporting his fat head. He's wearing a jacket and looks very out of place. Do you see him?"

It would have been hard to miss him. Kenzie's description was quite accurate. "*Sí*, he's still there. Is that a problem?"

"Yeah."

Fernando glanced several times at the man on the other side of the window. "What do you want me to do?"

"We wait. Don't suppose there's a back door to this place, is there?" Kenzie asked.

"*Sí.* It opens out to a small alley, but then what?"

"You go out the front door and get your truck and take it to the end of the alley. Keep it running. We'll be there as soon as we can. How far is it to this plane of yours?"

"Not far, about ten minutes. It's just up over the hill."

"The hill? What hill?" Kenzie asked.

"In Santa Rosalia, you have two choices — out to the sea or up the hill. We're surrounded by— *Señorita*, he's coming in," Fernando whispered quickly.

Kenzie and Cori backed away from the curtain. Kenzie saw the color drain from Cori's face, and the unmistakable sway of someone on the brink of collapse. Kenzie took a step forward and wrapped a protective arm around her. She could feel Cori shaking. "Shhh, it's going be okay," she whispered into her hair. "He doesn't know we're in here."

"But what if—"

"Then that's why I'm here."

Kenzie held her breath as she heard the sound of a set of heavy footsteps walking across the old wooden floor. They stopped just beyond the curtain. Cori must have heard them too, because she burrowed deeper into the security of Kenzie's embrace.

The footsteps shuffled and scuffed on the other side of the curtain. Kenzie reluctantly released Cori and gently pushed the young woman behind her, putting herself directly between Cori and the gunman. Kenzie brought her gun up, ready for whatever might happen.

"Excuse me, *Señor*, is there something I can help you find?"

The voice was young and female, with a strong Mexican accent. *Melita, the shop girl*, Kenzie realized. There was no reply to her question, but the footsteps moved on, away from them.

"Is this your first time in Rosalia?" Melita asked pleasantly. There was a muttered response, but it was impossible to discern what was said.

There were sounds of footsteps shuffling about, and Kenzie knew Cobra was scanning the entire store. Their change room was an obvious spot for them to hide, but with any luck, Fernando's presence would discourage further examination.

"*Adiós, Señor*. Enjoy your visit to Santa Rosalia." Melita's voice signaled Cobra's departure.

There was a long quiet moment, and then they heard Fernando's hushed voice. "He is gone, *Señorita*, but just one *momento* before you come out. I will bring my truck to the entrance of the alley."

"Be careful," Kenzie whispered. She turned around to face Cori, who was so scared she was visibly shaking. "Are you okay?" Kenzie tilted her head forward to look into Cori's eyes. She nodded, but turned her head away from Kenzie's scrutiny. "Hey, it's okay to be scared."

"You weren't scared?"

Kenzie could not help the small smile that lifted the corner of her mouth. She turned Cori's head and looked into her eyes. "I'm a highly trained professional, with years of experience under extreme conditions." Kenzie brushed the hair back from Cori's face and smiled. "Besides, who says I wasn't scared? My heart was pounding pretty good there, too, you know."

"I couldn't tell."

"You're not supposed to. If I wasn't scared, then I would be concerned," Kenzie said candidly. Feeling enough time had passed, she slowly moved back the curtain and looked about the store. Melita motioned them out of the hideaway with a wave of her hand. Taking Cori by the elbow, Kenzie moved beyond the curtain. Moving closer to the window, she scanned the street and the nearby stores, "Which direction did he go?"

"Left," Melita replied.

"Where's the back door?" Kenzie asked, keeping her gun close to her hip and out of sight.

"Back behind there." Melita pointed toward the far corner of the store, where a large blanket concealed the door. Kenzie nodded a thank you as she motioned Melita back to her position at the front of the store. "You stay here and keep an eye out. Don't do anything that might put you in danger." Melita nodded her understanding.

Guiding Cori by the arm, Kenzie moved them toward the exit. At the last moment, she turned back to Melita. "*Gracias*, for the clothes...and your help."

Pulling back the blanket, Kenzie uncovered an old plank door. "Just wait," she said to Cori as she turned the handle slowly. Kenzie cautiously peered out into the alley. It was narrow and littered with debris, but it appeared to be empty.

Kenzie moved out and away from the door, gun at the ready, as she looked left and right. There was no sign of Cobra or Viper. "Come on." She motioned Cori forward. "This way."

To the right was the ocean, and to the left was their escape, although at the moment it was partially blocked by boxes and broken crates. Looking beyond the barrier, Kenzie watched for Fernando, but so far there was no sign of him or his truck.

"We need to move that junk." Moving toward the pile of debris, Kenzie held her weapon in one hand and pulled at one of the crates with the other.

Cori quickly joined her. All she wanted was to be out of Santa Rosalia and far away from the man chasing them. She tried to ignore her shaking hands as they pulled the boxes and crates away as quietly as they could, opening their road to freedom. A rumbling motor echoed off the narrow walls as Fernando arrived in his pickup truck at the end of the alley.

"Let's go." Kenzie tossed the last crate out of their way, but the wooden box slipped off the pile and crashed loudly to the ground. The splintering sound resonated down the alley, and Kenzie knew it was enough noise to attract some very unwanted attention. Cori moved toward the truck as Kenzie glanced toward the seaside end of the alleyway. There was no one there and for that, she was very grateful.

She turned back to the truck and was about to follow Cori when something in the distance raised the small hairs on her neck. She stopped. If Cobra was not there, he was close. Bringing her gun into firing position, she shot a glance behind her for Cori, but the young woman was too far away, beyond her protection. "Cori?" she said as she kept her eyes and her gun trained on the distant entrance to the alley. When she didn't answer, Kenzie turned.

Cori was picking her way through the debris to Fernando's truck and had obviously not heard her over the sound of the motor. Kenzie wanted nothing more than to follow her, but her instincts dictated otherwise. Turning her attention back to the seaside end of the alley, the world slowed as Cobra's head moved into her crosshairs.

"Cori, get down!" she yelled, her 9mm shattering the quiet of the small town.

Cori screamed as she ducked down, instinctively covering her head with her hands.

The swelling in Kenzie's hand caused her to fire just an instant too soon, and the bullet intended for Cobra slammed into the concrete wall next to his head. Shattered pieces of stones, sprayed across his face, ripping at his skin. The concrete dust kicked up, stinging his eyes. He swore loudly, moving back behind the edge of the wall and out of the line of fire.

Keeping her gun pointed down the alley, Kenzie moved backwards toward Cori as quickly as she could. The moment she reached her, Kenzie grabbed her arm. Fernando's truck was too far away, and there was only the unacceptably rickety pile of crates for them to hide behind. Their best chance was back in Melita's store. Kenzie swore under her breath as she all but dragged Cori back into the store. "Are you okay?" Not waiting for an answer, she moved them past the frightened storeowner and out onto the main street.

Kenzie scanned the area and the people nervously looking about. The moment people started pointing, she knew they would have to move, and fast. Kenzie hurried them along the street, past a group of people standing in line at a taco pushcart. Not wanting to draw further attention, she nevertheless chanced a few glances over her shoulder as she suppressed the urge to run. "Cori?" she questioned without looking.

"What?"

"Are you okay?"

"I'm fine," Cori said in a surprisingly strong voice, "but I'm getting a little sick of people shooting at me."

"I know the feeling." Kenzie brought her gun in tight against her thigh, hoping no one was paying them close attention. "You need to get to Fernando's truck and get the hell out of here."

"I know," Cori answered as they hustled along. "What do you mean by 'you'?" She stole a quick look at Kenzie. "We need to get to Fernando's truck."

"Yeah, yeah," Kenzie answered agreeably.

A surge of defiance flashed through Cori as she slowed to a walk. "We...we, Kenzie, we are in this together."

"Fine, we, as in we don't have time for this." Glancing back over her shoulder, Kenzie saw Cobra emerge from around the distant corner. "There he is... Move it."

She propelled Cori forward, confident that there were too many witnesses for their assailant to attack them in the street, but apparently, Cobra wasn't so concerned. He brought up his weapon and aimed in their direction. "RUN!" Kenzie ordered. There was no sound of a shot, no pre-warning, just the feel of a bullet zinging past her. The corner was close and they turned it just as more bullets whizzed by them.

Fernando's truck was about a hundred feet in front of them, but in Kenzie's mind, it was too far for them to make it without putting them at risk.

"Go, get in the truck," she said as she turned back to face Cobra.

Cori took several steps before she realized Kenzie was not with her. Fear and panic gripped her. "You said 'we'!" she screamed in accusation. "Kenzie, you said 'we'!" It shocked her to realize that there was no way she wanted to keep going without Kenzie by her side.

"I'll be there, just go! Tell Fernando to take the next left, and to have that truck moving the second he sees me." She saw the hesitation on Cori's face. "Go. I'll be there. I promise."

From her vantage point at the corner, Kenzie watched Cobra moving swiftly in their direction. For a man of his solid stature, he had good speed. There were just too many people milling about for her to get a shot off. The pedestrians had apparently not heard the shots, but they seemed to sense panic in the air. Cobra was rapidly closing in on her and Kenzie knew she had to do something. Glancing back at Cori, she was thankful to see her just within reach of the truck. Kenzie waved for them to go and, as the truck moved away from the curb, Kenzie turned back to her target. It was an impossible shot, made even more so because of her damaged hands, so she did the next best thing. With her gun above her head, Kenzie squeezed off several rounds into the sky, creating instant pandemonium with the boom of her 9mm.

A screaming mass of people stampeded for cover as the ringing sound of gunfire reverberated through the sleepy little town. One of the taco handcarts fell over, entangling the people who had been standing in line in front of it. Locals and tourists alike found themselves in the midst of the maelstrom. Diversion accomplished, Kenzie took off running after Fernando's truck.

Cobra swore under his breath as he pressed past the frightened people. The sight of his gun added to the panic as he pushed his way down the street. He made it to the corner just in time to see Kenzie turning down the next road.

She knew Cobra would be right behind her, so she pushed her body to its limit. Ignoring the stabbing pain in her side, she raced toward the moving pickup.

Fernando's eyes were wide as he watched her approach in the side mirror. Lifting his foot off the gas, he slowed the truck, giving her a chance to get on.

Kenzie waved him forward. "GO...GO!" she yelled, urging him to pick up speed. A few more steps and her fingertips touched the rear of the truck. With one last bound, Kenzie reached for the tailgate and pulled herself from the road just as Cobra turned the corner behind her. The first *thwap* of a bullet hitting the tailgate was all she needed to launch herself into the bed of the truck. She grimaced as her body slammed to safety. Two more *thwaps* hit the box of the truck, and she slapped her open hand against the rear window. "Go go go!" Rolling over, she raised her gun and fired the last of her ammunition back at her assailant. Cobra buckled and collapsed to the ground, but as the truck rounded the next corner, she saw him slowly rising to his feet. With a deep sigh of relief, Kenzie leaned her head back against the truck and closed her eyes. They were alive, and for that, she was grateful, even if she did feel like crap.

A short time later, the pickup truck was bouncing up a dusty road. Cresting a small rise, Kenzie spotted a little Cessna, their ticket to Tijuana. It was old and patched together, but it had two wings, and that was enough. As they approached, she saw what was an almost non-existent runway — a hard packed road cut through the rocky, barren landscape. The pickup truck slowed to stop and Cori was out of the passenger seat and around to the bed of the truck before the dust they had created caught up to them.

"Are you okay?"

"I think so," Kenzie said as she moved slowly to her feet. Climbing from the bed of the truck, she looked Cori over. "Are you okay?"

Cori nodded, afraid that her voice would reveal that she was still shaking. "That was close," she said as Kenzie traced the bullet holes. Cori moved in next to her. "Who was that?"

Kenzie shifted her gaze to watch Fernando prep the plane. "I don't know his real name, just his call sign — they call him Cobra."

"So you've worked with him?"

"In a manner of speaking. He's an idiot and an asshole, but he's more than competent at what he does. Come on. Let's get out of here before he finds us again."

Walking toward the plane, Cori paused and looked back at the pickup. "How did he find us?"

"That's something I'd give a lot to know. However, we don't have the time or the ammunition to sit around and wait for him to show up so we can ask him."

Cobra's wound was only superficial, but it still hurt like hell. The locals surely would have called the cops by now and they'd be looking for him. He had no plans to stick around and answer any questions, besides he still had a job to do.

The town was in chaos. People were running about, talking excitedly amongst themselves as they cleaned up the aftermath. No one stopped him as he shoved himself into his stifling hot car. Pulling away from the curb, he put his hand into his shirt to check the extent of the damage. He noted the blood on his fingers with disdain. "You're going to pay for that, you bitch."

Driving as fast as he dared, Cobra followed the road his quarry had left on, out of town and up the winding hill. Once clear of Santa Rosalia, he reached under the seat and pulled out his satellite phone. He dialed a number and then placed the phone against his shoulder as he reached for his Blackberry.

"It's Cobra."

"This better be good news."

Cobra looked down at the Blackberry on the seat beside him. "It's not."

"What went wrong this time?"

"She got away."

Manuck cursed loudly. "How?"

"She got lucky. By the looks of it, some local is helping her."

"This woman has more lives than a cat!"

Cobra sighed loudly. "Well, don't worry, because I'm right behind her."

"Don't tell me not to worry. If she gets back to the States, we're all going to have a problem. Do I make myself clear?"

"Crystal." Cobra turned off the highway onto the bumpy dusty road. The fine dust in the air and fresh tire tracks disturbing the soil kept him on their trail. "I'm right behind her...or rather them. Their dust is pretty easy to follow out here."

Manuck leaned forward in his seat. "Them?"

"Yeah, she's not alone."

"Some local you said."

"Worse — or better, depending how you look at it."

"You're kidding! They're together?" Manuck mulled over the information. It was an interesting turn of events. However, it was not necessarily bad news. "Fine, if they're together, then get them both. If everyone had done their jobs right to begin with, they would both be dead right now anyhow. So if they're together, kill them both!"

Only half listening, Cobra slowed his car as a plume of dust rose above the distant hill. The roar of a plane drowned out the sound of Manuck's ranting. Cobra's shoulders slumped in defeat as the little Cessna flew right over him. "Yeah, they're together," he said reluctantly as his car rolled to a stop. Climbing from the car, he shielded his eyes from the sun as he watched the plane climb in altitude. "Colonel..." He attempted to interrupt, but Manuck was not listening. "Colonel...Colonel Manuck."

"What!"

"They're gone, I've missed them."

"What do you mean, missed them?"

"They're gone." Cobra seethed in anger and frustration as the aircraft grew smaller and smaller against the sky. "They just flew over my head in a small plane." The Cessna ascended out and over the Sea of Cortez, then banked hard to the left, heading north. "And Colonel, they're heading in your direction."

Chapter 10

Kenzie rested her head against the cool plastic window, but the vibration was more than her pounding head could handle. *Where had Cobra come from? How did he find us?* The thought unnerved her more than she wanted to admit, even to herself. The only phone call she'd made had been to Big Polly. *But Cori used a phone in Mazatlán to call her mother! And she used the phone on Manny's boat...* Kenzie turned to look at Cori. *No way!* She didn't want to pursue the questions churning in her mind, but she couldn't help it. *It's possible! At this point anything seemed possible. But if she called someone...who did she call?*

Cori saw the change in Kenzie's expression and she leaned across the seat. "You okay?"

Kenzie nodded. *Who did she call in Mazatlán? Her mother, she said...what if her mother's line was tapped...or maybe she didn't call her mother at all...maybe she called someone else.* She refused to follow that line of thought any further. Leaning her head back, she closed her eyes, almost thankful that the aching in her body kept disrupting her thoughts. *Thank God for Big Polly*, she sighed. He was going to save her butt once again.

Big Polly had gotten part of his name honestly. He was big, close to seven foot, but no one knew whether or not his name was really Polly, and no one dared to ask. He was Samoan, but he grew up on the big island of Hawaii. The rumor was that he had left the Polynesian Islands due to some questionable business dealings during his stint in the military, though he always insisted that he left for greener financial pastures. Which was the truth? No one knew and no one asked. His charismatic and friendly nature eclipsed his intimidating size. People were drawn to him and he knowingly used that to further his venture capital. If someone needed something, anything, legal or illegal, Big Polly was their man. He was an arranger, a mover and a shaker, and he made things happen without making noise. Many different types of people used his services, but Kenzie knew he really made his money on his dealings with those who paid under the table to have things done, no questions asked.

Her call to him from Santa Rosalia had been short and to the point. He had offered his services without question. It didn't surprise her that Big Polly had not hesitated, even when she told him they were coming in hot. He promised to have someone there to meet the plane. She had faith that he would have whatever she needed to get her and Cori across the border. To her way of thinking, once she and Cori were safely on her boat, she would be able to find the answers to the questions constantly tugging at her mind. She sighed heavily and tried to relax.

Kenzie's sigh caught Cori's attention. With a concerned eye, she let her gaze travel over Kenzie's new clothes. They were now torn and soiled from her ride in the back of the truck. She was holding her right shoulder awkwardly, which told Cori it was still sore. It was then that she noticed blood on Kenzie's side.

Without thinking, Cori reached for the edge of Kenzie's shirt. The moment the material moved, Kenzie's hand darted out, grabbing Cori's wrist. Kenzie's lightning fast reflexes caught her by surprise and she tried to withdraw her hand, but Kenzie's grip was unrelenting.

Seeing the fear on Cori's face, Kenzie's icy stare melted into compassion. "Sorry," she said above the loud rumbling of the plane's engine as Cori rubbed her wrist. "Reflex."

Having already seen some of Kenzie's reflexes, Cori didn't want to witness any more, especially when her own health was at risk. "You're bleeding again," she said.

Kenzie shook her head, not hearing or understanding what Cori said.

Cori gestured toward her side, "You're bleeding!" she yelled over the engine noise.

Kenzie glanced down at her shirt and nodded with a shrug, "I know. It's okay. I'll look at it later."

"I'd like to look at it now." Cori kept her hands to herself, but fixed her eyes firmly on Kenzie. "Please."

Care and compassion were not things Kenzie was used to. If she was injured, the only thing that mattered was completing the mission. Oozing wounds and broken bones were no excuse for failure, and pain was only a reminder that she was still alive. Right now, a little bit of bleeding coming from the wound on her side was not even a blip on her overly crowded radar.

"Just let me look at it."

"When we land," Kenzie said as she leaned back and closed her eyes again.

"Promise?"

"Promise."

"And what happens after we land? How are we getting across the border?"

Kenzie reluctantly opened her eyes and studied Cori's troubled face. The strain of all they had been through was clearly visible. Reaching down, she took the hand that she had just pushed away. "We'll be fine. I have a friend in Tijuana and he's gonna help us. Once we get to San Diego, I have a boat there, and access to a computer with a very high security clearance. We'll be safe there. It'll give us a chance to find some answers and regroup, then decide on the next step."

"I'm scared," Cori said unnecessarily. Kenzie could feel her whole body shaking through the tremors in her hand.

"It'll be okay," Kenzie said with confidence, even though she had her own doubts. "Come here."

Kenzie tugged her closer and Cori quickly accepted the offer, moving as close as her seatbelt would allow. Resting her head on Kenzie's shoulder, she was careful not to aggravate her wounded side. Leaning up, Cori pecked a kiss onto her cheek. "Thanks."

Kenzie smiled as Cori gently placed her head against her shoulder and closed her eyes.

There was not much more that Kenzie could do, so she leaned back in her seat and looked out the window at the desert and the ocean beyond. *What are you going to do now, Kenzie?* The question was without answers and she felt her own anxiety rising. She knew she needed to get to her computer. Somewhere out there, in the vast world of electronic information, were the answers. The steady buzz of the plane's engine lulled her into an exhausted sleep as one other question stuck in her mind: *was either of Cori's phone calls, supposedly to her mom, the reason Cobra found us in Santa Rosalia?*

True to his word, Big Polly had a car and driver waiting for them at the dusty airstrip on the outskirts of Tijuana. Forty-five minutes later, they pulled up in front of a small bar on one of the broken down back streets of the bustling border town. Built from brick and cinderblocks, its large arched windows were darkened to keep the daylight from shining on the shadowy figures within.

Crawling from the car, Cori squinted into the bright light as she took in their surroundings. The street in front of the bar was void of cars, its paved surface aged and broken. The wide sidewalks, dotted by well-worn power poles, were a mix of concrete, cobblestone, and broken asphalt. The businesses along the street were a jumbled blend of newer buildings and those with older, more flavorful craftsmanship. Regardless, it was the cleanliness of the old town that surprised Cori. It looked like everyone had gotten up early just to sweep off the sidewalks and roads.

Turning her attention back to the bar, Cori read the name scrawled in red neon just above the door — *Tequila Sheila's*. "Who is Sheila?" Cori asked Kenzie as she and the driver climbed from the car. No one answered her, but she hadn't expected them to. Not a single word had been exchanged among them since they landed. Looking over the building, Cori could not tell whether the bar was old, or if it was designed to look as if it were.

Walking up the steps into the front entrance of the bar, Cori glanced over and across the street. To her surprise, a police station was located just down the block. Numerous marked cars were out on the street or parked haphazardly behind a dilapidated chain-link fence. Several uniformed officers were hanging out around the front doors — some standing, some sitting or leaning against their cars — but not one of them paid any attention to the arrival of the two women.

Cori gestured with her head in the direction of the police station, "There is another option."

Kenzie barely glanced over as she moved toward the front doors of *Tequila Sheila's*. "You want to put your life in their hands?"

Without a moment's consideration, Cori knew there was only one person she would trust with her life, and she hurried to catch up to her.

The driver opened the door, revealing the darkness inside the club, "Head on in. You know where to go." It was the first time he had spoken all afternoon. He stepped aside, holding the door open.

As Cori stepped forward, Kenzie put a hand on her waist and pulled her closer. "Stay behind me," she said in a low whisper. It was hard to see at first, and that made Kenzie nervous. She refused to move until her eyes adjusted.

Once again, Cori was witness to an instant transformation as Kenzie quickly assessed the situation — taking in the layout of the bar and the locations of those now watching them. With great respect and a little admiration, Cori knew Kenzie had all of her options covered before she took a single step into the bar. Cori wrinkled her nose at the stale smell of cheap beer, cigarettes, and marijuana as she waited for Kenzie to proceed.

There was a tall, thin man behind the bar. The pen behind his ear and the clipboard in his hand told Kenzie all she needed to know about him. Another man, seated at one of the small round tables and eating a plate of something, was not of any interest to her either. Taking a few hesitant steps further into the bar, Kenzie's gaze fell on the two large men seated at one of the back booths, next to a closed door, Big Polly's office. They made no attempt to hide the guns strapped to their bodies or the automatic weapons within reach on the table.

One of the men nodded toward the closed door, granting Kenzie and Cori permission to approach. They crossed through the bar and one of the men stood up to open the door. One after the other, the two women entered the small, bare room. A naked light bulb hanging from the ceiling by a single wire dimly lit the cement floor and gray cinderblock walls. There was only one other door in the room, and there was nothing on it to indicate where it led.

Without warning, the door opened suddenly and a mountain of a man filled the doorway. His features were dark, "dangerous" was the word that came to Cori's mind, but the thought disappeared the moment he smiled at Kenzie.

"*Talofa*, my little lost *Señorita!*" His friendly voice boomed off the walls as he gathered Kenzie in for a crushing and painful hug.

For a brief moment, Cori wondered exactly what *talofa* meant, but that was forgotten as she found herself on the receiving end of the large man's contagious smile.

"I'm so glad you made it, and in one piece." He eyed her injuries and quickly changed his opinion. "A little damaged, I see, but in one piece, eh?" He gave her an extra little squeeze.

"Yeah, well." Kenzie stepped back and looked into the smiling face of the big man. "I better warn you, we seem to be attracting company no matter where we go."

"Really? That's interesting." Big Polly turned his bright gaze to Cori. "And who is this pretty young thing, eh?"

Cori returned his smile, but as she did, she saw a flicker of something ominous in his dark eyes. *This is not a man you cross*, she thought.

"Big Polly, this is..." Kenzie's mind ran through many different descriptions of what Cori was to her, but none seemed to fit. "This is my...ah...this is Cori. Cori, Big Polly."

The Samoan offered his massive hand and Cori took it hesitantly. Though he was still smiling, she could feel his eyes assessing her from the ground up. Standing tall, she refused to cower before his scrutiny.

"Do I want to see what the other guy looks like?" Big Polly said pleasantly as he lifted her chin to examine the bruise to her eye and lip. He couldn't help but notice her glance at Kenzie.

Interesting, he thought as he backed up and beckoned them into his office. "Well, come on in and let's see what we can do for you."

It was a large room with no windows, but the air was cool and, to Cori's way of thinking, smelled a lot better than the bar. There were two leather couches in the center, and against the back wall was a massive desk suited to someone of Big Polly's size. Next to the desk was a small bar with a couple of tall stools pushed up against its high, thick wooden top. Cori had almost expected crates of guns and ammunition, but so far the only weapons she had seen were two crossed American Civil War swords mounted on the wall directly behind the desk.

Big Polly walked over to the bar. There were several bottles of liquor at one end, with glasses stacked next to them. He pulled a bottle of Perrier sparkling mineral water out of the small fridge below the bar and handed it to Kenzie without her even asking. He obviously knew her well enough to know her beverage of choice.

"Big Polly, I need to make a secure call to the States," Kenzie said after she took a sip from her bottle.

"Not a problem," he answered. Moving out from behind the bar, he walked over to his desk and sat down. There were several phones within reach on the desk, but he opened a drawer and pulled out a small box of cell phones. "They're throwaways." He handed one to Kenzie. "Will this work for you?"

"Uh huh," she said, taking the phone from his hand.

"If you need a call back number..." He turned the phone over, showing Kenzie the cell's number taped to the back.

Kenzie nodded in understanding. "Thanks," she said as she dialed a number deeply embedded in her memory.

"Can I get you something to drink, Cori?" Big Polly offered as he returned to the bar.

"Do you have another one of those?" she asked, pointing to Kenzie's bottle.

He reached under the counter and retrieved another bottle from the small fridge. Cori smiled politely as she accepted the cold mineral water. She pulled out one of the stools beside the small bar, sat down, and silently observed Kenzie entering numbers into the cell.

After only one ring, the phone was answered and a woman's voice greeted Kenzie from the other end of the line. "Judge Woodward's office. This is Shelby, how may I help you?"

"Is the judge in?"

A judge? The inquiry took Cori by surprise, but she tried not to change her expression.

"No, I'm sorry. He's in court at the moment. Is there something I can help you with?" Her voice was pleasant, honeyed with a strong Southern accent.

Kenzie knew the contact she was about to make could be dangerous if not deadly for her mentor and friend. She hesitated for a long moment, but she knew she didn't have many choices. "I...ah...I need to get a message to him."

"I'm sorry, but he can't be disturbed while he's on the bench."

"Yes, he can, and we both know it. Tell him I have a collector's edition of a Zippo lighter if he's interested, and to call me if he can." Kenzie felt a little foolish using the code the judge had given her years ago. She had never had a reason to use it — until now.

Shelby's normally bright demeanor changed to a tone of concern. "Can you hold the line, please?"

"No, but I'll give you the number where he can reach me."

Shelby's pen was poised over a notepad, "Go ahead."

Kenzie gave her the number off the back of another cell phone. "Tell him to call me immediately if, and only if, he deems it safe to do so. Is that understood?"

"Yes. Where are you?"

"It doesn't matter, we're safe for now. Just tell him, if I don't hear from him, I'll try him at another time. Understood?"

"Understood."

Kenzie ended the call. She sat quietly for a moment, staring at the phone in her hand. Part of her wanted to call her commanding officer, to let him know all that had happened. It was the military thing to do — follow orders as directed. But she was not following orders, and had not been for a long time. Part of what she did, and part of who she was, required her to think for herself and to rely on only herself. She was not required to check in with anyone, not until the job was done. Then there were the questions in her mind, the ones that would not go away. And they pointed in one direction. Colonel Manuck was her supervisor, her superior, but he was also the one who sent her to Mexico. Kenzie placed the cell phone into the pocket of her pants.

"Okay, that's done, now come and tell me what the hell has been going on." Big Polly had patiently waited for Kenzie to finish her call. Now that the phone call was over, he wanted information. Taking a seat on the sofa, Kenzie gave a brief description of their recent adventures while on the run through Mexico.

Taking a sip of the bubbly, cool liquid, Cori took the opportunity to observe Big Polly as he listened intently to Kenzie.

He seemed friendly enough, but something told her that she didn't want this man as an enemy.

"Did you know the shooter?" Big Polly asked as Kenzie finished her story.

"No, not the one on the road," she said, shaking her head, "But the one in Santa Rosalia, I know by his call sign, Cobra. Do you know him?" Kenzie watched him closely as she waited for his answer.

"I've never dealt with him directly, but I do know of him. He would be a formidable adversary, I'm sure."

She nodded, both agreeing with, and weighing his words. "Believe it. So, can you set me up with a new bag?"

"Have I ever let you down?"

"No."

"Do you want me to load you a new bag here, or would you prefer it to be shipped to *Helen* in San Diego?"

Moving away from the bar, Cori sat down on the other sofa. *Helen, who is Helen?* Easing her tired body onto the fine leather, she waited with interest for Kenzie's answer.

Kenzie found herself slightly amused by the expression on Cori's face, but decided to satisfy her curiosity immediately. "Can you have it waiting for us on the *Helen*? I don't want to have to deal with anything else besides getting the two of us across the border," Kenzie said as she stretched out her injured side.

Big Polly noticed the dried blood on her shirt. "Battle scar?" he asked, pointing.

Kenzie waved off his concern, but Cori was a little wiser this time than the last time she had tried to intervene. "She's hurt," she said firmly as she screwed the lid back onto her bottle and placed it on the coffee table between the two sofas.

Big Polly looked at Kenzie in surprise. "Is it serious?" When she didn't answer him directly, his tone changed. "Is it serious?"

Looking a little more perturbed than concerned, Kenzie kept her eyes away from Cori's worried stare. "Like I said, we've had a little excitement."

"Let me see." Big Polly lowered his massive frame to the floor so that he was even with her side. He gestured with his fingers for her to show him and, without a shadow of modesty, Kenzie lifted up her shirt.

The wound was red, swollen and angry looking. There were splotches of fresh blood around the sutures Cori had so carefully sewn aboard the fishing boat.

"Jeez, Kenzie," Big Polly said, looking over the injury as Cori moved in to investigate.

"I knew it was bad, but she wouldn't let me look at it earlier." Cori touched Kenzie's warm skin. "And you're running a temperature."

Kenzie pulled away in annoyance at the unwanted attention. "The only thing I'm running is for the border. I'm fine."

Big Polly saw the look of determination on Cori's face and he was a little surprised. Kenzie was stubborn, that he knew, but this time around, he would put his money on the young blonde.

Settling back on her haunches, Cori looked intently into Kenzie's eyes. "And what is your plan when you start dripping blood on the border agent?"

"I'm not dripping blood," she answered, annoyed at Cori's hyperbole.

"But you're not exactly in any shape to be trying to cross a border, either."

Kenzie sighed deeply and looked at the large man. "Big Polly, we don't have a lot of time here. Everywhere we go, someone is right on our heels. We need some paperwork so we can get across the border and out of your hair."

He studied her for a moment, contemplating her words, knowing she was not one to exaggerate a problem. "Well, you're going to have to make time. You're waiting for a call, and I have to get your papers together, for which I'm going to need a photo of each of you. Plus, there's no way you can pass through the border looking like that. You don't want to be attracting any kind of attention to yourselves. A shower and some fresh clothes?"

"We also need to get that wound cleaned up." Cori turned to Big Polly, "Do you have any medical supplies? Antibiotics?"

He looked from Cori's determined face to Kenzie's steely-eyed stare. "Your friend's right, Kenzie. We need to get you fixed up and you both need to be cleaned up. I've got what we need, I'll be right back." Big Polly had to hide the smirk that crept across his face as he watched Kenzie glare at Cori. He knew Cori was in for a fight, but he was sure she could handle it.

Kenzie waited for the door to close behind Big Polly before she fired her first volley. "Why did you do that? I'm fine."

"Anyone can see you're not fine." Cori leaned forward, intent on looking at Kenzie's side, but the angry woman would not have it.

Kenzie slapped at Cori's outstretched hand and pulled down her shirt. "Back off!"

"No," Cori responded firmly. Once again, she reached out, determined to look at Kenzie's injury. Kenzie slapped at her hand so fast she barely saw it coming. Cori glared back at Kenzie, defiantly locking eyes with the woman she had once feared.

"You know, when this all started, that hard-ass tough-girl attitude would have scared me into the corner, but not today, girlfriend! I've been assaulted, kidnapped, shot at, set on fire, dumped overboard, smuggled across half the states of Mexico, and flown in a plane that was built by the Wright brothers, so don't even think that your little hissy fit is going to intimidate me!"

Kenzie watched her with surprised interest. This woman was very different from the woman with whom she had left Guadalajara. Kenzie regretted that she was one of the main reasons behind the change in Cori. "Look," Kenzie's tone was firm, but apologetic, "I don't need a mother, all right?"

"I never said I wanted to be your mother, I just want to look at your side. For reasons that should be apparent, I need you. I don't understand what's going on, but I do know that I stand a better chance getting out of it alive if I'm with you. It's not going to do either of us any good if you don't at least appear healthy when we get to the border. Now, can you please lift your shirt? I'd like to see your side."

Kenzie's stare softened. Cori's outburst had calmed her anger. She tilted her head in curious question. "Why is it that every time I turn around, you're trying to get your hands on my naked body?"

Cori's face instantly flushed a bright crimson. The comment caught her completely off guard, and she stuttered and stammered, not knowing what to say. The heat traveling up her neck told her that her mind had not forgotten the feel of Kenzie's bare skin or the kisses they had shared in Santa Rosalia.

Finding fun in Cori's embarrassment, Kenzie couldn't help but continue to tease her. "If you're trying to cop a feel, all you have to do is ask."

"I am not trying to 'cop a feel', I'm concerned with your well being, that's all."

"Nothing more?" Kenzie's eyebrow rose slightly as she played with her tongue against the inside of her cheek. "Really?" *Oh, blush some more, Cori. I thought you were cute before, but that shade of red is definitely your color.* Kenzie forgot why she'd been angry as Cori's face grew redder with each passing second. For a brief moment, she pondered what she would be like in bed. *A fireball, I bet.*

"I oughta slap you," Cori fumed.

"For what I'm thinking, you probably should."

Surprising even herself, Cori did — an open handed slap to the side of Kenzie's face. It was quick and justified, but unexpected. The sharp sound echoed around the room as the two women locked eyes, each waiting for a reaction from the other. Within moments, a white handprint emerged on Kenzie's cheek and the stunned woman reached to touch it. Her eyes narrowed as she worked her jaw back and forth. "I can't believe you just did that."

"You asked for it." Cori's words assigned blame, but her tone had lost its rancor. Cori broke their stare first, swallowing hard as she second-guessed what she had done. It wasn't fear that made her look away, but shame and embarrassment at letting her temper get the better of her.

The door to the office opened and Big Polly walked in with the medical supplies he had promised. It was immediately apparent to him that he had interrupted something. He watched with mild interest as Cori suddenly moved away from Kenzie's side.

"I think I got what you need. The antibiotic is a little old, but it should do." He sat down on the sofa across from Kenzie and placed a medical bag on the coffee table between them. "You need ah..." He stopped the moment he spotted the now red handprint on her face. "Nice," he said, nodding his head in her direction. "Deserved or undeserved?"

Kenzie lifted her gaze to Cori who was leaning silently against the bar. Cori turned to look at her, waiting for her answer.

"Deserved," Kenzie said as she looked directly into Cori's eyes. "Big Polly, could you umm..." She turned to look at their host. "Can you give us a few moments, please?"

He nodded in understanding. "I'll go get your paperwork and IDs started...after I get a photo of each of you." He held up a digital camera and motioned to the wall near where Cori was standing. "It'll just take a second. Cori should probably go first. That way your face can have a minute to absorb that handprint." Reaching behind the bar, Big Polly pulled out a long tube. "I've made arrangements. Your new bag is already on its way to your boat."

"Thanks. I'll wire your payment once I get there."

"Not a problem. I know you're good for it." He went over to where Cori was standing and positioned the tube horizontally on the wall. Pulling the tab in the center, he unrolled an off-white background screen. From a nearby closet, he quickly assembled two light standards that reflected their light onto the screen. Cori was watching him with interest and Big Polly smiled. "You can't have any shadow in the background of the picture or they'll know it's a forgery."

"Oh."

"Okay, let's take a couple of shots here, Cori," Big Polly directed. Cori stood at the wall, but her eyes were on Kenzie, not Big Polly. "You have to look at the camera, dear. You can deal with her in a minute." She turned to face him and he snapped the pictures quickly. "Okay, they'll do," he said as he reviewed the images on the camera's display screen. "Okay, Kenz, you're next."

"Fine," Kenzie said as she rose to her feet and moved to stand in front of the screen. She knew the drill. A couple clicks of the camera and she was done.

"All right, good enough. I know Kenzie doesn't have any real ID, but do you?" Big Polly asked Cori as Kenzie returned to her spot on the sofa.

"In my wallet." Cori reached into her pocket and produced a thin leather wallet, the only thing of hers that had survived their swim and then their hasty departure from Santa Rosalia. Opening it, she fished out two pieces of ID — her Washington state driver's license and her Mexican driver's license. She laid them in Big Polly's outstretched hand and then slid her wallet back into her pocket.

He nodded his head continuously as he examined the documents. "These are great. I'll keep them, if you don't mind. It will be better if I actually use one of these pictures for your new ID, instead of one I just took. It will lend some authenticity to the ID, and I won't have to doctor the picture."

"Doctor the picture?" Cori said.

He looked from Cori to Kenzie, "You both look like you've gone fourteen rounds in a very small boxing ring. It wouldn't be a good thing to have the same bruises and scratches in the pictures on your IDs. Now...you don't have anything else in your wallet with your name on it, do you?"

"No," Cori said. "Just that ID, and a little bit of money."

"American or Mexican?"

"Pesos."

"Good enough. Okay, I'll be back in a bit with some towels and stuff and a change of clothes. There's a shower and washroom just through that door." He pointed at the back of the room, in the direction of a dark wooden door. "Play nice," he said as he passed Kenzie on his way out.

When the door closed behind him, Kenzie turned her full attention to Cori, who had resumed leaning against the small bar.

The tension between them was palpable and Kenzie found herself unable to find the words to convey what she was feeling. She tried to read Cori's body language, but it was as if Cori was speaking in a foreign tongue. Regretfully, Kenzie knew she was the one who pushed too far and provoked Cori's reaction.

Feeling the tension within the room, Cori lifted her gaze from the floor and turned to look at Kenzie. She knew Kenzie was watching her — it wasn't hard to feel those golden eyes penetrating her thin veil of courage — but she didn't anticipate the feelings that surfaced with the look from across the room.

Kenzie unconsciously rubbed her cheek, but instantly regretted it when Cori looked away. It had not been her intention to hurt Cori's feelings again, but she knew she had. "Cori?"

Her tone was apologetic but she couldn't bring herself to say the words she knew Cori wanted to hear. She had screwed up and she knew it, but she was unsure of how to make things right between them. She collected the bottom of her shirt and slowly pulled it up over her head. Tossing her shirt to the side of the sofa, Kenzie reached down and touched her injured side. If she made a noise, she was unaware of it, but when she looked up, Cori was watching her.

"Please," Kenzie said as she leaned back against the sofa, presenting her wound as a peace offering.

Cori stood on the opposite side of the room, watching without moving, but it was only a moment before she pushed away from the bar. She said nothing as she took a seat next to Kenzie. She looked over the wound, but made no attempt to touch it.

"You can be a real bitch you know," she said keeping her eyes on Kenzie's stitches.

Kenzie nodded. "Yeah, I know."

There didn't seem to be much else to say, so Cori went to work cleaning up Kenzie's side. Big Polly's medical bag had everything she needed and soon there was a sterile dressing covering the injury and a full shot of antibiotic in her system.

"There. Hopefully this time you can keep yourself clean."

"Thanks," Kenzie said as she reached for her shirt.

Cori helped Kenzie put it back on, and once Kenzie was clothed and settled on the sofa, Cori gently placed a hand on her arm.

Kenzie turned at the touch and was surprised at the compassion on Cori's face. Feeling more than a little awkward, Kenzie fidgeted in her seat. "I ah...I'm sorry I said that...earlier. I didn't mean to embarrass you or to make you feel uncomfortable.

It's just that...I guess I haven't been around many women...or rather, a woman like you, in my life, and I guess I've forgotten how to act."

It was Cori's turn to watch Kenzie squirm and she had to admit that she liked it. "Funny, I got the feeling that you'd been around more than your fair share of ladies."

Kenzie found herself on the other end of a blush, and though she wanted to fire back with a snappy retort, she bit her tongue. It was the truth, after all, and sometimes the truth hurts. She looked away. "Most of them I wouldn't call ladies."

Cori was surprised at Kenzie's reaction to her comment, and it made her immediately regret it. *Tough assassin, maybe; tough woman, not so much.* She reached out and turned Kenzie's face back to her.

Why Cori was drawn to Kenzie, she didn't know, but she was. On the run or not, she could not stop the feelings she was having. Everything about Kenzie should have had her running in the opposite direction, but instead, she found herself wanting to get closer. She wanted to get to know her, in more ways than one.

Throwing caution to the wind, Cori leaned in and kissed Kenzie. It was everything she wanted it to be: soft, tender, and returned. Growing desire blazed through her body as she pushed her lips harder into the kiss. It excited her that Kenzie responded with an equal degree of passion, but a small voice of warning tried to quell her rising excitement. Feeling the heat radiating from Kenzie's cheek, she pulled back and looked into her eyes. "I'm sorry I slapped you."

Kenzie attempted a smile. "It's okay. I deserved it." There was an awkward moment of silence between them, something Kenzie was unaccustomed to. She struggled for something positive to say. "I've been pretty tough on you. I mean it's not like you're used to being shot at." Her smile this time was genuine, but Cori didn't smile in return.

"Are you?" Cori asked as she let go of Kenzie's face. "Used to being shot at, I mean."

"Actually...no. I'm usually on the other end of the gun...long gone by the time the chaos and panic set in." Kenzie pulled away from Cori's touch and rose from the sofa. She walked over to Big Polly's desk and looked over the phones still scattered on its surface.

"So do you do everything from far away?"

Kenzie kept her eyes on the desk and her thoughts to herself.

Rising from the sofa, Cori walked up behind Kenzie and turned her around. "From what I've gathered, you've lived your life from a distance, and that's not living, Kenzie that's existing. There's a whole world out there, and not all of it is filled with guns and wars...and dying." She took both of Kenzie's hands into her own. "There are millions of people working and playing, making love, having babies, going to restaurants and movies, enjoying their lives the best way they know how."

Kenzie's demeanor grew serious as she looked into the innocence of the woman before her, "And those people are living in denial, Cori. They no more control their lives than you or I do. Governments and corporations make the decisions on how this world will evolve. Their greed for power and money make this world go around. Those that want it will do anything to get it, and those that have it will do anything to keep it. Make no mistake — the rest of us are just pawns on a chessboard."

"I don't agree with you," Cori said, shaking her head.

"Then you're naïve." Kenzie studied her face for a moment, "Life is just a sexually transmitted disease and I hate to tell you this, but it's always fatal. No one gets out alive."

The sting of the comment splashed across Cori face, and Kenzie drew back. She had not meant to hurt her again, but she knew she had. Cori tried to pull her hands from Kenzie's grasp, but the stronger woman refused to let go.

There was a quick knock and the door opened. Big Polly entered with a stack of towels and clothing. Looking at their close proximity, he knew he had interrupted something again. "Sorry, but I ah..." He cleared his throat. "There's a bus leaving for the Tijuana Artisan Market in three hours and you need to be on it. Get in there, get cleaned up and changed." He placed his bundle on the edge of the sofa.

The phone in Kenzie's pocket buzzed. She reluctantly released her hold on Cori's hands, reached into her pocket for the phone, and flipped it open. "Yes."

"Katherine?"

The voice on the other end of the phone was loud enough for Cori to hear as she watched Kenzie's strong features relax. *Katherine?*

"Judge," she answered with a sigh as she closed her eyes. "I think I need your help."

Far away in Seattle, the judge pulled his chair up to his desk. "Whatever you need or whatever I can do, all you need to do is ask," he said as he reached for a pen. "Where are you?"

"Is your line secure?" Kenzie asked.

"I'm a judge in a federal court building. I sure as hell hope so."

"Yeah, me too. Look...I've run into some trouble."

"I gathered that much or we wouldn't be talking."

"The assignment I was on, well, something went wrong...very wrong."

"Are you okay?"

The concern came right through the phone and it caused Kenzie to smile. She looked down over her battered and bruised body and nodded. "Yeah, I'll be fine."

"What do you need, Katherine?"

"A couple of things. First, my extraction team never showed up and I need to know why."

"Okay. I'm not sure what I can find out about that, but I'll try. What else?"

"I want to know who ordered the hit."

"Then I'll need the name."

"Cori Evans," she said, spelling it out for him. "I also want to know who was in charge of the operation. I need to talk to somebody and I have no idea who I can trust."

"Have you talked to your commanding officer?"

"He was the one who sent me, and since someone also sent a back up, I have no choice but to suspect him. At the very least, I don't trust him, not with my life."

Judge Woodward pursed his lips as he wrote a couple of words down on the pad in front of him. "I'll see what I can do. Can I call you back on this number?"

Kenzie paused for moment, calculating the risks in her mind. "Yeah, but I hope to be on the *Helen* by this evening." She looked over at Cori who was watching her in return. "And Judge, please be careful."

"If you will promise to do the same, my dear."

The room in the back of Big Polly's office was similar to a cheap motel room. There was a bed with a small table, and a bathroom, which consisted of a shower, sink, and a toilet. Cori went into the shower first, and nothing had felt better to her in a long time. The water was hot and she savored the feel of it as she washed the dust and dirt of Mexico down the drain. A short while later, a smiling Cori emerged from the bathroom wrapped only in a towel.

"It's all yours," she said to Kenzie, who was sprawled out on the bed. There was no movement, so she took a few steps closer as she rubbed her wet hair with a towel. "Kenzie?" She watched the still form, sleeping peacefully, hesitant to wake her. Cori had had her opportunities to sleep — in the car, on the ferry, on the fishing boat, and on the plane — but the only time Kenzie had really closed her eyes since they'd met was when she passed out after Cori and Manny relocated her shoulder. She would have liked nothing more than to let her sleep, but she knew they were on a schedule, and that meant they had to be leaving soon.

Moving closer to the bed, Cori sat down carefully on the edge. Making the assumption that startling someone with Kenzie's training would not be a wise idea, Cori called to her softly, "Kenzie?" There was no sign of her waking, only the steady rise and fall of her chest. Cori reached out, but stopped with her hand just above Kenzie's arm. *What was it that the judge called her? Katherine.* The name sounded funny and didn't really seem to suit the sleeping woman, but Cori tried it anyhow. "Katherine?" This time she gently placed a hand on her arm as she called out to her. "Jesus, you're warm."

Eyes the color of gold opened slowly. She didn't lurch awake with fists at the ready and a gun in her hand, instead, she studied Cori's face for a moment and then smiled. "Hi."

"You fell asleep," Cori said, returning the smile.

Looking around the room, Kenzie didn't have to recall where they were or why. "Guess I did." Her gaze returned to the towel-clad blonde. "My turn?"

Cori nodded and started to rise, then stopped. "Can I ask you a question?"

"Sure." Kenzie smiled as she leaned back against the headboard.

"I'm serious."

"So am I. Ask away."

"What's your real name? I mean the judge called you Katherine, and that doesn't sound anything like Kenzie."

"That's really what you wanted to ask me?"

"Yeah."

Kenzie shook her head, "Of all the things I thought you might want to ask, that wasn't one of them. My first name is Katherine, but no one calls me that except for the judge. Everyone calls me Kenzie, which is short for Mackenzie. Feel better now?"

"Yeah, I guess. Thanks."

Cori started to rise, but stopped when Kenzie laid a hand on her arm. "Just wait a sec," Kenzie requested. "There's something I have to say. I'm sorry about earlier."

Cori studied her face for a moment and then looked directly into her sleepy eyes, "About what — the kiss or the comment?" She could only hope it was the latter.

"I am not sorry about the kiss. I'm sorry," Kenzie paused, "I'm sorry that I called you naïve. That wasn't right and it wasn't fair." Cori started to look away but Kenzie wouldn't let her. "Hey." She sat up straighter in bed and pulled Cori closer. "I mean it, that wasn't my intention." She brushed a wisp of hair back from Cori's face, tucking it behind her ear. "I didn't mean to hurt you...and I did. I promise I'll never hurt you again... You have my word."

Cori had no idea what to say, or how to say it, but the promise gave her a warm feeling of security as she reached out to touch Kenzie's face.

"I promise," Kenzie said as she leaned into Cori's caress, "we'll figure this out. Once we get to my boat in San Diego, I have the resources to keep you safe. I'll protect you with every ounce of my being." She placed her hand on top of Cori's. "No one will ever hurt you again."

Nobody had ever made her a promise like that before, at least not anyone with the ability to back it up. However, the promises seemed like impractical pledges, even for Kenzie. They didn't know who they were running from, or why, so how could she keep them safe? Cori considered Kenzie's words as she studied her unique eyes.

"You can't make that guarantee, Kenzie. I wish you could, but we both know you can't." Cori offered a smile, but her uncertainty affected its sincerity. Turning away from Kenzie's searching stare, Cori tried to hide her frazzled nerves. In the last several days, the quiet life Cori had been leading had exploded in an eruption of violence. It had shaken her to the very core of her being. She was scared and had been for what seemed like forever. Her eyes began to mist over and her lips quivered as she twisted the damp towel in her hands.

"Hey...hey." Kenzie saw the breakdown coming right before her eyes and she moved to get closer to Cori, but the young woman didn't want to be coddled.

Rising from the bed, Cori moved to the table and dropped the towel that she'd been using to dry her hair. Resting her hands on the back of the chair, she fought her growing fear. Kenzie's hand touched her bare shoulder and the dam holding back her emotions crumbled.

Kenzie felt the first shudder of a sob before she heard it. She turned Cori around and engulfed her in a hug. Cori collapsed into the warm embrace as she finally started to cry.

"It's okay, let it go," Kenzie whispered into her ear as she stroked her honey-colored hair. "Let it go." Cori was nearly naked, and her soft, clean skin was cool to the touch. Kenzie rested her cheek against her damp hair.

Cori buried her face against Kenzie's shoulder, letting go of the fear and anxiety that had been steadily growing inside her for days. The arms around her felt strong and safe, and they brought comfort to her. Kenzie's body was feverishly warm, but for just a moment, Cori indulged her own needs.

The sobs slowly began to subside, but the sniffles and tears continued, as did Kenzie's steady stream of encouraging words. "It's okay, I've got you." *And you've got me.* She sighed silently to herself as she began to realize just how much she had grown to care about Cori. They hadn't known each other for long, but the circumstances had been extreme, and she knew that time was not always measured in minutes. *Time.* She glanced at her watch. They were on a schedule. Kenzie was disinclined to break the embrace, but she knew she had to.

As if sensing Kenzie's reluctant need, Cori sniffed loudly and pulled away from Kenzie's damp shoulder. "Thanks, I needed that." Cori studied Kenzie's face, just inches away from her own. "You're awfully warm."

"You're awfully cute," Kenzie responded as she kissed Cori's forehead.

"Are you okay?"

"Are you?"

"Stop it, I'm being serious. You're very warm." Cori pulled out of Kenzie's embrace and touched her forehead. "I thought you felt warm earlier."

"I remember my mother used to kiss my forehead to check my temperature," Kenzie said with a smile.

Cori's features drew into a concerned frown as her hand slid from Kenzie's forehead to cup her warm cheek. "I'm not your mother," she whispered as she brought her other hand up to Kenzie's other cheek and pulled her into a kiss. This was no peck on the lips, but a woman's kiss of want and desire.

When Cori finally pulled back, Kenzie found herself a little breathless and more than a little sexually aroused. "You," Kenzie said as she licked her tingling lips, "are definitely not my mother."

"And you have a fever. Maybe we should stay here for a bit until you're healed," Cori pleaded. She felt safe in Kenzie's arms, surrounded by Big Polly and his men.

"We have to keep moving. Staying in one place for too long would be dangerous. It's only a minor wound and it will heal."

"Either way, I hope the antibiotic kicks in soon."

"Once I get cleaned up, it will look better and I'll feel better, trust me." She saw the concern on Cori's face, "I know all of this scares you, and it should, but you're going to have to trust me. A moving target is a lot harder to hit, so until we know what's going on, we're going to keep moving. Once we get to San Diego and onto my boat, we can pull up anchor and head out to sea."

"To where?"

"Wherever all of this leads us."

"And then what, Kenzie?"

"Then I'll do what I do best, because that's who I am."

Chapter 11

Transportes El Volanté was the local bus service that was supposed to deposit people at the US/Mexican border every fifteen minutes, but it ran on Mexican time and was seldom punctual. Every year, over twenty million people pass through the metal turnstiles at the Tijuana port of entry, so the buses were seldom empty. Kenzie hoped that no one would pay any attention to two more people in the ever-moving flow northward.

Big Polly had been true to his word, and both she and Cori had identification in the form of a California driver's license and a birth certificate. He had been adamant that they use the driver's licenses as their ID out of Mexico, or rather, their ticket back into the States.

Cori was dressed in a plain, teal-colored, cotton t-shirt and faded jeans; Kenzie in a button down, white linen shirt and a pair of khaki pants. The day was warm, but with the soon to be setting sun, there would be a breeze off the ocean, so Big Polly had also produced two lightweight windbreakers, blue for Cori and an emerald green for Kenzie. They were well worn but fit as if they owned them, and that was all they needed. Big Polly had arranged everything.

Kenzie glanced at Cori who was sitting close beside her. In her lap, nervous fingers clutched a black plastic shopping bag containing a couple of cheap t-shirts and a new leather purse, staple purchases for a tourist visiting Tijuana.

Feeling Kenzie's eyes on her, Cori leaned over and whispered in her ear, "The souvenirs are a nice touch."

"Speak for yourself." Kenzie glared at the bull shaped piñata on her lap. "At least yours are easy to handle and not so audacious." She'd had her reservations when Big Polly handed out the souvenirs, but when he assured her that her piñata held a special surprise, her reluctance turned to concern.

"They have x-ray machines at the border. What do I do when they want to x-ray this little fella?"

"It won't be a problem," Big Polly said with a knowing smile.

Kenzie was doubtful. "Really?"

"They can't and don't x-ray everything. Your little bull there won't fit through their x-ray machine."

Kenzie gave the piñata a little shake, but she felt nothing inside.

He smiled. "It's empty."

"Really?"

"No, but don't worry. I know for a fact that it won't be a problem."

"And if they do decide it's a problem and want to x-ray it?"

"They can't. I'm telling you — trust me."

"I don't trust people, Big Polly. You know that. It's not in my nature."

"You know me, and you know you can trust me. They can't x-ray it because it's too big. Don't worry, even if they were to shake it, it won't make a sound. They'll be looking for your reaction, that's when they'll decide if they want to look inside, but they never do. I'm sure you can handle it."

She nodded her reluctant acceptance. "So, do I want to know what's inside?"

Big Polly smiled. "A prize. Open it when you've cleared the border and are on the trolley heading north. The whole idea here is to blend in. You're a couple of women who just spent the day shopping in Tijuana. Once you're over the border, just follow the rest of the tourists. Use some of the cash I gave you and buy a few things from the locals. Be seen, but don't make a scene. Make some friends and everything will be fine. You know how this works, blend in."

Looking around at the other tourists on the bus northbound to Tijuana, she gave Big Polly his due. There was not a single empty-handed passenger on the bus. He was right. If they were going to pull this off, then they had to be taken for tourists.

It was something Kenzie found disturbing. She knew the protocols for her job. Unfortunately, her mind and body had been so badly beaten up that she had neglected one of the first rules of training: if you don't want to be noticed, then you have to learn to blend in and become part of your surroundings. *Walk like a duck, talk like a duck, and you'll be taken for a duck.*

"What did you say?" Cori shot Kenzie a puzzled look. "Did you just say...did you say that we look like ducks?"

"No," Kenzie said firmly.

"Yes, you did," Cori insisted.

Their short bus ride to the border lurched to a stop, saving Kenzie from having to respond. All but a few of the passengers rose to their feet at once, hoping to beat the mass exodus in escaping the stifling heat. The windows of the bus were open, allowing a steady breeze to swirl the dusty heat inside the rattletrap, but now that they had come to a stop, the temperature inside the bus would quickly become unbearable.

One of the few still seated, Kenzie wiped the sweat from her brow. A puff of diesel smoke billowed past the window. She took several shallow breaths, hoping to clear some of the fumes from her head, but it didn't seem to help much. "Come on, let's go," she said as she stood up and waited for Cori to move into the line exiting the bus in front of her.

They stepped out of the bus, away from the smell of diesel, dust, and sweat and into the ever-present aroma of Tijuana. Small carts and open-air stalls were cooking, making, and selling tortillas, burritos, and tamales, and the warm afternoon air was filled with their smells. The contents of many shops spilled out onto the uneven sidewalks: pottery, leather belts, jackets, t-shirts, ponchos, gold and silver jewelry in aged glass cases, velvet paintings of long dead singers and actors, and just about anything else a tourist might want to haggle over.

An elderly local held out silver jewelry as Kenzie and Cori passed them. "Ah, *Señorita*, come, take a look. For you or your friend." He held up an arm adorned with beautifully crafted silver necklaces. "Come, come." He beckoned them over, but they moved on with a shake of their heads, following some of the other tourists from the bus as they strolled along the wide walkway. The shops began to look pretty much the same as every merchant gleefully propositioned them to come into their shop. They did slow down for the occasional store, though it was more for appearance than to look for bargains. Kenzie had one thing on her mind and that was to get across the border.

The sloping of the sidewalk gradually lessened, as the pedestrian bridge over the cement banks of the Tijuana River came into sight. Several tables of trinkets lined the concrete walkway that zigzagged toward the bridge. Unlike the merchants in town, the women watching over these tables were silent as Cori and Kenzie walked by.

"You okay?" Kenzie asked as they proceeded up the ramped walkway.

"Yeah... Well no, I'm scared shitless," Cori answered honestly as she slid a nervous glance in Kenzie's direction. "If I neglected to mention it earlier, I'm glad I have you with me." She offered her best smile, but it quickly faded away. "Are you sure you're okay? You look a little flushed."

"I'm fine." She wiped the sweat from her face. "It's just the heat."

Cori was about to comment that it was not that hot, but as they rounded the last turn that would take them onto the bridge, she saw something that bothered her more than Kenzie's temperature. There, right in front of them, at the beginning of the pedestrian bridge, was a small red and white booth. Her eyes darted to the matching booth on the opposite end of the bridge. Both were marked with a faded but clearly written word: *POLICIA*. They appeared to be empty and she took a calming breath as they turned the corner and walked out onto the bridge. Her relief was short lived as they almost bumped into three uniformed officers partially blocking the entrance. Cori's heart thumped and her stomach dropped, but after one more reluctant step forward, she realized the trio was not even looking at them. The three uniformed officers were having an angry exchange with two young men and didn't seem to be aware of them.

Kenzie leaned over and whispered into Cori's ear, "It's okay. We're tourists heading home, remember? Just ignore them like everyone else is doing." Kenzie took Cori by the elbow and gently steered her around the group. Keeping their eyes away from the officers and their detainees, the twosome casually crossed the aging footbridge, carefully avoiding some of the large potholes in the older sections of the bridge. At some time in its past, there had been attempts to liven up the concrete by painting brightly colored squares with names all over the surface, but time, weather, and millions of footsteps had faded them to a memory. Neither woman spoke as they passed the halfway point.

"There's the border," Kenzie said. "See the fence?"

Cori looked beyond the cement riverbed to the exceptionally tall fast food restaurants signs and the palm trees that lined the streets of San Ysidro. "Then that would make that America."

"Yup."

Cori stopped and looked back over her shoulder at the busy streets of Tijuana. She was leaving Mexico, and that realization unsettled her. The lifestyle of the impoverished country was something that had initially been hard for her, especially seeing the children who had little more than the clothes on their backs. She recalled with vivid clarity the first time she had seen one of them eating in the middle of an open-air market. The flies had been buzzing around the mixture of refried beans and rice on the young girl's plate. The child barely noticed them as she scooped the food into her mouth with her fingers. It was a different world down here, and it took Cori a while to get used to the poverty, the heat, and the crime, but the people made it all worthwhile. Never before had she been around such a sense of community and family. They seemed to celebrate everything and they seemed to do it together. Family was everything, and everyone was invited.

"Cori?" Kenzie's placed a hand on Cori's back. "You okay?"

Cori turned and looked ahead to the end of the bridge. "Yeah, I was just..."

"There's no one following us, if that's what you're looking at. Even if there were, they wouldn't try anything here — too many people, too many eyes, too many cameras." Kenzie spoke reassuringly, but the caution inherent in her profession made her glance back over her shoulder as well.

"What about that guy in Santa Rosalia? The crowds there didn't seem to bother him."

"Cobra?" The name was barely a whisper off her lips as she scanned the vantage points that she would have used if she were the hunter rather than the hunted. The lay of the land would be perfect for a sniper — lots of uneven rooftops and billboards. The hairs on the back of her neck rose as her senses heightened. "I doubt he's following us. I winged him back at Santa Rosalia." Her eyes didn't find anything out of the ordinary, but she felt the sweat rolling down her back and between her breasts. "There are way too many witnesses here. But just to be on the safe side, stay in front of me."

Cori did as she was directed, her mind still working on the possibilities. "If he...this Cobra is out of the picture, would they send someone else?"

It was a good question, considering they had sent someone else because she had not done the job to start with. Even if they had, she didn't have the tools to deal with it at that moment, so there was no sense in worrying about what she couldn't change. "Probably. But they don't know where we are and they don't know where we're going."

"They don't know about your boat?"

"No one knows about my boat, except the Judge and Big Polly, and neither has been there. We'll be safe there, so come on, let's just keep moving."

Once they were off the bridge and down the ramped, zigzagging walkway, they found themselves in the middle of an open town square surrounded by more shops.

"Now where?" Cori asked.

"Big Polly said to keep going straight across the road until we pass the restaurant and the taxi stand. The Millennium Bridge to the border will be in front of us." Kenzie cursed under her breath as she transferred the piñata from her left arm to her right. The pain in her side had been throbbing almost continuously and, though she tried to ignore the pain, it was not going away. Despite her resolve to keep that knowledge from Cori, when the salty sweat from her body trickled down her wound, she couldn't stop the hiss of pain that escaped from between clenched teeth. Cori didn't seem to hear it, and for that, she was thankful. She shifted the piñata and their windbreakers back to her left side.

Cori did notice that. "You want me to take that stuff for a bit?"

"Nah, its okay, I've got it. Let's just keep moving."

It took only a few minutes for them to cross the square and find the Millennium Bridge that would take them over the road to the States. It was a lot more modern than the ancient footbridge, a lot narrower, too, leaving just enough room for two people to cross it side by side. Halfway across, Cori stopped in shock at the endless line of cars and trucks inching their way northward.

"Wow!" she said in awe, her mouth open at the sheer volume of vehicles converging on the Land of the Free and the home of the twenty-four hour shopping mall.

Kenzie joined her in looking over the traffic below. There were eleven lanes open to the border, hundreds if not thousands of cars idling their way northward past vendors desperate to sell their wares. She shot a glimpse over her shoulder, but she couldn't see the end of the line.

"Is that it?" Cori asked, drawing Kenzie's attention back to the direction they were heading. "That's where we're going, right?" There, in front of them, was the largest and most modern building in the entire area, and its identity was clearly spelled out in bold aluminum letters: United States Border Inspection Station.

"Yeah." Kenzie narrowed her focus to their immediate goal. Her head was still spinning and she squeezed her eyes shut several times, hoping to clear her vision and ease the throbbing in her head. "Let's get this over with."

They moved off the bridge and headed north. Cori was nervous, but she did her best to hide it. With each step, her heartbeat seemed to get louder.

Sensing her nervousness, Kenzie leaned over and whispered into her ear, "It's going to be okay. Just take a couple of slow, easy breaths, and remember, we were just down here for the day."

"I know...I know," Cori said, more to herself than to Kenzie. She took several deep breaths, blowing each one out slowly through slightly parted lips.

The sidewalk was not busy, though everyone around them seemed to be heading in the same direction. They reached the glass doors of the border station and Kenzie pulled one open for Cori to enter. She smiled and winked, hoping to help ease Cori's tension.

The building itself was warm. That was the first thing Cori registered as they moved forward with everyone else down the unfurnished corridor. She licked her lips several times, but it didn't help; her throat and mouth were too dry to furnish any moisture. The building was eerily silent except for the sound of everyone's footsteps echoing off the bare brick walls. At the end of the corridor, the foot traffic slowed as they approached the numerous inspection stations. There were four lines directly in front of them and all appeared to be moving quickly. Kenzie motioned to one of them and Cori silently followed her direction.

Everywhere she looked, Cori saw armed border guards. They all seemed to be looking at her and Kenzie, but she took another shallow breath and realized they were paying no more attention to them than to anyone else. A border guard enclosed behind a chest-high counter manned each of the four inspection stations. Cori and Kenzie could not actually see the border guard from where they stood, but his hands and arms poked out now and then as identification was handed over by the couple currently at the booth. They had several plastic bags, as most everyone had, and they passed them over to the guard's outstretched hands. After close examination, the bags were returned and the couple moved on.

Kenzie and Cori shuffled forward, closer and closer to the booth at the front of their line. As they drew nearer, Cori could hear mumbles and hushed words coming from people moving through the checkpoint. Before she realized it, they were at the front of their line.

"Next," a monotone voice said as a hand came out of the booth and waved her forward. Cori took a step forward and felt her heart rate increase as the cool whisper of fear suddenly gripped her.

Chapter 12

The judge had been tirelessly making inquiries, but the information he was seeking had eluded him. There were proper channels he normally would have followed, but the need for speed and discretion forced him to navigate shark-filled waters without making any waves. If he tipped his hand, he wouldn't be able to obtain the information he required without someone else knowing that he was looking.

There was a polite knock on his door and then Shelby opened it and poked her head inside. She held up several large manila envelopes. "These all just arrived for you by special courier."

"Excellent. Thank you." He stood up and gestured her in.

Shelby, a small sprig of a Southern raised woman, moved quickly across the thick-carpeted floor and set the envelopes on his desk. "Is there anything else I can get for you?"

Judge Woodward thought for a moment, then nodded. "Actually, yes, if you wouldn't mind." He went over to the closet to retrieve his wallet from his jacket pocket, counted out several hundred dollars, and then replaced the thin leather wallet in the jacket. Closing the door, he turned back to his secretary. "This is beyond your job description, so please don't feel obligated—"

"Judge Woodward, I have worked for y'all for how long now? Whatever it is that y'all need, I'd be happy to oblige."

He smiled at the woman he had chosen so many years earlier. Shelby had not been the most refined of the applicants he had talked to, but she had something that she referred to as "gumption". It had made him laugh, and he knew she was the administrative assistant he was looking for. "What would I do without you?" he said with a shake of his head.

"Let's hope we never have to find out, sir."

"I need you to pick me up one of those cheap, pay-as-you-go cell phones. You know — the kind you can get at an AM/PM or a mini-mart, and some phone cards, as well."

"Yes, sir." She nodded, almost bowing, before she turned to leave.

"Shelby."

She paused at the door and turned back to the judge, noticing for the first time how tired he looked. "Yes, sir?"

"If they need a name..."

"It sure as hell won't be mine or yours," she said with a wink, then left him to his envelopes.

"Next." The voice inside the booth sounded impatient, but Cori could not seem to move. Her feet felt like lead and her heart was pounding in her chest.

"Cori?"

She felt Kenzie nudge her forward, but her body refused to move. From the booth ahead, a face popped around the side, looking Cori over as he motioned her forward.

"Next," he commanded strongly.

A firm hand on the small of her back pushed her forward, giving Cori no choice. She reached the counter and smiled hesitantly at the stern face of the border guard. He didn't even lift his eyes to her as he held out his hand. Cori glanced back at Kenzie and then turned her attention to the detached government official.

"Identification," he said, waving his hand impatiently.

She swallowed hard, doing her best to appear relaxed. "Are we supposed to go one at a time, or can my friend join me?"

The border guard finally looked up at the young woman. He hesitated a moment, before answering, "It doesn't matter."

Cori looked back at Kenzie and motioned her up to the booth.

He leaned out to look beyond the booth to the woman standing next in line. "That your friend?"

"Yeah." Cori continued to gesture Kenzie forward.

"Next," the guard said sternly.

When Kenzie joined them at the booth, he looked the pair over, scrutinizing them from head to toe. "Identification." He held out his hand.

Cori was certain that he could sense her fear. If not, he definitely could hear her heart beating as she handed over her counterfeit Californian driver's license and fake birth certificate.

The border guard examined the ID carefully and then held it under a small desk lamp. He said nothing as he reached for Kenzie's ID. He held up the IDs and compared the pictures to their bearers.

It seemed to take forever but Kenzie remained calm and confident, though she could feel the heat radiating off her face and the sweat rolling down her back. She watched the border guard's eyes as he glanced over the documents.

Cori started to fidget, but the guard didn't appear to notice or care. He handed them back their papers without question or comment. Reaching out, he waved his fingers to the young Mexican couple waiting in line. "Next."

There was no "goodbye", no "thank you", and no "welcome to the United States of America". It was just — "next".

Kenzie guided them away from the booth as Cori tucked her fake ID into her wallet and slid the wallet into the back pocket of her jeans. *One down and one to go*, Kenzie thought to herself as they moved toward the x-ray machine. There were five uniformed border guards around the machine, two of them sitting and a trio standing. No one said a word to them and that was just fine with Kenzie. Apparently, it was just assumed that you knew what was to happen next after you left the guard at the booth.

Cori approached first, and one of the guards pointed to the moving conveyor belt of the x-ray machine. He didn't say anything, just pointed. She laid her bags down on it and then walked to the other end and waited for them to come through.

Kenzie transferred the piñata to her right hand as she placed the plastic bag and their jackets onto the x-ray belt. *This is it, Big Polly. You'd better be right.* She placed her piñata on the moving belt, watching nervously as it inched toward the opening, until it became apparent that it was not going to fit. Kenzie glanced up at one of the guards sitting next to the machine. "It won't fit," she said.

The guard barely looked up before he waved it off. Big Polly had been right again. The guards had no interest in either of them or the piñata.

With a sigh of relief, Kenzie reached for the piñata, but the hanging wire attached to the back became tangled in the handles of the plastic bag she had already placed on the moving conveyor belt. Try as she might to unwind it, the plastic only seemed to tangle more tightly around the wire hook as the conveyor belt persistently tugged at it. Other parcels and packages started jamming up on the conveyor belt, adding to the difficulty of untangling the little bull piñata.

Waiting at the other end of the conveyor belt, Cori saw Kenzie struggling with something, and though her demeanor remained calm, Cori knew her well enough to know something was going wrong. Glancing at the guards seated behind the x-ray machine, she saw they had not moved from their positions, but they were all watching Kenzie. *This is the last thing we need. Come on, Kenzie. Let's go.* But instead of moving on, Kenzie bent down out of her line of vision. When two of the border guard began to walk in Kenzie's direction, Cori panicked. *What's going on?*

She hurried back to see what the problem was and saw Kenzie pulling at the plastic bag wrapped around the wire hook of the piñata. One of the guards leaned down to assist, his leather gloved hand reaching out to grasp the papier-mâché piñata. Cori quickly leaned over and held back the mass of parcels, jackets, and bags that were pressing to get through the x-ray machine. Between them all, it was enough, and Kenzie released the plastic bag from the piñata.

"Thanks," she whispered as she snatched her piñata from the guard's grasp. "Sorry. I didn't know it wouldn't fit." She locked eyes with the border guard, "It's a gift for my nephew, but I think it's going to be more of a pain to get it home than it's worth." Kenzie smiled. "Do you want to look at it?"

The guard shook his head and waved her through, "Nah, don't worry about it." He turned his back with a wave of his hand, returning to the discussion with his colleagues.

Kenzie and Cori moved to the end of the belt where the troublesome plastic bag was waiting for them. Snatching it off the conveyor, Kenzie said to Cori, "Let's get out of here before we draw any more attention."

They were through and on their way, and Kenzie couldn't have been happier. The process had been easy, too easy, but she wasn't going to object as she crossed the hard tile floor.

"That's it?" Cori whispered to Kenzie, who was holding the door open for her.

A smile of relief spread across Kenzie's face. "That's it. Welcome back to the United States."

"Hey — you two ladies, stop right there." The voice of authority ruined their celebration. In unison, they turned to the guard summoning them. "Come back here, please." He motioned with his hand.

Cori looked at Kenzie. "What do we do?" she whispered.

For a brief moment, Kenzie looked beyond the doors. They were so close, but if they tried to run, there was no chance they'd make it past the doors. "Let's go see what he wants."

Nervous, Cori followed Kenzie back to the guard at the x-ray machine.

"In a bit of a hurry?" The guard's tone sounded accusatory as he glanced from Kenzie to Cori.

"Is there a problem?" Kenzie asked.

"You were down in Tijuana just for the day?"

"Yes," Kenzie answered for them both. *Where is he going with this?*

"You went down this morning?" He turned his full attention to Kenzie and the two locked eyes.

"Yes. Is there a problem, Officer?" Cori interjected as she watched the two size each other up.

The guard turned to Cori. "Should there be?"

"You called us back, I just don't know why."

The guard came around the end of the conveyor belt. "You forgot your jackets. It's kinda warm for jackets isn't it?" he said, holding out the two windbreakers.

"We weren't sure how long we were going to be. It can get a little chilly toward the evening," Cori said.

"Ah, sorry." Kenzie collected the forgotten items. "Thanks. I'm sure we'd be missing these later." The guard nodded and they turned and headed for the door.

Cori walked through the door and out onto the sidewalk of San Ysidro, California. They were back on American soil.

"So much for Homeland Security," she said as Kenzie stepped up beside her.

"What did you expect?"

"I don't know, but something better than that. They hardly asked us a thing. I thought that after 9-11 there would be better security."

"Security is a state of mind," Kenzie commented as she glanced over the busy sidewalk, her eyes stopping at the row of automated ticket booths. "There." She nodded toward them. "We need tickets for the red trolley. That will take us into San Diego." She transferred her piñata to her other hand, gently guiding Cori forward and away from the building.

They stood together in front of the ticket booth screen looking over their options. "What do we need?" Cori asked. When Kenzie didn't answer, she turned to her in question, but Kenzie's eyes were elsewhere. A tremor of fear rushed through Cori as she studied Kenzie's profile and her flexing jaw muscles. Her eyes were scanning their surroundings. "Kenzie? What is it?"

"Nothing," she answered but kept her eyes moving. "I don't know...something."

"What is that supposed to mean?" Cori wondered if she would ever be able to relax again as she looked around. "Something?"

"Nothing. The trolley should be here soon. It runs every fifteen minutes. Let's get our tickets and get out of here."

"Kenzie?" Cori placed a hand on the well-developed bicep. "Don't do that. I trust you and I trust your instincts. You got us this far. If there's something I should know about or worry about, you need to tell me. Trust is a two way street, you know."

Turning her attention back to the automated ticket booth, Kenzie punched in their destination on the trolley. *Cori is right. Trust is something earned and she's earned it, but...* She hadn't really trusted anyone since Mifflin. She waited for the machine to print out their tickets. *Who do I trust?*

As if hearing the question, Cori moved her hand to Kenzie's. "You can trust me, Kenzie."

Before she could deliberate on whether she could or whether she should, Kenzie turned her eyes to Cori's face. "I can't be certain, I haven't seen anyone, but if it was me...this is where I'd be — right here, waiting for us to come through the border crossing." She leaned down and retrieved their tickets. Her body ached with pain and exhaustion. She was tired, and maybe that was making her paranoid. When she stood up, tickets in hand, she automatically scanned the area again. She wanted to shake it off, but her instincts would not be silenced. That little voice of caution was screaming loudly. "Someone is out there. I can almost feel them."

"Where?"

"I don't know, but they're here. I'm sure of it." The red trolley came into view. "Let's go."

"Any idea who might be out there?"

"Isn't that what we've been asking ourselves since we left your apartment?"

There was no time for Cori to answer as the trolley came churning into the station. This was its final stop before turning around and heading north to San Diego. The modern light rail system, the main transportation for people traveling from Tijuana, handled thousands of passengers daily. The five-car trolley came to a stop almost directly across from them and the hinged doors flapped open loudly. The train emptied its passengers, and soon people were lining up to get on.

"Let's get out of here," Cori said.

"You took the words right out of my mouth. I'll feel a lot better once we get a few miles between us and Mexico."

By the time they got onto the front car, the only available bench seat was facing the back of the train. Sliding onto the red leather, Kenzie decided it was a fortuitous location. They would be able to watch the border station disappear as they pulled away.

"I knew you weren't feeling well."

"What?" Kenzie found it difficult to focus her attention on her traveling companion.

"You said that you'd feel a lot better. I knew you weren't feeling well."

"I never said that," Kenzie corrected as she moved the piñata around on her lap.

Cori watched her for a few moments as the rest of the trolley passengers squeezed on board. She was tired and more than a little frustrated. It felt like they had been on the run forever, and she thought that once they were over the border she'd feel better, but she didn't. In addition, knowing that Kenzie was not feeling well only added to her inner struggles.

"Would it kill you to admit that you're not invincible?" Cori said harshly, instantly regretting her tone. "I'm sorry, but if you're not feeling well then you're not feeling well. You're only human, Kenzie. I know you're supposed to be some tough-ass soldier chick, but sometimes you have to admit that you can't do everything by yourself. That's what friends are for — to lend a hand when you can't do something by yourself."

Kenzie rolled the words around in her mind and chewed on the inside of her cheek as she looked out the window. She didn't think that she was invincible, but at the same time, asking for help...it just wasn't done. Her training pounded in the necessity of being self-sufficient, reliant on no one but herself. All these years, she had only been responsible for herself...until now. *Now I'm responsible for both of—* "Son of a bitch!"

She had been watching the people hustling to make the trolley before it pulled out of the station. He almost blended in — that was his job after all, as it was normally hers — but something about him looked out of place and it caught her eye.

"What?" Cori leaned over Kenzie to look out the window.

"We've got company." Kenzie draped her windbreaker over the back of the piñata and then crammed her hand through the paper of the little bull's neck. Fingers searching inside, she felt for the contraband she'd smuggled through the border.

Cori watched Kenzie's hand disappear inside the piñata. "What the hell are you doing?"

"Cobra just got on the train."

The words sent a chill through Cori. "Oh my God!" Her eyes darted over the people aboard the train. No one was paying them much attention and she didn't see the man who always seemed to be one step behind them. "Where did you see him?"

Kenzie's fingers touched the gun. "He just got on the last car of the trolley," Kenzie said as a faint bell chimed and the doors to the train slammed closed. A moment later the trolley began its journey northward, making very little noise as it pulled out of the station.

"He's here on this train?" Cori felt cornered and an adrenaline rush ratcheted her anxiety to new levels. "What are we going to do?"

Keenly aware of the passengers closest to her, Kenzie pulled the torn paper bull toward her and repositioned her windbreaker to conceal what she was doing. "Nothing at the moment. He can't move between train cars while the train is in motion."

"And what happens when we stop?"

"We'll play a little game of cat and mouse." She glanced up at the station map posted high on the trolley wall. Wedged between an ad for Red Lobster and the announcement of new crab cakes at Joe's Crab Shack, a colored legend detailed their approaching stops. According to the map, there were twelve of them between their point of departure, the station at San Ysidro, and Old Town in San Diego. *Twelve stops.* She leaned back against her seat. *It's going to be a long game.* It was only then that she really noticed the woman sitting directly across from her. She appeared to be Mexican, with dark, curly hair and dark eyes cast downward. Looking intently at her hands folded neatly in her lap, the woman was trying hard to be invisible.

"What's your plan?" Cori asked, looking to Kenzie for the assurance she could not find in herself. "You have a plan, right? Tell me you have a plan, Kenzie. Tell me that we haven't been on the run for over a thousand miles for it all to end within an hour of your boat."

Kenzie actually smiled, then reached to touch Cori's hand. "I told you to trust me." She searched Cori's eyes. "And I told you I would protect you with every ounce of my being. I meant it. Trust me."

"I do...but that won't stop me from being scared."

"I know." Kenzie squeezed her hand, and then interlaced their fingers. "But we have a few stops before Cobra will reach our car. My guess is it will take about four stops."

"About?" She looked to Kenzie in question. "That doesn't give me much confidence in your plan."

Kenzie released Cori's hand and then carefully pulled the gun out of the piñata. Using the cover of her windbreaker, she attempted to slide the gun into the plastic bag on her lap, but the bag caught on the gun's rear sights and it tumbled to the floor.

Quickly she scooped up the firearm and shoved it into the bag. Disgusted with her clumsiness, she closed her eyes and squeezed them shut. Her head was swimming and she was having a hard time concentrating.

"What the... That was in there the whole time?" Cori whispered into Kenzie's ear. "What if you'd been caught with it at the border? What if the guards had searched the piñata?"

"They didn't, but if they had, we had a backup plan."

Cori was not pleased that this information was all news to her. "Do I want to know?"

Kenzie opened her eyes and turned to her. "Probably not, but let's just say we weren't alone at the border station, and there would have been a loud diversion."

"Great." Cori leaned back in her seat with a sigh. "I've come this far with a crazy woman."

"I wouldn't say crazy, just readily adaptable." With the gun safely stored away, Kenzie leaned over to the woman across from her. "Excuse me, do you ride this trolley often?"

The woman looked up with a smile and nodded politely.

Cori watched in astonishment as Kenzie started up a conversation with the stranger. Soon the two were chatting easily. Her name was Flora, she said, and she lived in Tijuana but worked in a warehouse south of San Diego. Once she got talking, she was quite chatty, and all Kenzie and Cori had to do was listen.

The first station came along faster than Kenzie had anticipated. The trolley car slowed to a stop, and she felt Cori's body tense. Kenzie leaned closer to the window, resting her face against the cool glass as she placed a reassuring hand on Cori's shoulder. The doors opened and several passengers departed. Watching and waiting, Kenzie spotted Cobra stepping out of the last car.

He stood out, breaking the number one rule: become part of your environment. He was not attempting to hide. He walked along the cement platform confidently peering into the windows of the trolley car next to his. *What an overconfident asshole*, she thought as she watched his every movement. Just as he got to the front of the fourth trolley, the bell chimed, signaling their imminent departure. Cobra quickly hopped through the opening before the doors slammed shut.

One car, one stop, but what about next time? If he moves faster, he could cover the two cars that separate us. Kenzie turned back to Cori as the trolley pulled out of the station.

"Where is he?" Cori asked.

"Two cars back."

"What are we going to do?"

"I'm working on something," Kenzie said as she looked up at the trolley map, scrutinizing the next several stops.

"Kenzie, we have one, maybe two more stops, and then he's going to be in this car."

Flora leaned forward between them. "Is everything okay? I don't mean to be nosy or anything, but, I mean, are you two in some kind of trouble?"

Unsure of what she should reveal, Cori looked to Kenzie. Despite Kenzie's calm and self-assured demeanor, her face was flushed and sweaty. Cori felt as if they were in trouble, even if Kenzie didn't want to admit it. She was certain Kenzie would be annoyed if she mentioned it, but she couldn't help confessing her fears to Flora. "Yeah, we're in trouble." Cori's concern grew when Kenzie remained quiet, almost too quiet.

Flora watched the two women. Everything about their body language told her much more than their earlier conversation had. The dark haired woman, who said her name was Kathy, appeared not to be well. The blonde had said her name was Laura, but Flora didn't think that was her real name. Part of her didn't want to ask. After all, she did not know them and she really didn't want to get mixed up in whatever they were involved with. Nonetheless, she had been in need once and a stranger had helped her out. Now she felt an obligation to that debt. Karma was something she strongly believed in.

"Is there anything I can do?" Flora asked as the women exchanged questioning glances.

"Actually, yes." Kenzie reached into her pocket and felt the wad of bills Big Polly had handed her before they left. "How would you like to make a couple of hundred dollars?"

"You don't have to pay me, Kathy. I want to help."

"Maybe you should wait until you hear what I'm going to ask."

The trolley pulled into the next station as Kenzie put her request to Flora. Cori listened intently, a little surprised at how easily Kenzie invented a plausible story about their predicament. When the trolley stopped, so did their conversation. Kenzie leaned against the window looking at each departing passenger.

Cobra stepped from the fourth car back, but he did not immediately turn in their direction.

"Is he there?" Cori asked.

"Yeah, but he's not moving." Kenzie narrowed her eyes and rubbed at her forehead as she tried to figure out what he was doing.

"What do you mean, 'he's not moving'?"

"He's just standing there... Wait. There he goes. He's checking the third car. But he's taking too long, the trolley only stops for—" On cue there was a faint chime, signaling their departure. Kenzie watched as Cobra had to hustle, jumping through the closing doors of the third car.

Kenzie leaned back in her seat and breathed a sigh of relief when the trolley pulled out of the station. "He didn't make it. He's on the third car now."

"Leaving one car between us." Cori's heart was beating hard against her chest. No one had to be told that the next stop was going to be the end of the line, especially if Kenzie's plan didn't work.

"Are you sure you want to do this, Flora?" Cori asked.

"My cousin, she too found herself on the run from an abusive husband." Flora leaned forward and patted Cori's forearm in understanding. "The family was there to help, and if they were all here now... Well, I'm sure you get the picture. I want to help."

Cori returned Flora's reassuring smile. "I don't know how to thank you. It's been a long and frightening journey, but the whole time we were in Mexico, everyone was so helpful and kind. It seems as if every time we've been in real trouble, someone has come to our rescue. And if they couldn't help, they had a friend who could."

"Or a cousin," Kenzie mumbled, her eyes shut, her head resting against the window as the trolley glided down the track.

Cori stole a concerned glance at Kenzie, "Or a cousin," she echoed, and then turned back to Flora. "It's something the rest of us could take a page from. When did we all stop being courteous and helpful?"

"People are too busy these days. In Mexico things are slower, and life is more appreciated." Flora leaned over further and whispered to Cori, "Is your friend going to be okay? She doesn't look very good."

It was not something that Cori didn't already know. Kenzie's condition looked to be deteriorating by the minute.

"I'm fine," Kenzie said. "I'm just...tired. Once we get to San Diego, everything will be okay."

"She'll be okay," Cori said, more to convince herself than to reassure Flora.

"Well, the next stop is Palomar Street, my stop, and we're almost there," Flora said, looking out the window.

Kenzie slowly opened her eyes and focused hard on Flora's face. "Are you sure you're up to this?"

"You don't worry about me, I can handle myself. Once I'm off the trolley, I'll be okay. It's a busy stop and there will be loads of people around, what with the end of shift and the afternoon rush and all." Flora leaned over to look out the window as she felt the trolley beginning to slow. "See what I mean?"

Cori and Kenzie turned in their seats to scan the approaching station. Flora was right. The area around the station was crowded with people.

"And look, there are some of the boys heading back to Fleet Street."

"Fleet Street?" Cori asked as she tried to look past Kenzie.

"San Diego is home to the United States Pacific Fleet," Flora said matter-of-factly. "You couldn't be safer than with all these Marines around."

Kenzie looked at Cori and a smile slowly spread across her face.

A large group of young men was gathering on the platform, waiting for the trolley to pull into the station. It was obvious from their short-cropped hair and clean-cut clothing of khakis and polo shirts, that they were Navy boys. They were loud and boisterous, having a good time, laughing and joking.

The trolley slowed to a stop and Kenzie stood up. She quickly handed her windbreaker and piñata to Flora. Stepping into the aisle, Kenzie joined the rest of the passengers disembarking in the afternoon rush. Cori slid over to Kenzie's vacated seat and pressed her head against the window. Her heart was pounding and her stomach instantly did a flip-flop when she spotted Cobra stepping off the trolley. She watched as he waited, his eyes constantly moving over the passengers as they exited. When most of the people had departed, he turned and made his way to the front steps of their trolley. Cori swallowed hard as she slid back to her original seat.

The group of military personnel made their way into the trolley. There were only a few seats left, so most of them had to stand. No one paid much attention to the thick-necked man who entered the front of the trolley car.

The only thing between Cori and Cobra was the group of Navy boys. *Okay, now or never.* The moment Cobra spotted her, Cori jumped to her feet. Bumping hard into one of the young Naval recruits, she clung to his muscled arm. She turned and stared heatedly into the dark eyes of her adversary. The moment he stepped toward her, Cori cried out with fear, "Oh God, no, please don't hurt me again." She pushed herself deeper into the tightly bunched throng of sailors.

Cobra's face showed no emotion as he moved down the aisle toward Cori.

"Please don't let him hurt me again." Cori grabbed one of the sailor's biceps as she hid behind him. Two of the young sailors who were sitting rose to their feet, blocking Cobra's path. "I'm not going back with you," she cried, her tears of fear cementing her case.

The boys of honor circled around the young woman, standing up against the thick-necked man approaching her. A young seaman named David McGary, born and raised in New Orleans, was the first one to speak out. "You heard her, buddy, back off," he said as Cobra approached. Seaman McGary had a younger sister around Cori's age, and in fact, they did look a little alike — minus the bruises on Cori's face.

"This has got nothing to do with you...boy." The muscles in Cobra's neck tightened as he emphasized the last word. "I never laid a hand on her. This is just business."

"He's my ex-boyfriend. Please don't let him hurt me again, I-I don't want to go with him," Cori croaked out as she moved further away from Cobra, putting more sailors between them.

"You heard her, buddy. She isn't going anywhere with you," Seamen McGary said as he stepped closer to Cobra, followed quickly by his brothers in arms. The show of force heightened the tension in the trolley car. "I suggest you back off, and take the next trolley in another direction."

Cobra studied the man in front of him, knowing that even with the sailor's youth and strength he was no match for someone with his own experience and expertise. Then Cobra's eyes scanned the rest of the sailors. His gun was within reach, but he quickly calculated the outcome, and the damage control that would necessarily follow. He knew LeGault had outplayed him again. That realization raised another question, a more pressing question. *Where the hell is she?*

The bell chimed, signaling the closing of the doors, but somebody hit the door release button and the doors slammed open.

"That's your cue to leave, buddy, and it's no longer a suggestion." Seaman McGary was not looking for trouble, but he was not going to avoid it, either. He stepped forward, moving closer to the woman's ex-boyfriend. "Get off the trolley!"

Cobra was still trying to decide what his best options were when he spotted Kenzie's dark curly hair moving swiftly outside the window of the trolley. Leaning over one of the benches, he could see the emerald green windbreaker in her hand. It was all he needed to know.

"I'll deal with you later," Cobra said, barely giving Cori a glance as he rushed for the open door.

"Oh my God." The words came out with a sigh of honest relief. Cori covered her mouth and took another deep breath. Her entire body was shaking as she watched Cobra disappear from her sight.

"Let's go, guys." Seaman McGary was on the move right behind Cobra. "Let's make sure he stays off this trolley and away from her." It was all his comrades needed to hear, and the sailors started for the doors.

One of the sailors who stood closest to Cori turned and looked her in the eye. "Are you going be okay, Miss?"

"Yes, and thank you. Thank you all so very much. You probably just saved my life."

"Not a problem. I'm glad we were here to help." The young sailor bowed and tipped an imaginary hat.

She smiled as he rushed down the aisle to catch up with his friends. Cobra was gone, and now all she and Kenzie had to do was to make it to the sailboat in San Diego. *Kenzie...*

The doors to the trolley closed behind the last young sailor as he ran to catch up with his buddies, who were following behind the abusive ex-boyfriend. The man was now following a woman carrying a piñata.

When he was close enough, Cobra put his hand on his gun, then reached out and grabbed hold of the arm holding the emerald green windbreaker. He spun her around and glared into the woman's surprised face.

"Not who you were expecting?" Flora said in a condescending tone.

"What the—?" he said as she smiled and pulled her arm out of his grasp.

"What are you doing there, buddy?" Seaman McGary put himself between Cobra and the woman in the windbreaker. "You going to rough her up next?"

Cobra looked back at the trolley as it pulled out of the Palomar Street station, and he sighed loudly. She had outfoxed him again. He turned back to the young men who surrounded him and threw up his hands in surrender. There was a time not too long ago that he would have loved to take them all on, but he was a little wiser now, and a little slower. It didn't take an Einstein to know when to walk away and when to run, so he did just that. Taking off like a jackrabbit in winter, Cobra sprinted down Palomar Street with twelve angry sailors right behind him. They caught up to him after only a few hundred yards.

Chapter 13

The doors of the trolley slammed shut and the passengers on the first car began to settle down for the ride into San Diego. The moment of excitement was over and they no longer paid much attention to Cori. Moving down the aisle toward the stairwell at the front of the trolley, she was happy to see Kenzie ducked out of sight, waiting for her.

"He's gone," she said as she knelt down. "Your plan worked."

Kenzie smiled slowly. "You say that like you had doubts."

"It was beyond doubt; I was scared shitless." The tone of her voice reinforced the truth of her words as she studied Kenzie's face. "You don't look very good." She stood up and offered Kenzie her hand.

"I'm just tired, that's all," Kenzie said, though she knew it was more than that. Apparently she was not fooling Cori. She studied Cori's concerned features and then took the helping hand and pulled her exhausted body off the steps.

"You keep saying that, but we both know it's not the truth," Cori said as they now stood eye-to-eye.

The intense scrutiny was more than Kenzie wanted to endure. Her head was throbbing and she felt weak with fatigue. She moved past Cori and made her way back down the aisle. She was thankful their original seats were still empty as she sat down. She didn't have to look to know that Cori was right beside her.

"Do you think Flora will be okay?"

Kenzie rested her head against the window and closed her eyes. "Yeah. He's not after her, he's after us. Besides...he's going to have his hands full with those Navy boys."

"I can't believe she was so willing to help us."

"I can...that's why I chose her."

Cori looked to Kenzie. Her eyes were closed and her features relaxed. "What do you mean?"

"She wasn't raised in the States. This so-called Land of Opportunity has raised a generation of people who don't want to get involved. They don't see anything because they don't want to be a witness. For the most part, they don't want to help."

"I don't think that's true. When people are in need, it's human nature to want to help."

"In a crisis situation sure... Nine-eleven, Katrina, people were there...but..." Kenzie sighed. "In their day-to-day lives, people don't want to help. They don't want to get involved."

"I don't agree with you. I think people do want to help."

"They help with a checkbook, from far away...but most don't even know their neighbors' names and they don't care. Family gatherings are becoming...obsolete. There's no respect anymore, no responsibility." Kenzie's words were growing softer and short pauses were becoming longer. "In the industrial countries...it's about money. In most other places in the world...it's about family."

With her final words barely audible, Cori was certain Kenzie had fallen asleep, leaving her to mull over what she had said. She had not seen her family in years. Other than her mother, she had not seen any relatives since she was a child. There were no grandparents in her life, nor any uncles or aunts. She thought about her time in Seattle, and was chagrined to realize that Kenzie was right. Her neighbors were strangers. She knew most of her co-workers, at least their first names. It was when she had moved to Guadalajara that she spent time with the "strangers" in her building. She played with the kids in the courtyard, talked to people in the hallways and on the street. It had been a community. They had looked out for her and, without realizing, she had been looking out for them. Most of the people in her computer classes were closer friends then anyone else in her life.

The trolley jostled along the tracks, stopping at its designated stations without any further incidents or excitement. A mother with a small child on her lap sat across from them for a while. Cori smiled at them, but neither made eye contact with her. When the mother and child got off, no one took their place, leaving Cori alone with her thoughts. She was tired, and wanted nothing more than to close her eyes and go to sleep, but she couldn't. Her heart was still pounding and her legs and hands were still shaking. To her surprise, Kenzie was finally sleeping. Obviously, she was used to such circumstances while Cori was not.

The city of San Diego was now just outside their window. The trolley cut through the streets, passing people who were living their everyday lives. An orange glow was beginning to spread over the sky, reflecting off the ocean. Sunset was not far off. They stopped at the downtown station where a majority of the passengers disembarked.

Cori looked up at the map and realized they were almost at their destination. The next stop was Old Town and that was where Kenzie said they would be getting off. The sailboat that would be their safe haven was not far away now. She was looking forward to a bed, a chance to regroup, and some answers to the questions plaguing them. Then maybe she could relax just a little.

Cori leaned over and whispered into Kenzie's ear, "We're almost there." The exhausted woman showed no sign of waking or of having heard her. "Kenzie." Concerned, she placed a hand on Kenzie's forearm and gave it a gentle shake. "Kenzie, wake up. We're almost there."

A frown wrinkled into Kenzie's forehead and she squeezed her eyes more tightly shut. She stretched her neck and rolled her shoulders, and a small groan escaped her lips. Kenzie rubbed at her tired eyes and then turned to look out the window.

"Old Town is the next stop," Cori said. "That's where you said we would get off, right?"

Kenzie cleared her throat, but only nodded as she licked at her lips. Her throat felt dry and swollen, and it was hard for her to swallow.

"Are you feeling any better?"

"Yeah," she finally answered as she turned to smile at Cori. "How are you doing?"

"I'm okay...I think."

The trolley began to slow and Kenzie reached into the bag on her lap and quietly checked to make sure there was a round in the chamber of her gun. "It's just a short taxi ride to the inner harbor where my boat is moored. I was hoping we would get there in the daylight, but the sun is about to set, so you'll have to wait until tomorrow to see *Helen's Gate* in her glory." She pulled the gun from the bag and slid it into her waistband.

Cori looked at Kenzie. It was easy to tell she was well beyond exhausted. "Do you think you'll need that?" she asked as Kenzie pulled her shirt over the butt of the gun.

"Who knows? At this point, nothing would surprise me, and I'd rather err on the side of caution. Let's go."

The trolley was rolling to a stop and Cori rose with the rest of the passengers. Kenzie attempted to stand but her legs wobbled beneath her, causing her to reach out before she toppled.

"Whoa, easy," Cori said as grabbed Kenzie's arm.

Kenzie squeezed her eyes shut and gave her head a little shake. "Sorry. Guess I got up a little too fast."

"I think it's more than that. You still have a fever. Big Polly's antibiotic was outdated and I don't think it's working." Cori took a firm hold of her arm and directed them both down the aisle of the trolley. "Once we get to your boat, I'm putting you to bed."

As they waited for the other passengers to step off the trolley, Kenzie leaned over and whispered into Cori's ear, "Is that an invitation?"

Cori scowled at her. Reaching for Kenzie's arm, she held it in a tight grip as they made their way off the trolley. The evening air was cool as the sun begun to slide into the ocean, leaving behind a sky of gold and pink.

"There." Kenzie motioned to the lineup of taxis on the far side of the station. No longer feeling the need for Cori's assistance, she pulled her arm out of her grasp. She regretted it immediately. She swayed unsteadily and almost missed the yellow painted curb marking the trolley tracks.

Cori steadied Kenzie with a firm grip on her elbow. "Let's get you into a cab."

Kenzie nodded reluctantly. She was not at the top of her game but she was still a professional, and as Cori directed them toward the first available taxi, Kenzie scanned their surroundings for whomever or whatever might be out there. It was so much a part of who she was — always looking, watching, and analyzing.

They climbed into the cab and Kenzie gave the driver the address of the marina. He attempted to strike up a conversation, but Cori only replied with one-word answers or not at all. The driver soon understood and turned his attention to his driving. Taking one of the many freeways criss-crossing San Diego, it didn't take them long to get to the building that was home to the University of San Diego's sailing team. The small building also served as the mooring office for Santa Clara Point and Sail Bay. Kenzie paid the cabbie and he disappeared into the night.

Cori looked around the shoreline of the bay, amazed at how tightly compacted the houses were. "They don't give you much space to breathe, do they?"

"For the price people pay down here for a little bungalow," Kenzie pointed out a small seaside shack that was no more than a few hundred square feet, "you could buy a ranch in Montana."

Cori shook her head in disbelief and then turned and looked at the assorted sailboats anchored off shore. "Which one is yours?"

"That one there," Kenzie said with quiet pride, pointing out a sleek, blue and white sailboat. "She's a twenty-eight foot Catalina Mark Two. Nineteen ninety-six Boat of the Year."

"How do we get to it?"

"We head over here to the mooring office and they'll run us out to her in a dinghy."

In the fading light of the evening, they walked slowly to the office. Kenzie didn't comment when Cori slid a hand into the crook of her arm. She did not want to know whether it was for Cori's benefit or her own.

"It's a nice boat, Kenzie."

"Thanks," she murmured as she opened the door to the office.

The office was bright, too bright for Kenzie's eyes as she followed Cori inside. A long counter separated the office from the waiting room, if one could call it that. There were two chairs, a small table covered with sailing magazines, and all the walls except one were cluttered with pictures of sailboats, old and new. The far wall was lined with trophies — big ones and small ones, some so new that their brass was still bright and shiny, and some so old that the engravings, long tarnished with time, were barely legible.

"Miss Etcher." A young man wearing an old tattered sailor's cap was seated behind the long counter. He jumped to his feet and his face offered a bright smile. "I knew you were coming in."

Kenzie's exhausted body sagged in disbelief at the news. "How did you know we were coming?"

"Because this arrived this afternoon." He held up a small, locked duffle bag. "I knew when this came in, you wouldn't be far behind it."

Big Polly. Kenzie sighed in relief as she ran her fingers through her curly locks. With the events of the afternoon, she had almost forgotten that he was sending her a care package. She was almost too tired to think and her body ached with fever. All she wanted was to get on her boat.

"Thanks, Dennis." She reached for the heavy canvas bag. "This is my friend, Laura." Cori nodded and Dennis offered a smile. "Can we get a lift out to the *Helen*?"

"Most certainly, Miss Etcher. Let me get my keys."

He walked to the back wall as Cori leaned over and whispered into Kenzie's ear, "Miss Etcher?"

"Shhh," she warned. "Did you think I would moor my boat under my real name? What would be the point of that?"

"I'm just wondering if Katherine Mackenzie is your real name."

"It is...for the most part."

Cori turned in question. "Meaning?"

Kenzie sighed. She was just too tired and sore to care. "Mackenzie is my middle name, my last name is LeGault."

LeGault. The name rippled something in Cori's memory. *LeGault.*

"Okay, ready to go," Dennis said. The young man's sudden reappearance prevented Cori from questioning Kenzie further about her name.

They walked down the aluminum gangplank to a small eight-foot dinghy. Within minutes, Dennis was maneuvering the small craft in and out of the moored sailboats to bring them alongside of *Helen's Gate.*

"Nice name," Cori said as she admired the scripted gold and blue lettering on the back of the boat.

"I named her after my grandmother."

"Here we go, ladies." Dennis grabbed hold of the rear railing.

"Thanks, Dennis," Kenzie said as she laid a hand on her beloved boat. Her arm felt heavy as she ran her fingers over the smooth surface of the hull. She could feel some of the tension leave her body when she finally stepped on board.

"Will you need a taxi pick up in the morning for breakfast?" he asked as he assisted Cori out of the dinghy.

Kenzie offered a hand to Cori and once she was safely on board, she reached back for the bag Dennis held out to her. "Actually, Dennis, I'll be pulling up anchor once I check everything out."

"You're leaving?" He was both surprised and disappointed. "But you're paid up 'til the end of the year."

"I'm leaving on business. You know how it is. I'll be back, though. Don't you worry."

"All right then. It was nice to meet you, Miss Laura. You have a safe trip, Miss Etcher," Dennis called as he powered his dinghy back toward the dock.

Kenzie turned to Cori and smiled. "Welcome aboard *Helen's Gate.*"

"Thanks. I can't believe we finally got here," she said as she looked over the sailboat. "Wow, I'm very impressed. Are you going to show me around?"

"You bet."

Handing Cori the duffle bag, Kenzie went to the base of the mast where she had a key hidden. She never knew when she would be aboard, so there was no point in packing a key with her. Cori was standing at the door that led to the accommodations below deck when Kenzie returned. Cori reached to turn the knob, just to see if it was indeed locked. The slight movement of the handle was all that was needed.

Ping.

Kenzie heard it and her eyes flew open wide in horror. A high-pitched whine — that most people never got a chance to describe — quickly followed. She flew at Cori with a full body tackle, taking them both over the side of the boat just as the propane tanks below ignited. *Helen's Gate* exploded in a massive fireball. The sound was heard all the way to Pacific Beach.

Cobra was sitting in the back of a taxi in a parking lot across from Sail Bay, nursing a swollen lip and a sore elbow, when the night sky around Mission Bay erupted with a large orange fireball. He didn't feel the blast, but he was certain those in the nearby vicinity had. He did not care about the loss of life and he did not care about the destruction of property. The new guy, Calvin, had done his job and Kenzie's boat was in a million pieces, and so were they — it was finally over. Leaning back in the taxi, he sighed in relief. The job was done and all he wanted to do was go home.

"Holy shit! Did you see that?" The taxi driver's eyes were wide as the fire and black plume of smoke climbed into the night sky.

"I most certainly did," Cobra said with an arrogant confidence. "I don't want to get caught up in the traffic, so you can take me to the airport now."

The driver nodded an absentminded acknowledgement as he glanced back and forth between the road and the flames. He pulled a u-turn in front of the wooden roller coaster, the famous landmark that marked the start of Pacific Beach. "You think it might be terrorists?" he asked, glancing into his rearview mirror at his passenger.

"Nah," Cobra answered. "Probably someone who wasn't paying attention to what they were doing."

The taxi picked up speed, leaving the burning wreckage behind them. "Which airport — international, commuter, or military?"

"Military," Cobra said, but then thought about it. "Actually, better make it international."

Dennis had almost made it back to the dock when the explosion lit up the sky. Before he knew what had happened, he felt the shockwave and then the intense heat. Looking back, he felt his stomach heave when he realized whose boat had exploded. His attention on the burning wreckage, Dennis failed to see the approaching dock and walkway. The small dinghy missed the dock, running its occupant head first into the aluminum gangplank and sending his limp body into Sail Bay.

Chapter 14

As she felt the full force of Kenzie's body slam against her, Cori's first instinct was to scream. They were in the air, falling toward the dark waters, when the fireball mushroomed toward the sky. The shockwave from the explosion pushed them hard into the water. Disoriented, Cori felt the cold blackness of the ocean engulf her as the fire above billowed over their heads. A heaviness dragged her down into the water. At first, she thought it was Kenzie pulling on her shoulder, then she realized it was the canvas bag. Letting it go would leave them once more with nothing, and that was not an option. Kenzie would need it. Only then did another thought erupt in her mind. *Kenzie!*

Kicking forcefully until she reached the surface, Cori breathed in a welcome breath of air. She searched the waters around her, but it was hard to see through the smoke and the burning debris. The fire was raging out of control. Twisting around, she swung the bag behind her and pulled the strap over her neck. That was when she saw Kenzie, floating face down, just out of reach. *Oh God, no!* Propelling herself with her legs, Cori reached her quickly. Pushing the scattered debris away from them, she flipped Kenzie over and lifted her face out of the water.

"Kenzie! Kenzie, open your eyes!" Panic swelled through Cori as she wiped the hair from Kenzie's face. "Oh God, Kenzie...please, open your eyes." There was no response, no sign of life in the still features. Fearing the worst, Cori pressed trembling fingertips to the side of Kenzie's neck...and waited as they bobbed in the water. Kenzie had a pulse and she was breathing. Cori closed her eyes and whispered a silent thank-you.

The intense heat of the flames refocused her on their immediate predicament. The water around them was littered with wreckage and some of it was on fire. However, thankfully those same flames also hid them from the onlookers beginning to gather along the shoreline. Everyone's attention seemed to be on the burning boat. Now if she could just get them to shore without being spotted.

Leaning further back into the water, Cori pulled Kenzie close to her and began the slow, arduous swim to the beach. She had not swum more than a few feet when Kenzie's body tightened and jerked.

A groan that was more of a gasp signaled Kenzie's return to consciousness as she struggled for air against the tight grip around her chest.

Cori stopped swimming and treaded water as she positioned herself so that she could see Kenzie's face. The gold-colored eyes had not yet opened, but Kenzie's grimace told Cori all she needed to know. "Kenzie...Kenzie can you hear me? Open your eyes," she pleaded.

"Can't...get...a breath," she answered with a grunt as her eyes fluttered open.

"Just hang on. I have to get us to shore." Cori was grateful that she was awake, but she needed to keep making progress toward landfall.

Kenzie tried to focus on her surroundings as Cori pulled them through the water. With slow, shallow breaths, Kenzie could feel the oxygen return to her lungs. Desperate for more air, she attempted a bigger breath, but it caused her to cough. The pain flashed through her body from multiple directions, causing her muscles to constrict, pulling her away from Cori and down into the water.

Cori had no choice but to stop. Pulling upward with every ounce of strength her small frame could muster, she was relieved to feel the sandy ground beneath her feet as she brought Kenzie's face back above the surface of the water. "Easy...easy," she said as she struggled to get them to shore.

With each cough, Kenzie's body protested her attempt to stand. Cori tugged, dragged, and stumbled into shallower water until Kenzie was able to help. "Come on, we're almost there."

"I can't...get a breath," Kenzie gasped, leaning heavily on Cori as she tried to get her feet under her.

Cori repositioned the bag on her shoulder and then moved in to pull Kenzie's arm around her neck. "Let me help you." A hiss of pain escaped through Kenzie's clenched teeth. "Is it your side?" Cori asked as they neared the shore.

"Amongst other things..." Kenzie tried to focus on the sandy beach. She felt weak and disoriented, but her training and her instinct for survival were strong. "We've got to get...out of here."

The words were quiet and lacked Kenzie's normal confidence. Cori was not sure whether Kenzie was talking to her or to herself. It didn't matter. She'd had the same idea.

Shouts and screams pulled Cori's attention away from Kenzie. People were pointing toward something floating near the dock. For a moment Cori wondered what it might be, then realized the distraction was what they needed to emerge from the water unseen. Cautiously, they moved together through the salty water until they made it to the shore. Only then did Cori turn to see what everyone was looking at, but there were too many people blocking her view for her to see anything.

Kenzie was quiet, but Cori could hear the difficulty she was having with her breathing. It was raspy and halting, and it was clear she was in pain. Now that they were out of the water, a part of her wanted to stop and tend to Kenzie, but Cori knew they had to get as far away from the flaming sailboat as possible. The shifting sand was hard to walk in, but as quickly as they could manage, they made it up the bank and onto the asphalt pathway that ran alongside the bay.

Curious onlookers had gathered on the shoreline. The flaming sea craft held everyone's attention. Some of the people had even moved into the water, searching through the floating debris for any victims. Fate was on Cori and Kenzie's side. They were far enough away that no one noticed the two women, huddled close together, moving slowly into the shadows.

Without the buoyancy of the water, Cori felt the weight of the bag. Grabbing the strap with one hand, she attempted to shift it higher on her shoulder. "Now where?"

Kenzie looked around and then gestured with her head toward a bike path that ran between two of the waterfront homes. It didn't matter at the moment where it led, just that it took them off the beach and out of view. They hurried the best they could away from the sounds of the burning wreckage, keeping close to the edge of the path and out of light from the lampposts. In the distance, sirens filled the warm night air.

Each step was a struggle but Kenzie kept her mind, and eyes, on the path. She could hear Cori's labored breathing as she strained under the weight she was carrying. It was only then that she realized it was not Cori's breathing she was hearing, it was her own. Her side was burning with pain, but she couldn't worry about that right now. They had to keep moving. The question was: to where?

Cori felt the resistance as Kenzie's pace slowed. "Kenzie, we have to keep moving," she pleaded as she tightened her grip.

"I know," Kenzie said, but her body would not respond to her mind.

"Come on." Fear was pushing Cori forward, fear and the fact that she didn't know what else to do. The sirens were growing louder and her anxiety pressed her beyond what her mind was thinking. The houses and cottages, packed tightly together, left no space for cover or any place they could hide. The night was still young enough for joggers and walkers, who thankfully paid them little attention, but she knew that wouldn't last for long. The explosion and the flames, along with the approaching sirens, were drawing people from all over the Mission Bay area.

Turning off the bike path into an alleyway, Cori spotted a covered boat parked against a fence behind one of the houses. "In there?"

Kenzie looked it over. She wanted to stop, she needed to stop, but she knew they had to move on. "No...you were right earlier...we have to keep moving."

Cori looked at Kenzie. "Shouldn't we just get out of sight for now?"

Kenzie closed her eyes. A place to hide would be good, but they couldn't stop. She wanted to, more than anything, but the training that had been drilled into her forced her onward. If she could just clear her head and think. Exhaustion was clouding her judgment, and the pain of each breath was pulling her down. *Move it, soldier. This is not the time to stop, LeGault. Keep it moving. Forward...always forward!* But she couldn't.

Suddenly Kenzie found her mind back in boot camp. Sergeant Carter was yelling at her to move. *"If you stop now, soldier, you're gonna die, and you're gonna take your entire platoon with you. Do you want to be responsible for every one of your friends dying? I don't think so, soldier. Move it, move it, move it!"* Each step was a struggle as she tried to shake Sergeant Carter from her mind. Though her mind tumbled in and out of time, she knew she was not in training. She was in an alley, running for her life. The sandy beach had been hard to run in... The sandy beach was suddenly the sands of the Middle East... *Cobra and Viper were there. And soldiers...*

Kenzie stumbled, and if Cori had not held her, she would have fallen to her knees. "Easy," Cori said as she strained to keep them both upright.

Kenzie shook her head and tried to keep her mind focused on the present, but she was just too tired. There were cars lining both sides of the alleyway and Kenzie reached out to steady herself against one. The simple movement brought a flash of unexpected pain and a wave of darkness. Her legs wobbled and she started a slow slide to the ground.

"Kenzie!" Cori did her best to hold on, but Kenzie's dead weight was more than she could bear. "Kenzie!" Fear and concern overwhelmed her as she dropped the bag and knelt down next to her fallen companion. Kenzie's eyes were open, but were distant and unfocused.

"Kenzie, look at me. Kenzie?" she begged as Kenzie closed her eyes with a grimace.

"I'm fine," she said with a groan. She was disoriented and having a hard time concentrating. "Just help me up."

"No, you are not fine! You're feverish. You keep mumbling to yourself and it's starting to scare me. I can't do this alone." Relieved that Kenzie was at least conscious for the moment, Cori looked up and down the alley to see if anyone was watching them. She was grateful to see that they were alone.

Cori's fear was enough to pull Kenzie's mind back together, at least for the moment. "Let's go."

"Can you stand?"

"Yeah...I'm fine, I just...slipped. Let's move on," Kenzie said as she steadied herself with her left arm. The movement was enough to dislodge her Colt .45 and, without warning, it clattered onto the ground, the sharp sound echoing loudly through the alley. Cori scooped the gun up and placed it into the front waistband of her pants before she assisted a grunting Kenzie back to her feet.

"Maybe we should rest here for a bit," Cori said, no longer having faith in herself or in escaping their situation.

Kenzie said nothing. It was taking all of her concentration just to get herself upright. Part of her wanted to rest. Her legs felt like tree trunks and her entire upper body felt like it was on fire. Her body was so hot she could feel the sweat rolling down her side beneath her damp clothing. She gingerly touched her side. The warmth oozing through her fingers told her more than she wanted to know. Pain was her friend, keeping her mind alert, telling her she was alive.

"We have to keep moving...now." She took a couple of uncertain steps and then turned to Cori, knowing she couldn't make it without her. "I'm okay, let's go."

Their progress was slow, but steady, until the alley ended at a long, high wooden fence. Looking left and right, Cori tried to decide which way to go. Kenzie was still standing, although every step was a struggle. As if sensing Cori's indecision, Kenzie lifted her head just as the sound of the sirens wailed to an end. The emergency personnel had arrived at the scene. "I think we should go right," she said.

Cori looked over at her and then in the direction she had suggested. "Isn't that back toward the bay?"

"Yeah," Kenzie said. "But if we go left, that will take us out to Mission Bay Boulevard — way too much traffic and too many people."

"Would that be such a bad thing? I mean, wouldn't we be safer with more people around?"

Kenzie hesitated, but only for a moment. "It might be safer, but I think we'd attract too much attention." She took a breath and swallowed hard against her own rising doubt and the pain that clouded her judgment. "We need to find a place to hide."

"What about one of these houses?"

"No, let's just keep moving."

Kenzie attempted to do just that, but her steps were slow and wobbly and Cori reached out to steady her. "I think you need to come up with a plan B." Cori moved closer to her, securing the bag on her shoulder as she attempted to wrap her arm around Kenzie's waist. "I can't pack you around San Diego all night."

"I'm okay," Kenzie said, holding up a hand to fend off Cori's assistance.

"No, you're not. You're a heartbeat away from passing out, and then what? We need to find someplace to rest, if only for a short while." She slid a sideways glance at Kenzie's pursed white lips. "And so I can take a look at that battered body of yours."

"Hmmm," she answered with a deep, rumbling grunt. "Any excuse to get your hands on my naked body again," she teased quietly, not taking her eyes off the path in front of her.

Cori shook her head in disbelief. "I'm glad to see your sense of humor was undamaged." *This woman is unbelievable.* "Your naked body is the last thing on my mind," she said. "Right now I'm more concerned with saving our asses by getting out of sight."

"I agree. Let's keep moving."

"Until what...you fall down...again?"

Kenzie refused to answer as they came to the end of the alleyway. They were back at the bay, the path blocked by several concrete cylinders that were in place to prevent vehicle traffic. The remains of Kenzie's burning boat still lit up the night skies while morbid spectators crowded the shoreline. Their detour down the alley and bike path had let them avoid all the onlookers.

Cori saw the anguish etched into Kenzie's tired face. Silently, she watched the embers floating upwards to the heavens. "I'm sorry about your boat, Kenzie," Cori said, almost regretting the intrusion on her privacy.

Kenzie sighed loudly and focused her attention on the woman beside her. "Material things can be replaced."

Knowing what the boat meant to her, Cori could only nod.

They watched for a moment as the emergency crew moved one of the fire trucks closer to the burning sailboat. Several small boats circled around, but it was the Coast Guard's Zodiac that caught Cori's attention.

"What's the Coast Guard doing?"

Kenzie squinted, trying to see what was drawing all the attention as two more small boats moved in next to the Coast Guard's vessel.

"Looks like they've spotted something in the water," Kenzie said as a diver flipped over the side of the rubber Zodiac and splashed into the water. A moment later, he lifted something up toward the outstretched arms of the men on the boat.

"Oh my God, it's a body," Cori said softly.

"Dennis," Kenzie said in a whispered breath.

Cori stared as they pulled the lifeless body from Sail Bay and into the Coast Guard's Zodiac. "Are you sure?"

"As sure as I can be from here." She swallowed hard against the regret rising in her throat. Collateral damage was what they called it, but this time it was more personal. "We need to get out of here, come on." She turned away from the wreckage.

"To where?" Cori asked as they set out on the paved path that ran alongside the water.

"Any place but here."

Moving away from what had been their original destination, they followed the water's edge to a large hotel at the north end of Sail Bay. The hotel's manicured lawns were brightly lit by rows of tall pedestal lights. The numerous volleyball pits were empty, but there were still too many people milling about for Kenzie's comfort.

Her eyes were on the move, searching for shelter or at least for a refuge away from the excitement around the bay. She saw another pathway lined with low-wattage ground lights, which directed hotel guests toward a tall wooden gate. "There." Kenzie motioned toward the gate.

Cori followed without thought. She trusted Kenzie and her instincts. However, as they approached the gate, a neatly printed sign dashed their hopes for an easy exit. GATE LOCKED — HOTEL GUESTS ONLY.

Cori tried the handle anyhow, in hopes that the sign was only a discouragement, but the gate was indeed locked. "Now what?"

Cobra had just paid his cabbie when his cell phone warbled in his pocket. "Yeah?" he answered curtly. He listened for a moment as he watched the cab pull away from the curb. "It's done." The voice on the other end of the phone responded sharply and Cobra's brow furrowed. "I said...it's done. I saw the explosion myself."

"And I'm telling you I want confirmation. Find their bodies and finish this! They're on American soil now and we cannot afford for this to become a story on the six o'clock news. Get it done, quickly and quietly, and I want visual confirmation. Understood?"

"Yes...sir." But the caller had already hung up.

"This is un-God damn-believable," he said to himself as he signaled for another cab. "You want visual goddamn confirmation. I'll give you visual confirmation!" He yanked the back door of the cab open and slid into the back seat. "Santa Clara Point in Sail Bay — now!" he ordered as he pulled his Blackberry from his pocket.

The cab ride was quick, though not quick enough for him. He threw some money at the driver and exited, slamming the door behind him. Cobra could smell the acidic smoke in the air as he moved quickly toward the flaming wreckage. The choppy water was littered with unrecognizable debris. There was nothing left of the boat. Several small boats and a Coast Guard Zodiac were buzzing about as he scanned the water for bodies.

A commotion near an aluminum gangplank drew his attention, and he smiled in satisfaction as he watched the men from the Coast Guard pull a body from the water. The smile slid from his face when he realized it was the body of a man. Cursing violently under his breath, Cobra scratched at the stubble on his chin. Hands on hips, he sighed as his eyes drifted over the crowd and the surrounding area. If they were not in the water, they had to be close by. Cobra moved slowly through the onlookers, his eyes never stopping as he pushed his way past a group of young men. They hurled insults at him for his rudeness, but he ignored them. Something had caught his attention at the north end of the bay. He quickened his pace as he watched the slow moving silhouettes. He was positive it was them. They were definitely women, and one was shuffling, her steps slow and unsteady.

"Gotcha," he said as he narrowed his eyes on his targets. He drew his gun and attached the silencer as he watched them come to a stop outside a tall wooden gate. It was easy to tell, even from this distance, the gate was locked. He had them cornered with nowhere to go.

Cori stared at the gate, willing it to open. "It's locked."

"We climb over," Kenzie said as she looked over her shoulder. No one was paying them any attention, but that was not what she was looking for. She felt something...or someone.

"You can barely keep upright and you think you're going to climb over this gate?"

Kenzie grudgingly accepted that Cori was right. She could feel that her side was bleeding again. She didn't want to look at it, knowing it would cause Cori even greater concern. "Let's go back and carry on along the pathway then. There have to be other exits somewhere further on. I don't want to be standing out here any longer than we have to."

"That makes two of us," Cori said.

They turned to head back the way they had come, when there was a *click* and the gate opened. A couple emerged from it, hand-in-hand, unaware of the women on the other side.

Cori offered a broad smile. "Hi."

The man smiled in return, but his smile faded as he scrutinized their appearance. "Rough night," Cori said with all the humor she could muster.

The man hesitated, then held the gate open as Cori reached for it. "Thanks. Saves us from having to dig our key out," Cori said lightly.

"No problem," he said as he and the woman continued on their way.

"That was a bit of luck," Cori said as they walked through the gate.

Kenzie turned to pull the gate shut and her eyes connected with someone moving swiftly along the bike path in their direction. "Goddamn it, he's like a fucking pit bull," she said. "Our luck just ran out!"

Kenzie's words filled Cori with panic. She looked back to see Cobra rushing toward the closing gate, his gun aimed directly at them.

"Go!" Kenzie urged as she tugged on the handle, but Cori was already moving. The gun made no sound, but the bullets striking the gate did as it solidly closed with a click behind them.

Racing away from Cobra, they found themselves in an open courtyard of the hotel. A curving brick pathway wound around large tropical plants and tall palm trees. Moving as fast as Kenzie could manage, they heard the sound of Cobra trying to break down the wooden gate. "That won't hold him for long," Kenzie said as the world wavered around her. Reaching out, she held onto Cori's small body for support.

"You don't have to tell me." Panic shortened Cori's breath. Feeling the taller woman sway against her, Cori looked at Kenzie. "Are you okay? Forget it, dumb question. We have to get out of here and find some place for you to rest." Looking over the courtyard, she searched for cover or an exit, anyplace to hide from the pursuing hit man.

There were a few people around and they turned with interest to the wet and battered women staggering hastily through the usually quiet hotel courtyard.

"There," Cori said, pointing to the glow of a red exit sign. The sound of breaking wood echoed behind them. She wrapped an arm around Kenzie's waist, ignoring her protests as she directed them to the exit. The brick path narrowed toward a door and Cori prayed it was not locked.

Kenzie was struggling to keep her focus as Cori reached for the handle and pulled open the door. They ducked through it without having seen Cobra. She knew he would not be far behind them. It was the first and only exit and he would see it, too.

They paused for only a moment as they found themselves standing on a residential street. Small one-story houses with manicured lawns lined the dimly lit road. It didn't matter where they went from here, and they both knew it. There was no plan, no destination, no safe place to run. Turning to their right, they headed for the nearest corner.

After only a block, Kenzie's breathing difficulty caused Cori to slow their pace. Moving through the dim light of a street lamp, she saw the blood Kenzie had been hiding from her. It was obviously a new and more serious wound as her entire right side was soaked in blood. "Oh my God, Kenzie!" Cori stopped and looked at Kenzie but the woman could barely lift her head. "We have to stop...now. You have a fever and you're bleeding...badly."

Kenzie wanted to argue, but she couldn't. She no longer had the strength.

Cori moved in closer, pulling Kenzie's left arm over her shoulder as she assessed the neighborhood for someplace, anyplace, to hide. Their options were limited, unless she wanted to knock on someone's door, which she did not. Moving out of the light, she spotted a large building with a perfectly manicured lawn dotted with perfectly pruned trees and large rocks. Looking skyward, she saw an illuminated cross on the roof of the building just beyond. A church. It was a perfect place to find refuge and maybe even some help for Kenzie. "Come on, just a bit further." Kenzie said nothing as she leaned heavily on Cori for support.

The heavy bag and Kenzie's weight slowed Cori's pace, but Cobra was not far behind them and that knowledge spurred her on. They were getting closer to the church and she could now see the neatly trimmed lawn belonged to a library. Cutting across the lawn toward the church, she began to question her decision to go there. Cobra was right behind them, and he would surely see the church's glowing cross, as she had. But what other choice did she have?

Crossing the empty street, they stepped onto the grass and Kenzie lifted her head to see where they were. The movement pulled Cori off balance and the two of them tumbled to the ground. Kenzie's groan echoed loudly in the quiet neighborhood. They came to rest next to one of the small trees decorating the library lawn. Cori flipped the bag off her shoulder and scrambled to her knees at Kenzie's side. Her eyes were closed and her breathing was erratic. Another moan escaped her lips.

"Kenzie?" Cori pleaded as she cupped her face in her hands. "Kenzie, open your eyes." She shook her head as she looked down the limp body. There was so much blood, she wondered how she had missed seeing it earlier. With as much care as possible in her haste, she maneuvered Kenzie over to one of the larger rocks near the trees and leaned her against it, eliciting a grimace. "Kenzie?" She didn't respond as Cori pulled back the corner of Kenzie's shirt. The wound that Cori had stitched was holding together, but just barely. Below that was a new gash, and it was bleeding profusely. "Oh, God." Cori glanced up at Kenzie's face and was surprised to see her eyes were open.

Moving closer to her face, Cori looked deep into the vacant golden eyes. "Kenzie, we have to get you some help. There's a church right over there. I've got to get you inside." She waited for a response, but none came. "Kenzie, can you hear me?"

Her head moved slightly and her eyelids drifted up and down.

Cori pulled the strap of the bag over her shoulder. Leaning down, she attempted to lift Kenzie to her feet, but couldn't budge her. Dropping the canvas bag, she stepped over and crouched in front of Kenzie to get a better grip. She struggled and strained, but to no avail. All that lifted were Kenzie's shoulders, and that made her groan. Reluctantly giving up, Cori crouched down. "I can't do it without you." She stopped when she saw that she was still talking to closed eyes. "Kenzie...Kenzie, you have to help me."

Kenzie struggled to open her eyes, to focus on Cori, but she could barely get them open.

Defeated, Cori's head dropped forward and she rested her chin on her chest. "I can't lift you."

"Cori." It was barely a whisper.

She lifted her head and was surprised to see Kenzie's eyes open. "Kenzie." The name was more a gasp of relief. She watched Kenzie's eyes grow larger and clearer.

"Why don't you just let her be?"

The voice behind Cori sent a hair-raising chill down her spine. She didn't turn around, instead she watched as Kenzie's eyes came alive with clear intent.

"Now stand the fuck up and move away from her slowly," Cobra said. Cori hesitated for a moment too long for Cobra's liking. He jammed the end of the silencer into the back of Cori's head. "Now!"

Kenzie pulled her eyes from Cobra and stared at Cori. Her nod was slight, but Cori saw it just as she felt Kenzie's hand slide up against her stomach, claiming the gun she had in her waistband. "You never cease to amaze me," Cori whispered to Kenzie as she lifted her hands in surrender. Straightening up, Cori stepped to the side, away from Kenzie as ordered.

Even though she had expected it, the boom from the Colt .45 in Kenzie's hand made Cori jump. The bullet slammed into Cobra's chest, stopping him instantly. His eyes grew wide in shock as he tried to lift his gun to retaliate. He never had the chance as the second bullet hit him directly between his eyes, dropping him where he stood.

The Colt .45 held its position for a heartbeat longer before Kenzie dropped it to her side. Her head tilted back as her eyelids slid closed.

Chapter 15

Cori stood for a moment, her heart slamming against her chest as her ears rang with the echoing thunder. She swallowed hard as she looked from one body to the other. *What am I supposed to do now? There's a dead body at my feet and a nearly unconscious woman next to it. I need to get help, but from where? There is no way I'm leaving Kenzie here alone, bleeding and... Awake!*

Kenzie was staring at her, her head lifted with apparent effort, watching in pained silence. Watching and waiting, as if reading the dilemma in Cori's mind.

A dog barking in the distance snapped Cori out of her impasse. They needed to move on, now. Kneeling in front of Kenzie, Cori grabbed the gun and shoved it back in her waistband. Then she once again slung the bag over her shoulder and prepared to hoist Kenzie to her feet. "I think we need to get out of here."

Lights were coming on around the neighborhood and it was enough to urge Kenzie upward. It was a painful struggle and she could not have gotten on her feet without Cori's help. Her steps were slow and heavy, but soon they were away from the library and away from Cobra's body.

"They're going to have a hard time explaining that," Kenzie muttered weakly as they came to the end of the block and turned down an alley behind the church.

"What's that, the shot?"

Kenzie had to take a couple of breaths before she could answer. "No. Cobra's dead body... If they ID him...the military would have...declared him dead...years ago..." Her breath came in a raspy rattle as she stumbled and swayed in an effort to stay upright. "Just like...just like me."

"Already declared dead?" There was no explanation to satisfy her curiosity.

Kenzie was relying more and more on Cori for support, her level of consciousness fading with each step. The alley was too dark to see anything, but Cori knew Kenzie was in bad shape. She was desperate to find somewhere to hide, someplace to rest and care for Kenzie. The fact that she was certain no one was behind them at the moment gave her very little assurance. Kenzie had made her aware that someone would soon be there to take Cobra's place.

The pavement in the alley was badly in need of repair. It slanted sharply to the center to form a spillway for the hard rains of San Diego. It made their progress even slower. There was a light on in one of the businesses across the alley from the back door of the church. As they staggered closer to it, Cori read the name: Grand Avenue Animal Hospital.

A hospital! Albeit an animal hospital, it was still a hospital...with a light on. "This way, Kenzie," she said to the unresponsive woman in her arms. "Come on, stay with me." Cori heaved at the weights dragging down on both her shoulders. She knew if they had to go any further, she herself might just drop where she was standing.

The back door of the veterinary hospital was open, but a heavy-duty security screen door covered it. Music was playing inside and she could hear someone moving metallic things around as she sang along to a lively country song. Her key was off, but her heart was in it as she loudly belted out the chorus. Cori cautiously moved into the light and banged on the door. The singing stopped instantly.

The motion of knocking caused the heavy canvas bag on Cori's shoulder to slip to the ground. She let it be. All of her strength was needed to hold onto Kenzie as she anxiously waited for someone to appear. Cori angled their position, hoping to hide their bloodstained clothing. Kenzie mumbled something but Cori couldn't make it out. She tightened her grip on Kenzie's waist, feeling the blood soaking through her shirt. Cautiously aware of their visibility, she looked both ways down the alley. At the moment, they were still alone.

Cori raised her hand to knock again and this time the volume of the radio diminished. Whoever was inside had definitely heard the knocking. Once again, Cori lifted her hand, but this time her knock stopped in mid-motion when she saw the silhouette of someone behind the security screen. "Hello?"

"We're closed, go away," an understandably nervous female voice stated.

"Please," Cori begged. "My friend...she's injured." She motioned toward Kenzie with her head. The movement caused Kenzie to flinch, which made her moan. "Please...we need some help." She could hear movement behind the door, but Cori still could not make out the woman behind it. "Please...can you just let us in?"

"I-I can't. It's against hospital policy to open the door after hours." The voice was closer to the door now.

"I-I can appreciate that." Cori tried her best to remain calm, sensing that playing on the woman's compassion might be the key to getting the door opened. "But my friend here is badly hurt." Cori moved a little, giving the person behind the door a chance to see the blood that covered Kenzie's clothes as well as her own.

"Holy crap, she's bleeding badly...I'll call an ambulance for you."

Cori panicked. An ambulance and more attention was not what they needed. "No! Please just let us in."

"I can't. I don't want any trouble. I'll just call you an ambul—"

"No, you won't." The time for niceties was over. Cori pulled out Kenzie's gun and leveled it at the form on the other side of the door. "Now...open the door!" Her tone sounded more confident than she was as she held the large gun firmly in her grip. She could not believe she was now holding a gun on someone, but she had no choice. "Open the door," Cori demanded firmly as she pulled Kenzie tighter to her side.

"You can't shoot through this door," the woman said with shaky certainty.

"That .45 will blow a hole through that door...and you," Kenzie said without lifting her head or opening her eyes.

Her voice was barely audible, but it was loud enough for the woman on the other side of the door to hear. There was a faint click and the security screen opened slowly. The voice belonged to a woman of appreciable size, with chestnut-colored hair, wearing hospital scrubs with puppy dogs on them.

"Please don't hurt me," she said as she came face to face with Cori holding the gun.

"That isn't my intention, but my friend here needs help." Cori grunted under the strain of Kenzie's weight as they climbed the step up and into the vet hospital. "Grab our bag, close the door, and lock it behind us," Cori said as she motioned to the door with the gun. "And turn out that light."

She did as she was directed and then turned back to face the two battered and bruised women. In the light of the back room, she got a better look at them and she was surprised to realize they didn't look that much older than she was, but it was hard to tell for certain. Their clothes were dirty, tattered, and covered in blood, and their hair was tousled and wet. Both looked like they were on the verge of collapse, especially the dark-haired one who appeared almost unconscious. The other woman still held the gun on her.

"My friend?" Cori reminded the woman as she watched her giving them the once over. Cori didn't care what they looked like, all she cared about was helping Kenzie.

"Oh...ah...this way," she said, directing them out of the back room.

"After you," Cori said with a wave of the gun.

They entered the treatment room of the small hospital, where the even brighter lights caused Cori to squint. It was a room similar to its counterpart in a human hospital with its medical equipment and supplies, just a whole lot smaller. There were several rooms off the main one, separated only by glass walls and doors.

"Put the bag on the floor," Cori said as she turned to examine Kenzie. "Kenzie...stay with me."

"I'm here," she mumbled. An attempt to lift her head only caused it to roll to the side.

"Where can I take her?" Cori asked.

"Here...but I don't think she'll fit on the table. It's not made for people, only animals."

"I don't care. Just give me a hand with her, and be careful."

She looked from the gun in the woman's hand to the semi-conscious woman at her side, and knew she would be careful for her own sake.

Cori watched with mixed emotion. Part of her was concerned only about Kenzie, but she could see the woman's fear and apprehension. "What is your name?"

The woman was uneasy about the question, but since it came with a gun pointed at her, she felt compelled to answer. "Heather... Heather Siddall," she said as she pushed up her round-framed glasses with her forearm. It was a movement of habit for someone who was used to having their hands otherwise occupied.

"Heather, I'm not going to hurt you...but my friend needs your help. So please," Cori stared hard into Heather's dark brown eyes, "help me."

"Are you gonna shoot me if I don't...or only after I do?"

Cori studied the woman's face and considered the honesty of the question. It was not that long ago that she had been in the exact same situation, only it was Kenzie holding the gun on her, but she was not the killer that Kenzie was, and her intentions were very different.

"I'm not going to kill you, shoot you, or harm you in any way...if you do as I ask. I just want to help my friend, and once she's looked after we'll be out of here. But," Cori made sure that Heather was paying strict attention, "if I have to choose between you and her, or keeping her alive...then all bets are off. Now please, help me get her on to the table."

After a moment of thought, Heather complied, and between the two of them, they got Kenzie onto the examination table. The only way to get her to fit was to keep her knees bent and her head at the very end. Heather was right — it was not made to accommodate the human form.

Cori backed away from the table. "Okay, now do something. Help her."

"What? I'm not a doctor...I'm only a tech."

"A what?"

"A technician. I'm not a vet."

Cori's shoulders sagged in exhaustion and defeat as she looked at Kenzie. Her eyes were closed, her face was flushed and glistening with sweat. "Just do something...help her." Cori looked at the woman with pleading, desperate eyes. "Please, Heather."

"Apparently you're not getting this. I work with animals, not humans."

"We all bleed and we all breathe, don't we? So do something," Cori demanded, her confidence returning after her moment of doubt. "Now!"

Heather looked at the tightly held gun, then at the still woman on the examination table. She didn't think the blonde would use the gun, but she'd been wrong before. Donning a pair of surgical gloves, Heather cut away the bloody top, revealing a wound about four inches long just two inches away from the other laceration Cori had recently sutured. She ripped open a package holding an abdominal pad and placed the sterile bandage on the wound. "Hold that," she said and Cori quickly complied.

The moment Cori applied pressure, Kenzie's eyes flashed opened and she looked from one woman to the other.

"Kenzie...it's okay...you're going to be okay." Cori looked at Heather as if willing her statement to be true. "Isn't she?"

"She has a raging fever and she's lost a lot of blood. I'm...I'm not sure what I can do."

Cori looked into Heather's face. "Do something," she said in aggravation.

"I keep telling you, this is a hospital for animals not people."

"That wasn't a request," Cori said. "Do something, and do it now!"

The rising volume of Cori's voice was enough to push Heather into action. After all, the woman was right — a person bleeding was not much different from an animal bleeding. She took a deep breath and steeled herself to comply. She reached up and pulled down a bright light with a magnifying glass in the center. She positioned the light onto Kenzie's side then reached for a handful of assorted dressings and bandages. Her hands were shaking so badly she could barely open the packet of gauze squares. She took another deep breath and started cleaning the area around both wounds. After a minute or two, she motioned for Cori to remove her hand from the abdominal pad. The flow of blood had slowed considerably, allowing her to examine the fresh wound as she dabbed at the oozing blood. She flushed it several times with a syringe filled with sterile water. Once the wound was clean, she pulled down the light and looked at it through the magnifying glass. "I think there's something in there," she said, more to herself than to Cori, "but I think I need to give her something for the fever before we do anything else." She didn't wait for a response as she unlocked and opened a side cabinet where they kept the hospital's supply of drugs and medications.

"She had a shot of antibiotic earlier today, but it hasn't seemed to help any. What do you mean...something in there?" Cori asked as she watched Heather picking through the different vials.

"I don't know. It's hard to tell. At the moment I'm more concerned with her fever. You say she had a dose of antibiotics?" Heather selected a small glass vial and read the label.

"Yeah, but it was past its expiration date. And, it doesn't seem to have made a difference."

Heather selected an antibiotic. "I'm not sure about this," she said as she inserted the tip of a small needle into the vial to withdraw some of the drug.

"Not sure about what?" Cori asked.

"Cephalexin." She held the small vial out for Cori to examine. "It's an antibiotic we would give animals that have an infected wound like your friend has."

"Anything would be better than nothing," Cori said.

Heather finished preparing the dose and then turned to her patient. Cutting away the top of Kenzie's pants, Heather exposed her thigh. She wiped the area with an alcohol swab and was about to inject the antibiotic when Kenzie suddenly reached out and seized her hand.

"What is that?" Kenzie said, lifting her heavy head off the table.

The mumbled question startled both Heather and Cori. "It's Cephalexin. It's for your infection," Heather said, looking into Kenzie's striking golden eyes.

Kenzie looked at Cori, her question clear.

"It's okay." Cori nodded. "That's what it is."

Kenzie rested her head on the table and closed her eyes. "It better not make me bark like a dog."

Heather was not sure how to respond to the patient's attempt at humor. She proceeded with administering the medication. Lidocaine was next, and once Cori gave her approving nod, Heather injected it around the wound site.

"We should wait a minute or so, until it takes effect. I wasn't sure how much to give her, but I used the same dosage that we use for a large dog." She examined her patient, wondering what she should do next. She was not a doctor and she was not a vet, but she was sure she had done everything right. "We should get her clothes off. They are no good to her now."

"Okay," Cori said, and then watched as Heather cut off the remains of Kenzie's clothes. Once they were in a heap, she unfolded a blanket and laid it over her.

Cori was relatively quiet, watching Heather as she re-examined Kenzie's side. She might not have the medical expertise, but she seemed quite competent in what she was doing, or rather, what she had been forced to do — at gunpoint. Cori looked down at the gun in her hand, having almost forgotten that she was still holding it. *What have you done, Cori?* The guilt was over-whelming. It almost brought her to tears as she laid the gun on the counter. "I'm sorry. What were you saying?"

"I think maybe we should x-ray her side. It looks like there's something stuck in the wound. I'm not good enough to go digging in after it, but I could x-ray it and that would tell me..." Heather looked up at Cori and was surprised to see her gun on the counter.

Cori stood there for a moment, looking down at the gun, her head dropped to her chest. She turned back and looked at Heather, no longer the woman with the power of a weapon, but a woman on the verge of tears.

"I'm sorry I pointed a gun at you, Heather," Cori said. "You have to understand, I was desperate." She placed a hand on Kenzie's forearm.

"Apparently," Heather said flippantly.

"I didn't know what else to do. I'm just as scared as you are, and almost for the same reasons." She covered her sob with her hand and then quickly wiped away the tears. "It wasn't that long ago that I was just a student, minding my own business, taking classes and worrying about whether or not I would have the grades to pass this semester, now here I am..." Her voice caught and she stopped, trying to regain her composure.

Heather watched her with conflicting emotions. She was a compassionate person and her heart went out to the woman. In any other circumstances, she would have gathered the woman in her arms, but she reminded herself this was different. Heather studied the haggard, dejected blonde. "I don't understand. If you didn't do anything wrong, why couldn't you go to a regular hospital?"

"It's a long story, and one that I don't have time to explain, but..." She looked down at Kenzie's face. It was the first time she had seen it so relaxed and peaceful. "We aren't bad people, but I can't say the same for the people chasing us."

"People chasing you?" Heather's eyes darted to the back door as if expecting the bad people to come through at that moment.

"Don't worry. They aren't chasing us anymore."

The truth dawned on Heather. "The gunshots...I heard gunshots earlier...and an explosion. Was that you?"

"No...yes...well, partly. The gunshots were her. She saved my life...again." She reached out and caressed Kenzie's scarred cheek. "Now it's my turn to save hers. Just tell me what we have to do. I have a year of pre-med, but I can guarantee that you know more than me." She raised her eyes and looked directly at Heather. "By the way, my name is Cori and this is Kenzie. I can't say anything more than that...actually I'm not sure if I know much more than that...but I promise you, we will not hurt you. We just need to get her fixed up and then we'll be out of here."

Heather believed her. They didn't look like bad people, but then again, she did not really know what bad people looked like. "We need to move her onto the x-ray table. It's in another room."

"Okay," Cori said with a tired sigh, "And thank you, Heather." She reached for the gun and slid it back into her waistband. It was a struggle, but the two managed to carry Kenzie's unconscious body into the next room and onto the x-ray table. Kenzie mumbled and moaned several times, but never woke up.

Heather was more relaxed as she took the x-rays. This was part of what she did on a routine basis, and it didn't hurt that she no longer had a large gun pointed at her. With the developed films in her hand, she returned to the room where Cori was standing over a semi-conscious Kenzie.

"I have the x-rays," she said as she held them up.

Kenzie nodded as she blinked hard several times, trying to focus.

Heather slid a film into a slot on the x-ray viewer and then flicked on the box light. Leaning in to study the film, Heather squinted in question as Cori stepped forward for a better view.

"What is that?" Cori asked, looking at a long, thin shard contrasting brightly against the dark of the negative.

Heather stepped back, tilting her head back and forth. "It looks like a sliver of wood, maybe."

Then Cori spotted something else on the x-ray that should not have been there. "What the hell is that?" she asked, her eyes focused on the abnormality.

Heather slid another film up next to the one in place and looked to see if the item in question was on both pictures. It was. "I have no idea."

Kenzie struggled to sit up, placing most of her weight on her left elbow as she studied the film. Her eyes narrowed as she glared at the small dot on the x-ray. "I do," she said angrily.

Chapter 16

The sun was setting on the West Coast and Winston Palmer was out on his sundeck enjoying an expensive, albeit illegal, Cuban cigar. Soaking in his pricey waterfront view, he did his best to relax. *Life is good*, he thought as he drew deeply and blew out the sweet-smelling smoke. He heard the phone ring. Not wanting it to intrude on his quiet time, he chose to ignore it. The second ring was cut short, and he knew that his driver had probably answered it. Moments later, the young Asian appeared with the phone in his hand.

"It's for you," Derek said.

As he accepted the phone, Palmer snapped, "Did you think it would be for anyone else?" He waited for Derek to leave. When the driver delayed, Palmer inquired brusquely, "Is there something else, Derek?"

"No, sir." He bowed slightly and turned away. "Rat dung," he whispered under his breath as he returned to the house.

Once Derek was out of earshot, Winston spoke into the phone, "Palmer."

Ennis Nelson was at his desk in the office next to Winston Palmer's, on the top floor of the Palmer Building, one of Seattle's tallest and most glamorous office towers. He had been Mr. Palmer's executive assistant for just over seven years. He enjoyed his job, despite the fact that there were times it required him to cross lines, both illegal and immoral. "Good evening, sir. I wanted to let you know that the last of our protestors will be arriving next week in Davos, Switzerland, for the WTO demonstrations. I have a meeting scheduled with them and will make sure everyone is on board with what will be expected."

"Very good, Ennis. It's essential that they understand what they've been hired to do."

"They do, sir. I don't think it will take much to ignite this group into a riot. They're quite passionate about their cause."

"I don't give a rat's ass about their cause. I just want a riot as big as the one in Seattle in '99. The riots, not the World Trade Organization, should be the lead story in European and Asian markets, as well as around the world."

"Our reporters and insiders have been advised what is to be mentioned and what is to be buried, but unfortunately, sir, we have no control over what is on the Internet."

"Well, thankfully, most people don't pay that much attention to the news on the Internet."

"Not yet, sir, but I think the time is coming."

"Ha. That's what people said about television. 'No one will read newspapers anymore,' they said. 'They'll be glued to their TVs for the morning news.' Bullshit. John and Joan Public still like to drink their morning coffee while they read their newspapers, filled with stories that are made of half-truths and glossed over media events. Trust me, Ennis. You get that riot big enough, and most people won't read anything more than what is under the headlines. Now, is there something else?" Palmer asked, anxious to get back to enjoying his cigar.

"No, sir. That was it. Will I see you in the morning?"

"At some point," Palmer replied with dismissal. He ended the call and placed the phone on the table, then leaned back and took a puff. The phone rang again.

"Palmer," he answered gruffly, annoyed at the new interruption.

"Calvin is on his way to retrieve the body," the caller said.

"Finally."

"Not her. Cobra." Bucannon sighed heavily into the phone. This was not a call he had wanted to make, but he had no choice.

"For Jesus..." Palmer slammed his hand down on the arm of the chair, knocking expensive ash all over his clothes. He jumped to his feet and attempted to brush it off, but only succeeded in rubbing the dark ash into his khaki pants. "Do you people not understand what's at stake here? How hard is it to kill these women?"

"Calvin set the explosive, Cobra confirmed it, but somehow they got away."

"Call Manuck. This is his mess, and he needs to clean it up."

"Yes, Senator."

"On second thought, don't bother. I'll make that call myself."

"Yes, sir."

Palmer seethed for several long seconds before he dialed the number. It rang twice and then a low, unhurried voice answered the phone.

"It's me." Palmer knew he didn't need to identify himself further. "It appears San Diego was unsuccessful, and we've lost Cobra."

"I know. Viper will be there shortly to pick up where Cobra left off." There was no immediate response but Manuck knew the senator was still on the line because he could hear him grumbling.

"You do realize the ramifications if Maquinar were to become public knowledge? Covert is supposed to be just that, covert."

"You don't have to tell me. We're all in this together."

"Jesus Christ, Manuck, I can't keep burying this. If the wrong person even gets wind of this, we're all going to jail...or worse." Palmer sat down in his chair and reached for the ashtray.

"Relax, Senator, no one is going to jail. Once we've eradicated the problem, everyone will lie low for a while, then we can reorganize and be back in business. Nothing has to change."

"Well obviously something has to, or we wouldn't be in this mess to start with. I told you we should have gotten rid of that woman in the beginning. If she has put it all together, we're all going down." Palmer bit hard into his cigar.

"That's not going to happen, Senator."

"You said that before, and look at the mess we're in now. The body count is rising and the collateral damage is out of control. And we have no damned clue as to where those two are!"

Kenzie's eyes narrowed as she stared at the small white mass that stood out so sharply on her x-ray. It was the size of an apple seed, though more rectangular in shape.

Heather and Cori turned to look at her, and Cori asked, "What is it?"

"Get it out of me," Kenzie said as she laid back in exhaustion.

"But what is it?" Cori persisted as she moved to Kenzie's side.

Her eyes were shut and her features were drawn. "It's the reason we've had someone on our ass at every turn."

Heather leaned closer to the x-ray. She had seen something like it before, but never in a human.

Cori felt the small hairs on the nape of her neck tingle. "Kenzie...what is it?"

"It's an identity chip," Heather said as she glanced from the x-ray to the women. "Isn't it?"

"In a manner of speaking." Kenzie opened her eyes to look at Cori. "It's worse than that. It's a tracker. This means they know I'm here." Kenzie felt defeated and betrayed. *When the hell did they put that in me, and why? Or do we all have one?* "Shit," she muttered regretfully as she closed her eyes. "We should have checked Cobra...to see if he had a reader." She took several breaths and then continued. "That's how they keep finding us." Kenzie opened her eyes and stared at Heather. "You need to get this out...now."

"I-I can't," she stammered. "I can't cut into you. I don't have the training for that."

"You have to. And do it quickly." Kenzie blinked several times as her consciousness began to fade. "Cori..."

"I'm right here." She settled a gentle hand on Kenzie's arm.

"She has to get it out...destroy it...crush it..." Kenzie's voice faded.

"Cori, I can't cut into her," Heather pleaded.

"We don't have a choice."

Heather looked down at the unconscious woman and then back at the x-ray. The device did not look as if it was very deep into the subcutaneous tissue, but still, she had never taken a scalpel to an animal, never mind...

"Now, Heather," Cori said.

Quickly, yet methodically, she gathered what she would need to excise the small tracking device, as well as the instruments she needed to remove the sliver of wood and stitch up Kenzie's wound. She was shaking on the inside, but her hands were steady. Flushing the wound first, she removed the wood before she sutured Kenzie's side and bandaged it. She and Cori then carefully turned Kenzie over so Heather had access to her back. They pinpointed the location of the device and Cori noticed it was under the small scar she had seen on Kenzie's back the night on the fishing boat.

"You're doing fine," Cori said as Heather hesitated, scalpel in hand.

Taking another deep breath, Heather slowly drew the blade across Kenzie's skin. A few moments later she pulled the electronic device out of Kenzie's lower back with a set of forceps and dropped it into Cori's waiting hand.

It was the size of a small vitamin caplet, but clear, and in the bright light of the operating room, Cori could see some of the electronics. Big Brother was indeed always watching. She dropped it to the floor and raised her foot to step on it.

"Wait." Heather held up her hand.

"Why? She said destroy it."

"But if you destroy it here, this will be the first place they'll look."

Cori shook her head at her own lack of foresight. Heather was right. She plucked the capsule off the floor and held it between her fingers. "Any suggestions?"

"Well...ah...let me think for a sec." Heather looped the suture twice around the tip of the needle driver and knotted another stitch into Kenzie's back. "Where are you heading from here?"

With everything that had happened, their eventual destination was the last thing on Cori's mind. They had nowhere to go and no means of getting there. She had a little bit of money in her American bank account, but something told her the moment she withdrew it, someone out there would know.

Heather watched the defeat wash over Cori's face. "You have a plan, don't you?"

"We did." She held the capsule in her palm and closed her fist over it, squeezing it tightly.

Heather watched for a moment and then returned her attention to finish Kenzie's bandaging. "I'm done, we can roll her back."

Cori nodded, her mind a whirl of possible destinations.

With Kenzie lying on her back, Heather went about cleaning up the surgical suite, periodically glancing at Cori, her sympathy growing with each look. "I'll be right back. I'm just going to go and get her some meds," Heather said, motioning toward the door.

Cori shrugged. If Heather wanted to escape now, there was no point in stopping her. She had done all that Cori had asked and more.

Cori was deep in thought when Heather returned.

"Okay. I have a bottle of Cephalexin for the infection. She needs to take two tablets, three times a day. The Meloxicam," Heather held out another bottle, "she needs to take two, once a day, to help with the infection and the fever."

"Thank you, Heather. I don't know what we would have done without you." Cori took the pill bottles and stowed them in the duffle bag on the floor where Heather had dropped it "We'll go now."

"Do you know where you're going?"

"No," Cori admitted reluctantly.

Heather looked from Cori's crushed expression to the unconscious woman on the table. "And how far are you going to get, lugging her around?"

Looking over at Kenzie, Cori bit at her bottom lip as she struggled to keep her tears of frustration at bay.

"You can't stay here."

"I know," Cori said quietly.

Heather was a big woman, with a big heart. These two women had entered her workplace and forced her to perform surgery, but she still felt compassion for them. She was convinced they were not bad people. She glanced at her watch and made a decision. "Tell me where you want to go."

"Pardon?"

"Tell me where you want to go and I'll take you...as long as it isn't too far. But we have to figure out what we're going to do with that thing." She motioned to the tracker in Cori's hand.

"I can't ask you to do that, Heather."

"You're not asking me. You're commanding me at gunpoint," she said with a slight smile. "At least that's what I'm going to tell my boss and the authorities...eventually...once you're long gone."

An angel with big, brown, bedroom eyes, Cori thought as she wrapped her arms around Heather's neck. "Thank you. I don't know when or how, but one day we'll pay you back. I promise."

"Whatever. Let's just get you out of here, and get rid of that."

"You're an angel, Heather."

"Actually," she said with a bright smile, "they refer to me as Princess."

"Princess?"

"P.I.C. — Person in Charge, or in my case, Princess in Charge," she said, emphasizing each word with a zigzagging snap of her fingers.

For the first time in a long time, Cori laughed.

They carefully dressed Kenzie in a spare tracksuit the hospital kept around in case someone needed an emergency change of clothes.

"Won't they miss it," Cori asked.

"No, it never fit any of us, so it serves them right, for keeping a size 10 track suit when none of us could fit into it," Heather said as they dragged/carried Kenzie outside to the tech's small pickup truck. It took some maneuvering, but they finally managed to get Kenzie into the backseat. She roused several times, but never for very long.

Heather checked on the animals in the hospital one last time before she locked the back door. She was leaving enough of a mess that the morning staff might be inquisitive, but not enough for them to be alarmed. And by that time, she'd have come up with a reasonable explanation of what had happened.

Heather climbed into the driver's seat beside Cori and started up her truck. "Where to?"

"I don't know. Let's just leave."

Heather drove out of the alley and came to a stop on Grand Avenue just as a city bus roared by. It stopped at a bus stop just down the corner from them and they watched as an older woman disembarked.

When the bus pulled away, an idea began to take shape in Cori's mind. "Heather."

"Yeah."

"Follow that bus"

When Manuck deplaned, he was not dressed in a uniform, nor was there anything about him, other than his rigid demeanor, that indicated his military rank or position of authority. The only things that identified him as military were the plane and the base where it landed. Colonel Manuck descended the stairs and before his feet could hit the warm tarmac, a large, dark SUV pulled up to greet him. There were no outward trappings that revealed who was in the vehicle, and he thought that a good thing. He opened the door and slid into the backseat.

Calvin was behind the wheel. He was ex-CIA and ex-military, so he found it hard not to salute a superior officer. "Evening, sir."

"Get us out of here, before someone starts asking questions."

Calvin nodded and followed the colonel's orders. Viper was sitting in the passenger seat, clicking away on a laptop. He turned slightly and nodded to his boss before turning his attention back to the screen to finish what he was doing.

"What do we know?" Manuck asked.

Viper stopped typing long enough to hand him a file folder. "That's not about the women, sir. All that is," he nodded at the papers in Manuck's hand as the colonel quickly flipped through them, "is the transcript of the initial call concerning the explosion at the marina. There was a body found, a...Dennis Squires."

Manuck lifted some papers and read the 9-1-1 call sheet of the emergency personnel. "Who the hell is Dennis Squires?"

"He worked for the marina and was an alumnus of the university sailing team," Calvin said as he exited the airport.

"And where does he fit into all of this?"

"He doesn't. He's just collateral damage," Viper answered callously.

Manuck looked up from the file. "Where are we heading?"

"Mission Bay, sir. That's where Cobra was found. We can stop there and regroup, then figure out what our next move should be." Calvin glanced in the rearview mirror. "I didn't think you'd want to be doing this at the division office or on the base. Too many questions all the way around."

"Good," Viper said, tapping away on the laptop. "I don't like hanging out with you ex-CIA spooks anyway."

Calvin's face tightened in contempt, his narrowed eyes illuminated by the light from the dashboard. "Yeah, well, beats hanging out with you and your jungle jarheads any day," he said.

"Bring it on, college boy. I know more ways—"

"Enough! We have other issues at hand, gentlemen. Once this mess has been cleaned up, if you two want to kick the shit out of each other, I might just pay to see that happen, but let's concentrate on the problem at hand." Manuck turned his attention back to the file. "Where is Cobra's body now?"

"At the morgue. He was found a few blocks away from the explosion. He'd been shot twice — once in the chest, and a money shot between the eyes. I spoke with the locals, and the coroner, don't worry, they saw the badge not a name."

"What story did you give them?" Manuck asked.

"Just said we were looking into the explosion, possible terrorist connection, and when the call came in that a body had been found that close without ID, we figured it was worth a peek. They bought it. I pulled rank, and got a few moments alone with the body. I got his microchip tracker and this—" Viper held up Cobra's Blackberry and then slipped it into his front pocket.

"Is it working?"

"Yup. I've downloaded the information onto my laptop."

"Where is she?"

"At the Greyhound bus station, near Old Town," Viper said with a sneer as he turned his attention back to the screen.

"What?" Manuck looked up in disgust. "Millions of dollars spent on training her, and she runs to the bus station to get out of town."

"She's desperate, or maybe she's injured."

Calvin pulled into a nearly empty parking lot just southwest of the remnants of Kenzie's boat. "Her boat was over there. I had everything set before you sent Cobra to the border. He was efficient...I think they just got lucky. You can still see the smoke, and the fire department and Coast Guard are still there. Cobra was found a couple of blocks north of here."

"How did they get to the bus station from here? They surely didn't walk."

"That we don't know," Viper said.

"Something doesn't add up. This is a highly trained soldier, black ops and special services, the works. I'm having a hard time believing that when her plans fell apart, she chose to hop a bus. This isn't a decision LeGault would make."

Calvin reached into his pocket and pulled out a flip pad. He balanced his wrist on the steering wheel while he searched for some information. "Cori Evans withdrew twenty-three hundred dollars, pretty much the balance of her one and only account, at three thirty seven this morning at a Money Mart — that's a check cashing place."

Viper's fingers tapped madly as he searched for additional information.

"Twenty-three hundred bucks isn't much to run on," Manuck said as he closed the file folder.

"Apparently it was enough. She purchased two bus tickets to Branson, Missouri."

"Missouri? Who the hell is in Branson, Missouri?"

Viper flipped to another screen, "Evans' mother lives in Springfield."

Manuck's brow furrowed as he looked down at his watch. It was almost five in the morning, and he was hoping to wrap up this catastrophe so he could be home by lunchtime. Going to Springfield was not in his plans. "What time does the bus leave for Branson?"

"Six thirty," Viper said.

Manuck thought for a moment and then tossed the file folder onto the dark leather seat beside him. "We don't want to get there too early and spook them, but I think we should drive past and take a look at the layout and then go from there."

Calvin obediently started up the SUV and set course for the Greyhound bus station.

Heather split her attention between Kenzie and the glass doors outside the ticket office. The last thing she wanted was for Kenzie to wake up without Cori there. She liked the young student, that was why she had offered to help them, but the woman with the golden eyes frightened her. *Who runs around with a microchip in their back — and doesn't know it?*

She impatiently drummed her fingers on the steering wheel. "Come on, come on." She scanned the parking lot, but she had no idea why. *Who am I looking for, anyway?* Several vehicles pulled up and dropped off passengers, but no one looked out of place. Most of them seemed to be families. They got out of their cars to give last hugs and kisses to those departing. Heather glanced at the clock on the dashboard of her pick up. *Cori had better hurry up with buying the tickets. There's not much time.*

Cori's plan was slow in developing, but once she had formulated the first step, everything seemed to fall into place. They had phoned around to the different stations to find out available departure times and destinations, and then it had just been a matter of Heather getting them to the station in time.

Heather turned in her seat to check on Kenzie. As far as she could tell, the fever had come down. At least the woman was not going to die. She turned back and looked at the glass doors of the ticket office, just in time to see Cori emerging. Seeing a quick thumbs-up, Heather sighed with relief.

Cori hurriedly crossed the parking lot and opened the passenger side door. "Two tickets," she said, holding them up triumphantly. "Now we just have to get Kenzie on board without a lot of questions."

"I think my hospital scrubs should help with that, as long as no one pays too much attention to the puppies on them."

"How can I...how can we ever thank you enough, Heather?" Cori said as she pulled the bag from the floor of the front seat and slung it over her shoulder.

"You already did," Heather answered with a small smile. "You didn't shoot me. Now, let's see if we can wake her up and then get you both settled in."

Cori reached into the back and placed a hand on Kenzie's forearm. "She's definitely not as hot as she was," she said to Heather. "Kenzie...Kenzie you have to wake up. Come on." She gently shook her uninjured shoulder.

An inaudible murmur escaped her lips.

"Kenzie, we have to go." Cori shook a little harder and pressed her thumb into Kenzie's shoulder. "Come on, Kenzie, wake up," she said, her tone lower and more commanding.

Kenzie's eyes fluttered open but there was no recognition in them.

Cori smiled. "Hey there, remember me?"

Kenzie blinked hard several times before looking around the small confines of the truck. "Do you think there's a chance I could forget you?"

"We've gotta go. Do you think you can walk?"

"I'll do whatever has to be done," she murmured.

Cori took hold of her arm, helping her to sit up, "We need to get going or we're gonna miss our ride." It was a struggle to get Kenzie out of the backseat, but a little easier than it had been to get her into it.

Head spinning and feeling weak and disoriented, Kenzie managed to make it to her feet. Her face was flushed and she was sweating. Heather reached to wipe her forehead.

Kenzie's hand snatched Heather's arm, gripping it tightly and holding it away from her face. It was not as fast as her normal reflexes, but it was a lot faster than the vet tech was expecting.

"I wasn't going to hurt you," Heather said as she looked into Kenzie's half lidded eyes.

Kenzie didn't respond, but she released Heather's arm.

Heather wiped the sweat from Kenzie's brow and then touched both of her cheeks with the back of her hand. "You're still hot, but I think your fever has gone down. Take it easy for a bit and I think you'll be fine." She turned away, but Kenzie reached out and took her hand.

"I'm sorry we dragged you into this," Kenzie said sincerely. "Thank you. You probably saved my life."

Heather studied the woman's face. She now realized Kenzie was just the same as everyone else. "You're welcome. Do you think you can make it to your seat?"

Kenzie looked over at the station. Her body felt like lead and it seemed impossible to focus, but she had been trained to push herself beyond her limits. "One step in front of the other, if I remember right."

"Let's go so we can get out of here," Cori said as she moved in beside Kenzie and took her arm. Heather took the other, and the three of them headed toward the station.

The terminal was busy and few people paid any attention to the three women slowly entering through the glass doors. The building was not very old, but abuse and neglect gave it an appearance that was scruffy beyond its years. The tile floor had lost its shine beneath the thousands of footsteps that had crossed it. The overhead fluorescent lights were bright, but not bright enough to cast away the shadows in the corners. The ticket kiosk was in the corner. There was only one woman working, and she was busy talking to someone on her cell phone. Her loud, grating voice carried across the hard surfaces and bounced off the dingy walls.

"I'm tellin' ya, Delilah, he's a catch. Y'all ain't gettin' any younger... That's not what I'm saying. He's good lookin' and he's employed, what mo' can y'all be..."

They moved away from the chatter and away from the other people waiting for their transport.

"How long do we have to wait?" Heather asked quietly.

"It shouldn't be long now," Cori said as she eyed the clock on the wall.

The dark SUV drove around the block a second time. The three occupants were quiet as each took in the lay of the land and all points of reference. Though it was early in the morning, the station was alive with travelers, workers, and those dropping off and picking up.

"There are a lot of people," Calvin stated as he parked the truck on the outer rim of the parking lot.

"That's probably what she's counting on," Viper commented as he looked through a set of high-powered binoculars. "I can easily take them out from here, sir."

Manuck shook his head, more in disgust than in disagreement. "And then we'll have an even bigger mess to clean up. No. We need to get them away from here. I think the best way would be to flush them out. Let them know we're here and force them out and away from the public."

Calvin turned in his seat to face Manuck. "What makes you think she'll run? Wouldn't she know that her best defense will be a public place?"

"No matter how smart the mouse, when the hunt is on, they don't always think ahead. They just concentrate on getting away." Manuck checked the time on his watch. "Where are they now?"

Viper checked his screen. "Inside the building. Without knowing the layout, that's about all I can confirm. You want me to download the floor plan, sir?"

Manuck shook his head. "I don't think that's necessary. It's not that big of a building. Viper, you stay here and we'll try to flush them out the front doors. Follow them...but for God's sake, don't shoot them here. Just follow them until you have a clean shot without a shitload of witnesses. Understood?"

"Yes, sir."

"Calvin, you take the side entrance that leads to the docking station where they load the buses. If you see them, let us know, and make sure they know that you've seen them. I'll go around back." He looked at both men and they nodded their understanding.

Calvin pulled out a drawer under the driver's seat, revealing a cache of small radios. He selected two and handed them over. When the radios had been checked, each man put his earpiece in and attached a tiny microphone to his lapel.

"Okay, let's finish this."

Cori nervously watched the doors. Kenzie was barely conscious, her head resting on Cori's shoulder. An ominous figure approached the door and flung it open with ease. Cori's heartbeat jumped and her stomach dropped. She shot a glance at Heather, uncertain as to what the vet tech would do, but her eyes were on the clock.

"Heather," she said, her voice filled with concern.

"Huh?" Heather turned from looking at the clock and Cori motioned with a slight nod of her head until Heather saw the official looking man walking into the station.

Cori looked away, desperately hoping they wouldn't be noticed if they didn't make eye contact. "You need to get out of here," she said to Heather in a whisper.

"Not until I know you both are safe and on your way out of town."

"You're not involved in this. This is about us."

"Apparently I am. Besides that...are you sure he's looking for you?"

Just then, his radio squawked and he reached down to his hip to turn it up so he could hear the transmission. Cori's eyes followed his hand to the gun on his hip.

"Let's get out to the platform," Cori said as she nudged Kenzie. "We gotta go. Can you walk?" Kenzie could barely muster a reply. "Come on, move it, soldier," Cori commanded.

Kenzie did her best to follow, but she was just too weak and she stumbled. Heather and Cori caught her before she slipped from their grasp.

Heather looked at the sign that read LOADING PLATFORM and then to the doors beneath it. She knew they would not make it without causing a scene. She quickly looked around and came up with an alternate plan. "Washroom," she whispered to Cori.

Manuck walked into the station and paused to assess the situation. "Low income, desperate people," he muttered. Taking a bus was beneath him. *If you can't afford to fly, maybe you shouldn't be traveling.* To him it looked like the entire station should be condemned. It was way past its prime, with poor lighting and stark décor. Pamphlets covered one wall, advertising every possible cheap hotel and tourist attraction. In one corner, there were the two doors leading to the men's and women's washroom, and on the opposite corner was the glass ticket booth.

There were a number of people milling about: husbands, wives, children, and people who didn't seem to fit in any category beyond their gender. He quickly scrutinized everyone in sight. To his dismay, there was no sign of either of their targets.

"Negative on the inside." Manuck spoke in a low tone to the mic on his jacket. "Calvin, what does it look like outside?" He pressed his earpiece to listen to the response.

"Clear out here so far, sir, but there are a lot of buses to check."

Viper listened to their exchange, his eyes glued to the front doors. "Negative from the front doors, sir."

Manuck cursed as he headed out to the platform to help Calvin search. The smell of warm diesel fumes assaulted him as he pushed through the heavy swinging door. He spotted Calvin hopping up alongside a bus, peering through the windows. There were four buses parked at an angle in their allocated spots, all but one in the process of loading. Calvin was at the second bus in line. Manuck pointed to the first bus and Calvin signaled that it was clear, so the colonel maneuvered through the passengers and their luggage to the third bus. He scanned the windows as Calvin moved to the fourth and final bus. Within a few minutes, they met up at the platform.

"Negative," Calvin reported.

"Goddamn it!" Manuck yelled. "They can't have just disappeared. Viper?"

"Negative out here, sir."

"Check your locator. They have to be here somewhere."

Viper put down his binoculars and turned the laptop so he could read the screen. He typed for a second and then ran his fingertip over the touchpad.

"She's inside the building, sir. Northeast corner."

"Back inside," Manuck said. They powered back through the swinging doors and stopped just inside the building. "Northeast?"

"Northeast," Viper repeated. "And she's not moving."

The three of them stood motionless inside the women's washroom, their backs up against the cold tile wall. Cori looked at Heather, who was checking her wristwatch. "How long have we got?"

"Just a few minutes. The stop here is only to pick up more passengers, and then it heads north."

"We can't wait in here much longer or we'll miss it." Cori stated the obvious as she turned to assess Kenzie's condition. "Kenzie...Kenzie, look at me." She snapped her fingers in front of her face. "Kenzie, come on, open your eyes. Just a few more minutes and then you can rest."

Kenzie struggled to open her eyes, but they only remained open for a moment before her head swayed and her eyes began to close.

"Kenzie, you've got to stay with us for just a bit longer. Okay? Come on," Cori pleaded as she gently tapped her cheek.

"I think we should go," Heather said nervously.

Calvin looked to the northeast corner of the station. "She's in the washroom. Should we go in and get her or wait for her to come out?"

"I'm not waiting any longer." Manuck reached inside his jacket and pulled his gun from the holster on his belt, keeping it concealed beneath his jacket. Calvin did the same as they walked directly toward the women's washroom.

"I thought you didn't want to make a scene," Calvin said.

"At this point, I don't care. I just want it over with, once and for all. We'll flash our badges and drag their corpses out by their hair if we have to."

The two men didn't hesitate as they approached the door and pushed it open. One step inside and their guns were drawn, but to their disappointment the bathroom was empty.

Heather, Cori, and a barely-conscious Kenzie, emerged from the washroom just as the pending arrival of the northbound Coast Starlight train was announced. Cori looked for the uniformed police officer whose appearance had sent them scurrying to the washroom. He had his back to them, chatting with the ticket agent behind the window. The three women moved out the doors to the train platform just as a distant whistle blew.

"Perfect timing," Heather said as they made their way down the cement platform.

"I'll be happy once we're on the train and away from here," Cori held Kenzie tightly, "and she's resting on the bed in our compartment."

"Do you think they've found it yet?"

"The microchip?" Cori asked, and Heather nodded. "I don't know, maybe."

The train pulled into the Anaheim station, thankfully on time. The large, cumbersome engine slowly brought the train alongside the waiting women, and then ground to a stop. There was no one there to take tickets, or check IDs or baggage. To Cori's surprise and comfort, there was no security whatsoever. The doors just opened and people got on or got off. The woman who had sold them their tickets had told Cori which car held their sleeping compartment, and where they should wait on the platform. Cori looked up at the car number and smiled. The ticket seller had been dead on. It didn't take them long to board the train, but it was a maneuvering challenge to move down the narrow corridor.

"This is it," Cori said as she read the number next to the door.

Heather opened the door and was mildly surprised at the size of the accommodations. It measured all of six feet by eight feet, but not much more. There were two chairs against the window, a set of small beds — one above the other, and an open door leading to a very small bathroom. "Apparently you have to go out into the passageway to change your mind," Heather said in jest.

"It has a bed and its private, that's all I want. No prying eyes and no questions," Cori said as they shuffled into the room. Kenzie had not said a word since they'd left the washroom, but she let out a low moan as they lowered her to the bed. "Besides, with your name on the tickets, which were paid for in cash, we should have a smooth trip. And hopefully enough time for Kenzie to heal."

"You've got her meds and the extra bandages I gave you?"

"Yes, and thank you again."

"Just keep a close eye on her stitches and if you don't see improvement, go to a real hospital, go to a real hospital — for people."

"I can't thank you enough, Heather." Cori opened her arms and hugged the large woman.

"Just get her healthy and don't get caught. I'll be looking for a postcard or something down the road to let me know you made it out of this mess." Heather smiled and closed the door behind her.

Manuck and Calvin stood dumbfounded in the women's washroom of the San Diego bus station.

"Viper! Get me a location," Manuck snapped into his mic. "There's nobody here!" Just then, a woman attempted to enter the washroom. "We're closed," Manuck yelled as he pushed her back out the door.

"She's in the northeast corner of the building... Hang on, let me pull up the city's site and get the building plans." Viper's fingers danced over the keys.

Manuck paced the floor, waiting for the information. Calvin was new to the team, but he had enough sense to stay close to the tile wall and out of his way.

"I got it," Viper announced exuberantly. "Okay, according to what I have, she should be right against the east wall, ten feet from the back north wall."

Manuck did the calculation and his eyes stopped on the metal waste receptacle attached to the wall. Without saying a word, he strode over and smashed it loose with his foot. It clanged loudly to the floor, spilling out wads of used paper towel and other assorted garbage.

"What the hell are you doing?"

A young woman was holding open the washroom door. Dressed in a pair of blue slacks and a white blouse with a gray vest over it, she obviously worked for the bus lines, and she was mad.

"You guys can't be in here! This is the ladies restroom, and that is Greyhound property you just smashed!"

Ignoring her, Manuck leaned over and plucked something from amongst the trash.

"You're gonna have to pay for that." She pointed at the damage to the wall and to the garbage can. "Excuse me!"

"Let's go," Manuck said to Calvin, and the two men turned to leave, but the young woman refused to move.

"I'm gonna call the cops. Someone has to pay for that!"

Manuck pushed her aside. "You do that, sweetheart, and when they show up tomorrow, I can guarantee they'll care just about as much as I do." With that, the two men were out the door and gone.

"Sir?" Calvin asked as they crossed the parking lot.

Manuck opened his hand and exhibited the electronic tracer.

"Now what?" Calvin asked.

Manuck stopped outside of the SUV with his hand on the door handle. "I don't know." He sighed loudly. "But we better figure out where she is and where she's going...and we better do it fast."

Chapter 17

Only after the train pulled out of the station did Cori finally take her first deep breath in a long while. They had made it. She checked on Kenzie, lying on the bed, and then flopped down in one of the high-backed seats next to the window and watched as the stadium of the Los Angeles/Anaheim Angels slowly moved out of sight. She tried to relax, but knew it would take putting a few miles behind them for that to happen.

Restlessly rising from the chair, she opened the door into the tiny cubicle of a bathroom and turned on the light. The woman looking back at her in the mirror was a stranger. Her face was dirty and still bore the yellowish green tinge of the bruising she had received over the past week. Her honey-blonde hair was tangled and tossed, and it looked as if it had been a month since she'd washed it. Suddenly she felt grimy, and looked longingly at the showerhead hanging from the wall. There was not really a shower stall, but it looked so very inviting that she couldn't resist it.

She returned to check on Kenzie again. She seemed to be resting comfortably, though her skin was still overly warm to the touch. Leaving her patient to sleep, Cori hoisted Kenzie's bag and dumped the contents onto the floor. She was looking for some of the clothing and bare necessities that they had purchased at an all-night Walmart on the drive up from San Diego. Her gaze fell on the bundles of cash and the assortment of weapons. She had known there were guns in the bag, but not what kind or how many. She let her fingers trail lightly over the black metal as she eyed the two stacks of money. *That's a lot of cash,* she thought. "Which is good, 'cause we're gonna need more than what I have left," she said. The train ticket, especially for a sleeping compartment, had been expensive, and the bus fare for two to Branson had been ninety-nine dollars each — two hundred dollars they no longer had.

There was a loud knock on the door and Cori jumped.

"Tickets, please," the male voice outside the door requested.

Cori hopped to her feet, grabbed the tickets from her back pocket, and then stepped toward the door. She reached for the handle, but stopped and looked back at the Colt .45 lying at the foot of Kenzie's bed. She grabbed the gun and held it in her left hand, concealing it behind the door as she opened it. A young man in a burgundy uniform stood smiling, his hand out.

"Good morning, ma'am. Tickets, please."

"Of course." Cori laid them in his hand.

"First time riding the rails?" he asked pleasantly as he flipped open the packet and pulled out the two tickets.

"Ah...yes, as a matter of fact." Cori watched him punch holes into both tickets.

"My name is Steven and I'm your train car steward. I'm here for whatever you need. The dining car is two cars up. Breakfast is at eight, lunch is at noon. They take seating for an hour before and after. Dinner service is from five until eight, and seeing as you have a sleeping compartment, your meals are included with your ticket. You just need to make reservations in the parlor car. Three cars to the back is the observation car that has a top bubble deck to enjoy some of the fabulous scenery, especially through Northern California and Oregon. The observation car also has a full bar that's open from three 'til midnight." He handed her the tickets and smiled brightly. "I'd be happy to come in and show you where everything is in your compartment and how it all works."

He took a step forward but Cori blocked his way, keeping the door only partially open and her hand firmly gripping the gun. "No, thank you. My friend isn't well. She's sleeping right now and I don't want to disturb her."

"Not a problem, I can show you at any time. Next to the light switch, on the wall by the bathroom door, there's a blue button. Just press that and one of us will be here in a jiffy to help you out. There's also a red button in case of an emergency. If you're hungry and you want a midnight snack, you can always run down to the café car. Anything else?"

"No, I don't think so." Cori hesitated for a moment as she slid the tickets back into her pocket. "The food on the train...our meals...can they be delivered?"

"I'm sorry, ma'am, we don't have a...um, room service, as such." He smiled apologetically.

"It's just...my friend is going to need to eat, but I don't think she'll be up to eating in the dining car." Cori glanced back at Kenzie sleeping soundly on the bed, and then down at the money and guns on the floor. "She's just gone through minor surgery and I—"

"There are sandwiches available in the café car," Steven said.

"Can you just hang on one sec?" Cori held up her finger. Steven smiled and nodded as she carefully closed the door. Pushing all of the contents of Kenzie's bag out of sight with her foot, Cori reached down and pulled out several crisp bills from one of the stacks. Opening the door once more, she held them up for Steven to see. "About that room service?"

Steven's smile never wavered as his eyes calculated the money in her hand.

"And I'll give you two more at the end of our trip, if you forget you ever saw us."

His eyes finally left the money as he turned his attention to the woman holding the bills, "I only travel as far as Sacramento, and then there's a crew change." When the bills started to move away from him, he quickly added, "But I have a friend I can swap with. He can double back my shift...he owes me."

Cori considered this for a moment. "Do we have a deal then?"

He nodded as he pulled the bills from her hand. "At your service," he said with a smile.

"Thank you. We're good for right now, but I'll let you know if we need something. You've been very helpful, Steven."

"It's my pleasure. Anything you need to make this a pleasant trip, just push that blue button and I'll be here." He bobbed his head and turned away to carry on down the passageway.

Cori closed the door and leaned back against it, sighing loudly. She closed her eyes and took a deep breath. *Dining car, observation car.* She snorted. "I have no intentions of leaving this compartment."

Gathering up what she needed, Cori went into the bathroom for a thorough washing and brushing. Half an hour later, a refreshed woman emerged. Feeling a hundred percent better, she gathered up the contents from the duffel bag that were still on the floor and separated what could stay in the bag and what they would need, and then she slid the bag under the bed.

The next order of business was to check Kenzie's wound and get her to take her pills. The wound part turned out to be quick and easy, but waking her up enough to swallow the pills was a challenge.

"Kenzie...come on, wake up." Cori knelt on the bed and gently shook her shoulder. Kenzie mumbled and groaned a bit, but did not waken. Repositioning herself at Kenzie's head, she pulled and lifted until she was kneeling behind her, with Kenzie's head on her thighs.

"Drink this," Cori commanded as she brought a glass of water to Kenzie's lips. It took several attempts, but finally Kenzie swallowed some water without coughing. A few moments later, she swallowed the pills Cori provided. By the time the ordeal was over,

Cori was mentally and physically exhausted. Finally feeling safe and secure, she curled up next to Kenzie and fell asleep.

On the plane, Viper and Calvin were both furiously tapping away on laptops. Just down from them sat Manuck. He was staring at the small capsule in his hand as he contemplated his very limited options. He pulled his cell phone from his pocket and made the call he had been avoiding for the last half hour.

"We lost her," he said into the phone.

"What? Where?"

"In San Diego."

"How did you lose her? What about her tracking—"

"It's in my hand." Manuck looked down at the minute microchip.

"Shit! Hang on. I need to close my door." Terry Bucannon crossed the room and shut the door. He didn't speak into the phone until he was back at his desk and in front of his computer. "What was her last known location?"

"Honestly...her boat, I think."

"You think? Jesus Christ on a cracker, Danny."

"Easy."

"You said you could get this done and you haven't."

Manuck looked down at the capsule he was jiggling in his hand. He held it for a moment longer and then placed it on the small table next to his seat. "We knew it wasn't going to be easy. The problem now is, I'm not sure when she found her little electronic babysitter. She had us on a wild goose chase all night, maybe longer."

"Great, and now she's just disappeared."

"That's what she's trained to do — eliminate and evaporate — and now you think we're going to find her? Ha! She'll find us long before we find her. Cover your ass, Terry, and keep your sidearm handy. That woman could unload a shitload of terror on us, and you know it."

Colonel Daniel Manuck knew just how bad the situation was. It had been his suggestion that they bring Kenzie into their little operation. He was the one who had done some of her early training, and he knew what she was capable of. After all, it was what she did. That was what she said to him not that long ago.

"Palmer suggested earlier that maybe the three of us should have a face-to-face," Bucannon said, breaking the silence.

"Palmer is an idiot, an asshole with money. He has no idea what's about to come down on him. If he was smart, he'd grab all of his money and disappear, forget he ever heard of Maquinar. Unfortunately, I don't think he's that smart. And I can tell you this, I'm not going to put all of us into one room together and give LeGault an easy target. If he wants to meet, it will be over her dead body. Are you having second thoughts, Terry?"

"No," Bucannon responded, though he knew it was not entirely true. He had nothing but second thoughts.

"Good, 'cause we have too much at stake here for you to start getting cold feet."

When Manuck went quiet again, Bucannon found the silence unsettling. "Where are Calvin and Viper?"

"Here with me. We're just leaving San Diego."

"Any idea where she'll be heading?"

"I can venture a guess." He didn't say goodbye, but the conversation was over and the line went dead.

Manuck sat and contemplated what their next move should be. If he was the one who had become a target, he'd have just disappeared, but LeGault was not him. He picked up his phone and dialed another number.

"Palmer, it's Manuck. We lost her." He sat silent for a moment, listening to the string of profanity coming from his phone. "Are you done?"

"How goddamn incompetent are you people?"

"Excuse me, Senator, but I'm not one of your flunkies. I'm a colonel in the United States Army, and I don't work for you."

"Well, Colonel, one of your little non-existent pieces of military property is running amok and she's putting all of us in jeopardy."

"You think I don't know that? If this thing becomes public, my entire career will be a footnote in the military manual under corruption and treason. We need to find her, and fast, before she starts to put it all together."

"And just what's your plan if she shows up on some Army base looking for you, Colonel?"

Manuck grew quiet. This possibility was not new to him and it made him uneasy. "And when she connects this to the rest of you, are you going to sleep easy at night, Senator? Despite all your money and power, how do you plan to stop a trained killer? Because believe me, it isn't a matter of 'if', it's a matter of 'when'."

"I wasn't aware that dealing with personnel was going to be part of my job. That was supposed to be up to you government guys. My job was to bankroll this little operation. We've all made a lot of money, but obviously we need to shut down Maquinar until this has been dealt with. I think the three of us should have a face-to-face meeting and come up with a plan."

"I think that might be a little risky right now, don't you?" Manuck said.

"I think, under the circumstances, we don't have any other options."

"I will pool my resources, at least as much as I can without drawing attention to the situation. I can't speak for Bucannon."

"Well, I would suggest that you and your CIA buddy find your wayward operative before she finds us." Palmer changed tacks. "What about the judge? Have you spoken to him yet?"

"Briefly, but he doesn't know anything."

"Are you sure?"

"No."

Palmer hung up, leaving Manuck to ponder the question. The colonel looked down at the capsule on the table and smashed it with his fist.

Cori took a seat next to the window and watched the outside world passing by. Periodically, she checked on Kenzie. Thankfully, she seemed to be resting peacefully. Cori leaned back in the tall seat and closed her eyes. *How did I wind up here?* She swayed with the movement of the train. *And what are we going to do now?*

Time passed slowly, but as the train moved further from Anaheim and San Diego, the questions in Cori's mind became more insistent. Despite their nagging, she felt herself beginning to relax. They were safe for now — or were they? Cori thought they'd been safe before, and each time, someone had found them. However, now there was not a microchip to tell their trackers where they were. *And who exactly are these people and who are they after? Me...or...*

Casting an eye at the bed, she wondered who Kenzie really was. *And why do I find myself attracted to her?* She recalled the kiss they had shared in Tijuana, and her body yearned in memory. She was attracted to her...everything about her: her confidence, her abilities, the way she moved, the way she spoke. "And apparently, how she breathes," she said quietly as she turned back to the window.

"Katherine Mackenzie LeGault, do you have any idea what you do to me?" She sighed in disbelief as she tried to focus on the scenery outside the window. It wasn't long before she was studying her own reflection in the window, and that of the woman on the bed.

Katherine Mackenzie LeGault... What is it about your name that rings a bell? She knew they had never met prior to Guadalajara because she would not have forgotten meeting someone like Kenzie. It was not her looks, though she was very attractive, it was more in the way she handled herself.

Cori left the chair, and went in search of a pen and some paper. Locating them in a drawer under the small counter, she returned to the chair and began making notes — where she had been, where she had worked, who knew about her and how they had met. Anything she could think of that might have connected her to Kenzie was listed.

Hours later, exhausted, Cori fell asleep with pages and pages of notes across her lap. She had found no connection, but the little bell in the back of her mind continued to jingle.

It was hunger that eventually woke Cori. She yawned and stretched her stiff body as she looked over at Kenzie's still form. It was easy to see from the steady rise and fall of her chest, that she was resting comfortably.

"I need food," Cori said as her stomach rumbled its unhappiness. She found the blue button Steven had mentioned and pressed it. Moments later, there was a soft rap on the door. It was Steven and he happily took her order. A short while later, she accepted a tray of soup and sandwiches with her right hand, holding the gun firmly in her left but hidden behind the door.

"I can bring it in for you, ma'am," Steven said with his ever present smile.

For the first time she was thankful for the small size of their accommodations. Everything was within reach. "No, thank you. I've got it." Cori placed the tray on the counter.

When Steven left and the door was closed, Cori sighed with relief. Moving over to the bed, she knelt down next to it and ran her hand over Kenzie's forehead. It was warm, but not feverish.

"I smell food," Kenzie whispered, her eyes still shut.

"Geez, you scared the crap out of me. I thought you were asleep."

A small smile lifted the corner of Kenzie's mouth. "Sorry."

"No you're not."

Kenzie opened her eyes. "You're right, I'm not." Her voice was hoarse, but her tone was light. "Where are we?"

"On a train heading north, far away from San Diego."

Kenzie surveyed the room and its cramped accommodations. "Works for me," she said with an approving nod. "What's that?"

"I got us some dinner," Cori said, looking over at the tray on the counter.

"Dinner? What time is it?"

"A little after six."

"Wow, really?" She pressed her head into the pillow and looked up at the ceiling. "Guess I slept through breakfast and lunch."

"We were on the road to Anaheim during breakfast, and we both slept through lunch." Cori motioned toward the seat next to the window. "You need to eat."

"I think we both do." Kenzie attempted to sit up, but all she could do was groan. "Christ, I hurt."

"Here, let me help you." Cori wrapped an arm around her shoulder and assisted Kenzie into a sitting position. Placing all of the provided pillows behind her, Cori helped Kenzie lean back against them. "I got soup and sandwiches. I wasn't sure what you liked or what your stomach could handle."

"I think right now it could handle anything. I'm not sure if I even remember the last time we ate."

"Neither do I."

They ate their meal in relative silence but their eyes connected several times, each watching the other for very different reasons. After their meal, Kenzie's eyelids grew heavy and she fell asleep. Cori cleaned up and, soon after, found herself dozing in the seat next to the window.

A little while later, in the dim sunset light, Cori woke to find Kenzie watching her from the bed. "Hi," she said softly. Kenzie smiled back, but Cori could see there was concern in her golden eyes. "What is it?" Cori moved slowly from the chair to join Kenzie on the bed. "What is it, Kenzie? What's wrong?"

"You tell me. I've been watching you for a while."

"I don't know what you're talking about. I was asleep," Cori said, but she could tell by the look on Kenzie's face that she didn't believe her. Taking a deep breath, Cori softly admitted, "I'm scared."

"I know. I can see it in your face, and in your body language."

"We need you healthy."

Kenzie lay back. "I know that, too."

"We're still in a pile of trouble, and I know I can't get us out of it." She studied Kenzie.

"You seem to have gotten us out of San Diego without any help from me."

The reality of it all seemed so overwhelming. "Most of that was luck and you know it." Cori laid her head on Kenzie's shoulder.

"Actually, I don't know it." She began to play with Cori's hair. "A lot of it I don't remember at all, and the rest is just a haze. How did we get to the hospital?"

"We walked, or rather I dragged you, after you shot that Cobra guy."

Kenzie's hand stopped. She had forgotten that. "I shot Cobra?"

"On the lawn of the library. Once in the chest and once between the eyes."

Kenzie didn't say anything for a long while, but she returned to stroking Cori's hair.

"You don't remember...any of it?"

"A little bit, but most of it is foggy. I guess I just reacted out of instinct," Kenzie said quietly.

"Well, your instincts saved my life."

"I would venture a guess that it saved both of our lives. I do remember the hospital, though, and the microchip...and a nurse. What was her name?"

"Heather."

"Yeah, that's it."

Cori smiled. "But she wasn't a nurse, she was a vet tech."

"Oh." Kenzie's eyebrows rose in question. "A what? You took me to a vet?"

"It's not like I could have dragged you into a real hospital," Cori said defensively.

"You took me to a vet hospital?"

Cori gave her a gentle poke. "Heather saved your life."

Kenzie pondered this information, trying to remember anything else. "How did you convince Heather to help?"

"It was quite easy once I stopped waving a gun in her face."

"What have I created?" Kenzie said with feigned horror.

Cori ignored her teasing. "We owe her, big time. Besides, it was her idea about riding the train. When we were leaving the vet hospital, I spotted a city bus. At first, we were going to put the microchip on the bus, but the more we thought about it, the more we were worried that someone else might get hurt as a result. So, we followed the bus around for a bit and came up with the idea of leaving the microchip in the women's washroom at the Greyhound station. Afterward, we withdrew all of my money from my bank account at a check-cashing place and bought a couple of bus tickets with my ID. Once we had those tickets in hand, we hightailed it out of town on the I-5 in Heather's truck. Next stop was the Anaheim train station and voila, here we are."

Kenzie watched Cori in amazement. "Pretty damn impressive for a student living in Guadalajara."

"It's actually pretty amazing what one can do when their life is danger," Cori said solemnly. "Besides, I still think most of it was luck."

Kenzie raised herself just enough to kiss the top of Cori's head. "Thank you."

"For what?"

"For everything...for looking after me, for saving my life...and yours, for everything." She shifted uncomfortably. "I've never had anyone look out for me like that."

"And?" Cori looked into her eyes and waited.

"I kinda like it," she finally answered.

The skies outside the large window were dark with night and the lighting in the train compartment was dim. Kenzie's moaning woke Cori, and for a moment she wondered where she was. The movement of the train swayed everything back and forth as she got her bearings. Kenzie groaned again and Cori gently placed a hand on her arm. "Shhh, it's okay," she whispered softly into Kenzie's ear.

Kenzie's eyelids fluttered, but did not open as she moaned again. Kenzie could feel a warm hand on her and she could smell the clean scent of shampoo. She hurt. Her entire body ached, but it didn't stop her from shifting a little closer to the warm body. She was surprised that something so soft could make her feel so protected.

Cori felt the movement and brushed the curly hair back from Kenzie's face as she shushed the moans. The tender caress of Cori's hand softened the sounds coming from Kenzie's lips. Cori whispered her name and Kenzie opened her eyes. "Hi." Cori offered a small smile. "Feeling better?"

"I think so," Kenzie said quietly.

Running her hand over Kenzie's flushed cheek and forehead, Cori shook her head. "You're still a little warm, but I don't think your fever is that much of an issue anymore."

"Is that how you check a woman's temperature?" Kenzie's smile was soft and lazy, but her eyes were alert.

There was no immediate change in Cori's expression, but she leaned up on one elbow and pressed her lips firmly against Kenzie's forehead. "No fever."

"Check again."

Their eyes connected in silent communication, each wanting, but both so unsure. Cori broke the stare first. Her eyes traveled down Kenzie's face and stopped on the lips that were waiting. Her movement was slow and very deliberate as she pressed her lips to Kenzie's. It was no surprise to Cori that the waiting lips were soft and warm, and very inviting. The kiss grew more intense and then Cori abruptly pulled back.

Breathless, Kenzie looked to Cori for an explanation. "What? Why did you stop?" Not answering, Cori moved her body away from Kenzie's. "Wait." Kenzie tried to stop her, but she didn't have the strength. "What just happened?"

"We have to stop," Cori whispered.

"Why?"

Cori leaned down and tenderly kissed the tip of Kenzie's nose. "Don't get me wrong, I enjoyed every minute of it."

"Just give me a minute to catch my breath, and I'll show you what enjoyable really is."

"We can't. I mean...we shouldn't." Cori sat up straighter in the bed while she watched the gamut of emotions on Kenzie's face.

"Excuse me?" Kenzie asked in confusion.

"I mean..." She took a deep breath and sorted her thoughts. "What I'm trying to say is...we shouldn't be doing this."

"We're both adults, so why the hell not?"

"Because a little more than twenty-four hours ago you were laid out on an operating table, nearly dead. That's why!" Cori's tone was harsher than she meant it to be, and it confirmed what she already knew.

"But I want to—"

Cori placed a finger on Kenzie's lips, silencing her words. "I know what you want to do, and believe me, nothing would make me happier... Ah ah." She shook her finger. "Nothing except you getting healthy."

"But—"

"No buts. We need you healthy."

Kenzie leaned back in frustration, her eyebrows drawn in a glare of annoyance.

Cori watched her for a moment, but Kenzie's face turned toward the wall. "You know I'm right," she cajoled without success. Cori waited, slightly amused by Kenzie's apparent pouting. "I'm not going anywhere unless you're by my side. And no matter how this all started...Kenzie, look at me." She turned Kenzie's face to hers. "No matter how this all started, regardless of the circumstances that brought us together..."

The mention of how they met evoked harsh realities that were enough to quell the desire throbbing inside of Kenzie. She closed her eyes to the truth, shutting off Cori's words. She didn't want to be reminded of how all of this had started.

"Kenzie, please look at me," Cori begged. "Look at me, please. I need you to look at me."

It took a moment, but she finally opened her eyes, and herself, to Cori.

"I need you to listen. You don't have to say anything. I just want you to know, regardless of how this all started...I need you." Kenzie started to interject but Cori placed her fingers gently on her lips. "Shhh, just listen, 'cause I've never said this to anyone before and I want to be sure you're hearing what I'm saying. We can't change the past. You told me that a while back and it's nothing I didn't already know. And I don't know what the future has in store for us, but I do know...that I care for you. I care what happens to you." She leaned down until she was inches from Kenzie's face. "I care because — well, believe it or not — I think I'm falling in love with you." She moved her fingers from Kenzie's lips and kissed her softly. Pulling away, she looked deeply into Kenzie's eyes. "Make no mistake, I would very much like this to carry on, but right now you need your strength to heal."

In her lifetime, Kenzie could never recall anyone ever saying they loved her, and she was at a loss as to what she should say in response. Did she love Cori back? It was a question she couldn't answer, but Cori didn't seem to be looking for a response. Instead, she kissed her once more and then curled up next to her and snuggled in to sleep, leaving Kenzie to ponder what she had said.

Chapter 18

Cori woke with a start. She looked around to determine what had woken her, and was surprised to see her arms and legs intertwined with Kenzie's. The sun was shining brightly through the hazy window, illuminating the compartment and the woman lying next to her.

A sharp rap on the door answered the question as to what had disturbed her from her sleep. Wiggling out from under Kenzie as quickly as she could, Cori picked up the gun and moved over to the door. She opened it slightly. "Yes?"

"Good morning, ma'am. Morning paper," Steven offered with a slight bow. "And I just wanted to make sure that you've found everything, and your journey thus far has been satisfactory."

"Yes, thank you." She took the paper and tossed it to the counter behind her.

"Am I correct in assuming that you'd like breakfast served in your compartment?"

Cori nodded, but was unsure of what to ask for.

"The 'Starlight Morning Bright' is very popular."

"That would be fine, for two people."

"Coffee, orange juice?"

"Both, thank you."

Steven repeated her order and left. She closed the door and locked it with an audible sigh.

"You handled that well," a low voice said from the bed. "I especially like the gun behind the door...nice touch."

"I had a good teacher."

Kenzie shook her head ruefully. "Of all the things I could teach you, how to handle small arms wasn't at the top of the list."

"The main thing you taught me is how to stay alive, to be more aware of my surroundings. Don't beat yourself up over it, because being alive is at the top of my list." Cori approached the bed. "Anyway, I thought you were sleeping."

"I was, but my pillow left me," Kenzie pulled herself up into a nearly sitting position, "and I got cold...and hungry."

"Steven, our train porter slash steward, will be delivering breakfast shortly," Cori said as she straightened her clothing and unconsciously ran her fingers through her disheveled hair.

"What I need isn't going to be delivered," Kenzie said, a slow smile growing on her face as Cori's cheeks flushed.

"What you need is to get cleaned up and put on a change of clothes," Cori said with a smile of her own.

The train chugged its way over and around the Siskiyou Mountains, heading northward toward Klamath Falls. The sun was coming over the snow peaked mountains and Kenzie watched the beauty of the scenery unfold from one of the seats next to the window.

"You okay?" Cori asked as Kenzie's eyes drifted away from the view.

"Yeah," she said quietly, turning to finish her breakfast.

"What's on your mind?"

Kenzie pushed the remains of her food around the plate with her fork. "My boat," she said with a heavy sigh. "I just can't believe she's gone." She turned and placed her plate on the counter. Her movements were slow, but not as painful as they had been. She settled back in her seat and closed her eyes.

"Are you sure you're feeling okay?"

"I'll be fine...it's just...how did they know about my boat?" A long moment of silence passed between them before Kenzie opened her eyes to the world rolling past. "None of this makes sense, it hasn't from the very beginning, but I do know one thing – Cobra wasn't after just you, he was after us, and now we know how he kept finding us."

"That tracker thing."

Kenzie nodded. "I'm beginning to think this whole thing was a setup." Her eyes narrowed as she considered what she had said. "I think they were really after me the whole time. The question I keep asking is, why?" The thought had been twirling in her brain as she wrestled with what she knew and what she didn't. She found it unsettling that she had no one to ask, no one she could turn to who was in a position to answer her questions.

"But why would they be after you? Don't you work for these people?"

"I work for the government, but the person I answer to is military... It's complicated."

"But why would they be after you?" Cori persisted. "Why would they want you dead?"

"I don't know, but...the last assignment I was on went bad. The whole thing was bullshit, and they tried to cover it up. Maybe they want to be sure I'm not going to talk to anyone about that." She was grasping at straws, and her words sounded desperate and a little deranged. "Where's the cell phone that I got from Big Polly?"

Cori shrugged. "I haven't seen it since our last swim in the ocean."

"I need to talk to the judge."

"There must be some kind of phone system or other method of communication on the train, I would think."

Kenzie glanced out the window of the fast moving train and a sudden realization slammed into her. *Why didn't I think of that before?* "Where are we going?"

"The only place I know – Seattle."

"We're going to Seattle?" Kenzie looked around their constricted box of a compartment as a feeling a dread flowed through her. "We need to get off the train."

"What? Why? We're safe here. No one knows where we are."

"You're right, but I don't think screaming into Seattle would be the smartest move for us right now. We have no idea who's behind this, or why. Are they just after me, or are they trying to get to you through me, or is someone really after the both of us?"

"I have no idea," Cori answered quietly.

"Well, until we do, I think we need to lay low for a bit and try to figure things out. Seattle isn't the place to do it." Kenzie was on her feet, pawing through the drawer and the small closet. "I need a map or a list of train stations, something that will tell me where we are...I need to know where we are."

"Hold on a minute, one thing at a time. I think I can get you a map," Cori reached for the blue button, "but then you're going to have to explain some of this to me."

"We have to get off this train."

"I understand that, but we can't while it's moving, so take a minute and explain." There was a quick knock on the door and Cori crossed over to answer it. She asked Steven for a map or a listing of the upcoming stations. He nodded and was back before they could continue their conversation. Cori opened the door for him, and he unfolded the train brochure as he stepped toward Kenzie.

"Where are we?" Kenzie asked.

"Just outside of Klamath Falls," he said as Kenzie snatched the map from his hand. He looked to Cori. "We're running a bit behind schedule, but that's normal."

Kenzie pored over the map in her hand, "When is the next stop?" she asked without looking up.

"We have a crew change in Klamath Falls, and then our next real stop is Portland. We're usually there for about half an hour."

"When is that?" Kenzie finally looked up at the young man. "What time do we get into Portland?"

Steven glanced at his watch and did a quick calculation. "At this rate...about four thirty-five. Is there something I can help with?" He directed his question to Cori rather than the agitated woman with the map.

"We can get off then?" Kenzie asked, her attention on the map and not on the glances exchanged between the other two.

"You can get off the train at any time, but you're paid all the way through to Seattle." He didn't know what the problem was, and he wasn't sure if he wanted to know, but he was concerned about receiving the remainder of his gratuity.

"Thanks, Steven," Cori said, reaching for the door. He nodded and stepped out as the door clicked and locked behind him. Cori turned her attention to the highly agitated Kenzie. "Why do we need to get off in Portland?"

"It doesn't matter whether it's Portland or not. We just need to get off before Seattle," Kenzie said as she spread the map out on the table and traced the northern path of the train. Their route was clearly marked and Kenzie stabbed her finger onto the glossy paper. "We're here," she said.

Cori leaned closer to read the map. "Yeah."

"Okay–"

"Stop, Kenzie. Why can't we carry on to Seattle?"

"Because Seattle is where I'm from, and I'm not stepping back into that hornet's nest until I know what's going on and who the players are. Coming in by train, we might as well put an ad in the paper. They'll be watching all incoming trains, planes, and buses."

"Who are 'they'?"

It was the key question and Kenzie still didn't have the answer. "I don't know...yet."

"But, Kenzie, that doesn't explain why you want to get off in Portland."

"I don't want to get off in Portland," Kenzie said as her finger moved along the route. "It's too big and too populated. Chances are there would be tight security at the station. If there are cameras, then there's a possibility we could be seen. With the facial recognition program, they would know we were there before we got out of the station. Right now...hopefully...they have no idea where we are, but I can guarantee they will be watching every mode of transportation. No, Portland won't work. We need something smaller, out of the way...like Tacoma." She tapped her finger on the port just south of Seattle.

"Tacoma?"

"Yeah." She turned the map over, looking for an enlargement of the port city. "Yeah. See." She pointed out the station. "The Tacoma station is right in the middle of an industrial area – fewer people, less chance there might be cameras."

Cori studied the road map enlargement of the area around the Tacoma train station. She shrugged her shoulders, not caring where they were going as long as they were going together. "And then what?"

"Then we need to start putting these pieces together and see what kind of a picture we get."

Later that afternoon Kenzie was resting comfortably on the bed when she felt the mattress shift as Cori sat down next to her. She lazily opened one eye. "What's up?"

"I need to change your dressing and you need to take some more of these." Cori held out her hand containing the antibiotics. "Here." She offered them along with a bottle of water.

Kenzie took her medicine without complaint as she watched Cori lay out the medical supplies needed. "You're getting pretty good at bandaging me, aren't you?"

"You've given me a lot of practice," she said with a smile. "Can you lift your shirt up?"

Kenzie complied by taking her shirt off. The movement was not especially painful and she realized she was not as sore as she had been. "I feel a lot better."

Cori did her best to keep her eyes and mind on the dressing rather than the half-naked patient. The bandages were clean and white, a sharp contrast to Kenzie's bronzed skin. "Well, there's no bleeding or seepage." Cori removed the tape and gauze carefully, noting the coolness of the skin. Kenzie's fever was gone. "You look a lot better," Cori said quietly while she went about replacing the dressing.

"I feel a hundred percent better," Kenzie answered as she studied the yellow bruises on Cori's face, so near to her own. All of that seemed so long ago. With everything that had happened, she felt like a completely different person. "I feel like a new me."

"Really? How is that?" Cori asked, her hands and eyes busy with taping the gauze in place.

"I feel..." She couldn't find the words, but she knew what she wanted to do. Leaning forward, her lips brushed lightly over Cori's cheek. Lingering for a brief moment, Kenzie detected the clean scent of shampoo and soap.

"Hey, hey." Cori pulled back and looked at Kenzie. "You may be feeling better, but I don't think you're well enough for that."

The color rising in Cori's cheeks told Kenzie more than her words did. She watched her gather up their limited medical supplies and, as Cori started to rise from the bed, Kenzie grabbed her wrist and pulled her back. Neither spoke, but when they looked into each other's eyes, the communication was clear.

Kenzie inched forward and kissed her softly on the lips. Leaning back, she placed her hand gently on Cori's cheek. "Thank you," Kenzie said softly.

"For what?" Cori whispered, not wanting to spoil the sudden change of mood.

"For everything – again."

There was a moment's hesitation and then Cori leaned forward and tenderly kissed Kenzie's lips. They parted, but Cori remained inches from Kenzie' face. "Thank you," she said.

"For what?"

"For not dying on me."

Kenzie's expression changed to one of amusement and her eyes shifted back and forth from Cori's eyes to her mouth. She wanted to kiss her again, but before she could, Cori's lips found hers. This kiss was harder, more demanding, and she realized she was not the only one who was wanting. Pressing harder against Cori lips, Kenzie felt her hand come around her neck, pulling her deeper into the kiss.

It was what they both wanted and the fervor of the kiss grew. Searching with her tongue, Kenzie separated Cori's lips, eliciting a moan when their tongues touched. Warm waves of desire flooded through Kenzie as she cupped Cori's cheek and pulled her closer.

Cori moaned as Kenzie slid a hand down to cover her breast. The t-shirt material was thin enough that she could feel the nipple harden in response to her touch. She squeezed firmly and Cori rewarded her with another low, needy groan. Running her thumb around the nipple in small circles, she waited for it to swell and then she gently pinched it.

Cori gasped at the sensation. Pulling away from Kenzie's kiss, she arched her back and thrust her breast harder against Kenzie's hand.

Taking advantage of the availability, Kenzie brushed back the hair from the nape of Cori's neck and began to kiss and nibble on her soft skin. Cori's low moans spurred her on, and she pressed her thigh between Cori's.

Fiery kisses and Kenzie's every thrust rocked Cori with waves of desire. The wetness between her legs growing, Cori wanted to touch and kiss every inch of Kenzie.

Lean hips flexed up off the bed when Cori ran her hand over Kenzie's bared breasts. Some of Cori's kisses were soft and tender, others were more demanding as she bit and kissed her way down Kenzie's neck, then nuzzled her way over the supple breast.

Her kisses didn't stop and Kenzie didn't want them to. She reached up and ran her fingers through the honey-blonde hair, pulling Cori's mouth down toward her chest. Her body tensed and pressed into Cori's as Cori rubbed across an engorged nipple. Kenzie hissed in a sharp breath as a flash of pain ripped up her side. It only seemed to intensify her desires.

Kenzie's reaction spurred Cori on as she captured Kenzie's nipple in her mouth. With her tongue, she teased in lazy circles, tenderly licking and kissing. Kenzie's moans grew louder, causing Cori to lick and suck harder. Pulling the whole nipple into her mouth, she grazed it gently with her teeth. When Kenzie cried out for more, Cori happily obliged. Leaving that breast in the care of her hand, her mouth moved in search of the other. Her body reacted to every one of Kenzie's moans, while her hips continued to grind against Kenzie's thigh.

As if knowing what she was thinking, Kenzie lifted her knee between Cori's legs and Cori groaned, the sensation causing her to forget her attentions to Kenzie's breast. Cori looked down at the semi-naked woman below her and drank in all of the body that she could see, but it wasn't enough. Reaching for the waistband of Kenzie's pants, she was surprised when Kenzie stopped her.

"One of us is wearing too many clothes," Kenzie said as she ran her hand up and under Cori's shirt.

More than willing to comply, Cori sat up and pulled her top over her head and tossed it to the floor. "Better?"

"Much," Kenzie murmured as her eyes wandered over Cori's breasts. She sat up and wrapped her arms around Cori's naked body and pulled her close. "You feel so soft and warm," she said, nuzzling and nipping Cori's neck.

Leaning away, Cori looked into Kenzie's eyes and then moved in to kiss her. Intertwined, they fell back onto the bed together, their hands roaming wantonly over needy flesh.

Kenzie's bandages were rough against Cori's skin, and she gently brushed a hand over them. "I don't want to hurt you," she whispered. "Are you sure we should?" Lifting her gaze to Kenzie's eyes, she was surprised at the absolute desire she saw there.

"I'm sure if you stop now, I may never recover," Kenzie said with a lazy grin. "I guess we're just going to have to be careful, that's all."

"Oh, I can be careful," Cori answered slyly. "Very... very...careful," she said as she placed soft kisses all around Kenzie's side. The result was instantaneous as Kenzie laid her head back and moaned, and the heat between them flared as Cori's hand roamed down Kenzie's body. Sliding easily over the bare skin and then down over her pants, Cori's hand came to rest on the mound between Kenzie's legs. She pressed hard and Kenzie groaned. Rhythmic stroking had Kenzie bucking into the hand with need, and she let Cori know it with each pleading "yes".

"I...want...you. Oh God, I want you," Kenzie pleaded.

Together they rocked, moaning with each exploring touch. Twisting and turning, grinding and humping, until Cori felt Kenzie's body clench as her hips rose off the bed. Kenzie's orgasm was enough to spiral Cori over the brink, and in a collective gasp, they tightened their grip on each other as a long, gloriously drawn out series of spasms washed over them and their bodies melted into a euphoric release.

"That was incredible," Kenzie murmured.

Cori snuggled in closer. "That was beyond incredible." Her words were soft, satisfied.

Kenzie pulled her in tighter. "I think I just might need my bandages changed a little more often."

Sliding past the pale blue roof of the Tacoma Dome, the Coast Starlight train pulled into the station an hour and twenty-two minutes late. Cori and Kenzie cautiously climbed from the train. To their relief, there was no one waiting for them. There was no one there at all. The long covered platform was deserted and quiet, except for the rumbling of the train.

The mighty engine churned behind them and the train lurched northward with a bang. Cori slung their bag over her shoulder and reached for Kenzie's arm as the train began to move. She leaned toward Kenzie's ear. "Now what?"

Kenzie looked left and right, getting her bearings as she breathed in the fresh air. It was fast approaching sunset and the sun hung low in the sky. There was a feel of moisture in the air and she tilted her head back to look at the dark clouds forming. It was a pity because she really was hoping to catch a glimpse of Mt. Rainier. She sighed to herself. She was almost home, but it didn't give her the comfort it should have. Surprisingly, the feel of Cori's hand on her arm did. "Let's see if we can find a taxi before the rain starts."

Moving away from the platform and away from the train station, they found one lone cab in front of the building, waiting patiently in hopes of a fare.

"Where to?" the cabbie asked, barely giving the two women a glance.

"We need a motel, something cheap. Anything north of here will be good."

The cab driver got them exactly that — a two-story, Mom and Pop motel, though the neon *E* was burnt out in the sign. It advertised free movies and wireless Internet access, but all that mattered was that it was cheap and north of the train station. A few extra bills were slipped to the night clerk, and they checked in without having to fill out a registration form. The rushing sound of Interstate 5 filled the silence between them as they made their way across the open parking lot toward their ground floor room.

Kenzie's progress was slow, partly because she was tired and sore, but the true reason for her cautious movements was even more ominous. She was checking exits, sight lines, and vantage points, looking for anyone who might be paying them more attention than they should.

Under the cover of the second story walkway, Kenzie unlocked their door. A musty, stale smell escaped from the room as she pushed the door open. Flipping the wall switch illuminated two queen-sized beds, a small table with two chairs, a dresser, and a TV. "It will do," Kenzie said as she stepped into the room.

Cori was right behind her. Dropping their bag, she closed and locked the door. "You know, in another few years these colors could be back in style," she said sarcastically as she flopped onto the bed. "But I don't care. It will be nice to sleep on a bed that isn't moving, swaying, or rocking."

"Funny," Kenzie gave the bed a quick push, "I didn't hear any complaints about the moving bed earlier."

Cori bit her lip to silence her retort, but the smile and flush on her face were revealing.

Kenzie went to check the bathroom. It was outdated as well, but by all appearances, it was clean. "Okay," she said as she stepped back into the room, "the first thing we need is another cell phone."

"No." Cori stood up. "The first thing I need," she slid her arms around Kenzie's waist, "is to kiss you...on solid ground."

Kenzie studied her face and looked into her eyes as Cori's lips drew closer.

"Without the confinements of a Mexican change room..." Moving ever so slowly, she stared into Kenzie's golden eyes, waiting and wanting. "And without the movement of a train, I want to kiss you." She was readily accommodated. The kiss was long and passionate, but she could sense Kenzie's tension. Pulling back from the kiss, she brushed back the dark curls. "I know we're still in danger, and I know we have to be careful, but I wanted you to know—"

Kenzie kissed her again. "I know. After all this time with you, I know. But there are a few things we do need."

"Like food...and something to drink." Cori leaned back with Kenzie's arms locked around her waist.

"Yeah, and some answers," Kenzie added. Releasing Cori from her embrace, Kenzie moved to the window. Pulling back the thick curtain, she stared out into the night as Cori sat down on the bed. It had begun to rain, but that was not new for the Pacific Northwest. She looked over the dark parking lot and was relieved to see no one in sight. Though she knew, if a pro was out there, they would not be seen.

Cori watched Kenzie surveying their surroundings. "It's fine, there's nobody out there."

Kenzie released the curtain without saying a word, letting the thick material fall back into place.

"Just tell me exactly what we need, and I'll go get it."

"No. I'll go."

"No, you won't. You're going to stay here and rest. Have a real shower...there's shampoo and stuff in the bag. I'll get us something to eat, and a phone," Cori added quickly.

"I would feel better, if it was me–"

"Kenzie, please, you need to relax." Cori hopped off the bed and stepped in front of her. Sliding her hands around her waist, she looked into her eyes. "Remember, we need you healthy. I can do it. I'll be fine."

"I'm not going to relax and have a shower while you're–"

"I'll be fine." Cori leaned forward and gently kissed Kenzie's lips. "You need your rest." She picked up the bag, and dropped it onto the bed. Unzipping the opening, she pulled out one of the bundles of cash that she had already dipped into for Steven's money. Folding a couple of the bills into her pocket, she turned to go.

Kenzie reached into the pocket of her jacket and pulled out the gun. "If you're going, take this."

Cori looked down at the firearm. "I'd rather not."

"If you're going out...you're taking this," Kenzie said firmly.

"I don't like guns."

"You don't have to like them to shoot them, and it could save your life." It was a battle of wills as the two women faced off with the gun between them. "You had no problem picking it up when we were on the train," Kenzie pointed out.

"That was different. I didn't know who was on the other side of the door."

Kenzie softened her voice as she looked hard into Cori's eyes. "And you don't know what's on the other side of this door, either." Kenzie pointed at the room door.

She couldn't argue Kenzie's point, so Cori grudgingly reached for the gun. "Fine, but I better not shoot myself."

Chapter 19

In his sparsely decorated, highly organized office, Terry Bucannon waited. It was late in the evening and most of his department had gone home, but not him. He was a nervous wreck. His palms had been sweating for several days. He had been trained to handle just about everything from criminals to terrorists, foreign and domestic, to volatile situations that could change the economic and power structures of the world, but not knowing the whereabouts of two women who could destroy his life and career was tearing him apart.

Winston Palmer was on the phone to him regularly, his anxiety was climbing hourly, and that alone made him edgy. Manuck was using his military connections, but too many inquiries would raise even more questions. If someone was watching them, the connection between them all was becoming evident, and that he didn't like. It was easy to pull the strings when everyone under him was conditioned to do as they were told and not ask why. If they weren't careful, everything they had been doing would become public knowledge.

Rising from his chair, he stood and looked out the window at the lights of Seattle. He could see the snaking stream of red taillights clogging the Interstate as everyone tried to rush home in the rain. Pushing his suit jacket to the side, he placed his hands on his hips and sighed. His eyes moved over the cityscape and he looked at all the other office windows still lit. *I'm not the only one still at work.* Then his gaze moved to the dark windows and the hundreds of dark rooftops, and a chill went up his spine. *Is she out there? Is she watching me now through binoculars, or worst yet, a sniper scope?*

He quickly backed away from the window and turned off the overhead light, leaving only his desk lamp to illuminate his office. "Jesus Christ, Terry. Get a hold of yourself," he said aloud. Rubbing at the day's stubble on his face, he took a deep breath. As far as they knew, LeGault and Evans were nowhere near Seattle, though he wasn't kidding himself. They had no idea where the two women had gone. Every mode of target acquisition they could think of was being monitored as well as they could without raising too much suspicion – bank accounts, identification providers, phone lines, air traffic, bus stations, train stations, and even the Sounder, Seattle's commuter train. So far, there had been no trace of either woman. Nevertheless, something deep in his gut told him this was the calm before the storm. She was coming, he knew it and Manuck knew it – it was what she had been trained to do.

When Cori returned to the motel room a short while later, the warm moistness of the room and the clean smell of shampoo told her the sleeping form on the bed had had a shower. Shaking the rain from her hair, she pulled the gun from her pocket and placed it on the second bed as she laid her bags down quietly.

"I'm awake," Kenzie mumbled.

Cori went around and crawled into bed next to her. She snuggled in tight against the warmth of Kenzie's body. "I got a prepaid cell phone, some basic essentials that I hadn't picked up before, and Chinese for dinner," she said, nodding in the direction of the white plastic bag.

Kenzie wrapped her arms around Cori, relieved that she was back. Cori's body was cold from being outside, and Kenzie held her tightly as they kissed. Wanting nothing more than to spend the evening in bed with Cori, she reluctantly rose from the bed. There were things she had to do.

"I need to phone the judge," Kenzie said as she went over to the table and picked up the cell phone.

"You need to eat first, so you can take your antibiotics. Please," Cori said as she pulled their dinner from the plastic bags. "Please."

Kenzie looked at the phone, and then slid it into her pocket. "Does that mean you need to change my bandages?"

"You need food," Cori said with a bright blush.

"You're easy to read, but sometimes hard to understand," Kenzie said with a chuckle as she accepted her take-out from Cori, pecking a quick kiss on her cheek. They ate in relative silence, watching the news on the TV. When they were finished, Kenzie turned the volume down and pulled out the phone. She hesitated for a moment, but then flipped it open and began dialing the judge's home number.

Cori reached out and snapped the phone shut. "What are you doing? You can't just call him. What if they have his phone bugged or wired or whatever?"

"I can guarantee that they do. But don't worry, I know what I'm doing." Kenzie flipped open the phone and dialed the number. Putting the phone to her ear, she let it ring once and then quickly closed the phone, disconnecting the line.

"Was it busy?"

"No. It rang once and that's all I need. The line was never connected so they can't trace the call, but I'm counting on him to have call display."

Cori let the information absorb. She considered herself very computer and tech savvy, but this was something new. "So he can get your number from call display but they can't trace the call because he didn't pick up, meaning the connection was never made?"

"Basically." She redialed the number, let it ring once and then hung up again. "The judge is a smart man, he'll figure it out." The phone in her hand vibrated.

She looked at the displayed number of the call coming in. It was not the judge's home number. "Hello?" she said guardedly.

"Katherine." His voice was hushed, the concern for her clear.

"Is this a safe line?"

"Yes." He sighed with relief. "Thank God you're okay. I've been worried about you. I tried the other number you gave me, but it was no longer in service."

"It's a long story. I'd love to tell you all about it over a chess game, but now isn't the time. What did you find out for me?"

"Just hold on a second. Are you okay?"

"I'm fine." She looked over at Cori, who raised an eyebrow in question. "A little beat up around the edges, but that's normal," Kenzie said truthfully.

"Where are you?"

"I don't want to say right now, but we're close."

"What's going on, Katherine?"

"I don't know. I'm hoping you can tell me." Kenzie looked at Cori who was listening to her every word. "Who was in charge of this mission? Who ordered the hit?"

"As far as I've been able to find out, there was no mission, there was no hit."

"Are you sure?" Her brow furrowed. "I saw the orders."

"Not according to those in the know. There was no mission. I even had them check flight logs...nothing. They've been wiped clean."

"That's not possible. I saw the orders, and I know I didn't walk to Mexico." A cold chill seeped through Kenzie as her mind raced with questions. "It was black ops, so you can't be sure. I need to talk to Colonel Manuck."

"Katherine...I'm sure. There is no one running anything in Guadalajara, nothing in Mexico. There wasn't even a record of your being there. As a matter of fact, there isn't even—"

"But I had orders," Kenzie said. "Somebody okayed those orders. Colonel Manuck has to answer to someone."

"Katherine...listen to me."

Cori watched with rising fear as Kenzie's expression and body language changed.

"Judge...maybe you missed it? I mean – you don't understand. This is high level security stuff. Maybe you..." Kenzie was beginning to feel the desperation of uncertainty. None of it made sense, and that was scaring her.

"I'm a federal judge, with some friends in very high places. I understand national security. I know about black ops and some of what they do. Katherine, you need to listen to me. There was no mission in Mexico, there is no record of you being sent down there. There's no record of you — period." He paused, giving her a chance to digest what he'd said. "Are you listening, Katherine? There's no government record that you even exist. You died several years ago in the line of duty."

Kenzie shook her head. "I know that," she answered with a shrug. "That was part of the deal. That's what I'm saying...we were running under the radar of even black ops. We were a kill squad. I knew that, I accepted that."

Cori studied Kenzie's face. She didn't like what she was hearing. *Kill squad, black ops? What have I gotten myself into?*

Kenzie suddenly leapt to her feet, her hand balled tightly into a fist. "That was part of the deal. If I didn't exist, and I was caught somewhere that someone like me shouldn't have been, then I was on my own. I had no backup, no government ties, and no country to blame."

"I understand all that. I understand why we need operatives that don't exist. What I don't understand is why somebody went to all the trouble of making your flight to Mexico disappear. What about this Colonel Manuck?"

"I don't know. He has to answer to someone. Somebody in the military had to okay this." Despite her protest, her words no longer had the strength of her convictions. "Somebody in the government had to know what was going on–"

"Katherine," the judge interrupted quietly.

"I had my orders. Colonel Manuck gave me my orders." The answers sounded hollow, even to her, as she contemplated what he was telling her.

Cori watched in growing apprehension as Kenzie lowered herself onto the bed.

"This isn't right, Judge. This isn't right." She swallowed hard as the dryness of her mouth thickened her tongue. "If there's no record of the mission in Mexico, then who ordered the hit? Who's calling the shots?"

"Katherine, have you talked to this Colonel Manuck?"

Kenzie wiped hard at her face. "No," she answered with an anxious sigh.

"No communication with him whatsoever?"

"No."

"Why not?" the judge asked.

It was not the first time that question had crossed her mind. Colonel Manuck was her superior, she answered to him, but he was much more than that to her — he was her mentor. Kenzie had trusted him like she had trusted no other. He was to have her back, so why had he not been there for her this time? "I don't know. I wouldn't know how to...he's always contacted me."

Judge Woodward listened to her words, letting them sink in before he commented, "Then why didn't he contact you when the mission failed?"

"I don't know. He couldn't. He had no way to." The truth was, she didn't want to know the real reason, because if Manuck was not with her, he was against her. That meant Kenzie really was out there all alone.

"Have you tried to contact anyone else?"

"Manuck was the only one I ever talked to. He was my only contact."

"There was no one else? What about in the case of an emergency? There had to be a number or a least a name of someone to call."

Frustrated, Kenzie lashed out. "No. I told you! I was to have no connection with the military or the government whatsoever! I was on my own."

Regretting that he'd had to push her into thinking beyond the familiar parameters under which she operated, the judge sighed. "Exactly."

The phone on Deputy Director Bucannon's desk warbled, echoing loudly inside the quiet office. "Bucannon," he answered curtly.

"Sir, its Agent Bisby. We just had something interesting on the asset's tap."

"Talk to me," he answered impatiently as he picked up a pencil and put it to paper. The asset referred to was the judge. It made their jobs less complicated if no one used names.

"A call came in a few minutes ago, but there was no connection. He didn't pick up the phone."

"He's home?" Bucannon queried.

"Affirmative, sir."

"So what...he was busy and he didn't want to answer the phone."

"It happened twice, both calls coming in within seconds. He didn't answer either of them, sir. It was out of the ordinary so I thought I would let you know."

"What was the number?"

"There was no number, sir, because there was no connection. No connection, no trace."

It was her. Bucannon was certain. "What did he do?"

"That's just it. He didn't do anything. He never picked up the phone. He didn't try calling the number back, nothing."

"What about his cell phone?"

"Inactive, sir." Agent Bisby waited. He was unsure whether he had done the right thing by disturbing the Deputy Director, even though it was his asset and his operation.

Bucannon's mind was racing with possibilities. *What is she doing? Trying to reach the judge, but why? Maybe we should get rid of him.* "Shit, he's a goddamn federal judge," he muttered to himself in disbelief at the thought that had crossed his mind.

"Sir?" Agent Bisby questioned in confusion.

"Just a minute, I'm thinking." Bucannon rubbed his temple and then began to tap lightly on his forehead. "What is he doing right now?" The agents had no idea who the judge was or why he was targeted. It was not their job to know, it was his.

Bucannon listened as Agent Bisby asked his surveillance partner. There was a long moment of silence before the other agent spoke, and the Deputy Director strained to hear what was said, but he couldn't make it out.

"He's what?" Clearly even Agent Bisby was startled by his partner's comment. "But we don't have anything on that—"

"Agent Bisby, what the hell is going on?" Bucannon angrily interrupted the two agents' discussion.

"Ah, sir, it would appear that the asset is on a cell phone, one we were not aware he had," Agent Bisby said.

"Well, whose phone is it? Where did he get another phone?" The fact that the judge had gone out of his way to acquire a spare phone confirmed what he suspected: the judge had been in contact with them.

"I don't know, sir. We've checked our records and as far as we know, he only had the one cell phone."

"Well, I would say you missed one! Get a patch on that other phone." Bucannon rose to his feet. "I want to know who the hell he's talking to!"

"We aren't set up for that, sir. We just have a mobile," Agent Bisby said, referring to the minivan they were crammed into.

"Son of a bitch!" the Deputy Director yelled as he paced. They had her, goddamn it, but he couldn't find her unless they could trace the call. "Do you have a cone?"

"A cone?"

"What exactly are they teaching you these days?" Bucannon fired off in annoyance. "A cone...a parabolic microphone."

"Negative, sir."

"I need audio! I need to know what he's saying!"

"Do you want us to break shadow?"

"No. We don't need that," Bucannon said, not wanting his agents to leave the anonymity of the vehicle. Then again, if the judge knew what was going on, he knew too much already. "Do you have the ability to acquire the asset?"

The question caught Agent Bisby off guard. They were there as surveillance not as a scoop squad, though he would do whatever was ordered. "We aren't set up for it, but if that's what you need, sir."

"Yes...no," he quickly corrected. "Just sit on him and try to find out who he's talking to. Let me work on it from this end." He disconnected the call and punched in Manuck's number.

"We have a situation."

"I'm well aware of that," Manuck said.

Bucannon ignored the sarcastic tone. "The judge is on a cell phone with someone, and we don't know who he's talking to."

"You can't trace it?" *You are inept, Bucannon. How did you get to be Deputy Director?* Manuck had been in a foul mood all day, and the incompetence of those around him was not helping any.

"It isn't a phone we were aware of. My guess is he picked up a clean one or has borrowed one, because there's no evidence that he purchased one."

Manuck didn't have to guess who the judge might want to call. He was more concerned with the why. "So she's talking to him. Interesting."

"What do you want to do? You want me to grab him?"

"No. He's our lead to those two and we need to find them." Manuck contemplated the situation for a moment. "You can't trace the call?"

"No, not at the moment, unless of course you want me to take the surveillance into the main war room. If we do that, though, we're bringing a lot of people into this. I think we need to keep this as quiet as possible."

"I agree. Can you get in and place some bugs?"

"That I can do."

"What do you mean – on my own? I'm working for my government, for my country."

"Are you sure?"

"Yes, goddamn it, I'm sure. I follow orders."

"Katherine, I think you need to look at this...and..." His voice trailed off.

"Judge?" Kenzie queried after a moment of silence on the phone.

"Just a minute," he answered quietly, and she could hear him moving around.

"What's wrong?"

"I'm not sure." The judge turned off his living room light and moved slowly toward the front window. "I think..." he cautiously pulled back the corner of the curtain, "I think I have babysitters," he said angrily as he eyed the van across the street.

"Any idea who it is?"

He slowly moved the curtain back into place, not wanting the surveillance to know they had been spotted. "My first thought would be to assume they're looking for you."

"You need to get out of there."

"I'm not going to go sneaking out into the dark like some common criminal."

"If they're after me, then it wouldn't be a stretch to say they'll be coming after you," Kenzie said with growing regret. She had put the judge – who was the closest thing to family she had – in danger. "You need to get out of there," she repeated.

"They aren't going to grab me out of my own home."

"You're right, they probably won't grab you. They'll just take you out of the equation."

"Katherine, I'm a federal judge," he said with authority.

"And I've taken out men a lot more powerful than a federal judge," she said clearly. "I don't know what's going on here, but I'd feel a lot better if I knew you were safe. You need to get out of your house. Get somewhere safe – you know how to do that. Then call me."

"What are you going to do?"

The question echoed her own thoughts. "I don't know. I don't know where to start to sort this mess out."

"In my experience, Katherine, trouble comes from greed for either money or power. Pick one, and don't let go until you find your answers. I would start with your Colonel Manuck."

Chapter 20

Agent Bisby was holding onto his headset with one hand and tweaking dials with the other. His partner, Agent Willow, was running a numeric algorithm on his computer, searching for a cell phone number he knew he would never get. The knock on the side door of the minivan caused them both to jump.

"What the hell?" Bisby looked at his partner in question.

Willow leaned back and peeked through the heavy curtain separating the back of the van from the cab. "It's the cops."

On cue, the officer outside the van banged impatiently. "Open up, Seattle PD."

"Shit." Bisby pulled off his headphones. "Bucannon isn't going to like this." He parted the curtains and climbed into the passenger seat, pulling the curtain shut behind him. He could clearly see the uniformed officers, one next to the van and the other standing near their patrol car that was blocking in the van. *Standard procedure*, Bisby thought as he reached for the door handle.

"Hands where I can see them," the officer standing at the door ordered. His gun was out, though aimed at the ground. "Hands where I can see them!" he demanded loudly.

Agent Bisby complied, his hands out in front of him as he slowly exited the van. "Officer, I can explain."

The judge's car reversed quickly out of his driveway, and both Agent Bisby and the police officer turned to look.

"Willow, he's leaving!" Bisby yelled as he slapped at the side of the van.

The cop turned his attention back to the occupant from the reportedly suspicious van. "Hands up!" the cop bellowed.

The door of the van slid open revealing Agent Willow in his dark navy slacks, crisp white dress shirt with the sleeves rolled up, and his gun in a shoulder holster.

"Gun! Gun!" the uniformed officer yelled, escalating the situation.

"We're CIA agents," Bisby tried to explain with his hands held high over his head. He watched in disbelieving anger as the taillights of the asset's car disappeared from sight.

"Hands up. Don't move!" The second cop had moved in and now pulled Agent Bisby's gun from his hip holster.

"We are CIA agents!" Bisby repeated in angry frustration.

The police officers weren't listening as one of them pulled Agent Willow from the van and confiscated his gun.

"Get on the ground! Get on the ground!" the cop directed.

"We are CIA agents. My ID is in my suit jacket in the van," Bisby said through clenched teeth. Deputy Director Bucannon was not going to be happy at all.

Cori gave Kenzie some space after she hung up the phone. Her conversation with the judge had obviously bothered her, but she didn't seem to want to talk about anything in detail. Cori understood the basics, and that was hard enough for her to process. A full stomach, a warm motel room, and a large bed soon proved to be too enticing for Cori.

Soft, steady snoring distracted Kenzie from the swirl of activity in her mind. Seeing Cori asleep, she began to feel her own exhaustion. She went over and sat on the bed. Cori's expression was so tranquil and at peace, that Kenzie was a little envious. She brushed back Cori's bangs, letting her fingertips follow the contours of her cheek. *Why did all of this have to happen now? Why couldn't we have met under different circumstances?*

"Hey."

Cori's whisper drew her attention, and Kenzie smiled down at the sleepy-eyed woman.

"Hey," Kenzie responded.

"You okay?"

"Yeah."

"Come to bed," Cori requested.

"Is it time to change my bandages?" Kenzie asked mischievously, forgetting for the moment all the problems they faced.

Cori tugged Kenzie firmly toward her. "We may get to that."

The next morning when Cori woke, she found reassurance in the fact that for the first time since she'd met Kenzie, Cori knew exactly where she was — in the same place she had fallen asleep. It was a nice feeling, but not as nice as the comfort she found in the warmth of the woman beside her. Kenzie's fever was a thing of the past, and her wounds were healing nicely. Cori smiled to herself as she recalled the evidence that Kenzie's strength and stamina were returning as well. They had made love long into the night, exploring each other's bodies with a sense of discovery. Kenzie was an incredible lover and, for a moment, Cori thought about waking her to tell her that, but decided to let her sleep. She was exhausted and still recovering from her wounds.

Cori ran her fingertips over Kenzie's naked back as she let her mind wander. All they had been through together, whether it was by choice or circumstance, was no longer part of her thoughts.

Regretfully, she finally disentangled herself from Kenzie's arm and legs, and padded barefoot to the bathroom. As much as she didn't want to rise, her morning pee was not going to wait. Once she was up, she knew she could not go back to bed. Besides, she didn't want to disturb Kenzie's much needed rest.

The motel-supplied coffee was perking and its aroma filled the air, waking Kenzie. She carefully stretched as her eyes opened to the woman hunched over the table. Her interest was piqued as she watched Cori scribbling away on a note pad. Crawling quietly out of bed, she moved with silence toward a seriously focused Cori. Standing behind her, she watched as Cori continued making notes on the pad of paper they had brought from the train.

"What's this?" Kenzie asked, causing Cori to jump.

"Holy crap, you scared me!" Cori brought her hand up to her pounding chest.

"Sorry, I didn't mean to startle you."

Cori took a moment to gather herself, then leaned back in the chair. "It's something I was trying to work out in my mind."

Kenzie looked over the notes with interest. "You have a lot going on in that pretty little mind of yours, don't you?"

"I was trying to figure out where I had heard your name before, but nothing is connecting. The only place our paths might have crossed would have been in Seattle."

"That would explain why you brought us back here."

"I hadn't really considered that."

Picking up the pad of paper, Kenzie flipped through all of Cori's notes. "I thought we had been over your time in Seattle."

"It's your name," Cori said. "I know I've heard your name before, I just can't place where."

"Heard it, or seen it?"

Cori thought about the question for a moment, but shrugged her shoulders. "I don't know."

Kenzie gave her the pad back and then turned her attention to the world outside their window. "The judge should be here soon," she said, more to herself than to the preoccupied Cori. He had called the night before after he had shaken his watchdogs. It took him a while to convince Kenzie that he would be okay and would see them in the morning. Reluctantly, she had given him their location, hoping the information would not put anyone else into jeopardy.

"I'm gonna take a quick shower," she said as she crossed to the bathroom. "Don't open the door for anyone, understood?"

"What about the judge?" Cori asked.

A second later, Kenzie poked her head out. "How would you know it was him? You've never met him."

"Point taken," Cori said as Kenzie disappeared into the bathroom. The sound of running water quickly followed.

Flipping over her pad, Cori wrote out Kenzie's full name for the second time.

Freshly washed, and with a cup of motel coffee in her hand, Kenzie walked over and offered her cup to Cori. She declined with a shake of her head. "How're you making out?"

"I'm just driving myself crazy," Cori said.

Kenzie leaned down and kissed the top of her head. "Don't do that. It will come to you, but not if you push it." She grabbed the edge of the curtain and peered out into the drizzly morning. Stepping closer to the window, she placed her coffee down without taking her eyes off the car that had pulled into the motel parking lot. "I think he's here." Moving away from the window, she grabbed her gun and quickly returned. As far as she could see, he had not been followed.

The motel was shaped like a large, square U, and Kenzie had chosen their room because it was located directly across from the driveway, giving them full view of who came and went.

The judge moved slowly across the wet, deserted parking lot, heading not toward them, but to the closest covered walkway. Kenzie glanced at him several times, realizing he was moving slowly so she could see if anyone was following him. To her relief, he was alone. Unlocking the door with her left hand, Kenzie put her back against the wall as she held the gun with her right. She urgently motioned for Cori to move to the bathroom, and the young woman quickly complied.

Kenzie heard his footsteps and cautiously opened the door a crack to watch the judge's approach. Using her foot, she opened the door to him, keeping her eyes on the parking lot. Once he was inside, she closed the door but felt little relief.

Judge Woodward looked around the room and then to Kenzie. She looked a lot different than she had the last time he'd seen her. The quiet, cocky, confident woman he had known was gone, and in her place was a woman who appeared nervous, exhausted, and...something he could not quite put his finger on.

"Katherine...I'm alone," he said solemnly. "I made sure of it."

"I know. It's just that every time we thought we were alone, someone was right behind us."

Curious about the woman his Katherine had been ordered to kill, he looked around the room, but it was obvious no one else was there. Then he realized the bathroom door was closed. "She's in there?"

Kenzie nodded as she sat down on the bed.

"You look tired," he said as he pulled out one of the chairs.

"But alive, which is more than we should be," Kenzie said. "Cori," Kenzie called out. The invitation was obviously loud enough, as the bathroom door opened.

Stepping into the room, Cori smiled politely as Kenzie introduced them. She held out her hand as the judge rose to his feet. He was bigger than she had pictured. He didn't really look like a judge, but he did have that air of authority.

The judge was studying her, just as Cori was studying him. She looked...he searched his mind for the right word — *contradictory*. She appeared meek, but strong, young but mature. She appeared confident, though in great need of some reassurance. "You look like you need a hug more than a handshake," he said in a compassionate voice.

Cori welcomed the bear hug she got from the man she had just met.

Kenzie watched the exchange with interest, surprised by the feeling of pride welling up inside her. They were strangers with one commonality...her.

"Katherine, you never mentioned what an attractive woman she was," the judge said, still holding Cori in his arms.

"I didn't?" Kenzie watched a smiling Cori step out from the judge's embrace. Her face flushed and her eyes shimmering with tears, she smiled at Kenzie. "I should have." Kenzie said, beginning to realize just how much she cared for Cori.

The conversation quickly moved to a full recounting of everything that had happened and what they each knew. The judge listened quietly, asking the odd question as he looked with admiration at the two women who had been through so much. When it came to the telling of the explosion aboard Kenzie's boat, the judge's expression showed grave concern. "But I thought no one but you and I knew about your boat."

"You and I...and Big Polly — that's it."

"And you trust this...Big Polly?"

Kenzie looked him in the eye, her face, strong and certain. "Unequivocally, as I do you, but I guess somehow they found out about it."

The judge's face turned to one of sympathy and regret. "Ah, Katherine, your beautiful boat."

"I've tried not to think about it too much. I mean it's just a material thing, right? I can replace it. I'm glad that it wasn't us."

"But it could have been. You were lucky."

"It wasn't luck," Cori cut in. She had been silent through the depiction of their near death experiences, sitting at the table, scratching away on her pad of paper. "This woman is amazing. She has gotten us out of trouble so many times."

"I'm not amazing, far from it. I've made lots of mistakes," Kenzie said, not attempting to hide her frustration. "Besides, you're the one who got us out of San Diego. And let's not forget, I'm the reason why we're in all this trouble to start with."

"Are you sure about that, Katherine?"

"I'm not sure of anything right now. After our conversation last night, I don't even know who I've been working for."

"You said it yourself — you were just following orders—"

"So was Oliver North," Kenzie interjected, "And he wasn't actually pulling the trigger — I was. I've been all over the globe killing people and now I don't know..." Her voice drifted off, leaving a heavy silence in the room. There were too many questions, and for the first time, Judge Woodward got a full sense of what the women had been struggling with.

"We'll figure it out, I promise." Even to him, his words sounded hollow and uncertain. There was a lot of power at play and he was well aware they might never find the answers they were looking for. He had done enough service in the military and had worked long enough in the government to know that no matter how quiet and non-existent an operation was, sooner or later someone talked. But it would only matter if the right person was listening. "Follow the money, Katherine. You're smart enough to know that. Follow the money and follow the power, and you'll have your answers. I'll do what I can for you, you know that."

"Yes, sir," she said quietly. "But I can't ask you to do anything more."

"You're not asking, I'm offering. You're not in this alone."

She wasn't alone, and she felt a warm feeling of contentment as she turned to look at Cori. The truth of what she knew, but had not wanted to admit, hit her hard. The target in Mexico wasn't

Cori. "They weren't after you," she said in realization. "They were never after you...they were after me." It had been a long night of thinking, and no matter how she turned the pieces, they only seem to fit one disheartening way. "Whatever is going on, I've been a part of it, unknowingly, but participating. I think when I told Manuck that I wanted out, somebody got nervous. I became the problem that needed to be eliminated."

"We don't know that for sure," Cori said.

"Cori thinks there's some kind of connection between us, but...I don't know. None of this makes sense."

He looked at Cori. "A connection?"

"Yes...sir...Your Honor...ah..." Cori found herself stumbling over how to address him.

"My name is Benjamin, but my friends call me Ben, well, with one acceptation," he said, looking at Kenzie.

"What?" She shrugged. "You don't call me Kenzie."

"Your name is Katherine," the judge said. "Now, what is this about a connection?"

"We haven't actually found one...Ben," Cori said, turning her pad so he could read it, "but I know there is one. Kenzie's name...I've heard it, or seen it...somewhere."

Ben looked over the notes Cori had been working on. "You're spelling Katherine's name wrong."

"What?" Cori turned the pad around and looked at how she had spelt Kenzie's name.

"You have it with a C, it's Katherine with a K and LeGault is L-e-G-a-u-l-t." The judge picked up the pen and in neatly printed, block letters wrote out Kenzie's full name. *Katherine Mackenzie LeGault*, and then twisted the pad so Cori could see.

Kenzie watched the change come over Cori's face "What?"

"Oh my God," she said slowly.

Chapter 21

The cold rain fell heavily on downtown Seattle, but Terry Bucannon was sweating profusely. The judge had disappeared and the men he had sent to watch him had returned to their regular assignment. It had only taken a phone call and the cachet of the CIA for the local police department to forget the previous evening's mess. They had no idea where Kenzie and Cori were, but they all knew the two women were close — too close.

The heated phone call he had earlier with Manuck left him feeling desperate and vulnerable. Staring down at his computer, he studied the official emblem on the wallpaper screen. This was not what he had signed up for and he knew now that it had all gone beyond what he could explain. He thought about running. He had enough money — Maquinar had been very profitable for all of them — but where could he go? He had been asking himself that question all morning.

His cell phone vibrated in his pocket and a quick glance told him it was the annoying but persistent senator. He answered it curtly, expecting to hear more complaints and demands. That was not the case.

"What are we going to do, Terry?"

"I don't know," Bucannon answered, his voice filled with dejection.

"I just talked to Manuck, and he still thinks we can quash this, but I'm not willing to lose everything if he can't. He can't even find one of his own."

"What would you suggest, Senator? I'm open to just about anything."

"Let's make her a deal."

"And how do you suggest we do that? If we could find her to make her an offer, then it would be easier to put a bullet in her head."

There was a heavy sigh of frustration on the phone as both men contemplated their predicament.

The senator had had enough. "Well, I'm tired of this phoning back and forth. I want to meet, all of us, and figure out what we're going to do. This sitting around is not the way to get the job done."

"You want a meeting?"

"With *all* of us."

Terry knew Manuck would be against a meeting, but it was not his argument. Senator Palmer had a point. "You call him. I've already argued enough with him today."

"What?" Kenzie and the judge said in unison.

"Your name." Cori pointed to the pad as she looked up at them. "It was your name. I saw your name when I was working at Trillium."

"Saw it? Saw it where?" Kenzie asked, her eyes narrowing with interest.

"Remember I said that sometimes I did payroll? Nancy was sick and I was entering payroll numbers into the computer. Well, when I was shutting down the system there was a window someone had left open, it was encrypted, but it piqued my curiosity, so I started to play around with it. When I was finally able to read it, I realized it was only a basic payroll file."

"Payroll?" the Judge asked.

"Yeah. I remember it as being strange because there were only a few names in a department that I had never heard of. Trillium International has hundreds of employees, but they are all split up into just three departments: management, development, and office staff. The names I saw were in a separate department, all on their own. They had no social security numbers assigned to them, and their payroll checks were issued under names other than their own. You have to have a social security number to get a payroll check, that's the law." Cori looked to Kenzie. "Your name was one of those that I saw."

"You worked for Trillium?" Judge Woodward asked Kenzie in surprise.

"I've never worked for Trillium. I've never even heard of them."

"Well, they were issuing Katherine Mackenzie LeGault's payroll checks to an S. L. Etcher," Cori insisted strongly. Then another thought flashed, "Etcher, isn't that the name you had your boat moored under?"

"Yeah...but..." Kenzie was confused.

"What else did you see in the file?"

"Nothing, just payroll."

"What was the name of the department you saw," the judge asked.

"Waste management. That was another reason why I thought it was strange at the time. Trillium doesn't do any kind of waste anything."

"But I've never worked for this Trillium under any name."

"Are you sure you haven't, Katherine?"

"Judge, you know as well as I do, I've never had a job other than the military. I think I would know."

"You got paid, didn't you? Well, who paid you?"

"Yeah...but...I don't know..." Kenzie scratched her head. "It's all done by direct deposit. I've never paid that much attention to it."

"Let's follow the money then," Cori said.

"And find out who owns Trillium," the judge added.

They agreed the easiest way to find out who was behind Trillium would be on a computer, so they went looking for an Internet café. Flipping through the Yellow Pages, they found several, but they opted for one of two in the downtown area of Seattle, near where Cori said the offices of Trillium International were located. The judge had wanted to go to the courthouse where he would have federal access, but Kenzie was adamant that someone would be watching the courthouse. They left the motel in search of answers none of them had.

Zipping up Interstate 5 in the car the judge had borrowed, it took very little time to reach Seattle even though the traffic was heavy. Cori gave directions as Kenzie sat quietly in the backseat, alone with her inner turmoil. She paid little attention to where they were going, too concerned with where she had already been. Coming home, back to Seattle, she had hoped the feelings of disorientation would be dispelled, but she was disappointed. The familiarity of her surroundings only made her question herself more.

Looking out the window, she watched as they drove past Quest Field, home to the Seahawks, and Safeco Field where the Seattle Mariners played baseball. It all seemed so normal, and yet she felt her world imploding. She had wanted to go straight to the base and confront Manuck, but the judge and Cori sharply disagreed with her.

"I think we should take it to the media. Let King 5 News sort through the shit and find the answers," Cori said.

"We can't do that, not until we have some answers. Katherine's work was under the umbrella of the government and we have to be careful. The last thing she needs is to be charged with treason."

"And let's not forget, the government declared me dead years ago," Kenzie said from the backseat. "And if it turns out I'm no longer working for them, then basically I've just been travelling around murdering people."

Cori turned around and looked at Kenzie. "You didn't murder anyone, you followed orders." She reached out to touch Kenzie's hand.

"That's a little hard to swallow right now," Kenzie said, keeping her emotions in check and her eyes away from Cori's.

The judge glanced in the rearview mirror and then turned his gaze back to the road. "Let's not jump to any conclusions. We'll see what we can find out, and go from there."

Fingering the familiarity of the gun in her jacket pocket, Kenzie continued to process the flood of information and questions. A simmering anger was slowly replacing her disbelief. She was going to get answers, and they were not going to come from a computer.

The Internet café was easy to find, nestled on the corner between the high office towers on Pike Street. It was a café and coffee shop/ bookstore all rolled into one. Dark chocolate-colored leather couches made it homey and comfortable. Large pane windows on both sides gave it an open-air feel. The small coffee shop was nearly empty, allowing the trio their choice of computers. Picking one near the back of the art deco café, the three of them hunched around the monitor as Cori's fingers flew over the keys. Kenzie considered herself computer knowledgeable, however Cori proved to be very proficient. Trillium International was easy to find on the Internet, but getting into their computer system was proving to be beyond Cori's ability.

After a lot of keystrokes and a long wait, Cori leaned back with a defeated sigh. "I can't get passed their firewall. We need a real hacker or someone with a lot more experience than me. I can't even get beyond the login without — proper ID." She began to type rapidly. "I'm in," she said victoriously. "All that security and no one thought to erase my old login ID." She rubbed her hands together, "Now let's see what we can find."

The names of those running Trillium were public knowledge. The names of who actually owned it seemed to be more elusive. "Someone has put a lot of time and energy into covering up who the actual owner is." Cori scanned the scrolling lines of information.

"What did you find?" the judge asked as he peered at the screen.

"Not much really," Cori said, tapping away feverishly. "A lot of corporate names," she added.

"Let me try my way," the judge said as he pulled a pen from his pocket. "Give me what you do have, and the address of Trillium. I've got federal connections that should be able to bypass some of this."

"I can also try the back door," Cori said, looking from the judge to Kenzie.

"What back door?" Kenzie asked. She wanted to do something. Sitting around a café, idly waiting was not something she did well, and it was gnawing at her patience.

"Money comes in and money goes out," Cori said as the judge scribbled away on his notepaper. "There are taxes, payroll, electricity, phone lines. Somebody is paying for all that."

"I'm going to make some phone calls and see what I can find," the judge said.

"You look your way and I'll keep looking through the utilities. They're usually easier to get into," Cori responded as he moved to a different table and another computer.

Manuck was expecting the call. Palmer was getting antsy and Bucannon's backbone was disintegrating by the hour, but not Manuck. He was a soldier. There was a job to do, and he was going to get it done. He still had Viper at his disposal, and he had all the faith in the world that Viper could complete the assignment. He debated whether to answer the call, but the annoying buzz was just too persistent.

"Manuck."

"We are meeting today, with or without you," Palmer said without preamble.

"That wouldn't be my first suggestion," Manuck answered.

"It's not a suggestion, Colonel." Fury filled the senator's voice. "These phone calls aren't solving the problem, and the problem is only getting closer."

"And you think getting the three of us together, out in the open, is going to solve anything? Because it's not, it's just going to make us easier targets. She's in Seattle; we're sure of that."

"You have confirmation of that?"

"Cori Evans just hacked into Trillium's computer system."

"Oh my God... Wait. How do you know that?"

"Because she used her own login ID, but it don't matter, now. I think we should just see what they're going to do."

"You want to wait... Need I remind you that she isn't looking for us, she's looking for you. You're the only one who's had contact with her. You know her training better than we do, and you know exactly what she's capable of."

He had considered those elements himself, but still he didn't like being told what to do and where to do it. "What time are you meeting and where?"

"In the underground parking, level C, at three."

Cori and Kenzie were huddled in front of the computer monitor as Cori manipulated the mouse and ran the cursor over the screen. They were backtracking Kenzie's payroll deposits to her bank account. The amount she was being paid startled Cori. Kenzie had mentioned that she was financially comfortable, but Cori could see that was a gross understatement. It had never crossed her mind how much someone in Kenzie's line of work would be paid.

"The name of the company making the direct deposits to S. L. Etcher is not Trillium, but when you trace the transit number back, the money is coming out of their account." The judge read from a pad in his hand.

"So they were paying me?" The information only served to unsettle Kenzie further. "But why...and who?"

"The 'why' I don't know, but the 'who' is Palmer Tectonics." The judge slapped his pad of paper down in front of Cori and Kenzie. When they looked up at him in question, he continued. "It helps to be a federal judge when you're looking for information. Under all the paperwork and behind several dummy corporations, Trillium is owned by Palmer Tectonics...which is owned by...Winston Palmer." He waited for a reaction, but none came. "Winston Palmer?" Kenzie shrugged and Cori shook her head. "Senator Winston Palmer."

Kenzie's brow furrowed. "A senator? Are you sure?"

"He's a senior senator in the U.S. Senate," the judge went on as Cori turned back to her computer and typed in the name Winston Palmer.

"And he's worth millions," Cori added as she scanned the monitor in front of her. "He has his fingers in a lot of different pies, but mainly pharmaceuticals and real estate."

"So he owns Trillium and Palmer Tectonics," Kenzie repeated, trying to make sense of the information.

"Actually," Cori looked from her screen and leaned over to look out the window at the tall office building rising above the others, "he owns a lot more than that. He owns that entire building." Kenzie and the judge looked out the window to the skyscraper located a couple of blocks from them.

"Why would someone like that be paying the wages of someone like me?"

"And it wasn't just you, Kenzie. I saw other names on that list, too."

"Whose?" the judge asked.

"It doesn't matter, right now." Kenzie looked at the judge. "Right now I want to know why a senior senator, under the guise of being the government, would be paying an assassin?"

"I don't know, Katherine, but whatever it is, if he's mixed up in this, then so is your Colonel Manuck."

"But why? What are they up to?" Kenzie turned her attention back to the tall building towering above the Seattle skyline.

The senator's Bentley wheeled down into the underground parking of the Palmer building. The tires squealed as it turned the sharp corners, spiraling down, deep into the concrete parking structure. The further down they went, the fewer parked cars they saw. It was damp and cold, even for Seattle, but the occupant inside the Bentley was unaffected. On the last corner, at the very bottom, two cars sat side-by-side, waiting. There was no signal or outward appearance of recognition as the expensive luxury car pulled up next to them. The engine was turned off, leaving behind a cool silence.

"Keep it running. This won't take long," Palmer commanded from the backseat.

The driver restarted the car and watched in silence as the senator slid the solid, soundproof divider into place. Two men climbed from the first car: Colonel Manuck, wearing his military uniform, heavily decorated on the left side, and another man, wearing jeans and a brown leather jacket.

Terry Bucannon exited the second car, dressed in his usual dark suit thin dark tie. He looked around nervously before entering the rear of the car.

Manuck did not attempt to sugarcoat his annoyance. "Okay, we're all here. Let's hear what you have to say."

The tension in the car was palpable as the four men sat in weighty silence. The colonel looked at the deputy director, and then at the senator, but neither seemed to want to speak first.

"Ah, for Christ sake, we're here. Isn't this what you wanted?" Manuck said.

"What I want is for your rogue agent to be found and disposed of. But since we can't find her and her computer hacking friend—"

"Did you bug the judge's house?" Manuck cut in.

"Yes," Bucannon said, "but he hasn't been back. There has been no action on any of his credit cards or his bank accounts, and he's cleared his docket for the rest of the week."

"What about any of her friends and colleagues?" the senator asked.

"She doesn't have friends or colleagues," Manuck snapped. "For all intents and purposes, this woman is dead. She does not exist. We have nothing to trace, nothing to follow, which is the whole principle behind an undercover black ops operative."

"So we just wait until she finds us?" Bucannon said. "Because you said it yourself, it's what she does."

Manuck had no answer as he sat and seethed in silence.

"Well, I for one am not waiting. I say we shut down Maquinar, get our money, and get out of town."

"That's easy for you to say, Mister CIA spook man. I'm a senior senator in Washington, D.C. I can't exactly disappear like you can."

"No one is disappearing," Manuck cut in. "And we aren't shutting down Maquinar."

"Actually, I agree with Terry on that one, Colonel, at least temporarily. Shut it down and get our money out of it. And then once this problem is taken care of, we can start again, only this time — no women."

"How would you propose we solve this problem, Senator?" Manuck asked. "Because if you have any suggestions, I'm listening."

The argument continued back and forth amongst the three. Viper remained silent, feeling a little uneasy about what he was hearing. He knew who they were after, but he was not a hundred percent certain as to why. He assured himself it didn't matter. He had not liked that bitch from the moment he met her, feeling even then that she was a risk to the operation. Nevertheless, he was interested in what this Maquinar was.

"Viper, what do you think?" Manuck asked, interrupting the assassin's thoughts.

"About what, sir?"

"You have the same training, the same background. How would you find her?"

He hesitated for a brief moment, staring stone-faced at his superior. "You got a file on her?" he asked without emotion.

Bucannon pulled a brown manila envelope from his briefcase and handed it to him. "In depth, on every level."

Flipping briefly through the papers, Viper was confident it was all he was going to need. "Consider it done."

"Don't call me until it is," the colonel said as he opened the car door, signaling the end to Viper's involvement in the meeting.

The door closed and Manuck laid into Bucannon, "Are you crazy? You mention Maquinar in front of him!"

"Do you really think your men don't have a clue as to what they're doing?" Bucannon shot back.

"If they knew, we wouldn't be sitting here."

Bucannon leaned forward and glared into Manuck's eyes. "What the hell have you gotten us all into?"

"You knew exactly what you were getting into, so don't hand me that crap. You sit in your fucking ivory tower, spying on the world with high tech gadgets, snooping through the trash, and screaming national security when you're caught with your hand in the proverbial cookie jar. My men are in the trenches, up to their asses in mud and squalor, doing what needs to be done so that the lunatics of this world never get the power to annihilate everyone and everything that we hold dear."

"Don't even try to convince me, or yourself, that you did this for God and country, Manuck. You did it for the goddamn money!"

"Gentlemen! Enough!" the senator said loudly. "We all had our reasons, and what's done is done. The question is, what do we do now?"

"Shut it down," Bucannon answered.

"Temporarily," Manuck said.

"I say we shut it down permanently." Palmer looked at the two angry men. "Two out of three, majority rules."

The colonel glared at him. "I wasn't aware this was a democracy."

"I want this over with," Bucannon said, ignoring the arrogance of the military man. "Let's liquidate what we have, divide it up, and be done with it."

"It isn't that easy," the senator said. "First we have to close down all the bank accounts, and that will take time. I'll have to go through the Maquinar file—"

Dumbfounded, Manuck stared at Palmer in disbelief. "You have an actual file?"

"Yes, at home in my safe—"

"You have a hard copy of all of this in your safe?" Bucannon asked in shock.

"I'm sure not going to keep it on my computer. Do you know how much paperwork is involved," Palmer answered. "I'll close the accounts and divvy up the money. What about Viper?"

"I'll look after my men," Manuck said with resentment. "You just make sure we get our cut. And be smart, Palmer, get rid of the all the paperwork before you get us all thrown into prison."

Chapter 22

The tall office building loomed over the Seattle skyline with authority and grace. Its windows, shiny and bright, reflected the intrusive gazes of all those who dared to look in. Kenzie glared at the monument of power as she struggled with the information coming to the surface. "If I wasn't working with the government, then who was I working for? What did Colonel Manuck get me into?"

"I don't know but I can guarantee it's highly illegal. I say follow the money, Katherine. Where it comes from and where it goes," the judge said philosophically.

"I don't get it," Kenzie commented, pulling her jacket off. She didn't like the feeling of confinement. She hung her jacket on the back of the chair behind Cori and began to pace. "I haven't been working for the government after all. I've been working for Trillium, or rather Palmer Tectonics?" Kenzie ran her hand through her curls and pressed her fingertips hard against her temples. It was all too much. "Why the hell would a senator be paying me to kill people?" The volume of her voice carried over the other conversations in the café and several heads turned to look in her direction.

"Easy, Kenzie." Cori placed a hand on her back. The attention Kenzie was drawing concerned Cori. She turned to the judge with a silent plea for help.

"Katherine, take a breath and calm down. We don't know who's behind this. It might be the senator, or it could be anyone inside the company. Let's not go off half-cocked. We need to look into this further."

"Does it really matter? I thought I was working for the military and I'm not!" An overwhelming sense of desperation ignited her anger. "I murdered those people," Kenzie said, loud enough for everyone in the café to hear.

"Katherine, we've only scratched the surface here. Please, let's not jump to conclusions." The judge's voice was calm and even as he quietly attempted to quell her rising fury. "Right now, you need to calm down. The last thing we need is to call attention to ourselves." He reached for her arm but Kenzie pulled back, her hands up in surrender.

Cori saw a flash of panic in her lover's eyes. "Kenzie?"

"I murdered those people. Orders or not, I murdered them." Looking at the faces of the only two people she cared about in the world, Kenzie felt the foundations of her universe crumble. What did she know? Who could she trust? She had put Cori and the judge into mortal danger. She looked at the customers of the café, who were staring back at her, and she saw fear. These people feared her. She felt the walls of the café closing in on her.

"I-I gotta get out of here," she said, pushing quickly past Cori.

"Kenzie," Cori cried out as she rose to follow her.

Judge Woodward stopped her. "Let her go."

"I can't, she needs me." Cori attempted to move past the judge, but he blocked her way.

Placing his hands on her shoulders, he looked Cori in the eye. "She does need you, but not right now. Right now, she needs to find herself. Give her some time to digest all of this. For someone like her, this is devastating."

Cori felt helpless as she watched Kenzie storm out of the café. She wanted nothing more than to be there for her, but the judge was right. With an audible sigh, she sat back down and returned to her search on the computer.

Kenzie burst out of the café and onto Pike Street. The rains had stopped, but the air was still cool and damp. It felt good on her flushed face. Looking up at the gray skies and the glass archway that covered a block of Pike Street, she still felt as if everything was closing in on her. She had no idea where she was going, but wherever it was, she was moving fast. She wanted to run away from it all, away from the truth that was plying its way into her conscience.

Viper perused the papers Manuck had given him. It made him a little uneasy to see everything they had acquired on her. He knew with little doubt there was a file just like it with his name on the envelope. He was not surprised to see that she had no family, neither did he, and neither did his colleague, whose body would go unclaimed in San Diego. Cobra's death had angered him. They had worked together only a few times, but Cobra was the closest thing to a friend Viper had.

Without lifting his eyes from Kenzie's dossier, he pushed open the glass door and exited the building. His plan was to go over the information until he found something the others had missed. He was not as confident in his ability to find her as Manuck had been, but then again, he was not all that concerned about it, either. If he found her, he would kill her. If he didn't, he could just disappear and no one would ever find him. "That's what you should have done, LeGault, just disappeared," he said to her picture as he flipped a few more pages. So far, there was nothing for him to go on. But then again, he was only skimming the documents.

The afternoon rush had started, and the sidewalks were overcrowded. Oblivious to where she was going, Kenzie bumped into several people. She neither stopped nor apologized. Horns honked beneath the fists of impatient drivers and tires screeched over wet roads, but the sounds barely permeated her thoughts. Kenzie was not aware that she was heading in any set direction until she found herself across the street from Winston Palmer's office tower. Her eyes scanned upward over the tall building with the shiny glass windows.

Wanting nothing more than to confront the man who had put her into this position, she sought him out in every window, even though she knew he wasn't there. According to the judge, as a senior senator, Palmer was not permitted on the premises of his own business – something to do with a blind trust, the ethics committee, and financial disclosure – but she didn't care as she stood rooted to the sidewalk.

A man reading a newspaper and carrying a briefcase bumped her hard in the side, sending a wave of pain through her. It was enough to bring her attention back to the present and she stepped out of his way, but that moved her into the path of two women discussing the recent activities of a cheating boyfriend. Stumbling slightly, Kenzie saw their looks of annoyance as they continued on their way. Trying to avoid any further collisions, she moved from the bustle of the middle of the sidewalk to the edge, closer to the shop windows. In an attempt to collect herself, she took several deep breaths, releasing the air slowly through her nose, until she saw him.

Kenzie's breath caught and she held it for a moment. It was Viper and he was here. She watched him as he flipped through some papers in a brown manila envelope. Only then did it occur to her that Viper had just exited the Palmer Building. A flash of anger blasted through her and Kenzie reached for her gun. It wasn't there. Kenzie had taken her jacket off and left it at the café. She had no weapon — no offense and no defense. She stepped back into the flow of the sidewalk, keeping her eyes on Viper.

A woman, her arms filled with shopping bags, was too busy trying to hold them and talk on her cell phone to notice Kenzie moving into her path. The two collided. The woman and her bags and her cell phone landed on the sidewalk while Kenzie stumbled to stay upright. The woman's shocked silence was quickly replaced by a stream of loud profanity, causing passing pedestrians to give her a wide berth.

The commotion drew the attention of almost everyone on the block, including Viper. He stared in disbelief at the target nobody had been able to find. The two trained killers locked eyes. The world around them became a blur as each assessed the other.

Kenzie knew what he was thinking, the same thing she was thinking. Neither moved as the throngs of people walked past them. The angry woman collected her shopping bags and cell phone, and continued on her way, but not before calling Kenzie a few more sexually inappropriate names. It didn't matter. Kenzie's full attention was on the man across the street. Many questions rose to the forefront of her mind, but they were all forgotten when Viper made the first move.

He stuffed the papers he'd been reading back inside the manila envelope, folded it in half, and casually slid it into the inside pocket of his leather jacket. She didn't have to see the gun to know it was there. When he stepped toward her, it set her body in motion. Turning back in the direction of the café, she heard a car braking hard on the wet road. The blast of a car's horn told her Viper had attempted to cross the street. Kenzie took several steps and then stopped. The last thing she wanted was to lead him right to Cori and the judge. Spinning around and changing directions, she saw Viper stop to let a honking car pass him.

Pushing people aside without a thought, Kenzie ran down the sidewalk in the direction opposite the café. Viper had now made it across the street and was hot on her heels. With each step, she waited for the sound of a gunshot, but none came. Her feet slapped hard against the concrete as she zigged and zagged her way through the people. It didn't take her long to realize that the damage done to her body since Guadalajara had taken a physical toll. After just one block of running, her body was screaming in pain. She dared not glance behind her. She knew Viper was there, and she knew he was gaining. Few people seemed to show any interest in the two people racing down the sidewalk. As she turned the corner, Kenzie dug deep for what little energy reserves she had and almost ran into one of the many trees lining the city street. Viper was catching up and the only way for her to avoid being caught was to use her brain rather than her unreliable body.

Risking serious harm, Kenzie cut into the oncoming traffic, creating instant chaos. Cars skidded and collided with a flurry of horns, crunching metal, and harsh angry words. She slid across the hood of a car that had slammed into the rear of a truck in the other lane. Chancing a quick glance behind her, she was alarmed to see how close Viper was. Scrambling back to her feet, she took off running in and out among the stopped cars. The next block was not that far away, but neither was her pursuer. Turning quickly, she crossed the street and ran into the first open door she saw.

It opened into a carpeted corridor with wood grain paneling on one side, large floor-to-ceiling windows on the other, and it veered continuously to the right. People were now turning to look at them in shock and disbelief as the two raced past them. An elderly security guard lounging sedately at his information booth saw them coming and hastily jumped to his feet. "Hey, hey, hey...what's going on here?" he yelled after them, but neither Kenzie nor Viper paid him any attention. He quickly retrieved his radio and called for backup as the two intruders raced out of sight.

They ran out of the corridor into a large open area, a hub with hallways that split off in different directions. Kenzie chose a path to the right. Around the corner, the surface changed from carpet to tile and she was thankful that she was wearing sneakers. Viper was not so lucky. His boots didn't have soles that gripped and he went down, sliding hard into the wall. Kenzie didn't even slow her pace.

What had been an elegant corridor was now a mall with shops and stores, and she was running straight toward a food court and an escalator. With all she had, she took the moving stairs two steps at a time. It was a struggle because her legs were not that long, but she made up for it with grit, guts, and determination. Grabbing hold of the handrail at the top, she swung the corner just in time to see Viper reach the bottom of the escalator. Leaning down, she slammed her fist against the plastic cover over the bright red stop button, breaking the plastic and stopping the escalator with a loud ringing alarm. The sudden stop toppled Viper to his knees, and Kenzie heard him curse loudly.

Kenzie saw the exit doors and hit them at full speed. The metal fire doors swung open, banging loudly against the building walls. She was now on the second level of an open concrete courtyard. It was only then that she realized she had just run through Seattle's convention center. She felt a little more confident knowing where she was, however, her confidence was short lived. She saw Viper ascending the inactive escalator like a staircase. Without hesitation, she ran to the edge of the courtyard and leapt over the three-foot concrete barrier.

Flying through the air, Kenzie reached out for tree branches to slow her descent to the bushes below. Landing hard, she felt a sharp pain blast through her body. It took her a moment to collect herself. Getting to her feet, she crawled out of the bushes as people screamed and scattered. She glanced back at the second story and was not surprised to see Viper jump over the wall the way they both had been trained. He was not as lucky as she had been. Being bigger, broader, and a lot heavier, the branches snapped under his weight.

Kenzie heard the crashing thump as Viper landed. Without waiting to assess the damage, she sloshed her way through the small pool and past the decorative waterfall. Scampering down the last few stairs, she shot a glance behind her. Viper had had the wind knocked out of him, but he was staggering to his feet.

Racing across the courtyard, she heard Viper splashing his way through the pool. From the sound of his progress, he was limping badly, but that barely slowed him as he hurried down the last of the stairs.

Kenzie was back at the street where she had started. A quick look back told her Viper, limping as he was, was still catching up to her. Dashing out onto Union Street, she encountered the rush of the one-way traffic, the air filled with the sounds of screeching tires and horns honking. Ignoring the pain in her side, she wove her way in and out of the downtown traffic. Viper was only a few yards behind her when she heard a horn, followed by a sickening thud and the smashing of glass.

She slowed and glanced behind her. Viper's body was sliding down the hood of a car, its smashed windshield clear evidence of the traumatic collision. Kenzie stood gasping for air as she watched and waited. Viper was moving, but the chase was over. He was not getting up. Taking several deep breaths, she turned to go then decided against it. She was tired of running and she wanted answers. She moved toward him as several people hurried to his aid, unsure of what help they might give.

"Is he dead?" a voice asked as Kenzie approached him.

"Someone call an ambulance."

"I didn't see him!" the driver exclaimed in shock as he stood next to his damaged car. "He just came running out in front of me...he didn't even look."

Kenzie barely gave the driver a glance as she knelt next to Viper's broken body. He opened his eyes and stared up at her.

Kenzie was still breathing hard, but her face was devoid of emotion. Looking down at the face of the former colleague who was trying to kill her, she found she had nothing to say to him.

"Oh my God, he's alive!" a woman screamed behind her.

Viper was alive, though Kenzie could tell he wouldn't be for long. Blood bubbled from his lips and trickled out of his mouth with each breath. She knew what she had come back for, and so did he.

Viper groaned as he attempted to reach into his pocket. "Take it," he mumbled.

"Hey...what are you doing there?" a man holding a cell phone demanded.

Kenzie ignored the stranger as she stared into Viper's darkening eyes. She pulled the manila envelope from his pocket.

Viper could feel his lungs filling with blood as his approaching death eased some of his pain. He looked into Kenzie's golden eyes. "I only did...I only did what I was ordered to do," he said, pausing to catch a breath.

"But why?"

Viper swallowed several times, struggling for a breath. He didn't have the answer she sought. "It was what...I was told to do."

"By Manuck."

He managed a nod. "Not just Manuck," he sputtered.

"I know."

"We shouldn't...have killed...them. You...you were right." He coughed and choked on his words as the blood oozed over his lips. Desperate to ease his conscience, Viper fought for his last breath. "You need...to end this."

"That's my plan," she said coldly as she watched the life fade from his eyes. The distant sound of a siren signaled Kenzie it was time to leave. And she was gone.

The chime rang signaling a customer's arrival, and Cori looked at the door. Once again, it was not Kenzie. Try as she might to concentrate on her monitor, every sweep of the minute hand seemed like an eternity.

The judge observed her expression of disappointment and knew there was not much he could do to comfort her. "She'll be back," he said, trying to convince himself as much as her. "Give her some time."

How much time? Cori wondered. She rose to her feet and walked to one of the coffee shop's large windows. "I'm not worried about whether she'll come back – I'm worried about when she does come back." She watched the pedestrians and the cars as they passed the window. "This whole...mess has to be overwhelming to her."

The judge watched Cori as she maintained her vigil at the window. Her body was tense. She crossed and uncrossed her arms repeatedly. This woman was a stranger to him, but he still felt the need to protect her, if not from the people who were out there trying to harm her, then at least from herself. "What about you?" he asked.

"What about me?" Cori echoed without taking her eyes from the constant flow of pedestrian traffic.

"How is all of this affecting you?"

Turning away from the window with a perplexed look, she addressed him very matter-of-factly. "You mean besides the shooting, the running, the explosions, the fires, and the not one, but two, near drownings? Or are you referring to falling in love with a woman whose life has been turned upside down and inside out? Because either way you slice it, I'm fine...or I will be once she walks back through that door."

"You love her?"

"I do." She turned back to the window, watching for Kenzie as an ambulance wailed past the café. "And don't ask me why because I couldn't explain it to you any more than I could explain the color green to a blind person. It's just what it is."

Kenzie was moving as quickly as she could without drawing attention to herself. Heading north, all she wanted was to get back to the judge, and to Cori. With great relief, she saw the glass archway and knew she was close to the café. Her pace slowed as she glanced down at the file and the blood on her hands. It was not her blood, but it could have been. She stopped and thought about where she was going. The manila envelope had her name on it, not Cori's. It was irrefutable confirmation that she had been the target the entire time, not the woman she was going back to. Cori was safe now, in the care of the only person left in the world that she trusted.

The sirens were getting louder and so was the voice of her conscience. How could she go back to them, knowing it was she who was putting them in danger? She couldn't, and she knew it. Raising her arm, Kenzie flagged down the first cab she saw.

"Where to?" the driver asked as she climbed into the backseat.

"Anywhere but here."

The cab driver glanced at her in the rearview mirror as the woman pulled a wad of money from her pocket. He could see blood on her hands as she peeled off a bill and handed it to him. Accepting the money, he decided it was not his concern, so he turned on his meter.

Leaning back in the seat, Kenzie took a deep breath of relief when the cab pulled away from the curb. Where she was going, she had no idea. When they passed the café, Kenzie spotted Cori standing in the window, her arms crossed and a look of concern on her face. Kenzie told herself that she was doing the right thing, but if that was true, why did she feel so bad?

"You got a cell phone?" she asked the driver. He nodded and pulled one from his pocket. Kenzie handed him another bill. "I just need to borrow it." And he passed it back to her.

She was not sure what she was going to say, but she didn't want them waiting at the café any longer.

The judge, focused on his computer monitor, almost missed the vibration of the phone in his pocket. He looked at Cori as he answered the phone.

"It's me," Kenzie said in a tired voice.

"Where are you?"

"That's not important at the moment. Look, you need to get out of there."

"Are you okay, Katherine?"

"I'm fine. I just need you to take Cori and go. Get out of there, now. Find some place safe. I have a couple of things I need to do, but I need to know that she'll be safe."

"Katherine, what are you going to do?"

"I trust you, Judge. I trust you with her life and yours."

The judge persisted. "Katherine, where are you?"

"Please...just look after her, okay? I'll contact you." She closed the phone, ending the call.

Cori snatched the phone from the judge's hand. "Kenzie!" But she was gone. "Where is she? Is she okay?"

"She said she was fine, but we need to go."

"What do you mean, go? If she's fine then why are we leaving?"

"Because she told us to leave," the judge said as he gathered up his things.

"I want to know what she said, what's going on."

"Not now, Cori. We need to go," he said, taking her by the arm.

Cori pulled from his grasp and stood defiantly still. "I'm not going anywhere until you tell me what she said."

The judge looked around the café, and then out the windows. No one appeared to be paying them any special attention, but that didn't ease his concern. It all seemed so unreal to him, everything except the frustration on Cori's face. "Katherine didn't tell me what was going on. All she said was that we needed to leave and to get somewhere safe. That was all. So might I suggest that we leave...now."

Reluctantly, Cori scooped up her papers and pulled Kenzie's jacket from the back of the chair. The weight of it sent a cool shiver of fear through her.

Judge Woodward saw the change of expression. "What? What is wrong?"

She silently reached into the pocket of the jacket and showed him the butt of the gun. "It's her gun!"

"Put that away," the judge said in a hushed whisper. "We attracted enough attention earlier."

"But it's hers... She has no gun...no way to defend herself."

The judge stepped toward Cori. Putting his hand on hers, he slid the gun back into the jacket. "I'm not comfortable with that, so let's leave it where it is." He wrapped an arm around her shoulder and they headed for the door. "I wouldn't be too worried about Katherine being defenseless. I know her and I know what she's capable of. She is more than proficient in the art of defending herself, with or without a gun."

Staring out the taxi window, Kenzie tried to decide where she was going and what she was going to do. Pieces of the puzzle were starting to fall into place, yet she still didn't have an idea what the big picture was.

The judge had told her to follow the money, so she decided to do just that. The money came to her from Trillium, and it came to Trillium from Palmer Tectonic. If she was going to start anywhere, it might as well be at the top.

"Do you know where Winston Palmer lives?" Kenzie asked the cab driver.

He shrugged. "Who?"

Kenzie pulled a couple of bills from her pocket and held them up to him. She watched his eyes as she asked again. "Senator Winston Palmer."

"I think he lives out on Lake Washington somewhere."

She added several more bills to the collection, and the driver eyed each of them greedily. "Somewhere?" she asked, offering him the bills.

"On McGilvra Boulevard, about half an hour or so from here." He took the money and changed direction.

Chapter 23

The skies darkened with the approach of evening as the cab made its way northward toward Lake Washington. The homes grew in grandeur as the gates and fences grew in height. The taxi slowed as they wound through large, lavish residential properties in search of Senator Palmer's home.

Engrossed in the information she had taken from Viper, Kenzie had not been paying close attention to their direction. It was her entire life typed and neatly assembled inside a manila envelope. The more she read, the more defeated and disheartened she felt. They had it all – from the addresses of her bank accounts to the zip code of her bike mechanic, and scrawled in the margin of one of the papers was the marina where she had kept her boat. They, whoever they were, knew everything about her.

The driver slowed the car as they approached the senator's gated home. "We're here."

Looking up from the file, Kenzie peered out the car window. "Don't stop. Pull up there, beyond those trees."

He did as directed, curious as to what was going to happen next. His fare had intrigued him since he saw the thick roll of money in her pocket. She had been quiet if not anxious, or maybe frustrated. He watched her looking about the neighborhood.

Kenzie pulled three more bills from her pocket. "Give me half an hour. If I'm not back, redial the last number on your cell phone and give him this." Kenzie held up the brown manila envelope and then laid it down on the backseat. She started to pass him the cash, but had second thoughts. Ripping the bills in half, she handed over three halves, "Just to make sure you wait."

He took the torn bills and looked at her quizzically. "And if you don't come back?"

"The man on the phone will reimburse you for your time and trouble."

Exiting the cab, Kenzie quietly closed the door. She walked past the large mansion the cab driver had pointed out as Palmer's, examining every detail of the fence, the gate, and the security system. It told her the man who could afford all of this had a lot of money, and a lot of enemies.

Climbing a large tree next to the stone wall gave Kenzie a better view of the grounds around the senator's home. There were only a few lights on, but with a house that size it would be impossible to tell if he was alone or even home. Checking the area, she tried to ascertain whether there were any in-ground sensors, but she wouldn't know for certain until she was standing on the neatly trimmed lawn. After a quick glance back to assure her the cab had not left, she scaled the fence and dropped into the unknown.

Holding herself in a crouch, she listened for the sound of an alarm. To her relief there was only the quiet serenity of an affluent neighborhood. No barking dogs or raised voices, no signs of life beyond the fences, everyone was safely tucked inside their homes. Moving cautiously in the shadows, she was on alert as she made her way down past what she assumed was a large garage. Kenzie's heartbeat was strong and steady as adrenaline pounded through her. The grass and bushes were wet from the afternoon showers, but she paid them little attention as she crept along the side of the house. Rounding the corner, she ignored the million-dollar view of Lake Washington as she glanced from window to window. Stepping with care onto the multi-level cedar deck, she was not surprised to find the first set of double doors locked. Treading cautiously, she tried the second set of doors and a couple of windows, but they were all locked as well. Picking up a small potted plant, Kenzie moved to the last set of double glass doors. Swinging the ceramic pot back with enough force to smash the glass, she hesitated a moment and tried the handle. To her amused surprise, the door was unlocked. Kenzie returned the potted plant and stepped silently into the house.

She found herself in a massive kitchen. Expensive looking stone countertops were bare and cold looking. The stainless steel fridge was unadorned, without even a picture or magnet. In the center of the kitchen was a large island, shadowed above by a copper and iron grid that held pots and pans. The only thing out of place was a single dirty plate next to the sink, its cutlery placed neatly in the center. Someone was definitely home.

In the stillness of the evening, a muffled voice came from deeper inside the house. Leaving the kitchen, Kenzie followed the faint sound. Moving through the house, she ignored the elaborate design and the impeccably positioned furnishings, concentrating all her senses on one destination. The art on the walls and the Italian furniture meant nothing to her. All she wanted was to locate the person who was talking.

She made her way to a wide hallway, which ended with a set of dark double doors. Moving toward them, she could see that one of them was slightly ajar. The voice she'd been following was now clearer. The speaker had an English accent and the voice was obviously coming from a television within the room. Approaching with caution, she stopped several times and looked back in the direction from which she had come. Kenzie was thankful when she found nothing but the stairs leading to the second floor. Inching closer to the open door, she heard the sound of fingers tapping on a keyboard. Kenzie chanced a quick peek into the room.

There were two carpeted steps down into the sunken room, making the ceiling seem even higher than it actually was. There were bookshelves on three sides, with a single draped window on the far side. Best she could tell, there were no other doors. In the center of the room a man sat at a massive L-shaped desk, totally engrossed in what he was typing. Kenzie knew from pictures she had seen on the computer at the Internet café that this was Senator Winston Palmer, and he was alone. It was all she needed to know.

Without making a sound, she moved stealthily into the room, taking it all in. The room's elegant décor was washed with a male hand. The shelves were lined with books, leather bound and expensive. A framed degree from an Ivy League school was prominently displayed on one shelf, surrounded by pictures of the senator with several presidents. Scattered across several shelves was a collection of miniature swords perfectly placed in little stands. Kenzie moved to the TV and pressed the off button.

Silence and tension instantly filled the room. Palmer's hands froze above the keyboard. "They said you would show up," he said without turning around.

Kenzie was not concerned by the comment, but by his use of the word "they". Putting her back to the one wall of books, she quickly looked back and forth between the senator and the hallway. "So you know who I am?" She waited to see if he had alerted someone else in the house, but no one arrived.

The senator leaned back in his chair. Calmly, confidently, he put his fingertips together and turned to face her. He observed Kenzie with interest, respectfully curious about the woman who had ruined all of their plans. "Yes, I know who you are, and I've been expecting you."

"Really?" Her senses in overdrive, she warily watched his every move.

"You've had more lives than a cat, Miss LeGault." He looked her up and down, the woman who had eluded them. "Though you do look a little worse for wear."

Kenzie remained silent.

"Funny though, I thought you'd be taller...and maybe a bit smarter. You shouldn't have come here."

"If you knew I was coming, then I don't have to ask if you're involved in all of this." Kenzie took in his air of rich arrogance and his scheming political smile. If he had been expecting her, then she might have walked into a trap. There was no time to waste with idle chitchat. "Why has Trillium been paying me?" He chuckled and she wondered if it was from nerves.

"Is this where I'm supposed to confess all my sins and answer all your questions?"

"That would be the easy way to do it," her gaze was steely, "but make no mistake, Senator, I am leaving here with answers. The easy way...or the hard way, I really don't care. And before you shoot back another sarcastic quip, keep in mind that you've been paying me to kill people. Adding you to that list wouldn't bother me in the least." She watched and waited for his reaction. "I want to know why."

The smile on Palmer's face didn't fade, but the gleam in his eyes darkened. "Quite simply, my dear, you're very good at what you do, and I employ the best."

He sat calmly in his overstuffed, expensive chair, his overconfidence annoying her. "You're a senator. You're not supposed to employ anyone, certainly not someone like me. You and Colonel Manuck had me convinced I was working for our government, not a private party like you." Kenzie included her mentor's name to gauge Winston Palmer's reaction. He didn't show one. It confirmed what she already suspected about her commander: Colonel Manuck was involved!

"Maybe you should have read the fine print, or maybe taken a better look at one of those fat checks you received. The military sure as hell doesn't pay that much." Palmer studied her, impressed by what his money and power had bought him. She was good, he had no doubt, good enough to thwart all their attempts and still be standing there in front of him. "Are you here to kill me?"

"If I have to," she said honestly.

"What is it that you want, LeGault?" He dropped the friendly, relaxed façade. "Money?"

"No," she said, irritated by his attempt at bribery. "I want answers."

"Really?" He chuckled. "Money is much more fulfilling."

Ignoring his flip comment, Kenzie pushed on. "I'm supposed to be working for the government, so why have you being paying me?"

"Why?" He laughed outright, motioning with his hand matter-of-factly. "To kill people — isn't that what you do? You're very good at it, by the way."

The senator's comment didn't bother her, but it brought to mind her comment to the colonel, and the reason she had gone to Mexico in the first place. "Why Cori Evans?"

"Miss Evans saw the wrong thing at the wrong time. Simple as that."

"Simple as what?"

"She saw a payroll file that she shouldn't have seen. It was a connection to me, through my company, I could not afford to have made. It would be a little...difficult to explain why I had been funneling money to pay for a bunch of soldiers that were supposedly dead."

"So why have your company pay for Cori to move to Mexico to go to school? Why not just kill her here?"

"Because killing her here would raise too many questions. We couldn't have a bunch of state police sniffing around. We didn't know who she had talked to and we certainly couldn't afford to have her death be connected back to me. It was cheaper just to send her away."

"So then why send me down there to kill her?"

"If you had done your job, and Vasquez had done his, then both of you would be dead."

Vasquez? The name of the shooter she had killed north of Guadalajara. "So he was there to kill me?"

"We had no choice. When you mentioned that you wanted to opt out of our little program, we had to do something."

There is that "we" again, Kenzie thought as she scrutinized him and considered what he was saying. Winston Palmer was not nervous and he surely didn't look concerned, and that bothered Kenzie. "Who's the 'we'?"

He chuckled slightly, "Don't know all the players yet, my dear? Frustrating isn't it? Not sure who to trust, even those close to you have sold you out, that has to be annoying."

"But why? Why have you been paying me to kill people?"

Dropping his hands to his lap, he grew serious and stared hard into her eyes. "Are you really that naïve? For the money, of course."

"How does my killing people make you money?"

Palmer grinned smugly. "Taking out the right person at the right time puts you in control. When you control governments and companies, you manipulate how they do business and with whom.

It's very profitable. Government contracts, medical supplies, munitions – it's a great money making circle. You start the wars, supply the guns, treat the wounded, and on the outside fringe you control the prices of the commodities. It's a license to make money, and you, my dear, helped to keep it all in play."

He moved his chair slightly and Kenzie knew he was up to something. *Is he stalling...or waiting for someone?*

"I've been making money off you for years, and you had no idea."

Kenzie's stomach churned with the truth of what he was saying. It was too much for her mind to grasp as she tried to keep herself aware of what he was doing and what he was saying. "I never would have gone along with it if I had known what you were doing."

"That's a little irrelevant now, isn't it?"

"Do you think I'm going to let you continue doing what you've been doing?" She moved slowly down the book-lined wall. She placed her hand on the edge of the shelf and concentrated on the man she knew she was going to kill.

The smile returned to the senator's face. "You can't stop me. After all the people you've killed, you're no different than I am. You did your job for the money, just like I did. I just invested better."

His smile froze and Kenzie saw the muscles in his neck grow taut. His gun cleared the desk as she grasped one of the miniature swords from the shelf behind her. In one fluid motion, she flung the lethal weapon as she dropped to the carpet a moment before he fired the gun. It was a small caliber pistol but the sound filled the room, echoing in her ears as she rolled to her feet. She stood before him, her body tensed for action, but it wasn't necessary. The miniature sword she had thrown was buried up to its tiny hilt just above his collarbone. It was not the target she had aimed for, but the spurting arterial blood told her she had succeeded nonetheless.

Senator Palmer had his hands to his neck, but he couldn't stop the flow of dark red blood oozing from between his fingers. His eyes were wide with surprise and disbelief as he watched her move slowly across the room toward him.

Kenzie climbed onto his desk and knelt in front of him. "I'm nothing like you! I didn't do my job for money," she said. "I followed orders because that was what I thought I was supposed to do."

The reality of death suddenly frightened him more than Kenzie did. "You bitch," he spat as the color drained from his face.

Kenzie's features turned dark with anger. "Who else is in on this with you besides Colonel Manuck?"

The senator coughed and sputtered as panic filled him. "Go to hell!" he said, tightening his grasp on his neck in a futile attempt to stem the escaping tide of blood. A cold chill slithered through his body, sucking the strength out of him. The feeling of helplessness was new to him, but he would not have to endure it for long.

"Was it just you and the colonel?" she demanded. The life in his eyes began to dim and Kenzie grabbed him by the hair. "Who else was in on this? Who else was involved?" She needed to know, but he had no answer. He was dead. "Who else!" she screamed into his face. She needed the information, but it wouldn't be coming from the senator.

"I can tell you."

In one fluid motion, Kenzie let go of Palmer's hair, scooped up his gun from the desk, and spun around. "Who the hell are you?" she asked the young Asian standing in the open doorway.

"My name is Derek." He stood rigid, then bowed slightly. "Derek Lee. I was his," he gestured toward Palmer's slumped body, "driver slash assistant. Although slave might be a better name for what I was."

Kenzie kept the gun aimed squarely at his chest. Her mind was spinning with everything she had learned from the senator and she didn't know what she should do. "What are you doing here?"

"I live here. I heard the shot and I came to see what happened." Derek looked over at the still body of his former employer. The only real emotion he felt was relief.

"Were you aware of his business dealings? Did you know what he was doing?"

"Not all of it, but yes, some of it. I believe you're referring to Maquinar."

"Maquinar?" Kenzie recalled seeing the word written several times inside her file. "What is Maquinar?"

"You are. He is...or rather was. Him, Colonel Manuck and — I think the answers you require...may be in there." He bowed his head toward Palmer's desk. "May I?"

Kenzie gestured him forward with the gun, but she kept the weapon trained on him as he descended the steps and crossed the room. Going behind the desk, Derek knelt down in front of a floor safe and spun the dial.

"You have the combination?"

"Senator Palmer considered me insignificant and invisible, doing things in front of me that he should not have, but I'm astutely observant...and far more honorable than he was." He opened the safe and pulled out a thick white portfolio with the name MAQUINAR written on it in red. "I don't know all that they were involved in, but I suspect it was totally illegal and highly immoral."

Kenzie laid the gun on the desk and accepted the package. Did it really hold the answers she was looking for? Judging by the weight, it held a lot of something.

"You need to go," Derek said cautiously. "Someone may have heard that shot. I can give you five minutes and then it will be my duty to inform the police. He was a senior senator, after all, though it was self defense."

Moving toward the doors, Kenzie stopped and looked back at Derek. "Why are you doing this?"

Standing over the man he had loathed for so long, Derek felt no loss or remorse. "Like I said, he was not a lawful or moral man, and he did not live an honorable life. But I did not have the courage or ability to stop him. He promised me years ago that he would help my family come to this country. Instead, they work for one of his companies in Thailand, under deplorable conditions for very little money. I did not have the means to bring them here, or to give them their freedom at home." He stepped away from the man who had financially restrained him, and looked at Kenzie. "I'm free now, and so are you, but you must leave...now."

She took a step toward the door and then turned back to the desk. Scooping up the gun, she spotted Palmer's cell phone and grabbed that as well. Her gaze fell on the open safe. Moving to the other side of the desk, she collected the stacks of crisp new bills and handed them to Derek. "I don't think he'll need this anymore. You deserve it, you and your family."

Holding the cash in his hands, he shook his head. "I could not accept this. This money was made from people like my family."

Kenzie stopped at the open doors and turned back to him. "That's why they deserve to have it."

Derek pondered her rationalization and then bowed. When he straightened, Kenzie was gone.

Kenzie was thankful the cab driver was still waiting for her as she climbed back over the stone wall.

"Where to now?" the driver asked as she slid into the backseat.

That's a good question. "Just drive," she said as she unwound the string securing the white portfolio file. The file was thick and she knew she would need time to look through it.

Chapter 24

Cori and the judge booked themselves into a hotel and waited. The minutes ticked by at an agonizingly slow pace. The judge had spent the afternoon on the phone doing what he could to keep himself busy, hoping to connect some of the pieces of the never-ending puzzle. Cori paced, picked at her nails, watched some TV, had a shower, and then paced some more. She decided that being on the run with Kenzie was better than waiting and wondering where she was. The judge assured her that Kenzie was well-trained and could take care of herself, but it did little to quell Cori's rising anxiety. Standing at the window and looking out into the dark of the night, she wondered for the umpteenth time where Kenzie was and whether she was okay.

It was well after midnight and neither of them was tired or sleepy. They had not heard from Kenzie and the judge was beginning to worry about how long he should wait before he started to make some of his questions more official. If something had happened to her, how would they ever know? Looking over at the young woman lying nervously on the sofa, he wondered what he was supposed to do about her. If something happened to Kenzie, could he keep Cori safe?

The cell phone on the end table rattled noisily, startling them both. The judge scooped it up and quickly flipped it open. "Hello?"

"It's me."

The judge nodded, affirming it was Kenzie, and Cori breathed a loud sigh of relief. "Where are you?" Judge Woodward asked.

"At a gas station, somewhere downtown." Leaning against the trunk of the taxi, Kenzie rubbed her tired eyes. "I've been riding around in the back of a cab half the night."

"We've been worried about you," the judge said, watching Cori.

Kenzie closed her eyes as an ache of loneliness welled up inside her. She wanted nothing more than to wrap her arms around Cori and leave the rest of the mess to someone else. Unfortunately, Kenzie knew if they started to run now, they would never stop. They would never be safe unless she brought all of the players down. She had to finish Maquinar.

Physically and emotionally exhausted, Kenzie sighed loudly. "The senator is dead," she said abruptly.

"What?"

"Senator Palmer is dead. It was self defense," she interjected before the judge could ask.

"Are you okay?"

"I'm fine. Tired, but fine." Kenzie knew she was way past tired. She had read the file and had a pretty good understanding of what had been going on, and it made her physically ill to know that she'd had a part in it, however unwitting. Feeling raw and exposed, she realized how much she hated who she had become. There was no honor in what she had been doing. "Have you ever heard of Maquinar?" she finally asked.

"No. Who is it?"

"It's not a 'who', it's a 'what'." She glanced over as the cab driver emerged from the gas station mini-mart with two large coffees. "The good senator was kind enough to have everything in a file. It lists names, places, dates, you name it. I don't understand it all yet, but I get the general idea of what was going on. "

"Bring it to me."

"No, not yet. I want answers from Manuck. He and the senator were behind it all."

"Katherine, if the file has what you say it has, you don't need to do any more. Come in. Let me take the file to the proper authorities."

Kenzie accepted her coffee from the cab driver, and then waited until he was back behind the wheel. "I can't. I need to do this for me. I need to see him. I need to hear it from his mouth."

"Just turn yourself in, Katherine."

Kenzie felt lost, disillusioned. "To whom, Ben?" she asked, using his first name for the first time since they had met.

"Then come in, or at least meet us somewhere."

"I can't do that. I'm too hot right now, and I won't put either of you in any further danger."

"Katherine–"

Cori had heard enough. She could tell the judge was getting nowhere with Kenzie, so she grabbed the phone from him, cutting off his plea.

"Kenzie."

The simple sound of her name whispered by the woman she loved was almost enough to make her forget it all. All she wanted was Cori.

"Are you okay?"

Looking up at the blinking red lights atop Quest Field, Kenzie knew she didn't have an answer, even for a question that simple.

"Kenzie, are you there?"

"I'm here. I'm sorry I walked out on you today. That wasn't my intention when I left the coffee shop."

Just hearing Kenzie's voice gave Cori the relief she was looking for. "Things happen, right?" Cori's eyes welled up with tears of release.

"Yeah," Kenzie answered softly, not trusting her own voice.

"Are you gonna be okay?"

Kenzie sighed deeply, unsure of the answer. "Depends. Are you going to be sticking around after this is all over?"

"That was kinda what I had in mind," Cori said as she smiled through her tears.

Standing alone, leaning against the cold trunk of the taxicab, Kenzie questioned her own intentions. Maybe the judge was right after all, it might be better to hand the whole thing over to someone else. Let them sort through it. In the time it took her to formulate that thought, she realized the government rarely admitted to its mistakes, and when it did, it was those at the bottom of the ladder that found themselves in the deepest shit.

"Kenzie," Cori's whispered plea brought her back, "come back to me."

"I'm working on it."

A half-empty bottle of Crown Royal sat in front of Deputy Director Bucannon. He had not slept and he had no intention of trying. Sitting on his sofa, he swirled the alcohol in his glass and then tossed it back, draining the remains. He leaned forward, poured himself another liberal libation, and then reached for his phone. No one had called him all night and he was beginning to feel like he was no longer part of the solution, but part of the problem. Dialing the senator's number from memory, he had to wait for only one ring before an unfamiliar voice answered the phone.

"Senator?" he slurred.

"Who's calling?"

"Who is this?" Bucannon asked, sitting up a little straighter.

"May I ask who is calling?" the authoritative voice repeated.

"No, you may not. Who is this and where's the senator?"

"This is Detective Montenegro, Seattle PD. Now it's your turn... Hello...hello." Bucannon quickly hung up the phone.

The detective turned to a junior officer. "Find out who that was."

Terry Bucannon's heart was beating loudly as he licked at his dry lips. *Seattle PD! What the hell are the cops doing there? Calm down, calm down.* He dialed the senator's cell phone.

Kenzie was sipping her coffee in the back of the taxi that was still in the parking lot of the gas station. When she told the driver she had nowhere in particular to go, he asked if they could just stay where they were. He explained that the cost of the gas came out of his pocket, and she understood. Also, it was easier to read from the file sitting still.

The cell phone on the seat next to her lit up and vibrated, dancing in an erratic circle on the worn upholstery. She picked it up, looked at the name on the Caller ID, and recognized it from the file. Terry Bucannon. Glancing down at his file, she noted his picture neatly stapled to the corner of his dossier. For the first time she knew the name of the man she had dubbed "Kevin", the man who had sat across the table from her so long ago when Colonel Manuck had recruited her.

The phone vibrated again in her hand as she climbed from the cab. She opened the phone and put it to her ear.

"Jesus Christ, Palmer. I just called your house and the cops are there. What's going on?" His voice was slurred with alcohol and panic.

"Deputy Director, Terry Bucannon, NCS, National Clandestine Service, CIA," Kenzie read from the file. "Graduated Harvard law, in 1976. Joined the CIA in—"

Just the sound of the woman's voice was enough to shut him up as the air slowly escaped from his lungs through his open mouth. He didn't need to ask, but he did anyhow. "Who is this?"

"I think you know who I am. We met once before, though we were never introduced."

"LeGault!" he said. "Where's the senator?"

"He's dead." There was a long pause and she could almost feel his rising panic through the phone. "I know about Maquinar. I have the file."

"Jesus Christ!"

Kenzie glanced through the window at the file spread out over the backseat of the cab. "It has all been meticulously documented: names, dates, assignments...bank accounts."

Bucannon sat back as an eerie calm came over him. It was over, and surprisingly enough, he felt relief.

"The only thing I don't understand is...why?" Kenzie said, "Was it all just for money?"

Foregoing the glass, Bucannon put the bottle to his lips and took a long drink. He welcomed the burn of the alcohol as it slid down his throat. Placing the bottle back on the table, he wiped his lips before he answered her. "It wasn't for the money, at least not for me, not in the beginning."

"Then explain it to me."

Taking a long, slow breath, Bucannon wondered how he could have let things go so far. Their plans in the beginning had seemed so honorable and just. He wondered how he could put it all into perspective for her. "If we could have taken out Osama bin Laden before 9-11, what would that have been worth to the people of the world?"

"Him, I would have done for free. But isn't that part of what the NCS is about – fighting terrorists?"

"Yes. The National Clandestine Service was created in the wake of the 9-11 attacks, but you have to understand—"

"I do understand, but we weren't killing terrorists, Mr. Bucannon."

"We only call them terrorists after they have committed an act of terrorism. What if we could eliminate them before they have a chance to kill thousands of people, or what if we could take out a dictator before he becomes a tyrant putting lives and freedoms in harm's way? People questioned why no one stopped Hitler before he murdered millions of Jews and tried to take over the world, but by the time we knew what he was doing, it was too late."

"So Maquinar was created to kill these people, these civilians, before they did anything?"

"They weren't civilians," Bucannon said defensively.

"Cori Evans is a civilian."

The statement and the name caught him off guard, and it took him a moment to respond. "That was different. That was Palmer's remedy to his own problem. Cori Evans knew too much about the distribution of the money. She put the whole operation in jeopardy."

"So it was about the money?"

"It wasn't about the money," Bucannon said with conviction. "It was about saving lives and trying to bring stability to a world out of control."

"So by killing people, you gain control of the governments and their leaders, thereby getting control of their money."

"Yes...no, it wasn't about the money." But Bucannon was no longer convincing even himself. "At least not in the beginning."

"Well, it's all over now. Maquinar is finished. Your career is finished," she said with disdain. "And when I've found and dealt with Manuck, I'm coming after you."

"Don't bother," Bucannon said as he reached into his side table, pulled out his gun, and put it into his mouth.

The rolling ticker at the bottom of the TV screen had been announcing the senator's death for over an hour. Manuck desperately wanted to know the particulars, but there was no way for him to make inquires without drawing unwanted attention. He knew LeGault had a hand in it, just as she had with Viper's death. He kept asking himself where she was now, and how much she knew.

His phone rang, and when he looked at the call display, he smirked. The senator was dead, so there was only one person who would have the guts to call him from the senator's cell phone. "I wondered how long I was going to have to wait to hear from you."

"Colonel." Kenzie addressed him with his military rank more out of habit than respect. "The senator and Bucannon are dead."

He had been concerned when he hadn't heard from Bucannon after the news about the senator broke. Now he knew. Not surprisingly, the information did not bother him in the least. It was one loose end he no longer had to tie up. "I didn't know about Bucannon, but thanks for the update. So now what? Are you coming after me?"

"I want to meet."

The colonel laughed. "So you can put a bullet in my head? I think not. I'm not that stupid."

"I don't need to kill you. This is over. I'm finished, and so is your career."

The truth of her statement burned inside of him. He didn't trust her, but he was curious. "Why meet then?"

"Because I want answers and only you can provide them," she said honestly.

"So, ask away."

"Not on the phone. I don't trust you any more than you trust me. I want to be able to look you in the eye."

"Again I say, so that you can kill me?"

"You pick the place and the time."

He thought about it for a moment, quickly weighing his options. It had to be someplace public, but not too public. There would have to be people, even at this time of the morning, and it would have to have good access in and out. If he played his cards right, he could finish her off, then lay low until the whole mess blew over. Maybe a meeting wasn't such a bad idea after all. "The boardwalk at Waterfront Park, in front of the fountain. Two hours."

The judge, Cori, and a subdued Kenzie sat edgily in the car in the public parking lot across from Seattle's Waterfront Park. Lined with benches and lampposts, the wide wooden boardwalk ran the length of the harbor between piers 57 and 59. It was home to shops, restaurants, charter boats, and the Aquarium. It was early, the sun had just come up, and the boardwalk was already busy with tourists and locals alike. The rush hour was humming along above them on the Alaskan Way Viaduct as Kenzie, Cori, and the judge waited for Manuck's arrival.

"He'll be early," Kenzie said as she watched the South Lake Union Trolley lumber past them, "looking for any sign of a setup."

Cori placed a hand on Kenzie's thigh. "I don't like this. You're making yourself a target and he has nothing to lose." She was relieved when Kenzie had finally returned to her, and she was not happy to have her in harm's way again. "How can you trust him?"

"I can't, and I don't, but he won't trust me either." She put her hand on top of Cori's and gave it a comforting squeeze. "I have to do this or I'll never be able to live with myself. He has answers nobody else can give me. I need to do this for myself."

The judge was quiet in the front seat. His thoughts echoed Cori's concern as he scanned the boardwalk with binoculars.

"It's time. I have to go." Kenzie looked into Cori's worried eyes. "You stay here. The judge will keep you safe."

"And what about you?"

Kenzie gave her a reassuring smile and leaned in to kiss her. "I'll be fine."

The gentle peck was not enough for Cori and she pulled Kenzie into a deep, emotional kiss. "Please, be careful," Cori whispered, as they parted, "so don't do anything foolish or heroic."

"We should have thought of that before we put all this into action," Kenzie said, and then she looked at the judge. "Are we set?"

Not trusting his voice to hide his apprehension, he turned and nodded.

"Keep her safe," Kenzie said as she started to climb from the car. Cori reached out for her hand, and they connected one last time. Kenzie looked into her eyes, not wanting to let go but knowing she had to.

"Come back to me," Cori whispered.

"That's my plan." With one last squeeze of Cori's hand, Kenzie exited the vehicle. Leaving them behind was harder than she'd thought it would be. However, she knew she had to block them out and concentrate on what she had to do. She crossed the trolley tracks and waited for a break in the traffic.

Colonel Manuck was dressed in civilian clothes, though he still walked like a military man. Weary but alert, he strolled casually down the weathered boardwalk. He had checked the rooftops on the east side on his first pass of Waterfront Park, and the west side on this second. There were not many places LeGault could set up without witnesses, but that did little to ease his mind. Several times in the last hour, he had questioned why he was there. He wondered the same thing again as he approached the large, bronze, cubical-shaped fountain.

Not wanting to sit down and give her an easy target, if she was out there, Manuck kept moving, amongst the trees and around the fountain. His back to the ocean, the colonel scanned the buildings, the boardwalk, and the throngs of people. There was no sign of her and that heightened his anxiety. She was out there, he knew it. He just didn't know where.

"Hello, Colonel."

Manuck spun around at the sound of her voice and watched as she climbed over the hand railing that separated the boardwalk from the ocean. "You're a little late," she said as she hopped down beside him.

"So are you."

"Just wanted to make sure you came alone." She eyed the man she had once respected. He looked tired, and a little too confident for her liking.

"Armed?" Manuck asked.

Kenzie unzipped her windbreaker, held it open for him to see, and then turned in a circle. She had no weapon, but she was sure he did. "You?"

"Of course." Manuck pulled back his sport jacket, revealing the butt of a gun.

With Manuck's back to the judge, she was certain he had not been able to see the weapon. Nonchalantly, Kenzie ran her fingers through her curls, signaling the judge that the colonel was armed.

"You look like shit, soldier," Manuck said, noting her numerous scratches, scrapes, and bruises. "But then, most of the other guys are all dead, aren't they?"

"Their blood is on your hands, not mine. I only did what I had to do to stay alive."

"So...why the reunion, LeGault?"

"I know about Maquinar," she said. "I know I have not been working for the government. We've all been hired assassins, paid in full by you, Palmer, and Bucannon."

"You brought me here to tell me that?" He didn't believe it for a moment. "What do you really want to know, LeGault?"

"Whose decision was it to bring me into Maquinar?" It was one of the questions she wanted to ask him face to face.

"Mine."

Kenzie felt deflated. Her mentor, the man whose military career she had emulated, had betrayed her right from the very beginning. "Why me? Why did you pick me?"

"Because you were exactly what we were looking for — the model soldier. You followed orders without question. Your abilities and instincts made you an ideal candidate for what we were doing. You had no family and no friends, no ties to the community. Once we got rid of Mifflin, the rest just fell into—"

"You killed Mifflin?" That information was new to her.

"Well, not me directly. It was one of your colleagues. Viper, I believe."

In shocked disbelief, Kenzie swayed under the weight of the information. "You killed Mifflin." Her tone and wording drew no attention from the passing crowd. "Why?"

"We needed you to learn to work alone."

"You had him killed so that you could get me into your kill squad?"

"Call it...collateral damage. It needed to be done. Viper made it a clean kill."

"You fucking bastard!" Kenzie stared at the man who had been her commander, feeling as if she had been gut-kicked. "He was one of us, one of the good guys." In a flash of memory, she recalled the look on Viper's face when they met before the mission in the desert. What a shock it must have been when he recognized her.

"Mifflin was a problem. He was in the way of what we were trying to accomplish," Colonel Manuck said.

"Just like those soldiers you sent us to murder in the middle of the goddamn desert?" Kenzie inquired angrily.

Only then did Manuck realize how much she had changed. Showing emotion was never a part of her training. "What does it matter? You didn't follow orders then, either, did you? Instead you ended up in a fistfight with two members of your own squad."

"I want to know why the three of us were sent to murder our own men."

"Are you really that naïve? You've been around this world and you've seen things most people have not. People die for a lot less than what those soldiers died for."

Kenzie stepped to within an arm's length of him and glared into his eyes. "I want to know why we were sent to murder our own soldiers!"

"Because they were in the wrong place at the wrong time, wearing the wrong uniforms," he fired back. "They were sent there to assist in a coup, and if they'd been caught and identified as US soldiers, the ramifications would have been catastrophic."

"For you or for them?" she asked, knowing he wouldn't answer. Kenzie had read some of this in the Maquinar file, but reading the words were a lot different than hearing them. "To assist in a coup? That isn't exactly how I read it. It sounded more like they were there to overthrow the local government."

She saw the car door open and the judge step out. *Why are you getting out? Stay there*, her mind screamed. Then she saw both the judge and Cori standing in front of their car. It was an unneeded distraction and she fought to concentrate on the dangerous man in front of her.

"So those soldiers' deaths were all part of Maquinar, and your bid for money and power?"

"War is a very profitable business, LeGault. A lot of people become very rich and powerful because of it." Manuck eyed her suspiciously. Something about her demeanor had changed and it made him leery. He turned his attention from her and quickly scanned the boardwalk.

"Colonel!" Her tone caused him to turn back to her. "Who sent those soldiers there in the first place?"

"It doesn't matter."

"It does to me!" she shouted. "Who sent them there?"

"I did!" he yelled back, uncharacteristically. "It was my decision, my orders!"

Kenzie was stunned. How could she ever have looked up to this man? He was the epitome of what Bucannon had described as the reason behind the founding of Maquinar – an out of control tyrant, killing his own people for money. "I can't believe I followed your orders so blindly."

"That's what soldiers do in time of war."

"This was not a time of war. This was your way of trying to start a war so that you could make more money. Most people don't start wars to make a profit. You did. You had me assassinate people so that you could manipulate and mold foreign governments to your will — all for money," Kenzie said, disgusted by the man she thought she knew.

"And power," Colonel Manuck said firmly.

"You are not God, Colonel. You can't play with people's lives like that." Kenzie didn't want to take her eyes off of him for fear that a simple glance would alert him to the judge and Cori crossing the street.

"With enough money you can."

Kenzie had the answers she wanted and they left her feeling shattered. It was over and she had heard enough. "All the money in the world isn't going to get you out of this," she said as the judge and Cori approached walking up the boardwalk.

"Sure it will," he said smugly as Kenzie stepped away from him.

Tilting her chin toward her chest, Kenzie sighed deeply. "I hope you got that, General," she said.

Colonel Manuck glared at Kenzie and she stared back at him in utter disgust. "It's over, Colonel, and it's all on tape for everyone to hear." Kenzie lifted her shirt to reveal a small microphone taped to the center of a Kevlar vest.

"General... What the hell?" Manuck looked at Kenzie for answers, horrorstricken by what he had admitted to. "What the fuck have you done, LeGault?" He looked to the left and then quickly to the right as the MPs came out of hiding and began to move in. Surrounded, he had no escape, no way out. "You bitch," he said as the circle of military police tightened around him.

"You did it to yourself, Colonel. General Coquette was very interested in the whole Maquinar file and in everything you had to say." Kenzie pulled off the microphone.

Turning to face her, he realized the full extent of what he had said. "You gave the file to General Coquette?"

"All of it," she said, glancing over his shoulder. She managed a small smile as the judge and Cori approached.

"Are you stupid? You're just as guilty as I am, and they now have that on tape, too."

"I'll answer for what I've done, but so will you, Colonel."

Anger erupted inside of Manuck, but before he had a chance to act, the MPs had his arms. "You bitch! You goddamn bitch!" The colonel continued to make a scene while the military police moved in to keep back the curious crowd.

Ignoring his outburst, Kenzie walked contently toward Cori. *It's over. Let the chips fall where they may.* She reached out to embrace the woman who had captured her heart.

Cori held Kenzie tightly, relieved that it was finally over. General Coquette had made no promises to Kenzie, but Cori believed that justice would prevail once the truth came out.

"I told you I'd be fine," Kenzie whispered into her ear.

"I believed you." Cori opened her eyes and looked at Kenzie, "But it was too hard to just sit there and watch, knowing so many things could go wrong."

Behind Kenzie, a scuffle broke out between the MPs and the colonel, and Manuck suddenly had a gun in his hand. Cori saw the gun come up and the utter determination on the colonel's face as he pulled the trigger.

Unaware of what was happening, Kenzie only felt Cori's tug turning her body as the gun discharged. Cori's body bucked in Kenzie's arms. "Cori?" Kenzie questioned softly as screams of fear and panic filled the air. Three rapid shots quickly followed the first and Colonel Manuck died with the gun still gripped firmly in his hand.

"Cori!" Kenzie gingerly felt her back. It was warm and wet, and Kenzie knew without looking that the wetness was blood.

"Oh, God, Cori!" She laid her gently to the ground, keeping one hand pressed firmly on the wound on her back. "Medic!" Kenzie yelled. "Get me a medic!" She turned back to Cori, her voice filled with fear. "What did you do?"

Blinking several times, Cori looked up at Kenzie. "I did what you would have done for me."

"Why?" Kenzie could hear the siren of the military ambulance that had been parked and ready nearby. The judge was there by her side, but all of her attention was on the woman whose blood was covering her hands. "Why?"

The ambulance arrived and its siren died away as Cori's eyes slowly closed. Kenzie panicked. "Stay with me! Cori, please...look at me." It all seemed surreal as she brushed back Cori's blonde hair, smearing blood across her forehead. After everything they had been through, it couldn't end this way. "Cori, sweetie, open your eyes."

It was a struggle, but Cori did as she was asked, smiling up into Kenzie's face.

"Stay with me, please," Kenzie begged as she held her close. Never before had she wanted something so much, and been so powerless to obtain it. "You have to stay awake...please."

"Okay," Cori said softly.

Tears slid unheeded down Kenzie's face. "Why...why did you do that?"

"Because I love you."

It was the top news story in Seattle that night. Jean Enersen, one of the anchors for the nightly news, spoke solemnly to her TV audience.

"The military has released little information about the shooting this morning during a mock exercise at Waterfront Park. According to sources, the maneuvers early this morning were a simulation of a response to a National Security threat. However, reports from eyewitnesses state the exercise appeared to be very real, including real blood, real bullets, and real body bags.

In other news, there has still been no arrest made in the murder of Senator Winston Palmer during an apparent home invasion..."

Chapter 25

The judge looked down at the address one more time, confirming he was at the right place. He had two favors to do for Kenzie. The first was to wire funds to some fishing boat captain, that he had already done, and the other...

He sighed as he looked up at the hospital. It didn't look like much, but he had not expected it to be. He would have preferred to be with Kenzie. She needed him right now more than ever. Somewhere in a backroom in Washington DC, she was sitting in front of a committee that did not exist as they tore apart her career and questioned her about everything she had done. It had been a long and arduous proceeding, adding to the strain she had been under, but it would soon be over. General Coquette had assured the judge that he would look after Kenzie's interests. After all, he was the one, when he was still a colonel, who had pulled the strings for the judge to start Kenzie's career in the military.

The judge parked in front of the hospital, pulled the keys from the ignition and sat for a moment. When he was done there, he was climbing onto a plane and heading to DC to be with his Katherine. He knew when the hearing was finished and the committee had all their answers, she would be gone again, this time for good. That made him regretful. He would not change what he had done for her, but he knew he would miss her.

Exiting slowly from the vehicle, the judge soaked in the warmth of the California sun as he climbed the steps. The glass door jangled when he pushed it open and stepped into the hospital.

"Can I help you?" asked the young woman at the front desk.

"Yes." He slid the address into his pocket. "I'm looking for a Heather Siddall."

The young woman smiled. "Heather's in the back. I'll get her for you."

A moment later, a woman with chestnut-colored hair and wearing hospital scrubs came through the swinging door. "I'm Heather, can I help you?" she asked, her brow furrowed in question.

The judge didn't know what to say so he just reached into his pocket and pulled out a set of keys. "These are for you," he said as he held them out to her.

She looked from the elderly man to the keys with the tag still on them. "Excuse me?"

He jiggled the keys and offered his best smile. "They're a gift from a couple of friends," he said, placing the keys into her hand, and then he added, "I was asked to deliver them." The judge motioned to the shiny new pickup truck he had parked out in front of the hospital.

"What?"

"It's all yours...a thank-you gift."

"What...what are you talking about?" Heather asked as she and her co-worker moved to the large window. "For me? I don't understand. A gift...a gift for me?"

"From what I heard, you earned it," he said with a smile. "A couple of women I know said to delivery this — because a new truck is better than sending you a postcard."

Suddenly, she understood. "Oh my God! Are they okay? Did everything work out?"

The judge could only offer a smile as he pulled the registration papers from his pocket and handed them to her. "Enjoy it," he said as he left the startled woman and her new pickup truck.

It was the last thing that Kenzie had asked him to do, and he had been happy to comply with her wishes.

The waters of the Pacific Ocean sparkled brightly in the late afternoon sun. A sailboat, anchored off Vancouver Island's rocky shore, bobbed gently up and down in the incoming tide. Kenzie was alone on deck, doing some routine maintenance on the mainsail while the light was still good. Dressed in a fleeced-lined yellow windbreaker, she ignored the tangle of curls brushing over her face as her mind reminisced with her past. Many moments of regret and flashes of haunting memories would catch her off guard at times. However, for the most part, she was living with what had happened. The committee had closed the book on Maquinar and she had earned her freedom, but at a cost. She could never go back to who she had been. Her military career was over, tainted with the broad stroke of a whispered scandal, leaving her to deal with the lives she had taken for all the wrong reasons. *All those people who died for all the wrong reasons...*

With a heavy sigh, she looked over the deck of her new boat. *Hel'n Back Again* was a bit larger and a lot faster, but it wasn't *Helen's Gate.*

"Where's your head at?" Cori whispered into Kenzie's ear as she wrapped her arms around her.

Kenzie snuggled into the embrace. "Nowhere."

"I find that hard to believe."

Kenzie smiled but Cori saw a shadow of something darker. "What else is going on in that busy mind of yours?"

"Lots of things...too many things."

"Now that I do believe."

"If I could turn back time and take it all back, I never would've met you."

"I don't accept that. I think we would have found each other eventually."

Kenzie turned around. "I found you and then I almost lost you. That I wouldn't want to live through again." She brushed back the blonde hair but she could not look Cori in the eye. "You aren't the naïve and innocent woman I met in Guadalajara. That woman would not have stepped in front of a bullet, especially not one meant for me."

"No, because that woman was Cori Evans and she's dead. She died in Seattle months ago." Lifting her chin, Cori forced Kenzie to look at her. "My name is Maureen Gibbins, and I love you." She kissed Kenzie on the lips, and then smiled as she studied the bronzed face before her. "You aren't the angry, lost woman who came busting into my apartment. We learn and we grow and we forgive. It's a new start for both of us, with new names and new places to go."

Golden eyes began to shimmer as Kenzie fought to control her emotions, but Cori would not let her go, not this time.

Kenzie sniffed loudly, "So much for my tough girl image."

A smirk lifted the corner of Cori's mouth as she held Kenzie's face in her hands. "Sweetie, you lost that long ago with me." Cori gently kissed her. "I love you, I love being with you, and no matter how it happened, I love that you came into my life." She kissed her again, harder and with more passion.

It took a long moment for Kenzie to trust that her voice would not betray her emotions. "I'm the happiest when I'm with you. I feel complete and content. I wasn't sure how this was going to work out. I mean, you could have died and I could have wound up in jail."

Cori placed her fingers on Kenzie's lips, silencing her. "But I didn't die, and you were rightfully given amnesty."

"I'm thankful you're in my life. I love you," Kenzie whispered, tears beginning to spill over. They grew quiet for a while, each lost in their own thoughts and memories as they held each other close. The ocean waves lapped gently against the hull of the sailboat. A light breeze fluttered her hair as Kenzie leaned back and watched as a gull played in the wind. "I was thinking...maybe we should head into Victoria and do some shopping."

"Shopping — you? Really?" Cori's voice exuded excitement.

"Well, for you shopping, for me, I have a package to post...a Zippo lighter I need to send to an old friend."

Cori's face warmed with a smile. "I think he'd like that."

They curled up together under a blanket at the stern of the boat and watched as the sun sank down below the horizon. Kenzie had found the happiness she had been searching for, and a place she could finally call home.

I know who I am. I know what I have done,
But I am no longer alone in the shadow of one.
I trust who you are, you saved more than my life,
You stopped me from walking on the edge of a knife.
Justice is blind and, in a way, so was I,
It's hard to see through a web woven with lies.
But the game isn't over, there's still one in play,
'cause someone's still watching you from far away.
With his sights dialed in, his target is true,
From a distance he watches and the target's still you!

~ CL Hart

CL Hart, author of *Facing Evil*, resides outside of Vancouver, British Columbia, with her partner and their 3 dogs, one cat and two guinea pigs!

An avid outdoors woman, she enjoys hiking, kayaking and playing guitar & banjo. Visit her website at www.clhart.com or drop her a note at sinful@telus.net

CPSIA information can be obtained at www.ICGtesting.com
Printed in the USA
269996BV00001B/57/P